Spirited

JULIE COHEN

ORION

An Orion paperback

First published in Great Britain in 2020 by Orion Fiction
This paperback edition published in 2021 by Orion Fiction,
an imprint of The Orion Publishing Group Ltd
Carmelite House, 50 Victoria Embankment,
London EC4Y 0DZ

An Hachette UK company

1 3 5 7 9 10 8 6 4 2

A CIP catalogue record for this book is
available from the British Library.

ISBN (Mass Market Paperback) 978 1 4091 7989 4
ISBN (eBook) 978 1 4091 7990 0
ISBN (Audio Download) 978 1 4091 7991 7

Typeset at The Spartan Press Ltd,
Lymington, Hants

Printed and bound in Great Britain by Clays Ltd,
Elcograf S.p.A.

www.orionbooks.co.uk

Also by Julie Cohen

Dear Thing
Where Love Lies
Falling
Together
Louis & Louise

This book is written in the spirit rather than the letter of the truth. The places are imaginary even when they have real names; the clippings are a mixture of true and false; and all the events are fictionalised even when they really happened.

A page from The County of Dorset Calendar of Prisoners Tried at the Autumn Assizes, Holden at DORCHESTER on Thursday, the 21st day of October, 1858.

The large calendar has been folded many times, and then flattened and bound into a book (Dorset History Centre archives item D-698/6). It is heavy duck-egg blue paper, printed in black ink in columns. The edges are water-stained, brown and buckled; the right-hand side has been damaged.

No. 7
Name. Viola Worth
Age. 21
Trade. None
Date of Warrant. 28th Aug., 1858.
Offence as charged in the Commitment. Fraud against Mr Theo. Selby, on 27th Aug., 1858, at Fortuneswell, by trickery and deception, selling to him what is claimed to be the image of a ghost.

Chapter One

They were married in mourning.

Viola's black day dress was simple, as were all her clothes: close-fitting in the bodice with bell sleeves and a modest crinoline. Jonah wore black morning dress and a black tie, black crêpe tied around his hat. Neither of them had new clothes for the wedding. Viola's dress had been made up so recently that it seemed hardly worth buying a new one for her wedding day, and Jonah hadn't been back from India long enough to order a new suit.

The only lightness was Jonah's white shirt, and the strand of white pearls that Viola wore around her neck. Strictly, she shouldn't be wearing them whilst in full mourning, but they had belonged to her mother, who had worn them on her wedding day. The locket with her father's hair lay under her dress, out of sight, close to her heart and Viola's chestnut hair was tucked underneath a black bonnet. Jonah's face was tanned from the Indian sun, but still managed to be pale; his eyes, blue in her memory of summers past, were grey. Viola felt that her own face was as colourless as the weak spring sunshine.

Mrs Chapman stopped them outside the vicarage, before they got into the carriage that would take them to the church. 'Your father wouldn't mind these,' she said to Viola. She held two knots of the violets that grew in the vicarage garden. The housekeeper tucked one knot into the band of Viola's hat, and the other into

Jonah's buttonhole. 'There,' she said, standing back, 'you can't marry without flowers.'

The words were kind, but the tone was bleak.

'It's a new beginning for you both,' Mrs Chapman said. 'And the first and last wish of your father's heart.'

'I know,' said Viola, and she pressed the hand of this dear woman who had been with her nearly all her life. She wanted to glance at the face of the man she was about to marry, but she was afraid that when she looked at him, she would see only her father – his waxy face, eyes open, mouth open, a bristle of white on his chin which he had always so carefully shaved every morning as the sun rose; his hair no more than a dishwater wisp. It had nearly all gone, at the end.

Her father had died six weeks ago and since then she had seen his dead face. It floated before her when she closed her eyes to sleep. It appeared at the table when she tried to eat, his mouth open to show the missing molar, his tongue a sandpaper sponge. She had washed his body herself, tied the bandage around his head to close his mouth, and his skin had been – not cold, but not warm. His skin had been an object. He had ceased to be a person and become an appendage of the bed in which he lay, a carving of a naked skeleton which she cleaned as gently as if he were a newborn baby.

'Viola?' said Jonah softly, and she started. He was holding out his hand to her to help her into the carriage.

She stared at his black-gloved hand with the sudden conviction that, were she to touch it, the flesh underneath would be as dead as her father's.

'Thank you,' she said, and turned away to climb into the carriage without assistance. Jonah followed her and settled beside her, closing the door. In the enclosed space, his clothing rustled and his breath was a soft hush. The cloth of his jacket touched the side of her skirt. There was a faint scent of camphor. She heard the driver chirrup the horses and they started off. Without looking, she knew that Jonah was staring straight ahead, as she was, at the wooden opposite wall of the carriage. These same horses had driven her father's body the same route to the Kimmerton church, along the same lane he had walked at least twice a day.

A carriage is larger than a coffin. He'd had white lilies, not violets. They weren't going to the Kimmerton church but to the church in the next parish, and in another hour this carriage would be driving them back to the vicarage, man and wife. The first and last wish of her father's heart.

She couldn't breathe.

'Are you unwell? You're unwell. I'll ask Langley to stop.'

Jonah raised his hand to knock on the carriage but she said, quickly, 'No,' and he subsided into his seat.

'It isn't far,' she said. 'We should have walked.'

'I'm not confident that your legs would carry you, Viola. And it will rain.'

She should have let him help her into the carriage. It was a weakness on her part. Two summers ago, before he'd left, he'd taken her hand as they walked through the field strewn with poppies, and his fingers had been warm and his eyes the brightest shade of blue she could imagine.

'I won't melt,' she said now, hating the reedy sound of her own voice. It had diminished, it seemed, with the rest of her. She couldn't help but recall how Jonah had looked at her last week, when he returned to Kimmerton. They hadn't seen each other for over two years. She'd always been slim, never blooming, prone to freckles if she wasn't careful enough with bonnet and parasol. She'd always wished for rosier cheeks and brighter eyes, womanly curves instead of her wan, straight body. Her hair was the only part of her that she liked. It grew bountiful and glossy, conker-red, whilst the rest of her was meagre. It had to be combed and tamed and twisted and pinned.

She hadn't looked in a mirror for weeks, even before her father had finally died and all the mirrors in the house had been covered with crêpe. But when Jonah returned from India, she saw in his shocked expression how much she'd changed from the girl with whom he had walked, hand in hand. She was no longer the girl whom he'd said he loved.

He'd changed, too; but he'd been away, doing things. He had been caught up in a war. He had saved a life. He was a hero. Those things would leave a mark. She had failed to save anyone.

She cleared her throat. 'Tell me about sunshine.'

'You know all about sunshine,' he replied with a smile.

'Tell me about India.'

'No,' he said quickly.

'But you've hardly said anything about it since you've come back.'

'There's nothing to say.'

'There's lots to say. I want to know more about it. The good things. Did you see monkeys?'

'I said, I don't want to talk about it.' His tone was sharp.

She looked down at her lap, at her black gloves.

'I'm sorry,' Jonah said.

'We shouldn't be doing this,' she said.

He didn't answer straight away. The carriage jolted and she heard a splash as they went through a puddle.

'You think we should've waited?' he said at last. 'But where would you have lived? Who would have looked after you?'

'I think a bride should be full of joy and not sadness.'

'Oh, Viola,' Jonah said, and he made a move as if to take her hand. She flinched slightly before she could control herself. He noticed it, and returned his hand to his own lap.

'You're sad,' he said. 'It's natural that you're sad. Your father was a wonderful man. I loved him as if he were my own father. It was an utter shock to hear he had passed away. I had no idea he'd been so ill for so long. Your letters…'

'I didn't want to worry you, or make you feel that you should come home. You'd been through enough, and you had to recover.'

'I wish I'd been by his side when he died.'

'No,' she said, unable to repress a shudder. 'You do not wish that.'

'But you must see that this is the best thing for us to do. I wish we could wait longer, until you're less sad, until you're well. But we have no one else, now, except for each other. We're both alone in the world, and you need someone to look after you. The sooner we're married, the sooner we can start anew. As Mrs Chapman said.'

'A new beginning should be fresh and bright. Not ... not like this.'

'It will be,' he said. 'I'm determined that it shall.' He drew himself more upright in his seat. 'I'm conscious of my duty to you, Viola. I won't fail you.'

It was raining by the time the carriage stopped outside the church at Bonner Green. Langley hopped off the driver's seat to help Viola down. She allowed herself to lean on his arm, swathed in his thick, wet greatcoat, as she stepped down into the muddy lane.

'Blessings on you both, Miss Goodwin,' Langley muttered. 'It's just what your father, God rest him, would have wanted.'

'I know, Langley. Thank you.'

Jonah appeared at her elbow and held an umbrella over her head. It wasn't quite large enough to shield her dress completely, and she felt rain falling on the silk, spoiling it, as they walked hurriedly up the path to the church.

A tall, reed-thin man with dusty black clothes and pure-white whiskers was waiting for them in the porch. 'Oh,' said Viola. 'Mr Adams. I wasn't expecting to see you.'

'I'm here to give you away, Miss Goodwin,' said the man who had been her father's deacon.

'Oh,' she said again. 'That's very kind, but there's no need, it's not at all necessary.'

'I'm a poor substitute, but your father would never forgive me if I didn't.'

She hesitated. She'd insisted that she and Jonah marry in Bonner Green church rather than Kimmerton, which had been her father's parish, specifically because she did not want any reminders of her previous life. Mr Adams' bony figure had hovered at her father's elbow over countless Sunday sermons, and occupied a regular seat at their table at Sunday lunches. As a bachelor, he was often present at other meals, too, or ensconced with her father in his library, smoking and talking. He had stood by her father's sickbed, turning a worn Bible over and over in his hands. He had led the psalms at her father's funeral.

Now, standing in the porch with his battered hat and old coat and a small drop at the end of his long nose, he looked like a crow perched on a tombstone.

But refusing him would be selfish. 'Of course, Mr Adams. It's an honour.'

He smiled his thin smile and he wiped at the end of his nose with a black-edged handkerchief. 'It's my honour, Miss Goodwin. Your father was … he was … I don't know how I'll do without him, and without you, once you and Mr Worth are gone.' His watery eyes welled up.

'Cheer up, Mr Adams, it's our wedding day,' said Jonah, and his words were forced. He patted the deacon on his back.

'Yes. Yes, I don't know what … I'm sorry, I …'

Viola pulled off one of her gloves so that she could remove a few violets from the posy in her hat. She gave them to Mr Adams. 'For your buttonhole, sir.'

He nodded and gulped. Jonah turned to Viola. 'I'll go in.'

He left her with Mr Adams in the porch. Viola drew on her glove and tried to use the boot scraper to brush some of the mud off her shoes. Mr Adams, obviously embarrassed by his show of emotion, busied himself with wiping his eyes and arranging the small flowers.

She hadn't pictured her wedding day like this. She'd imagined it sunny, the stained-glass windows of her father's church casting dancing rainbows on the stone floor. She had seen herself in a sea-green dress, with roses in her hand, entering the church on her father's arm, holding fast to the man who'd supported her all her life. She'd seen Jonah standing at the altar, red and purple light in his brown curls, his well-known smile greeting her. He would hold out his hand and she would take it and step into her new life, from her father's care into Jonah's.

It would be a moment like a jewel, to be treasured and taken out to polish and admire and cherish. Her father would take a photograph afterwards and they would keep it on the wall of their home to look at whenever they wanted to remember.

When Jonah returns and we marry, she had thought, over and over and over like a refrain. When her father started coughing and could not visit his parishioners. When his voice grew too weak to read his sermons and she sat next to him and read the news about what Jonah had done in Delhi. *When Jonah returns and we marry, Father will get better. He's so proud of Jonah. Happiness will cure him.*

When he had to stay in bed and the doctor visited, in the night, she forced the refrain to repeat in her head and sat in her chair by the fire in her father's bedroom, changing the cool cloths on his forehead, all through the dark hours until the sun rose, mentally rehearsing the cheerful letters she would write to her fiancé who was under the Indian sun, recovering from his ordeal. Even in war and death, Jonah had saved a child. Happy endings *were* possible. *When Jonah returns and we marry.* The sunshine would surely come.

A sparkling jewel. The happiest day of her life.

In the last days, she hadn't been able to see it. Not clearly, in her mind. She thought the words, the refrain, over and over, but sunshine was beyond her imagining. She set up the camera in her father's bedroom at his bidding and she uncovered the lens, and when the exposure was done, she said it aloud, 'Jonah will like to see that photograph. When he returns and we marry.'

Her father was asleep by then. Her words sounded hollow, bodiless, a lie.

That was the night she had written to Jonah and begged him to come home, as soon as he could. It was the first urgent, and truthful, letter she had written to him since he had left. It never reached him; he was already at sea by that point. Jonah only heard of her father's death three weeks ago when he was greeted at Dover by cheering crowds waving British flags, and her second letter on black-edged paper. He had gone straight to London to sort his affairs and engage an agent to find them a house, and then he had come here to marry her.

'Well,' said Mr Adams. He went to the church door, opened it, and peered in. Then he returned and held out his bony arm to Viola. 'I think they're ready. Shall we?'

She couldn't avoid taking his arm. When she did, it felt brittle, like a bundle of twigs wrapped in wool. But he smiled down at her, that clear drop still hanging at the end of his nose, and that made it better. They walked in together.

The interior of the church was the same colour as the rain and even colder than outside. Grey walls, windows without light, a long stone aisle in front of them. Their footsteps echoed. Mr Adams walked slowly, his shoulders stooping. She knew Mr Morris, the vicar, who watched their procession. He attempted a smile at her, a baring of teeth.

Ahead of them, Jonah waited at the altar. He gazed straight ahead, not looking back at her as she approached.

For the first time since he'd returned, from this distance and without his eyes to avoid, she could look at him. He, too, had lost weight; his suit was too big for him in the shoulders, and gaped at the back of his neck. He stood almost unnaturally upright, hands by his sides. His hair had been flattened by his hat.

Although Viola had known him nearly all her life, she realised with a jolt that if she hadn't known that this was Jonah, she wouldn't have recognised him.

They drew abreast. Jonah's jaw was set. Viola recalled the words he'd said about duty.

She couldn't blame him for not wanting to marry her. She should've been strong and broken off the engagement, for his sake. But it seemed as if the promise of this day had been the only thing keeping her alive. If she'd known it was going to be so grey and thin and cold, would she have clung to its prospects so much?

'Are you ready to begin?' Mr Morris said.

Viola hesitated. It wasn't too late to release Jonah. But then what would she do? Her father had left her almost nothing. She couldn't remain in the vicarage; it was needed for the new vicar. She couldn't live somewhere else alone. This limbo, between two men, between death and marriage, could not last indefinitely. If she didn't marry Jonah, she would have to find another man to marry – and who would that be? How could she marry anyone aside from Jonah, who had been a fact of her life for as long as she could remember? How could she possibly like another man?

'Viola?' prompted Jonah softly. Caught off guard, she glanced at him. And there it was: underneath the resignation, the stiffness, the pallor, there was his dear face. The face of her playfellow and her first, best friend. The old Jonah hovered there like a ghost standing just behind this new, sombre Jonah. He was a slender bridegroom, wearing violets at his breast, his eyes as blue as the summer sky.

'I'm ready,' she said.

He took off his right glove and she took off her left so that he could slip the slim gold band onto her finger. The ring had been her mother's, kept for her by her father until the day she married.

Her left hand lay in his gloved palm. It was a cold, small thing, a naked animal. As he slid the ring onto her fourth finger, the tips of his own fingers touched hers. They were chilled here in this empty church, cold and clumsy, and Viola had to think very hard about sunshine, about violets, as the man whom she had promised to love forever put the ring of a dead woman onto her own finger.

Chapter Two

And then they were man and wife.

Jonah stayed behind to pay the vicar who had married them, and Viola walked out with Mr Adams onto the porch.

'Well, God bless you, Mrs Worth,' said Mr Adams, gazing at the relentless rain and shaking the tail of his coat as if it were dull feathers.

'Mrs Worth,' she repeated. 'Just like that.'

'You will be very happy together,' Mr Adams said, as if he hadn't heard her. 'The two of you were inseparable as children. I remember you tumbling into the drawing room at teatime and upsetting all the tables.'

'Yes, we used to do that, didn't we?'

'And now you're married. And our Jonah Worth is a famous man. I'd be surprised if he didn't get a medal from the Queen. When will you go to the coast?'

'Tomorrow morning.' She held her left hand, the one with the ring, out from the shelter so that she could feel the rain. It pattered on her glove.

'Your whole life is ahead of you,' he said to her. 'Never found the right woman myself. It's too late now.'

'It's never too late,' she said, but it was automatic.

Jonah opened the church door and came out, putting on his hat. Mr Adams shook his hand. 'I wish you joy,' he said.

'I'm sure we'll have lots of it,' said Jonah. 'Would you like to share our wedding breakfast? Mrs Chapman is bound to have outdone herself.'

He said it so naturally that Viola nearly failed to notice how smoothly he had transferred mastery of the vicarage from Viola to himself. No matter how many times Viola's father had urged Jonah to consider the house his own, he had always been very conscious of his status in the Goodwins' home as a ward, not a natural son. Until ten minutes ago, he would have left the invitation to Viola.

'Yes,' she said, though with an awareness of the mere form of her assent. 'Please do, Mr Adams. I know how you enjoy Mrs Chapman's cooking, and this may be the ...'

It would be the last time. After the newly-married Worths left tomorrow, Mrs Chapman would be going to Trowbridge to live with her sister. She'd refused their offer to take her with them to Dorset; she'd never left Wiltshire in her life and she wasn't about to start now. Viola wasn't sure if she would ever see her house-keeper again, and if she did, it would never be the same. Mrs Chapman had been with them for as long as she could remember. She had let the young Viola play in her kitchen, and taught her how to sew. Her father's death had ended that relationship, as well.

'We'd like it very much if you joined us, after your kindness,' she said instead.

Mr Adams wavered, but the thought of Mrs Chapman's pastry lit a greedy light in his thin face. 'I wouldn't want to intrude.'

'Not at all,' said Jonah. 'Mr Morris is coming as well, and his clerk. I hope that's all right with you, Viola.'

She swallowed. 'Of course. The more the merrier.'

Breakfast finished, guests departed, neither of them as merry as she might have hoped, Viola walked between the pale forms of the dust-sheeted furniture, feeling insubstantial. Jonah had leased a furnished house for them on the Isle of Portland, so that Viola could take the sea air. His own belongings had gone there already. Only her personal things from this house would follow them. The Kimmerton living, and this house, would go to a new vicar. Other people would sit in this chair, use this table, take a book from this case. Would they think of the people who had gone before them?

Jonah found her in the library, running her hands over the wooden crate that held her father's books.

'Shall we do the last boxes?' he asked her.

'I've been dreading it,' she admitted.

'I've already written to Burnham about your father's photographic equipment,' Jonah said, 'and he's willing to take anything you don't want to keep. He has some students—'

'No,' she said quickly. 'No, I don't want to sell it.'

'Then we'll take it all.'

Outside, Jonah opened an umbrella for her and they hurried across the garden to Papa's studio in an adapted outbuilding. She hadn't stepped into this place since she had developed the last photograph of her father, a week before he died. That photograph was already packed, folded among her clothes to keep the gilt frame from breaking.

She had carried the camera upstairs, taken the photograph of him in his bed. His body weight had hardly dented the pillows. In the photograph, his hands were folded on the neat coverlet. His wedding ring was loose, but his nightshirt was starched, hair combed, face shaved, sideburns trimmed. His eyes glittered with fever. But he smiled and gazed straight at the camera lens, because she stood behind it.

When she looked at the photograph now, she could see the echo of his love captured in the image. She treasured it, but it was too difficult to look at except in glances. It was like holding a knife by the blade.

Viola unlocked the green wooden door with one of the

keys at her waist. Even though it was still pouring outside, the white-painted studio was lighter and airier than the inside of the vicarage. A chair and small table sat in the centre of the room in front of a screen that her father had painted to look like a formal garden. His tripod faced the chair, waiting for him to place his camera upon it. As always, the chemical scents of photography greeted her nostrils. The rusty twinge of ferrous sulphate, the lavender oil in the shellac.

It was as if her father were there just out of sight in the dark-room, making prints, and she had only to wait for him to step outside and greet her, to hold out his hands stained black with silver nitrate.

Viola stifled a sob. Jonah turned to her quickly.

'I can pack all of this,' he said. 'I know your father's equipment almost as well as you do. Why don't you take a rest. It's been a tiring day.'

'But I should do this. It…'

She was putting her father into a coffin again.

'You put the albums together,' he said to her kindly. 'I'll get you some brown paper and string. And I'll do his equipment.'

She nodded. She began to stack the heavy albums of prints together, without opening them, though she knew the contents of each one. This room was where her father had taught her to prepare a plate, how to frame a composition. He had stood behind her and taught her the names of every chemical he used to fix the image and print the negative; discussed with her the difference between a daguerreotype and a calotype, outlined the advantages of the newer wet-plate method, his gentle voice in a red-lit room.

'The house in Portland,' Jonah said, from across the room where he was carefully wrapping her father's wet plate camera, 'was built by an artist. It has a studio in the attic. We could work side by side. The agent says there's even a place for a darkroom.'

She wrapped a shroud of brown paper around the stack of albums.

'I don't think I'll ever want to take another photograph again,' she said.

Jonah had come to them when he was eight years old and Viola was six. His parents lived in India and he was going to spend this summer with them in Kimmerton until he started boarding school. His parents wanted him to have a proper English education. He would spend every holiday with them too, until he was grown up.

'You must look after him, Viola,' her father had said. 'He came all this way from Delhi without his parents, and he doesn't have any family in this country. You have lost a mother, so you know what it is to miss a parent. Only speak of it if he wishes to. Try to talk of pleasant things and make him know that he is welcome here.'

It was a hot day in July with heavy bumblebees weighing down the flowers in the garden. They were still making calotypes then. She and her father had set up the tripod on the lawn and she was dressed as her idea of an Arabian princess, draped in pink and orange scarves and with a pheasant's feather, one of her treasures, tucked behind her ear. Father was adjusting the lenses when she heard the carriage draw up in the front of the house. She ran around in time to see Jonah Worth step down, next to Mrs Chapman who had been to fetch him from the station. He was slender and tanned from the sun, and wore a linen suit that was too short for him in the arms and legs. He must have grown during the journey from Delhi. His hair was a jumble of curls. *He has no one to comb it for him*, she thought with pity, although when she thought it through when she was older, of course even if his mother were in England instead of far away in India, she wouldn't be combing Jonah's hair any more. Her own mother had died the year before, but Viola had been brushing her own hair since she was four.

She had never met a real person from India before. But aside from the tanned skin, he looked very much like a child who had grown up in England.

'I'm Viola Goodwin,' she said to him, and although she wouldn't do this with her playmates, she held out her hand as she had seen her father do with his contemporaries. He took it, and shook it in what seemed like a kind of daze. He had a narrow face, pink lips, large blue eyes. With his abundance of curls he looked as pretty as a girl, which pleased her.

'Jonah Worth. You're Mr Goodwin's daughter?'

She nodded. 'My father and yours were best friends, you know. They were at school together.'

'I know. My father told me all about it.'

'Was the boat trip very long to get here? Months and months at sea? Who looked after you?'

He shrugged narrow shoulders. 'Mrs Brownlee, whose husband knows Father.'

'Was she kind to you?'

'She was seasick. I kept busy drawing. Why do you have a feather behind your ear?'

She released his hand. His palm had been a bit sweaty, so she wiped it on one of her scarves. 'Father's taking photographs and I'm Scheherazade. You can be Aladdin now that you're here. Come on, we'll find you some better clothes.'

He followed Viola around the house to the back garden and to the studio. Father had moved to the back of the camera now and was only a black shape under the cloth. 'I'll introduce you in a minute, when he's finished,' Viola said, passing him. 'There's no point interrupting him when he's busy. He won't even hear us. We might as well go to the studio and find a costume.'

'I thought your father was a clergyman?' Jonah said, staring at the spindly-legged camera and the black cloth in the shape of a man, the piles of cushions and the potted palm plants arranged on the lawn.

'He is. Photography is his hobby, and it's mine too. We'll teach you all about it this summer.' She unlatched the door of the studio and headed straight for the racks of costumes. Only when she turned to speak to Jonah did she realise that he had stopped just inside the door, gazing with wonder at the equipment around him. She went over to hand him a curved sword which she had made herself of cardboard and covered with silver paper.

He took the sword without looking at it. 'Can you really use all of this equipment yourself?'

'I can. It's very delicate, though, and expensive, and you must be very careful. Some of the chemicals are poisonous. I'll show you how to use it safely.'

'I like drawing,' he told her. 'I want to be an artist one day.'

'Then you can draw, and I can photograph. We can do it together.'

They didn't talk about his parents or her mother all that summer. They didn't need to: there were photographs to take, and countryside to explore, and scenery to draw, and books to read, and games to play until it was September and he went to school until his next holiday.

Two years later, when they'd had the news that both his parents had died of typhoid, he came to them for the Easter holidays wearing black. She put her hand in his and he squeezed it. 'Let's not talk about it,' he whispered to her. So they didn't.

They drank tea in the dining room because all of the furniture in the drawing room was covered. Jonah sat on one side of the wide mahogany table and she sat on the other. Just as they used to sit, when they were children, with her father between them at the head of the table.

Now they were husband and wife. Conversation had run out

and Viola was weary to her bones. The silence stretched between them like the expanse of glossy table.

Outside it had grown dark.

Mrs Chapman came in with another plate of fruit cake and set it on the table between them.

'Thank you,' Viola said to her. 'Please don't stay up on our account. I'll take these to the kitchen after we're finished.'

'Oh no no no, I wouldn't hear of it. It's your wedding night, Mrs Worth. You shouldn't be carrying crockery.' Mrs Chapman hesitated. 'You gave no instructions as to where you would choose to sleep tonight. If you let me know which room, I'll have a fire lit. I'm sorry, I would have lit a fire in each of the rooms, but with everything ready to go, I didn't want to cause extra mess.'

Viola's eyes widened. With everything to do, with the weight of her loss on her shoulders, she hadn't thought of bedrooms. She had thought of tonight only as the last night in her childhood home, not the first night of her marriage.

Her bed was narrow, as was Jonah's in his room. The only bed big enough to fit both of them comfortably was ...

Cold horror seeped through her.

'Thank you, Mrs Chapman,' said Jonah. 'You've been very kind to us today. We don't need a fire.'

'Much joy to you both,' she said, and left them alone together.

Jonah lifted his cup. He put it back down again without drinking. 'You're not well, Viola.'

Her throat was dry. 'My father died in that bed. I can't.'

He recoiled, as if he'd been slapped. 'You think I'd make you sleep in your father's bed?'

'I think that – I think that we're married now.'

'But that doesn't mean ... I wouldn't ...'

She couldn't look at him; she looked at the gold rim of the tea pot. 'I honestly haven't thought about any of this, Jonah. I've been living through each moment as it happens, watching one foot step in front of the other. I haven't been able to glimpse the road ahead.'

'You're not strong. It would be cruel to insist upon ... upon starting that aspect of our marriage at present.'

Viola nodded. The silence stretched out between them again. In another room, muffled by cloth, the clock struck nine. She'd been awake since before first light this morning.

'You're exhausted,' said Jonah. 'And tomorrow will be tiring, too. We should go up.'

They walked up the stairs side by side, Jonah holding the candle. Their shadows loomed large on the flocked wallpaper along the staircase: two heads, one taller, two sets of shoulders, one broader. The angle of the light and the fullness of her skirt made it appear as if their divided shadows grew out of one body below the waist, like conjoined twins.

He paused outside her bedroom. 'Goodnight,' he said. 'Sleep well, Viola.'

It was no different than the hundred, the thousand other times he had bade her goodnight before they went to their separate rooms. She hesitated, touching the unfamiliar gold ring on her left hand with her thumb, and he stooped and placed a swift kiss on her cheek.

'I'll see you in the morning, bright and early,' he said, and gave her the candle, and walked to his own room at the end of the corridor.

When she was in the privacy of her own room, she put her hand to her cheek where he had kissed her. Her first kiss as a married woman.

Viola undressed slowly, hanging her dress in the wardrobe that was empty save for the even plainer black travelling costume she would wear tomorrow. She unlaced her corset, pulled her lawn nightdress over her head and buttoned the sleeves and neck. She unpinned her hair and brushed it, sitting on the edge of her bed instead of at her dressing table with its covered mirror.

She'd pictured her wedding day many times, over and over. She hadn't given her wedding night much thought at all. Only, perhaps, the idea of Jonah helping her with her gown. Perhaps him taking the brush to smooth out her hair. She had thought of him removing his jacket and waistcoat and standing before her in his shirtsleeves, but she couldn't picture him without his shirt. She had never seen him without a shirt on since they were children.

Her father's chest, the skin draped loosely over bone as she had bathed him for the last time.

Viola shivered. She washed quickly, said her prayers, blew out the candle, and climbed into her bed. The sheets were cold and her teeth chattered as she lay on her back, gazing up at the black ceiling and breathing in the smoke from her candle. She should sleep. Tomorrow would be another long day. And the day after that, and the day after, in a new town by the sea. She would be known there only as Mrs Worth; Miss Goodwin would be gone forever. All of her days stretched out in front of her, as wreathed in darkness as her bedroom.

Several rooms away, Jonah would be getting ready for bed. What did he do? What did he wear at night? Did he still pray by his bed, as she did by hers? Did he hope, unlike her, that his prayers might be answered? Why hadn't she asked him while they were sitting in silence at that table? She knew him, but she didn't know him. She had grown up with him and she had promised to cleave to him forever but now that they weren't children any more, his thoughts, his tiny intimate actions, were hidden from her.

It seemed like so much to know. So much effort.

She knew this house better than she knew her husband, and yet she was leaving it. This house was old and draughty; the floors creaked. She listened hard, wondering if she could hear Jonah. Instead, she heard the soft familiar tread of Mrs Chapman coming up the back stairs to bed, and a few minutes later, the lighter tread of Nora the maid. The chiming of the clock. A distant drip of water. Perhaps a leak in the roof. She didn't have to worry about the roof any more.

Jonah would have got into bed by now. Folded back the bed-clothes and climbed beneath them. Perhaps he had lit a candle and was reading. He had used to like poetry, but lately he had been reading Gibbons. The only sound in his room would be the turning of the pages of his book. Now he would be closing his book, placing it on his bedside table. Laying his pillows flat. Blowing out the candle. Closing his eyes. Did he sleep on his side, or his back? Curled up or straight?

Once she'd come across him sleeping in the studio on a pile of cushions, curled up like a child. His pencil and drawing pad had slipped to the floor. But he had been twelve then, maybe thirteen, and she had put a shawl on him and crept away.

Chapter Three

May, 1858
Geneva, Switzerland

Mr Selby was coming.

It was whispered in the back of theatres, spoken with satisfaction over games of whist. Mrs Henriette Blackthorne heard of it as she was on her way back to her lodgings from her visit with Lady Fanshawe. She had sat all afternoon in the dowager's bedroom, holding her paper-dry hand and passing on messages from her eldest son, who had died in the Crimea. The Honourable Robert Fanshawe, even after death, liked to talk about the weather and horses, and Henriette was quite weary. Lady Fanshawe, however, found this conversation very stimulating and she had actual colour in her cheeks when she patted Henriette's hand and said, with surprising vigour for a dying woman, 'Thank you, dear. It has given me such joy to speak with my Bobby. Tomorrow, I shall call for my solicitor and ensure you are remembered in my will.'

Henriette had, of course, protested, but only enough to seem gracious. 'You'll outlive us all,' she said to the dowager, and drew on her gloves to leave, wondering if Lady Fanshawe would remember Henriette enough for her to be able to pay the debts she'd incurred in London.

She wasn't having much luck with widows, lately. She'd had some hope of Madame Fournier, but it turned out that all the jewels that Monsieur Fournier had given his wife throughout their marriage had been paste – a fact that M. Fournier had not seen fit to impart during his long conversations with his wife from beyond the grave. Henriette had been bequeathed a match-ing 'emerald' necklace and earrings, both of which she gave to her maid. Elise wasn't fond of them, either.

Hat settled on her head, she headed towards her lodgings near the cathedral. In the Place du Bourg-de-Four she encountered Mr Munro. Or rather Mr Munro encountered her. 'Madame Blackthorne!' he called from across the square, and bustled over to her, watch chain gleaming, sisters trailing behind like three grey goslings. 'Have you heard?' he said, kissing her hand. 'Mr Selby is coming.'

'Mr Selby?' she said, feigning ignorance. Though she knew who Mr Selby was, by reputation. Mr Selby, who had written about the Fox sisters, and Mrs Hayden. Quite perceptively, she thought, though his educated language barely hid his contempt. It was a sort she recognised: the fury of a man who looked at a woman he'd thought to be a virgin and whom he now suspected of being a whore.

Selby never investigated Daniel Dunglas Home, or Paschal Randolph; he had never been interested in Henriette herself, until after her husband Ethelred had died. Henriette wondered if he had been romantically scorned by a female medium, or if he simply hated women. It was an idle wonder: she intended never to find out.

'He's corresponded with Madame Richard and Herr Müller. And to you, too, perhaps?' The financier's pale eyes blinked up at her. His sisters had caught up by now, and were listening.

'You must have had a letter from Mr Selby, Madame Blackthorne,' said Miss Sally, the youngest (at forty-seven). Miss Sally had been their father's favourite and as a result she had an independent income. She'd been using it to pay Henriette, in secret, for messages from her piano tutor for whom she had shared an unspoken passion before he died in a boating accident in 1819. The passion was much more spoken now than it had been in Sally's youth.

'How glorious it would be for him to meet *you*, Madame Blackthorne,' said Mr Munro. 'All his doubts would vanish in an instant, I know they would. He would no longer be a sceptic. And the cause of Spiritualism would be furthered!'

'I haven't read my post,' she said, extracting her hand from his as gently but firmly as she could. 'I've been with poor Lady Fanshawe. But I'll look, right away.'

'So gratifying that he would come to Geneva!' said Miss Evelyn. 'It *must* be to witness your work!'

'Quite,' agreed Henriette. 'Thank you for telling me.'

'We shall see you at Herr Müller's this evening?'

'Yes, of course,' said Henriette, her mind already on boat trains. She bade them farewell and made her way, rather more quickly, to her lodgings. Mr Selby's letter lay on the table in the entranceway, with all the rest of today's post. She put the letter straight into the fire, unread.

It took her very little time to pack her trunks. She had done it so many times before. It took hardly any longer for her to write letters to her landlord, to Herr Müller, and regretfully, to Lady Fanshawe. By the time the cab arrived at her door she was ready to go, changed into a black travelling suit and a hat with a veil. She did not allow the driver to take the small battered satchel, a contrast to the well-appointed matching steam trunks which she directed him to instead. Instead she carried the satchel herself into the back of the cab: a stained and cracked leather bag, marked near the handle in ink with the initials H.S. She cradled it on her lap like a child.

An extract from The **Spirit Moves Me: Spiritualism and Feminist Spectacle** *by Elisabeth Nwabara, published by Pennsylvania State University Press, 2012, page 114.*

The Isle of Portland in the south of England is connected to the mainland by the thinnest of threads, a pebble beach. It is most famous for its limestone and its lighthouse, its prison and its role as a major embarkation point for D-Day. But in the summer and autumn of 1858 this island in Dorset became a very different sort of battleground – between science and religion, between male law and female spirituality. A battle that culminated with one woman jailed and another vanished, while men in courtrooms debated the legal reality and economic worth of life after death.

Chapter Four

June, 1858
West Weare, Isle of Portland, Dorset

So this was what scientific discovery was like. Jonah wiped rain from his eyes. His hat was dripping, his coat soaked through, his feet squelching in his boots. Sea, sky and cliff all melded together in one sheet of grey and red and brown. He scrambled over slippery rocks to where his new acquaintance, Mr Field, had been digging.

Mr Field was practically dancing with joy. 'We must document the position of the skull and the teeth we find; it will make reconstruction so much easier.' He waved his brush in the air like a magic wand.

Jonah extracted his sketchbook from the inner pocket of his coat and unwrapped it from its oilcloth covering. He peered at the fossil and began to sketch its outline, trying to shield his paper with the oilcloth as he drew. Raindrops fell on the paper and blurred his pencil lines.

'The skull,' enthused Mr Field. 'The skull is always a special find. This is so much more than ammonites. We are looking a creature in the eye, who lived thousands of years ago. Thousands of years, Mr Worth! A creature who never saw the Garden of Eden. It's the death knell of Christianity.'

Mr Field sounded positively joyful about the death of what many people considered a perfectly good religion.

All religions are true, or none of them are. The voice was quite clear in Jonah's head. He wished it weren't.

He stooped down to get a better look at the skull. Closer, he could see more of its shape emerging from the mud. It wasn't dissimilar to the head of the crocodiles he had seen basking in the sun on the banks of the Yamuna River. In India, crocodiles were sacred. But this was – so Mr Field said – an ancient fish, worshipped by no one.

'I take it that you're a good Christian,' Mr Field commented.

'I'm …' He straightened and corrected the lines of his sketch, adding the spikes of teeth. He'd met Mr Field the week before, by chance. Jonah had been crouched at the side of a disused quarry, drawing a bee orchid, when a well-spoken but very dirty man had hailed him as a fellow scientist. It soon transpired that they lived within a mile of each other on the south side of the island. 'You must come and hunt fossils with me,' Mr Field had said, and so here they were. Jonah hadn't, however, anticipated a theological discussion on a muddy cliff.

All, or none. He cleared his throat. 'I was raised by a clergyman, my wife's father. My father-in-law hoped that science and religion could be reconciled.'

'Oh, no no no. Not at all. We're in a brave new world, Mr Worth. This skull is only one instance of the ascendancy of science. A society built purely upon reason and understanding, with every fact subjected to scrutiny and proof. Can you imagine how beautiful it will be, eh?'

Mr Field went back to painstakingly brushing clay from the skull. The dead animal was interminable. It was impossible to get an idea of scale when it was found in so piecemeal a fashion, each fossil removed and taken to a safe, dry location. Jonah, who preferred to draw landscapes and botany, could not put the ichthyosaur together in his head from the parts. It was a puzzle in a mash of mud and rock, not something that had once lived and breathed.

Something glinted in the red earth. He stooped again. 'Mr Field, there's a piece of jewellery here?'

Mr Field didn't look up. 'I'm not here to look for treasure, my son.'

'It's not treasure, it's …' He dug with his fingers into the mud. The rain and sand had covered it up already, but he found it eventually: a child-sized silver bangle. He held it out on the palm of his hand to the fossil-hunter.

'Oh,' said Mr Field. 'Oh yes, that is mine. I must have dropped it. My littlest one, Gracie, gave it me this morning. For luck, she said.'

'Luck in finding fossils?'

'No; luck in not being buried alive. Gracie's heard the stories of Mary Anning's dog, who was killed by a landslide further up the coast. I lost my pickaxe in a slide last week, and she's worried. I indulge her too much.' He tucked the bracelet into his breast pocket, inside his oilskin. 'These cliffs are constantly collapsing. We're lucky that all the fossils weren't washed out to sea long ago. One day, all of Dorset will be in the sea. This island will be gone.'

Jonah eyed the cliff to see if it were about to move. The island's famous stone was made out of dead things: shells and bones. This ichthyosaur's bones had been underground so long that they had turned to rock.

People would do the same. The body of a person, left abandoned on a floor soaked with blood. All the bones of someone you loved, slowly fossilising as their memory faded away.

He turned away swiftly towards the hard grey sea. Gulls screamed overhead.

'I daresay that on a day like this, you'd as soon be inside in front of a fire with your pretty new wife, eh?' asked Mr Field, with the air of someone who would rather be nowhere else than here, on this muddy shifting cliff full of fossilised bones. He'd been a London barrister before giving up the Old Bailey in favour of digging up ancient creatures and starting a family with a younger wife.

Jonah forced a smile. 'She's willing to sacrifice me in the name of science.'

'Well.' Mr Field gazed up at the sky, which was a bit of a mistake as at that moment, the heavens opened and the rain turned from a drizzle into a deluge. 'Duty before pleasure, eh?' he yelled over the sound of the raindrops and the surf.

'Duty,' said Jonah. 'Always duty.'

Their house was built on a hill with other houses above and below, so from a distance it looked as if they were layered on top of each other, like sedimentary rock. It wasn't large: three windows on the bottom and three on top, with the attic skylights in the roof. Not quite the fairy castle he and Viola had imagined living in as children, and much smaller than the haveli he still owned in India. But it was new and well-built, and large enough for the two of them whilst being suitably modest.

Inside, he bent to remove his boots and saw that they and his trousers were coated with clay. In the gaslight it looked shockingly white, as if from knee down he had turned to bone.

'Oh my goodness, you're soaked through,' said Viola, coming into the hallway. He straightened quickly.

'It's all for science. Mr Field found a whole skull today.'

'A skull! Incredible. Go up and get changed. I'll make you some toast.'

Dry linen and shoes made all the difference. When he came down to the sitting room, Viola was kneeling in front of the fire, carefully toasting a slice of bread on a long fork. A tray of tea and cake sat on the table.

A fire, a devoted wife. It was enough to make any man happy. Jonah reminded himself of this fact.

'It's ready,' she said. 'Sit down and I'll pour you some tea.'

The toast was exactly as he liked it, golden and brown with a pat of melting butter. She had used to make toast for them both at teatime when they were children. He'd thought, then, with great satisfaction about this future that they were living now. He'd pictured it much as it actually was: a comfortable routine, with a helpmate and companion to make his house a home.

His younger self didn't have the imagination or the knowledge to picture a marriage as anything greater or lesser. At thirteen, sixteen – even twenty – he wouldn't have known how a life that should be perfectly content could be hollowed out in the middle. How it could have a deep, immovable coldness at its heart. Growing up, it would have been unthinkable for him to keep secrets from Viola, especially something so dramatic and important. And now ... now, he had no choice.

She needed him. She had no money and no protector, and he had enough inheritance for them both. During his own illness in Calcutta, he'd thought about ridding himself of his Indian property and investments, tearing up the deeds and the lists of figures that he never could understand. He didn't want to be tied to a system that he knew was wrong, that could lead to such death and hatred. But his drawings hardly raised any money, and he was useless at any kind of business. He could not ask Viola to live in poverty. He could not tell Viola anything about it.

So here he was, in this house paid for by other people's labour, being waited upon by other people.

Like Viola, he wore mourning – it was almost a relief at being able to wear it openly. Sometimes he'd seen her holding the photograph of her father that she'd taken weeks before his death. She'd gaze at it as if her will could bring her father back to life. He should feel compassion for her, but his first emotion was envy.

She had buried her father, but Jonah had lost someone he loved too. He had watched her die. He didn't know what had happened to the body. Sometimes at night he woke alone in the darkness from a dream in which he'd been the one left behind, gasping his life out with no one to save him. And then he lay there catching his breath, trying to calm his heartbeat. Feeling all the miles and uncertainty, the wound that would never stop bleeding.

As miserable as Viola was, at least her father had died peacefully in bed, and she had been able to hold his hand. She had his photograph, and she was allowed to grieve for him in public. Jonah had none of that.

And then he felt ashamed. Viola wasn't the girl he used to know: she was hesitant and solitary. It wasn't only because of the death of her father. She'd been ill when they came here, but she was better now. The sea air and good food were working their magic on her, and her body was stronger, though her manner was a shadow of the confident girl she'd used to be.

It was his fault, although she would never say it. His fault that every night they went up to separate bedrooms. At first it had been because she was tired, and then for the sake of her health. But they had been married three months now. He took long sketching walks all over the island, collected botanical specimens, went on fossil-hunting expeditions, shut himself inside his office to pretend to look at business papers and correspondence from India. He gave her his drawings as gifts and he gave her none of his thoughts. He did everything to put distance between them when he should be drawing her closer.

It was all his fault. Everything here; everything in India.

'Tell me about the skull,' she said. The request, like the tea and toast, like the way she'd made this rented house cosy and homelike, was designed to please him. She worked hard to keep conversation flowing between them, though sometimes the silence was an immovable wall. 'Was it very grisly?'

'It wasn't grisly. Here, look.' He passed her the sketchbook, and she bent her head to the drawing. 'I don't know enough to tell you about the creature it came from – some sort of giant fish. But we can learn more together. Mr Field invited us to dinner tonight. I said yes.' And, as an afterthought: 'I hope that's all right.'

'Oh. Yes, of course. I could, yes. We haven't been very social, have we? You must be bored.'

'No, no I'm not bored. But I thought it would do you good, to have some lively company. We don't have to go. I can send a note.'

'No, we should go. We should get to know the neighbours. In Kimmerton I knew everyone.'

He sat back in his chair, relieved. Any society was better than none, and definitely better than another evening of silence between them. Or, even worse, a conversation that circled round and round and left them both still strangers to each other.

'I have to warn you, though – Field is an avowed atheist.'

'I shall try my hardest not to quote Corinthians at him over the soup.'

He took a large bite of toast. 'What did you do today?'

In Kimmerton she had always been busy. She helped her father with his photographs and his parish duties. She read his sermons for him and she visited the sick and poor. She was a dutiful daughter and now she was a dutiful wife. But here there was nothing for her to do.

'I wrote some letters,' she said. 'It was too wet to walk.'

'I was thinking that it would be interesting to photograph Mr Field's fossils, instead of drawing them. It would be fitting to use a chemical process to document scientific discovery.'

'I don't wish to take any photographs, Jonah.'

'Of course. I understand. It's just … it would give you something to occupy your time, and it might do some good.'

She was silent. Of course a dutiful wife would not contradict her husband. They were both trapped by this duty.

He put down his tea. 'I want you to be happy, Viola. It's what I want most in the world.'

'What about your happiness?'

'I'm already happy,' he lied.

Chapter Five

The Fields had six children and they did not believe in having a nanny or governess. The door was opened by one of the children, a small grave creature in a green frock, who curtseyed and let the Worths into the cluttered hallway. While Viola stood looking around her at the specimens of birds and butterflies in glass cases, Mr Field rushed to greet Jonah and take their dripping umbrellas. 'Thank you so much for coming, Worth,' he whispered. 'Laeticia has invited those Newhams from Weymouth. He's her second cousin. Unavoidable. It will be good to have another sensible person in our midst.'

'Sensible person?' Jonah repeated, mystified, and surprised to see the head of a stuffed fox glaring at him from the top of the coat rack.

'Mrs Newham has Ideas.' He handed the umbrellas to the green-frocked child and ushered them through to the drawing room, where Jonah accepted a glass of sweet sherry from another child with sticky fingers.

'Ideas?' But he was being borne down on by a large, pink-cheeked man with a large white moustache and bushy white sideburns and very little hair on his large, pink head.

'Admiral Newham,' said Mr Field quickly, and with the air of self-defence. 'This is my neighbour, Mr Jonah Worth.'

'Jonah Worth,' boomed the Admiral, shaking Jonah's hand

vehemently. 'Jonah Worth. Think I've heard that name before, somewhere. Not from Portland?'

'No, my wife and I recently moved here. I grew up in Wiltshire, mostly, though I was born in India.'

'Worth. India,' mused Newham. 'Now why is that familiar?'

'It's a common name,' said Jonah quickly. 'This is my wife, Vio—'

But Viola was gone, drawn aside by a woman nearly as large and as pink as her husband, who was talking down at her. There seemed to be no sign of Mrs Field.

'I'm a Weymouth man, born and bred,' said Newham. 'My wife Louisa's from London, makes me spend the winters there, but I'm happiest right here by the sea. What brings you to Portland, Mr Worth?'

'We came for the air and the views. I'm an amateur artist. Though today I've been drawing Mr Field's ichthyosaur.'

'Ah yes, fossil hunting,' boomed Newham. 'Nice little hobby, that. I've found an ammonite or two in my day.'

'It isn't a hobby,' said Mr Field, testily. 'I am a palaeontologist.'

'A paleo-what? Isn't that head bumps or some such?'

'The science of the shape of the head is phrenology, Thaddeus,' called Mrs Newham from across the room. 'Remember, we attended a demonstration of phrenology and mesmerism by Mr Elliotson in Hanover Square.'

'Oh yes. Fascinating stuff. Fascinating. Do you know that you can tell by the shape of someone's skull whether he has criminal tendencies or not? Your whole fortune is in your skull.' Admiral Newham rapped his own large head with his knuckles. 'My wife knows all about it.'

'Palaeontology is the study of the great lizards, through using the fossil record,' said Mr Field. 'It is a science. Unlike phrenology, which has no scientific basis and has been soundly discredited.'

'You study old bones,' said Mrs Newham, bustling across the

room, Viola in her wake. 'How can you tell anything about the creatures you study without looking at their skulls?'

'A skull can tell us what a creature ate and what its relative intelligence was,' said Mr Field. 'It can't tell us whether the creature had criminal tendencies or was destined for genius. Isn't that so, Worth?'

'Fortunately,' said Jonah, 'I don't believe that fish are capable of committing crimes.'

'You have the most extraordinary skull, Mr Worth,' said Mrs Newham. 'Don't you think, Thaddeus? Such a noble brow. There's a distinct lack of interesting skulls in this part of the world.'

'Are there?' asked Viola.

'Oh yes, child, you have only to compare the skulls in Dorset to the skulls in London. There's a huge variety in the metropolis. Here, everyone is the same. Interbreeding, for generations.'

A child, even smaller than the other two, appeared at Jonah's elbow. 'Dinner is ready,' it said in a piping voice, and Viola took Jonah's arm to walk into the dining room.

'Are you all right?' he whispered to her, and she nodded.

'I don't think Mrs Newham finds my skull very interesting,' she whispered back, and Jonah smiled. Perhaps this was all they needed: more society, more to talk about together, and they could find their way back to who they once had been.

'Do you think the children will serve the dinner?' he whispered. 'I'm worried that I won't be able to tell the difference between the scientific specimens and the food.'

Her chair, when he pulled it out for her, had a doll on it. A person, presumably Mrs Field, who was presiding over the table with a baby on her hip, swooped in and removed the doll, giving it to the baby. 'The children had their lessons in here this afternoon,' she explained, blinking her eyes rapidly behind spectacles, before she shepherded the miscellaneous children out of the room.

The dining table was, to Jonah's mingled disappointment and relief, skull- and specimen-free, but there was an ink stain on the cloth near his fish knife. He moved his plate to cover it. Viola saw his action and their eyes met, and she covered her mouth with her hand. It was like old times, when they'd exchange covert glances over the tea table, stifling their laughter during Mr Adams's detailed enumeration of his health problems.

'Fancy saying that phrenology has no basis in science!' Mrs Newham was saying as she entered the room. As soon as Mr Field was seated at the head of the table, the servant began to ladle the soup, even though the mistress of the house wasn't present. 'It has been extensively proven by the best minds of the day. The *best minds*.' She raised her chins. 'I am a good Christian, and a woman of science.'

Mr Field made a noise into his soup, and Viola said, 'My father always said that science was the best test of religion, and religion was the best proof of science. He said everything that we understood as faith, would be explained one day with fact. He was a clergyman and also an amateur chemist,' she explained, turning to Mr Field, her voice soft and warm. 'He would have been fascinated by your discoveries.'

'Exactly!' cried Mrs Newham. 'Science and religion, hand in hand!'

'By God! You're Jonah Worth!'

Admiral Newham's exclamation rang across the dining room, cutting over Mrs Newham.

'Yes?' said Jonah cautiously.

'Worth! I have it now! Knew I recognised you! You're the Hero of Delhi!'

His stomach sank. 'Oh. Well, that's what the newspapers said, but I hardly think that I—'

'Louisa! It's that fellow I was telling you about! Front page of the *Evening News*! He saved the life of a child, in that city full of savages where they were killing every white man, woman and child they could find! Brought her out in a laundry cart or something, didn't you, Worth?'

'A laundry cart, yes. But you can't call the Indians savages, they—'

'I knew it,' said Mrs Newham. 'Your head struck me as extraordinary as soon as I laid eyes upon you, Mr Worth. Didn't I say: such a noble brow? We may expect great things of a young man with a skull like that.'

'I didn't know you were a hero during the Sepoy Rebellion, Worth,' said Mr Field.

'I'm not a hero,' said Jonah. 'We managed not to die, that's all. People do it all the time.'

He felt the weight of everyone's eyes on him, including Viola's.

'You must come and give an Evening for us, Mr Worth!' said Mrs Newham.

'An Evening?' enquired Viola.

'Just a little thing I do on occasion, to host intellectual gatherings. We have missionaries, reformers, philanthropists, exceptional people. It's my little way of bringing a flavour of the capital to Weymouth. It would be quite thrilling to hear of your Indian adventures.'

'It's kind of you, but I'm not much of a public speaker. I'm sure people would much rather hear about skulls, or ... or whatever other topics you find.'

He took a spoonful of soup, in a desperate signal to end the conversation.

'You have missionaries?' Viola said. 'And philanthropists? I would like to hear them, one day.'

'You must come, Mrs Worth. You must come to them all. You will meet the best people in Weymouth, and improve your mind. On Friday we have *Mrs Blackthorne*!'

She announced it as if she were announcing the Queen. Mr Field grunted, but Jonah was grateful for the change in topic.

'It's quite a coup,' Mrs Newham added. 'She's come all the way from Geneva. I'm sure you've heard of her.'

'I can't say that I have,' said Viola.

'In London, she flew,' said Mrs Newham. 'Positively flew around the parlour of Mr George Dubbins.'

'*Flew?*' said Mr Field, with a dangerous quiet to his tone.

'Oh yes,' said the Admiral, comfortably. 'In front of dozens of witnesses, too. I can't say I'm entirely convinced that it's a respectable thing for a woman to be doing. Not in skirts, at least. Mr Daniel Dunglas Home flies all around London, I hear, inspired by spirits. It seems more of a man's habit, flying.'

Mr Field stared at Admiral Newham across the table. Admiral Newham gazed back, unperturbed.

Silence.

'Well,' said Viola, 'it's very kind of you to invite us. I've never seen anyone fly.'

'Do you have any children, Mrs Worth?' asked a voice from the end of the table.

The company, except for Mr Field, turned and stared. Mrs Field had, at some point during the previous conversation, joined them at the table and was calmly spooning soup.

'I ... do not,' Viola said.

'I have six daughters,' said Mrs Field. 'How many children are you hoping for?'

'I ...' Viola glanced at Jonah, who, to his own dismay, flushed deeply. 'We will be content however God sees fit to bless us.'

'And does this Mrs Blackthorne have any children?' Mrs Field asked Mrs Newham.

'That is – I cannot say for certain, but I think she does not. She's a widow.'

'I supposed as much. One has very little time for flying when one has children.' She turned back to Viola. 'Have as many as you can, my dear. They have been the great joy of Erasmus's and my life, and it is the natural purpose of a woman. Perhaps you have one on the way now?'

Jonah dared to look at Viola. She was utterly pale, her hands folded in her lap. She did not look at him.

'Start while you're still young,' Mrs Field advised her. 'A woman's body is designed to care for children but as one ages, one loses one's natural elasticity and strength. Start right away, and you will find it easier.' She settled back in her seat with an air of great satisfaction. 'This soup isn't very good, is it?'

Chapter Six

Viola was learning very quickly that it was rarely any use protesting against anything that Mrs Newham decided. Because it was still raining, their new acquaintance insisted on carrying Jonah and Viola in the Newhams' carriage and dropping them off on their way back to Weymouth, even though the distance was less than a quarter of a mile. 'People dine so early here in the country that it will barely be midnight when we get home,' she said, bustling them into the carriage, wishing an imperious goodnight to their hosts. Although Jonah and Viola were slender, the Newhams were both large people and Viola found herself pressed up against Mrs Newham's fragrant crinolines.

'Too many children and dead things in that damn house,' Admiral Newham was muttering. 'Can't think what my cousin had in her head, marrying that fellow.'

'People on the island are always a little strange,' said his wife. 'It is so fortunate that we have met you both now, so we can show you some society. Weymouth isn't what it used to be, but there are still plenty of people to speak to. We will see you on Friday, yes, for our Evening? We'd be pleased to send our carriage to you, if you don't want the trouble of using yours.'

'It's very good of you. I'm not certain...' Viola glanced at Jonah, trying to see his opinion. He had seemed uncomfortable earlier, when Admiral Newham wanted to talk about what he had done in India, so she was surprised when he said, 'Thank you, yes. We shall be there.'

The carriage stopped, hardly any time after it had set off. After effusive goodbyes from the other couple, Jonah descended and opened his umbrella for Viola.

'They're very kind,' she said, as they climbed onto the porch and Jonah opened their front door.

'Yes.'

'And very... enthusiastic.'

'Yes.' Jonah folded his umbrella and put it in the stand.

'I know you don't like speaking of what happened in Delhi.' She had the sense of taking a risk as she said it.

'It was good to get acquainted with our neighbours,' Jonah said, turning away. 'You are isolated here.'

'I don't mind isolation so much as—'

Their maid, Alice, appeared, and Jonah handed her their sodden coats and hats. Viola waited until she had gone to say what had been on her mind all evening – before this evening – but had seemed unspeakable.

'What Mrs Field said. I...'

How did one say such a thing? Standing in the hallway, not even in the parlour, with the hem of her dress dripping on the tiles?

How did one say: *I used to be a person, with work and occupation, and now I am merely a woman? People knew my name, my history, and now they know only that I am a wife.* Tonight not one person had spoken to her of herself. Her father was gone, Mrs Chapman was gone, all of her friends were gone. She could not take photographs. She knew no one except for her husband, and even he wouldn't talk with her about the most important thing that had happened to him.

There was only one future ahead of her, and they had not yet taken any steps toward it.

She swallowed and dared. 'Don't you want children, Jonah?'

'Of course I do,' he said.

'You like them. You always used to play with the Colchesters' children, after Sunday school.'

'Children are wonderful.'

'So shouldn't we … try?'

He nodded. 'It's late. Go up. I'll join you soon.'

The house was square and made of Portland stone, with shells trapped in the walls. Aside from the servants' rooms upstairs it had a master bedroom and another bedroom, which was presumably designed to be a nursery. Viola had the master bedroom to herself. She and Jonah hadn't discussed this; the arrangement seemed to make itself. He ensured she went to bed early, that there was a fire in her room on cold nights, and he slept in the second bedroom at the end of the hall because he didn't want to disturb her. At first she hadn't been well – grief and months of caring for her dying father had taken their toll – but rest and sea air were helping her recover her strength. And yet nothing had changed. He bade her goodnight every night with an affectionate kiss on her forehead. Nothing more.

He was a gentleman. He was considerate of her needs, the same way he'd always been. He put his comfort and desires behind hers. Her gentle, kind, sensitive Jonah, who was only trying to make her happy.

If they'd had a proper wedding night, this wouldn't be a problem now. It would be habit to be together as husband and wife. But that night had set the pattern for all their other nights, the pattern of their marriage: they behaved as the companions they'd always been since they were children. Something less than that, because there was supposed to be something more.

She wished she knew how to flirt or tease. But she'd been brought up by a clergyman and his housekeeper, and neither of those were exactly a role model for learning feminine wiles. She'd considered trying a new hairstyle, or maybe wearing some scent.

But she'd feel self-conscious and silly – and besides, Jonah never seemed to notice what her hair looked like or how she smelled.

Perhaps if they'd waited to be married until they were out of mourning, it might have helped. Perhaps if they'd gone away, taken a wedding journey instead of packing up everything and coming straight here to live. Bright colours and foreign sights might have made them somehow into two different people.

But the facts of their marriage were these: she had little to do, and her husband and she slept apart. They never talked about it, not once since they'd been married. She knew she loved him – she had never loved anyone as much, except for her father – and she believed from all of his actions and words that he loved her. As his wife, it was her duty to attract him.

Now, Viola tried to get ready for her husband. She had no special nightgown, but she chose her newest, laid it out on the bed, and hesitated. What was she meant to wear underneath? Not her corset? Her shift? Nothing? How should she have her hair: loose about her shoulders, or plaited as she usually did before going to bed? Each choice seemed weighted with significance, and she'd never had a mother or an aunt or a female cousin to teach her what was meant to be done, what she was meant to wear, and how she was meant to behave. She'd thought that she would take her lead from how Jonah acted and what he did. But he hadn't done anything at all.

She removed her corset and underclothes and didn't glance at her naked self in the mirror as she pulled on the nightgown. She removed her locket and carefully laid it on the bedside table. She left her hair unbound, loose and hanging down her back. Jonah had used to like to play with it when they were children. She scrubbed her face until it felt fresh and tingling, and washed herself with scented soap in the basin.

She crawled into bed, keeping herself carefully on the right-hand side, blew out the candle, lay down, and waited. Her heart was beating very fast and although she'd felt fine earlier, she felt distinctly ill now. But that time was over; she wasn't going to use illness as an excuse any more.

It seemed a very long while until Jonah came up. She heard him first; his steps were measured, almost careful. He opened the door and hesitated before coming in.

'Are you still awake?' he whispered.

'Yes.'

He shut the door behind him. He was a shadow in the darkness, a faint gleam of white shirt. She heard the rustle of his clothing as he unfastened it. There seemed to be so much of it – layer after layer. A muffled bump, and a little gasp from Jonah.

'Are you all right?'

'Hit the chair ... my trousers ...'

More rustling. And then his footsteps, shoeless now though still careful, approached the bed. He pulled back the bedclothes and the mattress dipped under his weight as he lay down beside her.

They both lay on their backs, not touching. Viola could barely breathe. They had been this close many, many times before; they had been nearly this close when they had spoken at the door an hour ago. But Viola couldn't think of a single word to say.

Jonah's breathing was soft and steady. Viola held tight to the edge of the sheet. If only she could say something, anything to make them both comfortable. To remind herself, and him, that they were intimate friends, old playfellows, now man and wife, instead of two strangers who lay untouching and contemplating how to begin some momentous and mysterious act.

But the only things she could think of to say were unspeakable.

What do we do first?

Where do I touch you?

Should I expect it to hurt?

Have you done this before?

And he was so quiet, and so still. Had he fallen asleep?

She shifted, turning her head to try to make him out, tilting her body so she could – what? speak to him? reach out to him? – and at her movement, Jonah let out a sigh, a noise almost like despair if that were possible. He turned over and pressed his mouth to hers.

It was unlike any kiss they'd ever shared. Lip to lip, his mouth open on hers, wet and warm. Their teeth clicked together and their noses bumped in the dark. He smelled and tasted strongly of wine. His chin with its day's growth of beard rasped against hers. Tentatively, she brought her hand up and touched his hair, winding its curls around her fingers. Trying to make this more familiar, with that familiar touch.

Jonah seemed not to notice. He kissed her harder, rolling his body so that he was half on top of her.

He wasn't a large man, but lying over her he was much bigger than she ever thought of him as being. His limbs were heavy. The scent of the wine he'd drunk filled her nostrils. He'd had more since dinner. His hands moved over her nightdress, first at her waist and then up over her bosom. She barely had time to understand what it was like to have her breasts touched, before he had shifted and was rucking up her nightgown to her waist.

He'd stopped kissing her and buried his face in the pillow beside hers. She tried to turn her head to kiss his cheek but his head was lying on her loose hair, pinning her in place. Instead she tried to help him with her nightclothes, and when that didn't work – his body was in the way, she couldn't reach any of the loose fabric – she put her hands on his chest. His own nightshirt was open at the throat and almost by mistake her palms touched warm, bare skin. She recoiled, and then made herself touch him again.

'Viola,' he muttered. By now he had pushed up her nightgown and his fingers brushed against her bare hip, making her shiver. 'Viola,' he said again, louder, as if reminding himself of who she was.

And then ... nothing.

He didn't kiss her again. He lay there, half on top of her, one of his bare legs pressing against the inside of hers. His breathing was harsh and rapid. Her nightgown was balled up between them in a wad around her stomach.

'I'm sorry,' he said. His voice was loud in the silent room.

'Jonah? What's wrong?'

'I can't.' He rolled off her and sat on the side of the bed.

'What did I do?'

'You ...'

'Did I kiss you the wrong way? Did I do something wrong?'

'You haven't done anything wrong. I ...' He stood. In the darkness she heard him gathering his clothes. She pushed her own nightgown down to cover herself, even though he couldn't see her.

'Jonah?'

'I can't, Viola. I just ... can't.'

The door opened, then closed.

Chapter Seven

Before first light, Jonah was striding up Verne Hill. He knew he was cowardly. But he couldn't bear to face Viola this morning.

He'd tried last night. He'd sat alone in the dining room, drinking glass after glass of claret, thinking of Viola. The soft grey of her eyes, the hollow under her ear, her pink lips. The way she had kissed him when she had promised to be his wife. He'd drained his glass, refilled it, and tried to picture her without clothing and couldn't.

'Being with my wife isn't a betrayal of someone else,' he'd said to the dining room curtains. 'The past is gone. Viola's my wife now. I belong to her.'

If only he could believe it. Jonah drank more wine to try to swallow down his guilt.

Nothing that had happened had been Viola's fault. He'd sworn to make her happy; he swore to that when he was still a child. She shouldn't suffer because of him, because he was mourning a life that could never exist and that he should never even have imagined.

The wind blew cold from the sea. He pulled his coat tighter around himself and walked faster, climbed higher.

He'd thought it would make it easier if the room was dark, but it was more difficult. No sooner had he kissed Viola and touched her than his mind had filled in details that he couldn't see, and all of them belonged to someone else. The person in his bed was not

48

the person in his heart, and all he could feel was a creeping sense of dismay. When she touched him, and her scent was of lavender water and cotton, he tried to remind himself who she was. Of all that Viola meant to him, of all that he owed her.

He was so desperate to perform that he had deliberately called up an image in his head. In London, in '56, a sultry spring morning when he was down from Oxford, he'd climbed narrow dusty stairs to a room in Lambeth. The light was better here by the river, Blandford said, with tall windows on the first floor to catch it, but Jonah suspected his Oxford friend had chosen the location because the rent was cheaper. Until he entered the room and understood why Blandford had really chosen it.

In the middle of the room was a sofa, and on it lay a naked woman. Her breasts were large, her nipples dark; between her legs was a thatch of hair shaped like a small animal. Blandford was sketching her with bold strokes of charcoal. Jonah backed immediately away, averting his face.

'Don't be so shocked, Worth,' Blandford laughed, putting down his charcoal and adjusting the woman's knee with a deft touch to expose her more. His fingers left black smudges on her pale skin. 'I've set up an easel for you. You need to try to draw something more exciting than dandelions.'

'I've – done life drawing.'

'Withered men, and women in classical drapery.'

'I prefer still life.'

'You're a man.' Blandford pushed a piece of charcoal into his hand. 'You need to know what a fine woman looks like, and Black Maria is a very fine woman.'

Blandford was a year older; at Oxford he had been part of a more sophisticated set. They talked about Art and Life and spent money like water. They seemed to know everything, and Jonah nothing. When Blandford held parties in his rooms, the laughter floated down the staircase to where Jonah sat huddled over his tiny desk, squinting at textbooks in candlelight. For some inexplicable reason Blandford had taken Jonah under his wing when he found out he enjoyed drawing, invited him upstairs to his parties, and now to this room, set up as a studio.

Jonah stole a glance at Black Maria. Presumably she got her name from her hair, a mass of raven curls both on her head and elsewhere. Black Maria was gazing at him in mingled boredom and amusement. 'And she … doesn't mind?'

'Easiest money you ever made, isn't it, Maria?'

'Cep' for the old 'uns what fall asleep before they can undo their trousers,' said Maria. 'That's easier, but this ain't bad.'

Jonah's face was aflame; his hands were wet. Blandford chuckled and went back to his drawing. 'You're off to India in a few months, Worth. You should learn about Englishwomen before you take your fill of the dusky beauties in Delhi.'

In the end, the only way he could bring himself to draw Black Maria was in the same way that he drew a still life: looking at her as an object – a flower, perhaps, cataloguing her individual features in detail, giving his attention to parts rather than the whole. A curl of toe. The lobe of an ear, a plump orchid. The round volume of a breast. A glimpse of pink through dark hair, like a poppy emerging from a bud.

When they were finished, Black Maria shrugged on a robe and rose from her couch. Jonah busied himself wiping his hands clean of charcoal on a cloth, but he knew where she was; felt her lean against his arm and whisper in his ear. 'You ever want to learn how to be less shy, love, you come an' see me here again, on your own.'

He had rolled up the drawing into a tight and furtive tube, and thrust it under his overcoat. He vowed to burn it before he returned to Wiltshire, but he did not. It lived at the bottom of his trunk, unopened, during the entire Easter holiday. At night he thought about it, felt the grit of charcoal between his fingers, pictured the smudge on her leg, the scent of linseed oil and warm bodies; ashamed and aroused, until the night before he was due to go back up to Oxford he took it from his trunk and went barefoot across the wet moonlit lawn to the pond where he unrolled the picture and plunged it in the water. He held it down, watching the lines of Black Maria blur and dissolve and drown.

Last night, in the dark bedroom with his wife, he had tried to call up the sketch again in his mind. To superimpose the image of Maria, splayed and bored, on the shadow of Viola in his bed – desperate for even this furtive arousal. It hadn't worked, except to make him even more disgusted with himself.

Jonah stopped. He stood on the lip of the cliff, gazing at the sea crawling beneath him, seeing nothing.

Teaspoons and knives on porcelain, the rustle of Jonah's napkin, the everlasting sound of gulls outside. Faintly, the sea.

'Did you have a nice walk?' Viola asked.

Jonah finished chewing before he answered. 'Yes. Are you … well this morning?'

'Quite well.'

He inclined his head.

'Would you care for a kipper?' she asked him, offering.

'No, thank you.'

Viola buttered a piece of toast for herself. Scrape of knife on bread. Jonah's spoon made a brittle sound as he scraped his boiled egg from its shell.

Her chewing was loud in her own head. Sometimes she wondered if it were as loud to Jonah, if he could hear it nearly as well as she could, in the silence of the dining room, but then again she couldn't hear him chewing, normally, so perhaps not. Unless she were a louder eater than Jonah was. Jonah's manners were always so beautiful, like everything about Jonah.

Her thoughts were loud, as well. But those she knew were only in her head. She couldn't tell what Jonah was thinking, not without looking into his eyes, and he hadn't looked up from his plate.

If she had a photograph of him, here at the breakfast table, boiled egg in a silver cup before him, coffee, newspaper at his elbow, she could look at that instead. His face might be readable in that, if it were captured.

She glanced at his hands. He had long, tapered fingers, the hands of an artist. There were fine hairs at the bases of his fingers. Those hands had been on the skin of her belly, last night. On the inside skin of her thigh, there and gone, as if made of imagination. He brought his spoon to his mouth and she looked away quickly, at the sugar bowl.

'It should be fine today,' she said. 'The weather has changed.'

'Yes.'

'It's Mrs Newham's Evening tonight.'

'Ah, is it? Yes.'

'Will you come?'

'If you wish. What was it?'

'The flying woman.'

'I didn't think you were interested in things like that.'

'I want to go, Jonah,' she said. Her voice sounded high. 'I can't just sit here and wait for you.'

'I never said that you should.'

'And yet that's all I can do.'

'I don't think that a flying woman is going to change anything.'

'I'm lonely, and you don't want me. What else am I supposed to do?'

Silence. He cleared his throat. He put down his napkin. She waited for him to say something. Anything. To explain what had happened, what she'd done wrong.

'I should look over some correspondence.' He stood.

She opened her mouth to say words about what had happened in the darkness, something conciliatory and loving, something that would make everything better, but he was already walking out of the room.

Chapter Eight

Fifteen years earlier...

September, 1843
Upcross Hall, near Wareham, Dorset

'What's that book?'

Francis leaned against the doorway to Hetty's bedroom. The room was slope-eaved and lit by a single guttering candle. Hetty shared the room and the narrow bed with Jane the first under-parlourmaid, but Jane's mother was ill and she had gone back to Wareham this morning.

'Why do you care?' Hetty didn't lower the book or the blanket pulled up to her neck. Her nightgown was third-hand at least and thin from many washings. 'I doubt you can even read.'

'I can read,' said Francis. Even from here, she could smell the stables on him. Hay and horseshit and the odour of his own stale sweat.

'You shouldn't be up in the house,' she said.

'I go where I want.' He took a step inside the room and closed the door behind him. 'I've had my eye on you a long time.'

'Well, I haven't had my eye on you, so you can go back to your own business.'

'Go back to your own business,' he repeated, in a mocking tone. 'Don't play the fine lady virgin with me, little girl. Everyone knows you've spent half your time on your back since you've been here.'

'Not with you.'

'And that's what I'm here to change.' He came up beside the

bed and leered down at her. His breath was onions and beer. 'You're wasted on Charlie.'

'Charlie has clean hands and his face isn't all over pockmarks.' She wrinkled her nose theatrically, despite the way her heart was pounding. 'And he smells better.'

'Charlie's a nancy. He's got soft hands and curls like a girl. What you want is a real man.'

Charlie was safe and a protector. Charlie, big Charlie the footman, with his broad shoulders and simple pink-cheeked face, had got her this job. When she'd met him, she was working in the scullery of the Red Lion where she'd worn the skin of her hands red and raw washing glasses and dishes and floors. She'd worked there two years already, since she was thirteen, and she was sick of it. So when he came for a glass of porter on his days off she made sure she had an excuse to be in the yard when he came out. She smiled at him and flirted, and they walked out together and soon more besides, and she wheedled him into putting in a word with her with Mrs Watson the housekeeper so she could leave the heat and stink of the Red Lion and work in a big house with a view of parkland. 'Think of how close we'll be, Charlie,' she whispered to him, out in the meadow on a fine day or under the thatch behind the stables when it rained, as he kissed her tits through her rough dress and pulled up her skirt to paw her thighs, his face pink with lust. 'If I worked at Upcross Hall, we could do this every day, not just Sundays.'

Within a month she had a position as an under-housemaid and she never touched another pint glass again. The house itself was like heaven: quieter than anywhere she'd ever been before, and she had a proper room in the servants' quarters instead of a straw mattress in the back room of the Lion. She could touch fine things as she dusted and polished, breathe lemon and linseed, catch a glimpse of herself every now and then in the gilt-framed mirror in the parlour. She listened at doors to cultured laughter, slept in an actual bed and ate meals at the long servants' table in the kitchen presided over by Mrs Watson and Mr Moore. She felt a million miles away from the Red Lion, and even further from the cottage where she'd grown up, with the walls dripping with damp and her father drunk and asleep or drunk and raving.

And then there was Madame, who didn't own Upcross Hall, but glided through the rooms as if she did. Hetty could never have imagined a woman like that.

What Charlie did to Hetty was worth it, because it meant she got to work here. Charlie said sometimes, soft with pleasure afterwards, his hand on her breast, whispering sleepy words in her ear, that he would marry her. He'd save up his wages and they'd move somewhere that he could buy a shop. She could work behind the counter in a pretty frock, be the clever one totting up the accounts with a baby on her knee.

She neither agreed nor disagreed. She just smiled and pressed his hand closer to her. It was a version of the future: a safe Charlie version. It wasn't what she dreamed about – a shop counter and an endless stream of blonde babies sucking at her – but who ever got their dreams?

Now, in her bed with Francis leering down at her, she wished for Charlie. If only she'd whispered to him at supper to come to her tonight. But she'd wanted to read. Jane objected to the candle when she was trying to sleep. Hetty had looked forward to being alone, not thinking that anyone else would be watching her to see that she was.

'Pull down the blanket and spread your legs,' Francis said. 'Or I'll do it for you.'

'You're not a man,' Hetty said, 'you're an animal. Get out.'

But her voice caught on the last word, and he laughed.

'One cock's as good as another when the lights are out, eh?' He sat on the bed, which sagged under his weight. 'You want me to put out this candle first?'

'No. I'm reading.' She brought the book up in front of her face.

She knew that it would be useless to scream. Mrs Watson, alone and imperious in her housekeeper's room, did not like trouble.

At night, when she and Jane were curled around each other in bed waiting for sleep to catch up with their exhausted bodies, Jane, who was two years older, shovel-faced and strong, whispered about Mags, the housemaid who'd slept in this room before Hetty. One night Mags had risen in the darkness while Jane was sleeping and used a twisted wire to try to get rid of the baby she was carrying. Jane had only awoken when the bed grew cold. When she got up, whispering 'Mags?' she put her foot straight into cooling blood.

No one had answered Jane's cries for help and when she finally ran to Mrs Watson's room, treading bloody footprints into the rush matting on the floor, she was told to shut up, use one of Mags's petticoats to try to staunch the blood, and cover her with a blanket until morning.

'Stupid girl,' the housekeeper had muttered, closing her bedroom door in Jane's face. 'Deserves all she gets. And you, see that this doesn't keep you from work in the morning.'

At sunrise, the grooms Francis and Paddy came to carry Mags away. 'I think she was still alive,' Jane whispered to Hetty, knees tucked behind her knees, cold hands clasped at Hetty's belly. 'I held her all night. They said they were taking her to a doctor but I don't know. They barely looked at her. She never came back. Then there was you.'

Now, Francis tugged at the book in Hetty's hands. His fingernails were black with dirt. 'Don't play the coy lady with me. Charlie told me all about you.' He pulled the book away, glancing at the pages. 'This ain't even English.'

'It's French. Not that you would know what that was.'

He threw it into the corner where it landed splayed open. 'Oh you are the lady, aren't you? Don't worry, fine miss, I know how the posh ones like it. Filthy, like animals.'

'I don't like you. Go away.'

She pushed at him, but he rolled over her to pin her with his body. He grabbed her wrists in one hand and pressed them down on the bed over her head, and with his other hard hand he covered her mouth. She bit him and he swore, raised his hand, and slapped her hard. Blood flooded into her mouth; she spat it in his face.

'Cheeky bitch,' he growled, and punched her on the side of the head.

Darkness.

When she woke up, the candle was still lit and he was working away at her. Grunting, squeezing her with his filthy hands. She tried to speak, to pull away, but she was dizzy and sick and he just held her down with his hand at her throat until he was finished.

She looked up at the flickering ceiling and thought of Madame.

The next morning Mrs Watson took one glance at her and said, 'Clean yourself up.' There wasn't a mirror in Hetty's room; when she glimpsed herself in the bowl of a spoon she saw that her lip was split and her eye swollen shut – which she already knew – but also that when she had washed herself with the cold water in her jug she had missed a dark crust of blood on her chin and along her hairline. She went back up to her room and washed again, watching the water turn brown.

She brushed out the grates and laid the fires, starting at the top of the house in the nursery and then working her way down. Master's bedroom, Mistress' bedroom, their dressing rooms, the room of the eldest son and his new wife. Her employers were snoring lumps in their beds; she moved quietly enough not to disturb them, carrying away what they had voided in the night, and when they woke their rooms would be warm and lavender-scented and their chamber pots spotless. She wondered sometimes if they thought it all happened by magic.

She emptied the slops in the yard. She was limping and her hands were clumsier than usual. Breakfast room, morning room, library; Mistress's parlour, dining room, salon. Every breath she took smelled of urine and tasted of ash. One day, she would live in her own house and none of her rooms would be cold. She thought of the cooking fire in the house where she had been born and how often it went out because they didn't have enough fuel. She remembered peeling yesterday's porridge, congealed to paper tracings, from the side of the pot, and going through her father's pockets while he was in a drunken sleep hoping to find half a penny for food.

She banished all of these thoughts, screwed her unswollen eye up against the pain, and instead of going to the kitchen for her own breakfast she crept up the stairs and stood outside the nursery door.

Madame laid and lit her own fire. Madame had breakfast brought to her in her room by one of the kitchen maids. Madame heard the children's French lessons every morning at eight o'clock.

Hetty pressed her ear to the door, holding her breath. Madame's voice was musical and lilting. Her hands were small and smooth. She was, perhaps, thirty, older than Hetty's mother had ever been, and wore no wedding ring, though her ears were pierced with small gold hoops. Her black hair had one or two threads of silver, her dress was forest green and she had a single gold bangle on one wrist and dark eyes that had seen Paris and Calais. According to rumour in the servants' hall she was the granddaughter of aristo-crats who had been beheaded in the French Revolution. She dined neither with the servants nor with the family but took her meals in her room alone. She took walks in the grounds, glided silently through hallways, and once Hetty had seen her pull a locket from her bosom, open it, and contemplate a single curl of hair as black as her own.

Hetty listened to the lesson going on beyond the door. Quietly, so she would not be heard, she mouthed the conjugation along with the children: 'Je deviens. Tu deviens. Il devient. Nous devenons, vous devenez, ils deviennent.'

There was a sound from along the corridor, and Hetty started up guiltily and hurried down the back stairs. On the landing, she paused, and drew herself up, not allowing herself to wince at the pain in her ribs and between her legs. She held up her chin, in an imitation of how Madame stood, her upright posture suitable for a descendant of French nobility.

Under her breath, she tried the unfamiliar shape of the words in her mouth. 'Je deviendrai.'

I shall become.

It hurt her mouth to smile, but she put one on for Charlie when they met in an upstairs corridor, late morning. His eyes were cold.

'What happened to your face?' She knew from his tone that he knew. Betrayal rose up in her throat like bile.

'He hit me,' she told him. 'He forced me. I told him I was yours.'

'That's why you didn't talk to me at supper last night. Why you didn't tell me to come up. You wanted him instead.'

'Why would I want him? He's an animal. He forced me, Charlie. He held me down by the throat.' Her words caught.

'Or you liked it. Francis said you liked it. He's been laughing at me all morning. He said you asked for more and then afterwards you bashed yourself to get him in trouble.'

She shook her head. 'It wasn't like that. Why would I want him when I have you?'

'Because that's what you are. You love fucking.' The word was unnatural coming from his always-genial face. 'I knew you were beautiful but I didn't know you were a whore. I'm a fool. How many others have there been?'

'None. No one but you, please believe me. Francis forced me.'

'Now I know why you wouldn't promise to marry me. Too many others out there and you couldn't keep your legs shut. I'm the last to know, aren't I?'

She'd be alone again tonight, Francis would come again. She grabbed his sleeve. 'Please, Charlie, please believe!'

He pulled away. 'Don't talk to me. You never loved me.'

'I did, I do. Please …'

'Liar.' He spat on the floor at her feet and thundered away. Hetty watched him go, heart thudding, knowing it was true. She was a liar. She didn't love him. There had been others. It was how she'd got that job at the Red Lion.

Lies, and her beauty, were the only things she had.

Chapter Nine

June, 1858
Weymouth

It was an improvement on Dover, where she was cold in a cheap inn room.

Mrs Henriette Blackthorne stepped down from the train carriage in the new station of Weymouth, steam and coal dust filling the air. Out of habit, she glanced quickly around for men with the shiny suits and broad shoulders of debt collectors, and instead was greeted by a footman. He appeared to be about sixteen years old, and was in actual livery, with polished buttons.

'Mrs Blackthorne? The Admiral sent me to fetch you, ma'am. Mrs Newham is waiting in the carriage. May I take your bag?'

The accent, with its pronounced Rs, was familiar. She had not heard it in a long time. She lifted her chin, satchel firmly under her arm, and said, 'Thank you, no. But my trunk is in the baggage car, if you'd be so kind.' He scurried away and she put the coin she'd reserved for the porter back into her purse, where it would do her more good.

Mrs Newham, her benefactor, was exactly as Henriette had pictured her: fat and loud and with her strident words hiding a deep well of desperation. Her letters, sent to London and forwarded to Geneva, spoke of science and the brave new world of Spiritualism, but Henriette had long years of experience with widows, sisters, mothers, daughters. Science was all very well and good, but these women were not yearning for Progress. They were yearning for the loved ones they had lost, and were willing to pay good money to get them back, if only for a moment.

The men sometimes yearned for something quite different, and it was part of her never-ending dance to whet that yearning without ever satisfying it.

Henriette, charming, answered questions about her journey, about Geneva and London, asked about the weather in Weymouth, exclaimed over the view of the sea from the carriage window, and all the while she read the lines and pouches of Louisa Newham's face like a map of a route she had walked a hundred times before.

The carriage stopped after a short journey and the child footman helped her out. Henriette Blackthorne stood on the Esplanade and looked about her at what, for the time being, was her new life. The carriage had set them down in front of a row of tall Georgian houses. They were painted white and looked showily respectable, like starched shirt fronts. On a sunny summer day like today, holidaymakers thronged the pavements, wearing straw bonnets and crinolines, parasols and nosegays. Bathing machines stood sentinel on the sandy beach amongst donkeys and winkle-sellers. Cut into the chalk hill curving the bay, King George rode ramrod-straight upon his white horse. Henriette took a deep breath of sea air, salt and charcoal and horseshit, and smiled at Weymouth, the pleasure grounds of a dead mad king.

How Ethelred would have hated it here.

'I've taken the first and second floors for you,' said Mrs Newham, who had alighted from the carriage with surprising agility. 'It's a very fashionable address and I'm sure you will be very comfortable – and of course you must stay with us here for as much of the season as you can. I'm certain that you will find that the society of Weymouth is quite superior, as good as anything that you have been used to on the Continent.'

'I expect to meet many new friends. You shall have to tell me all about everyone. I have never been in Dorset before.'

'Your reputation precedes you. Weymouth is abuzz! And of course I-I have been ...'

Mrs Newham faltered, and Henriette, used to the symptoms, interrupted smoothly, 'I have the distinct impression that there is someone who would like to speak with you. They've been tugging at my sleeve from the moment I met you. They've small hands ... quite impatient. Has it been a long time?'

The other woman, struck dumb, nodded. It was a new town, a new house, new people, new benefactors, and the same old story. Time for Henriette Blackthorne, born Harriet Smith in Wareham, to sing for her supper.

She followed Mrs Newham up the stairs into her new lodgings and shut the door behind them.

A newsprint copy of an engraving, cut and mounted on black card.

The heads and shoulders of two women, each drawn in isolation. The one on the left is in her thirties. Her thick dark hair has been secured in coils and her chin is rounded and strong, her eye clear, her brows thick and precisely arched, her neck a smooth column above her black dress. The artist has given her Grecian features, the imperial expression of Hera, though she wears a necklace with a cross. The slightest of smiles touches her lips.

The woman on the right is pale and blonde, with her hair loose about her face. Her chin is pointed, her features gamine, her eyes large and liquid. She is younger, shy, wearing a filmy white gown. Her mouth is half-open, as if about to speak.

Underneath, the legend:

MRS HARRIET BLACKTHORNE AND HER SPIRIT GUIDE, FLORA BELL.

Chapter Ten

Jonah and Viola drove along the road between Chesil Beach and Portland Harbour in near-silence. Viola looked out the window at the water, tipped by frothy waves and dotted with pleasure craft. She hadn't been off the Isle of Portland since they moved there. Jonah tried his best to make some unexceptional remarks about the weather. He'd spent the day with Mr Field on his dig, careful not to mention where they were going that evening, only returning in time to dress hurriedly before going out again.

He would have to speak with Viola about what had happened sometime, but after avoiding the subject this morning, he had no idea how to broach it, how to explain himself. How did you even talk about these things that happened in silence in the dark? What language could you use that wasn't crude or vicious or hurtful?

And he would have to lie.

Painful as it was, silence was easier than lying. Seeing the ghost of uncertainty on Viola's face was more bearable than seeing the slow wince of pain.

The Newhams lived on Trinity Road on the south side of the harbour, directly across the water from the Custom House, in a double-fronted house with bay windows on the ground and first floors which overlooked the road with its foot traffic and the harbour with its constant coming-and-going of boats. Jonah imagined that very little happened in Weymouth without the Newhams being able to observe it first-hand.

Viola took his arm as they walked into the Newhams' house but dropped it as soon as they were inside. It was still light out but the curtains had been drawn and the gas had been turned down so low as to almost cast no light at all. Mrs Newham bustled over to them, all glittering eyes and self-importance, and drew Viola's arm into her own. Jonah let them go, not without a feeling of relief.

'Oh, my dear Mrs Worth, you're here just in time. We're about to begin. You must be very quiet, you know.' She lowered her voice to a whisper. 'Otherwise the spirits won't come.'

Spirits?

'Is this . . . are we here to see *ghosts*?' Viola asked.

'Of course! Mrs Blackthorne is a spirit medium. Didn't I tell you?'

'You may have left that part out.'

Two days ago she might have exchanged a glance of complicity with him, shared the sense of the absurd. Now, she merely allowed Mrs Newham to lead her into the parlour, and Jonah followed. The darkened room was crowded with stolid and prosperous Weymouth citizens, in their watch chains and jet beads, starched collars and net gloves. No one looked like a ghost, or as if they could fly.

A circle of chairs ringed the room and guests conversed in low voices. A large table covered with a white lace cloth sat in the middle of the circle. On the table lay various musical instruments: trumpet, tambourine, mouth-organ, drum. It was almost impossible to see them, with the lights turned so low. Jonah squinted, and thought he also saw slates and several rolls of paper. At the head of the table was a large, heavy wooden chair with stout arms and a high back. Some sort of apparatus had been rigged up around it: a wooden frame with curtains attached. There were several lengths of rope on the seat.

Mrs Newham led Viola and Jonah to seats near a couple whom she introduced as the Davises. Then she went to the head of the table, clapping her hands for attention. The conversation ceased instantly.

'We are *extremely fortunate* that Mrs Henriette Blackthorne has agreed to favour us with one of her séances. Before we begin, she has laid down some rules.' Mrs Newham held her finger to her lips as if telling the already-silent guests to be quiet. 'Spirits are sensitive to light, so we must lower the gas even further, once we begin. They are sensitive to sound, so I must ask you to keep your conversations quiet. And they are very sensitive to thoughts and feelings. They require an open and receptive atmosphere.' She tucked her chin and gazed around the room, eyes glittering. 'If you don't believe in the existence of spirits – if you doubt their ability to manifest in our earthly sphere, and to talk to us, sing to us, even touch us – you should leave now.'

She paused dramatically. Jonah glanced around the room. The other guests were suitably impressed, it seemed. Viola caught his eye, and then looked down at her lap.

Did she believe in this stuff? He'd never asked her. She was a vicar's daughter; she went to church every Sunday. So did he. Repeating prayers, singing hymns, all of them empty. They weren't empty to Viola. When she prayed, he heard the tremble in her voice, her fervently whispered 'Amen'. He thought of Mr Field's exultation on the cliff: *It's the death knell of Christianity.*

He had heard the death knell of all religion in that ruined temple in Delhi. He had seen it in the bodies lying on the dusty earth. Everything since then had been an exercise in hypocrisy.

'Then we are all believers,' said Mrs Newham. 'Shall we sing a hymn to begin?' She immediately launched into a booming version of 'For Those In Peril On The Sea'. Jonah, lips moving, glanced at Admiral Newham, who was sitting on the other side of Viola, singing his heart out in a hearty baritone that was only slightly deeper than his wife's. Four verses. Were they hoping to communicate with the spirits of sailors, or was it a tribute to their seaside location?

The last note faded away, Admiral Newham's the last to disappear. There was a noise; a door opening at the far end of the room. As one, all heads swivelled as a shadowy figure entered the parlour. It almost appeared to glide across the Turkish carpet towards them.

'Mrs Blackthorne!' whispered Mrs Newham, a thrill in her voice. 'We are ready for you!'

Complete silence for a moment, aside from the whisper of a dress's hem on the floor, soft as breathing. The faint light caught the figure's form and Jonah was able to discern a woman dressed in black. For a confused moment he thought she had no face, but then she passed closer to the gaslight and he saw that she was wearing a black veil. She was tall, as tall as a man, but with a woman's rounded figure and narrow waist. She moved with leisurely grace, as if she knew the eyes of everyone in the room were focused upon her and she intended to make the most of their collective interest.

Mrs Blackthorne passed through the centre of the circle, past the table with its collection of musical instruments. Such was the stillness of the room that Jonah felt the air move as she walked by, and he caught the scent of neroli. A murmur rose up in her wake. He distinctly heard someone whisper, 'I wonder if she will fly!'

Jonah gritted his teeth. This woman might cultivate a walk like a goddess come to earth, but she was made of flesh and blood. Even in the near-dark it was obvious that she hid no wings under the close bodice of her dress. Or perhaps she had winged shoes, or a flying device secreted beneath her crinoline?

Even as he thought it, he was aware that his irritation wasn't with the irrational nature of what they were doing, but with himself.

Mrs Blackthorne took her place at the head of the table, in

front of the curtains and the chair. Mrs Newham reverently stepped back to allow her room. The medium did not raise her veil, but spoke in a clear, musical voice: 'I wonder if any of the gentlemen in the room would mind tying me up?'

No one moved or spoke. Jonah could only assume that the rest of the room found this as extraordinary a request as he did. But then, why would it be extraordinary? If a medium claimed that she could pass through the barriers of life and death, presumably she also wanted to prove that she could pass through the more mundane barriers of several hemp ropes?

He stood. Beside him, he felt Viola start in surprise. 'I will.'

Mrs Blackthorne inclined her veiled head to him. 'Thank you, sir. And someone to assist you?'

Admiral Newham cleared his throat and also stood.

Mrs Blackthorne took the ropes from the seat of the chair and gave them to Jonah. 'They are good, strong ropes, are they not?'

He tested them in his hands. 'Yes, they appear very strong.' He handed them to Admiral Newham, who also tested them and agreed.

'Very good,' said Mrs Blackthorne, and although her face was still obscured by the veil, Jonah could hear a smile of approval in her voice. She sat gracefully in the chair, laying her arms along the armrests. 'Please secure my wrists and ankles to the chair, with as many knots as you like.'

Admiral Newham gave half the ropes to Jonah and they bent to their task on either side of the chair. From this side, the little light was blocked out by the chair and Mrs Blackthorne's body, and Jonah had to peer closely to see what he was doing. He wound one of the ropes around the arm of the chair and Mrs Blackthorne's wrist. She wore black gloves and her dress, which he could not help touching, was made of silk with small black frills at the sleeves. From here, he could smell her perfume more clearly.

'You may wrap them tightly,' she said to them both. 'Please

don't fear that you will cut off my circulation. I am quite used to being bound.'

'Well, I've tied up some interesting creatures in my time, but never a woman before,' said Admiral Newham, bluffly, but neither Jonah nor Mrs Blackthorne answered him. Jonah pulled the ropes tighter and tied one knot and then another, tucking the ends into one of the coils. Jonah could hear the steady softness of her breath under the veil.

'And my ankles to the legs of the chair, if you please. I would like you to both be quite satisfied that I am not able to move from my seat.'

Jonah knelt at the foot of the chair. The medium's skirt was dark as night, and the floor was entirely in shadow. He could see nothing, not even his own hand. He touched material: the hem of her skirt.

'You shall have to lift my skirt a little,' she murmured. He cautiously nudged the material aside and ventured further, encountering the warm leather of her boot. With his other hand he found the chair leg, and by feel, began wrapping the rope around it and Mrs Blackthorne's ankle.

To be bound this way, she must be sitting with her knees apart, each of her feet flush against the foot of the chair. It was an unnatural position for a woman to sit, with her legs spread.

Except for Black Maria, he thought, and sweat sprang up underneath his collar.

The hem of her skirt brushed the backs of his hands. Quickly, he tied the rope and tightened it, trying his best not to touch Mrs Blackthorne any more than necessary. Despite his efforts, as he was tying the second knot his thumb encountered soft wool, warmed from skin.

Her stocking. He recoiled as if pinched. Mrs Blackthorne did not move at all, made no indication that he had taken an inadvertent liberty.

'You are quite satisfied with your work?' she asked.

Jonah nodded, and then, realising that she couldn't see him, said, 'Yes.' His voice was very loud in his ears. He scrambled to his feet, hoping his red cheeks were invisible in the darkness.

'I'm satisfied,' said Admiral Newham, who puffed slightly as he straightened.

'Very good. Then will you please do me the favour of drawing these curtains about my chair?'

They pulled the curtains closed, rendering Mrs Blackthorne effectively invisible to everyone sitting in the room. Jonah glanced around the back edge of the curtain and saw her sitting in her chair, bound hand and foot, head upright as if this were the most normal thing in the world.

'Now, please lower the lights further, Mrs Newham,' she said, 'if you don't mind. We have several spirits close tonight, but they may be shy.'

Mrs Newham bustled noisily about. As they crossed to their seats, Admiral Newham whispered to him, 'Nice bit of leg, eh?'

Jonah didn't answer. He hurried to his seat before it became so dark that he couldn't find it. Such was their hostess's zeal that she turned the gas lamps right off, and the only light in the room came from two candles, both set in the sconce nearest the door from which all the guests had entered, on the opposite side from where Mrs Blackthorne sat behind her curtain. Jonah blinked several times, trying to adjust to the darkness.

Beside him, Viola was sitting perfectly still. He wondered what she made of all of this. He knew that she had once loved the setting of a stage: she enjoyed dressing up for photographs, or dressing up others, creating a scene. But it was always in fun. The costumes were a play act, and only temporary. Viola was a practical person, not someone given to theatricality or displays of emotion.

In all the time he had known her, he'd only rarely seen her cry. Once, when they were very young, she had put her foot in a rabbit hole whilst they were walking together and fallen and broken one of the bones of her arm. The pain must have been incredible, but as he had helped her back home, only one tear fell from her eye. He'd admired her bravery, and told the boys at school – particularly Edward Freeman, who had broken a toe the autumn before kicking a rock, and wailed as if he were having his foot amputated.

As the daughter of a vicar, she visited the sick and the poor, and sometimes she'd tell him about the suffering she'd seen. But although her voice was sombre, she never swooned or cried or did any of the things that young ladies were popularly supposed to do.

When he returned from India, she'd lost weight; the bloom had gone from her cheeks and instead of her habitual white lawn she was dressed in full mourning. But these were the only outward marks of her mourning, or of the long months that she had spent nursing her father through his last illness – months when Jonah had been recovering his own strength in the Indian sun. Perhaps she'd wept when she was alone in that empty house that had used to be so full. She may have wept at his funeral, which had happened while Jonah was on a boat crossing the Indian Ocean, avoiding small talk with his fellow passengers, spending hours in his airless cabin alone. But he had never seen her cry for her father, even though he knew how much she missed him.

Jonah glanced at her. He hadn't thought of it – he'd been too busy with his own conscience. Did Viola hope that her father's spirit would be here at this séance?

He couldn't see her face clearly. Hesitantly, in the darkness and silence, he reached out to touch his wife's hand.

There was a rattling, metallic crash. Jonah started, someone shrieked. The crash came twice more and Jonah realised that it was the sound of the tambourine from the table being struck. He tried to see who had picked it up but all he could make out was a metallic glint catching the candlelight. As he watched, the tambourine rattled and shivered and he saw the glint rise higher, towards the ceiling.

Was it ... *floating*?

The trumpet blared and Jonah jumped again. Mrs Davis, on his right side, gasped. A rap sounded somewhere – on the table? in the walls? – and the tambourine fell to the table with a clatter.

'The spirits wish to speak.' Mrs Blackthorne's voice emerged from behind the curtain, so clearly that she could be standing in the middle of the room rather than tied to a chair. 'They hover, beyond the veil, waiting for a voice. Can you feel them?'

A few murmurs.

Jonah felt something like a breath of air on the back of his neck. Instinctively he reached up to brush it off, as if it were an insect. There was nothing there.

Spirits. Instruments that played themselves. What nonsense.

And yet, he'd tied the medium to the chair himself as tightly as he could. Who was moving these instruments? Another guest? An accomplice? But how would one have slipped in without their noticing?

A hand laid itself on his shoulder.

Jonah whipped his head around. He saw a pale hand, a pale arm, seeming to slightly glow in the darkness. A light-coloured dress, and above it, a face: perfectly oval, features hardly discernible except for the eyes, which were black hollows.

Someone cried out.

'It's Flora Bell,' said Mrs Newham in a shrill voice. 'Her spirit guide.'

Jonah could not breathe. The hand on his shoulder was light, but it had the effect of freezing him to his chair.

'Is it you, Flora?'

The figure stooped. 'A person is with me,' it whispered into Jonah's ear. If it was a spirit, it was a spirit with breath; his hairs stirred, and he felt gooseflesh crawl up his arms and over his neck.

'Who?' He choked the word.

'P of the white and red.'

His throat closed again.

'Flora, speak to us!' cried Mrs Newham.

The hand left his shoulder. The figure moved back further into the shadows.

He could not see or hear or think. He knew he only needed to escape that figure, its words and what they meant.

Jonah stumbled unheeded through the darkness, through the room. The tambourine quivered and raps sounded all around him. In the dim-lit hallway, he rushed past a startled maid and outside onto the street. He didn't care what direction he went, as long as it was away from the house.

The words were from a spirit. Spirits were dead. White and red, blood on white cotton. Even after everything, after all of the death, the corpses in the Delhi streets, on the floor of that temple, he'd cherished a small guttering flame of hope that, somewhere, the person he loved might still be alive.

And then he would not be to blame.

He'd never seen Delhi again, not after that night in May – he'd recovered in Calcutta, and as soon as he was well enough, left for England. He had heard accounts of the siege that had followed the rebellion, read about it in the newspaper, seen the lithographs of mutineers hanging from gallows, hands tied behind their backs; the ruins of the Kashmiri Gate, shelled and bullet-ridden; the vast open empty spaces, devoid of people. Delhi – the Delhi where he'd been born and that he'd known for those few vivid months – was no more. It was a city gutted by revolution and vengeance, stained with the blood of the innocent.

One innocent in particular. *P of the white and red*.

Jonah stopped. He was on a bridge. Beneath him the water shivered, promising oblivion. If he were brave, the sea could purge his guilt. It could erase these thoughts of spirits, of love, spin them into nothingness forever.

He leaned against the parapet, put his hands on the cold stone, and thought about climbing up over it and dropping down and into the water to be washed out to sea.

Chapter Eleven

When the lights went up there was a crush around the medium. Viola could barely see above the shoulders of the other guests but she gathered from the movement and calls for brandy that Mrs Blackthorne was being revealed, untied, and revived. She caught a glimpse of the woman being helped to her feet and then she was swept out of sight.

'Wasn't that extraordinary?' said Viola's neighbour, turning to her. She had been introduced before the séance as Mrs Davis. 'The message she gave to Mr Andrews from his sister about the pearls. Have you ever heard anything like it in your life?'

'I haven't,' said Viola. She bit her lip, agitated, feeling an unfulfilled yearning, a sense of anticlimax. But why should she hope to communicate with her father's soul? Wasn't it more comforting to think that he was safe in Heaven, rather than floating around playing tambourines?

'It's proof of the material basis of the human spirit,' said Mr Davis. 'That souls have weight and volume, that they survive after the body is decayed and gone. It is incontrovertible evidence in favour of Christianity, Mrs Worth. Nothing less than that! We live in a scientific age indeed.'

'Mrs Newham told me that you are in mourning for your father,' said Mrs Davis. 'I'm sorry that Flora Bell didn't have a message for you from him. I was rather hoping that my papa would put in an appearance. There is some dispute about his will, you see; he could have sorted it out in an instant.'

'Is that admissible in probate?' Viola said, but neither of them seemed to take the least notice.

'And Flora Bell appearing right behind your husband like that! I believe that her hand was actually on his shoulder. What did it feel like, I wonder? Was it warm or cold, firm or ephemeral?'

'I thought she whispered something to him,' Mrs Davis added. 'Do you know what it was?'

'I couldn't hear what she …' Viola turned to Jonah to draw him into the conversation, but he wasn't there. 'Oh.'

'Perhaps he went for some air,' said Mrs Davis. 'He looked very pale. And who could blame him, being touched by a person from the beyond! Mrs Blackthorne is exhausted, look.' She craned her neck. 'I wonder if she'll have any more messages for us over supper. Papa never meant to bequeath the property in Shropshire to my older brother, I know he did not, we spoke about it in particular detail before he died.'

'I hope that your husband isn't ill,' said Mr Davis. 'Would you like me to look for him, Mrs Worth?'

'Oh, no, thank you, no, I will find him myself.'

She squeezed her way between people, towards the door. Why didn't Jonah tell her that he was leaving? She should've noticed it, but she was too busy trying to catch a glimpse of the medium, like everyone else in the room. In that shocking moment when the lights came up and the curtains were opened and Mrs Blackthorne was revealed – bound in her chair and half insensible, the veil slipping from her deathly pale face – Viola had not thought about her husband in that moment, at all.

A maid lingered in the corridor outside the room. 'Excuse me,' Viola asked, 'have any of the guests left the house in the past few minutes?'

'One gentleman left the house, ma'am. Did you see the ghosts?'

'Yes. Did he take his hat and coat?'

'I don't know, ma'am. I don't think so. Maybe he's coming right back. What were the ghosts like?'

'I only saw one, and she was very beautiful. Thank you.' Viola hurried to the door and slipped outside. It was dark now, and the air outdoors was much cooler and fresher than in the house.

She remembered how her father's fever had come upon him suddenly, and at first he had thought that the house was too warm. She had found him at the bottom of the garden, hatless and in his shirtsleeves, holding on to a tree to keep himself upright, perspiration dripping from his forehead.

'Jonah?' she called. She looked up and down the street. Light from the houses spilled out onto the streets and there was a full moon overhead, but she saw no trace of her husband. 'Jonah!' she called again.

'Have you lost someone?' said a voice behind her. Viola turned; the tall woman on the pavement wore a black dress, but no hat or veil. Her hair was dark, her eyes even darker, and although Viola had not seen her face clearly she recognised her at once from her dignified posture and her musical voice.

'Mrs Blackthorne? I thought you were inside.'

'I wanted some air, so I slipped out the back door. I've had to learn how to make a quick escape, on occasion. Messages imparted by spirits are not always popular with those who hear them. Who's Jonah?'

'My husband. He … I think he may be unwell.'

'Your husband? The gentleman who tied me up? Young, like you, dark hair in curls, silver watch chain, artistic and handsome?'

'He … well, yes.'

'I'll help you look for him. Do you know where he would have gone?'

'No. I don't know Weymouth.'

'If he wanted air, he would go towards the seafront, don't you think? Let's try that first.' Mrs Blackthorne held out her arm, and Viola, at a loss, took it. The other woman was taller than she was, and more womanly, as if she had been made on a bigger scale than Viola herself. She tucked Viola's arm close to her side.

'I'm sorry not to stand on ceremony and introductions,' said Mrs Blackthorne, 'but I find it rather superfluous when I've been tied up and unconscious in your company for an hour. What's your name?'

'Viola Worth.'

'And what do you do, Viola Worth?'

'Do?' Viola was looking around for Jonah, only half-listening to her companion.

'Yes. What do you do all day?'

The question was an odd one. She didn't think she had ever been asked that in polite conversation.

'I don't do much all day. I go for walks, or write letters.'

'What would you like to do?'

'I used to take photographs,' she said. 'But I don't seem to be able to any more.'

'Why not?'

'It reminds me too much of my father.'

'And you don't care for your father?'

'What? No! I cared for him a great deal. But he's dead.'

'It seems like the best way to keep him alive, in my opinion: to remember him.'

'Better than calling up his spirit from the dead?'

Mrs Blackthorne laughed. It was a deep, rich, sound, and Viola, who had been craning her neck to try to see ahead of them along the shadowy street with the harbour on their left, looked at her instead. Without her veil, Viola could tell that she was quite beautiful, with a generous mouth and arched dark brows. She was perhaps ten years older than Viola.

'He isn't here,' said Mrs Blackthorne. 'Shall we try in the other direction?' She turned them around without waiting for a reply, and then asked, 'Did you enjoy the séance?'

'Oh, yes,' Viola said, and then was conscious that she wasn't telling the truth. 'That is, I found it very interesting, and a little sad.'

'Some people find it sad. For others, it's inspiring and hopeful.' Viola's arm was pressed against Mrs Blackthorne's side; she could feel the vibration of the other woman's voice as they walked. 'I'm often unaware of what happens during a session. Did you receive any messages?'

'No.'

'Were you hoping to?'

'I ... don't know. I desperately want to talk to him again, but if I did receive a message, I don't know if I would find it comforting, or upsetting. And I wouldn't be sure if it were really from him, unless it were quite specific.'

Mrs Blackthorne glanced down at her. 'You are an honest young lady.'

'Not always.' It burst out from her before she'd known she was going to say it. Something about being outdoors, and this physical closeness with the other woman. Aside from with Jonah, she had not been so physically close to another human being since her father's last embrace. And with Jonah ...

'I don't like to hurt people's feelings,' she added quickly. 'So sometimes a white lie or omission is necessary. That's what I meant. I hope I didn't hurt your feelings by saying I'm not certain whether my father would really send a message through you. I do believe that our souls live on after death – so did my father – but I am not sure that they communicate through raps and playing the tambourine. It seems so – so mundane, somehow, for something that's the greatest mystery of our lives.'

'You haven't hurt my feelings at all. I think a good healthy dose of scepticism is necessary in a world like ours. Your husband is not a believer,' Mrs Blackthorne said.

'How – how did you know that?'

'Because of what I do, the barriers between other people and me are thinner than they would normally be. I believe the spirits help me understand how other people think and feel.' She smiled, and Viola saw a flash of teeth. 'He also took great care to fasten his knots very fast and tight. Usually this is a symptom of some-one wanting the séance very much to succeed, or very much to fail. In his case, it was the latter.'

'I don't think that he wanted you to *fail*,' Viola said, and Mrs Blackthorne laughed.

'Now that's a white lie.'

The other woman stopped walking and pointed ahead of them at the stone bridge that spanned the narrow part of the harbour. A man was standing at the railing, silhouetted against the lighter night sky.

Viola squinted. At this distance, she couldn't tell if it was Jonah. And what did that say about her, about their marriage, that she couldn't recognise her own husband at a distance, when a perfect stranger had discerned something vital about him merely from the way he tied knots?

Mrs Blackthorne released her arm. 'Go to him. He needs you.'

'How do you know?'

The medium merely smiled and turned away.

Jonah didn't look around as she approached. He was gazing downwards, at the moon reflecting on the sea. In the cold silver light his expression was clear to her: it was the expression she had often seen since they were married. His mind a million miles away from this world and his wife. He was focused, attentive on something, and his eyes were desperately sad.

'Jonah,' she said, and hesitantly touched his arm. 'Are you unwell?'

His expression changed. 'Viola. No – no I am well, I ... it was very hot in that room.'

His voice was unsteady, though he was clearly making an effort. He still looked sad. Viola thought of how naturally she had taken Mrs Blackthorne's arm – how the touch had been somehow at the same time comforting and energising – and wished she could do the same right now for her husband. But the stiffness of his posture, the way he was avoiding looking into her face, made her think that if she did, he would shrink from her.

'We should go home,' she said gently.

'Yes. Yes, I need to care for you. That is why I ...' He seemed to see her for the first time. 'You have come out without your hat or coat.'

'So have you,' she reminded him. 'When you disappeared, I was worried, so I came out to find you. What happened? Why did you need to leave like that?'

'You'll catch a chill. Why do you never think of yourself?'

'I'm not cold.'

He took off his jacket and wrapped it around her shoulders. His shirtsleeves were bright. The jacket smelled of his shaving lotion and his hair, and was warm from his body. She didn't feel cold at all, but she drew it closely around herself.

'Mrs Blackthorne said you needed me,' she said.

He didn't answer, merely began walking across the bridge towards Trinity Road. The breeze blew his curls back from his face and she could see his high forehead, the dark slashes of his brows, the liquid sadness still in his eyes.

She realised he didn't want to speak, kept deflecting her questions. With his jacket around her, surrounded by his scent and his warmth, she felt all the distance that had come between them. It was even worse since last night.

What was he thinking of in those times when he forgot that she existed?

'Mrs Davis thought – *I* thought – that the figure whispered something to you,' she said. 'I heard something, but I couldn't make out the words. When it touched you.'

They had reached the Newhams' house. 'I'll order our carriage. Please go inside and get warm.'

'What did it say, Jonah?'

But then the door to the house opened, he ushered her inside and went off to find the groom, and she was left standing quite alone, except for the maid.

Chapter Twelve

Mrs Blackthorne was staying in lodgings on the Esplanade. Jonah sent his card up and waited in the street.

Overnight, guilt had transformed itself into clear, bright anger. It was a welcome change. He took deep breaths of the morning air, trying to steady himself. This person was a stranger and she at least put on the semblance of a gentlewoman. He would be calm, and reasonable, cordial, and cut through all of this mystic rubbish.

A maid appeared and nodded to him without speaking. He followed her up the stairs to a sitting room with windows looking out over the harbour. Mrs Blackthorne was sitting in an armchair. Jonah had never seen her face properly, but he recognised her. The room smelled faintly of her perfume.

'Mr Worth,' she said, holding out her hand. 'It's nice to put a name to the knots.'

Her voice was amused, almost mocking, and it made him forget all of his resolutions. 'How do you do it?' he demanded, ignoring her outstretched hand.

'How do I do what?'

'Escape from the ropes?'

She smiled. 'It's quite simple. I don't.'

'Then who's your accomplice? A friend? Your maid? The maid who let me in is blonde. Is it her?'

'I have no accomplice, other than my spirit guide.' Mrs

Blackthorne withdrew her hand, apparently not at all nonplussed by Jonah's rudeness, and resumed her chair. 'Please, sit down.'

'I won't sit, thank you. I came here for answers.'

'What about?'

'You know full well.'

'I'm afraid I don't, Mr Worth. Was something done last night to upset you? Did you receive a message?'

'You know that I did.'

'I know very little of what happened last night. I went into a trance soon after you drew the curtains around me, and I didn't awake until the lights went up. If you received a message from Flora, I can't take responsibility for it.' Her expression was maddeningly calm; she reached for a cup on the table near her elbow. 'Shall I ring for some coffee?'

'No.'

Mrs Blackthorne raised her eyebrows. She spoke in a soft voice. 'You're angry.'

'And you are manipulative and cunning.'

She smiled slightly. 'You really must have some coffee. I'll call Greta back.' She lifted her hand to pull the bell.

'I don't want coffee! I want you to tell me who you think "P" is.'

Mrs Blackthorne didn't pull the bell. She took a sip of her own coffee, with infinitely provoking calmness.

'Your wife tells me you are not a believer, Mr Worth.'

'You've spoken to my wife about me?'

'I have. Yesterday evening, when she was looking for you. I told her to help you. Did she?'

He set his jaw. 'I don't need help. I need answers.'

'I've met plenty of sceptics in my time. I don't need to be tied up, Mr Worth. The spirits come whether I am restrained or not. The knots are there to satisfy men such as yourself, particularly men who don't believe women.' She took another sip of coffee. 'But it wasn't enough for you that I was bound hand and foot?'

'Who is "P"?'

Mrs Blackthorne put down her cup. She folded her hands in her lap. 'I don't know. From your anger, I hazard that perhaps you do?'

'Who's Flora Bell?'

'You have the advantage of me there, Mr Worth. I've never met Flora Bell, though we've often been in the same room. All I know of her is what others have told me.'

'But she's meant to be your spirit guide. She's meant to come through you.'

'She and I have an intimate connection, yes. I am her channel. But that's not to say I know her, any more than two people who live in the same house together but don't open their hearts to each other.'

He ground his teeth. 'I'd thank you to stay away from my wife.'

'Your wife needed help. As do you, I think.'

'I told you: I don't need help!'

'And yet you're angry. As I've said, I've met sceptics in my time, Mr Worth. They've been mocking or contemptuous. They've treated me as a deliberate trickster or as a scientific specimen or as a gullible fool. But they have only rarely been angry. This makes me think that whatever Flora told you, there was a glimmer of truth.'

'Truth? What kind of truth? "P" could be anyone. Everyone knows someone whose name starts with "P". Or it doesn't even have to be a name, it could be a title or a place. It's a lie, it's a guess.'

'This spirit must have told you more than their initial, for you to be so upset.'

'That message could have gone to anyone in that room and they would have made meaning of it. Red and white could mean anything. Flowers, a flag, a dress ...'

Blood on white cotton. He swallowed.

'But Flora chose you,' she said. 'This is what you want to know, isn't it? Not how I do it, or who she is, or what that message even means. You know what that message means, and you don't care about me or Flora. You want to know why she chose to give the message to you.'

'There's no meaning to it,' he said. But it came out as nearly a whisper.

Mrs Blackthorne stood. Jonah's card had been left on a small table near her chair, next to her coffee cup. She picked it up and walked to a desk near the window, where she opened a diary.

'As I told you, I'm not aware of what Flora does and says while I'm in a trance. If you need answers, you'll have to ask her.' She picked up a pencil and looked down at her diary. 'Can you come on Wednesday afternoon?'

'Wednesday? Spirits take *appointments*?'

'No, but I do. A séance tires me out, especially a well-attended one like that. I shan't be able to channel Flora until I've had some time to recover.' She touched the pencil to her lip. 'Say, three o'clock?'

'Very well.'

She wrote it down. 'I'll be prepared.' She smiled, that irritating, condescending smile. 'Will your charming wife be accompanying you?'

'Mrs Worth isn't interested in spirits.'

'And neither are you.' She approached him, hand extended again. 'Goodbye, Mr Worth.'

This time, manners won out, and he shook hands with her. She wore no gloves, so they were bare palm to bare palm. He had a brief memory of her legs, as he had bound her, and he felt his cheeks warming. 'Goodbye,' he said, quickly turning to go before he could see any more of her knowing smile.

'Mr Worth?'

He paused, hand on the doorknob, still not looking back. 'Yes?'

'You didn't come here for my advice, but I will take the liberty of giving it to you: it's not wise to keep secrets from your wife.'

Extract from a poem attributed to Bahadur Shah Zafar, last Mughal emperor of India, after his exile following the capture of Delhi by the British after the Indian Rebellion of 1857. Although numbers are uncertain, it is estimated that the mutiny and its reprisal caused the deaths of 6000 Europeans and 800,000 Indians.

Delhi was once a paradise,
Where Love held sway and reigned;
But its charm lies ravished now
And only ruins remain.

Chapter Thirteen

Fourteen months earlier...

April, 1857
Delhi

The rest of the household were taking their afternoon siesta, but Jonah couldn't sleep in the heat. There was no relief from it: it beat down on you with the sun when you were outside, and inside it suffocated you, despite the punkah-wallahs and their fans, despite the scented and wetted reed blinds on the open windows. His clothes were damp with sweat within minutes of his putting them on. Only when the sun went down could he feel any comfort; in the twilight, it could almost be high summer in England. Except, of course, for the insects, and the birds, and the chattering of the monkeys that swung onto the railing outside his room and scampered across the garden, and the low conversation of the servants talking to each other in their native language.

Until the age of seven, he had grown up with all of this, had taken it all for granted as much as the sweet voice of his ayah, who sang to him in Hindi at night. But his years in England had stripped it all away. He was used to the green and blue of the Wiltshire countryside, the grey and gold of Oxford's spires. In India, which should have been his home, so much of what should be familiar was strange, and he walked as if in a fever dream.

His hosts, the Hamiltons – though strictly speaking Jonah was *their* host – had also both been born here in Delhi, but had never left. Robert had fought in the Anglo-Sikh wars and Patience had borne three children. They ate kedgeree for breakfast, curried mutton and chilli chutney, while Jonah could stomach the thought of nothing heavier than a sliced, ice-cool mango.

'You'll get used to it,' Mrs Hamilton had said, smiling kindly to him when he had arrived from Calcutta. He was still a bit wobbly from the stomach bug he'd picked up on the journey. 'Everyone's sick at first. And everyone is too hot. Give it another month and it will be as if you've been here your entire life.'

He doubted it. But he would trade any number of cool days in Wiltshire for a single night in Delhi. At night, the stars were brighter than any he remembered. It was hard to believe they were the same stars he'd seen from his window in England. The sky wasn't black but the deepest, lushest, midnight blue, and at night the scent of jasmine was released into the gardens and lay over the city like the perfume of a fascinating woman. Bats flitted on silent wings and the city became more alive, something mysterious and throbbing, full of shadows and incense. He walked through the streets and heard strange lilting music and conversations in words he did not understand. They said that the old Mughal Emperor was a poet, and at night Jonah could believe this city was ruled by poetry.

In the afternoon, it was a city ruled by the heat. Jonah rose from his bed, took up his sketchbook and pencil, and walked through silent rooms.

This house was his. His father had bought the land and had the house built before Jonah was born. A haveli, it was entirely unlike an English house, built in three stories around an aangan or central courtyard, with the rooms all open to the air. Jonah had some memories of it – a white curtain fluttering in the breeze in the nursery, his mother's parlour with its lamps and flowers. He recalled running across the courtyard chasing a lizard, bare feet pattering on tiles. His parents had died here, in the room where Robert and Patience Hamilton now slept. The Hamiltons had offered it to him but he'd said no.

They'd changed the furniture when they took tenancy and so,

although the bones of the house were the same, the face of it was altered and strange. Like the whole country, he didn't yet feel that he belonged in this house even though it was his birthright.

Jonah crossed the courtyard and passed through an archway outside, walking on heat-seared grass. He ducked his head under the force of the sun as he made his way across the grounds to a stone building on a slight rise, a ruined temple which had come with the land that his father had bought. It was a small building of weathered red brick, with crumbling terracotta ornamentation of scrolls and curves that looked tantalisingly like human bodies. The doorway and windows were pointed arches, and the roof was gone, replaced by a peepul tree whose limbs twisted around the structure. When he got closer, he saw that the embrace of the tree was probably the only thing holding up the listing walls.

It was smaller than he remembered. His head brushed against the arch of the doorway as he entered and he ducked to avoid dust or spiderwebs in his hair. Inside the air was cooler, shadowy and dappled with green from the tree, smelling of foliage and sap and earth. He looked first at the ground, blinking to adjust to the dimmed light after the blaze outside. He had nearly been stung by a scorpion on the journey from Calcutta.

Thus he saw the person's legs and feet first: feet in sandals, legs in white pyjamas. It was a young turbaned Indian man lying on the floor of the temple. A book lay open on his chest. He was fast asleep.

Jonah stepped back and the slight noise woke the young man, who started and jumped to his feet, book in hand. 'Oh my dear, I am sorry, sahib, I must have fallen asleep reading.'

Jonah held up his hands. 'It's my fault. I'm very sorry to have disturbed you. I'll leave you to your book.'

'No, no, there's no need. I am intruding, I will go.' He tucked the book under his arm and Jonah recognised the cover.

'Tennyson?' he said, in some surprise.

'Ah, yes. Hamilton memsahib allowed me to borrow it.' He looked down at it. '*In Memoriam A.H.H.* You have read it?'

'Not exactly cheerful stuff. I preferred *Maud*. Though that didn't have a happy ending, either.'

'Poets prefer tragedy,' said the young man. 'It is considered a higher literary form, even though it is not what one would want to live through.'

'Maybe that's the point of literature,' said Jonah, laughing. 'The worse the event, the higher the art. I don't believe we've met, have we? I'm Jonah Worth.'

'Pavan Sharma. I believe you have met Rajesh Sharma, who is my brother.'

Rajesh was a young Hindu whom Hamilton employed as an accountant in the Customs House. He often came to the house to discuss business with Hamilton – 'Fiendishly clever, some of these natives, if they're taught correctly,' Hamilton had remarked at dinner the night before. Jonah could see a family resemblance now in the large dark eyes and the slightly curved nose, though Pavan had no beard and his face was rounder than his brother's, and Rajesh did not wear a turban.

'Well, I am pleased to meet you.' He held out his hand to Pavan, who placed his palms together and bowed from the waist in the customary greeting. Jonah, a little embarrassed at his gaffe, did the same.

'Rajesh mentioned you, sahib,' said Pavan. 'He said you own this house, and therefore – ' a slight nod of turbaned head – 'this temple.'

'It came to me when my parents died. But I haven't lived here since I was a child. I hardly recall it. I remember playing here, though. I would pretend it was a castle, and I was a king.' He gazed around the space. Most of the windows were overgrown and there was a dais on the far side, choked with ivy. 'It's smaller than I thought it was. I don't even know what god it was dedicated to.'

'It was dedicated to Radharani, who is a consort of Krishna.'

'I hope Radharani wouldn't be offended by my playing here.'

'Our gods are, in general, I believe, more playful than the Christian one.'

'There's so much I don't know,' admitted Jonah.

'Perhaps there is room for mystery, sahib.'

For the second time, he laughed. 'You're a philosopher, Pavan.'

'I study at Delhi College.'

'Philosophy?'

'Mainly mathematics, which is a philosophy of its own.'

'I'm hopeless at mathematics. My father hoped I would follow in his footsteps and take charge of his investments, but everything here is so much past my understanding.' He said it with sadness – much more sadness than he had allowed himself to express to anyone, especially his hosts.

'You do not like India?'

'Oh, I'm sorry. This is your country, and I don't mean to offend. I like it very much. Everything here is so beautiful, especially at night.'

Pavan inclined his head. 'I must go. Should I return this book to the Memsahib?'

'No, please keep it if you are enjoying it. Perhaps we can discuss poetry another time.'

The young man didn't reply; he pressed his hands together again in the customary goodbye, and, tucking the book under his arm, was gone on silent feet.

'I met Pavan today,' Jonah said that evening, when they were gathered on the verandah sipping brandy and soda. The Hamiltons' two elder children were racing toy wooden horses with their ayah, while their parents watched them with pleasure.

Mrs Hamilton looked surprised. 'Pavan Sharma?'

'Yes. I surprised him quite by mistake during his siesta.'

'Both Rajesh and Pavan are very talented,' said Hamilton.

'Rajesh is a magician with numbers. I've never met a white man who was any better, and that's saying a great deal. Pavan is meant to be even cleverer.'

'I am surprised that Pavan spoke with you,' said Mrs Hamilton. 'He's usually shy.'

'They seem quite an ambitious family.'

'There are only two of them: their parents died and they came to Delhi, I believe, so that Pavan could study here. They lived in Agra, I think. It's brave of them to have come away from their extended family. They left all manner of aunties and cousins behind.'

'He was reading your volume of Tennyson. I told him he could keep it until he's finished; I hope that's all right.'

Mrs Hamilton gazed at Jonah thoughtfully. 'Don't be offended if he doesn't reappear for some time, or never. As I said, Pavan is very shy. He assists his brother at times, but I believe he mostly comes here for my library. Where did you see him?'

'In the disused temple in the back of the grounds.'

'That old thing is falling down,' said Hamilton, comfortable in his chair. 'You should think of having it demolished, Worth, when you have the time. It's an eyesore.'

'I think it's picturesque. It was built to worship Radharani, who is Krishna's consort.'

'Superstitious nonsense.' Hamilton drew on his cigar. 'The sooner we have all the natives converted to Christianity, the better. Make this country run properly, for once.'

Chapter Fourteen

June, 1858
Fortuneswell, Dorset

'It seems like the best way to keep him alive, in my opinion: to remember him.'

The studio was empty except for early morning light. Viola stood in the middle of it, unpacking crates.

In his life, her father's camera had been an intimate part of him. His hands had held this wooden box and his eyes had looked through this ground glass. Viola had been his first subject, and he had been her last.

She lifted out a heavy album of prints. They were all calotypes, carefully pasted into the album with gum; her father had been a devoted follower of Mr Fox Talbot's developments and had corresponded with him. They had visited him at Lacock Abbey when she was a child, though she only had a vague memory of an arched window and honey-coloured stone.

Here she was as a baby dressed in white with a bonnet twice as big as her head. Her hand, holding a rattle, was blurred where she had moved it. And another of her asleep (her father had clearly learned the risks of photographing infants). A chubby toddler on a blanket; a young girl holding an apple. She could chart the course of her growth through photographs.

'Why do you like it so much?' she had asked him once, half out of exasperation, when they had spent yet another entire day in cold drizzle lugging equipment and costumes to the beck, where she would pose as Titania. When Jonah was with them he made these expeditions more fun, and also helped with the carrying, but this time he was at school.

'Because it's truth,' he'd told her. 'Everything you see in these pictures is true, and we are capturing it forever.'

She tugged at the heavy case. 'If we're capturing truth, why do we have to carry these costumes with us? I'm not really a fairy princess.'

He had put his hand on her shoulder, and kissed her hair. 'Oh, yes, Viola. You are.'

Here was the photograph – Viola as Titania near a stream, her loose hair strewn with wildflowers. Viola ran her fingers lightly over it.

The sun had cleared the clouds and, in the end, she had felt like Titania that day. She remembered the husky green scent of the water; how the moss had felt soft under her bare feet and how it had dampened the bottom of her skirt. But although the photograph captured a kind of truth, it didn't capture all of it. Because her father had been there, too, also with his shoes off to feel the moss between his toes.

A tear fell onto the album page and she quickly closed the book so that she would not ruin the prints.

She was better than she had been. She could think of her father in his prime, with mud spotting the cuffs of his trousers, fingers stained brownish black with silver nitrate, helping her to make a daisy chain. He was no longer the fleshless, cold body in the bed, waiting to be washed and wrapped in a shroud. She no longer recoiled from touch or felt a constant chill.

She still wore black, but she was better.

So why were things so silent between her and Jonah?

Perhaps he didn't want children. They had never discussed it, much as they'd never discussed becoming engaged. It had always seemed like something natural and destined to happen. But what if Jonah's vision of their marriage was entirely different from hers?

She couldn't discuss it with him now; he was hardly home and when he was, he avoided her eyes.

Mrs Blackthorne, the medium, had told her that her husband needed her, but she wasn't sure that was true.

Viola let out a short, sharp breath. She hadn't come here to the studio to muse about her life. She did that endlessly in her own drawing room. She had come here to escape those circular thoughts and to *do* something.

Once she'd started, it was second nature to set up the studio with her father's camera and tripod, a cloth draped over a screen to make a backdrop. It took more time to remove the contents of a small box room adjoining so she could block off the windows with cloth and set it up as a makeshift darkroom. Her father's voice was in her ears as she did. 'The wet plate is an improvement on Mr Fox Talbot's calotype, Viola, because the glass plate negative is so much more durable than a paper one, you see.'

She paused for a cup of tea, and then unpacked the trays and spirit lamps, the demijohns and bottles, the plates and chemicals. She sniffed each bottle gingerly, and each one was a thousand memories: ether, ethanol in the prepared collodion, ferrous sulphate in the developer, potassium cyanide in the fixer. She had mixed these solutions months ago. It was impossible to know for certain if they'd lost their efficacy until she took a photograph. To be safe, she should mix them all again – and usually she took a great deal of pleasure in measuring and mixing – but today she was impatient to get started, after so long lying fallow.

It was mid-afternoon; there would be enough light, if she made haste. Before she left the house, she asked Mrs Diggory and Alice to carry water up to the darkroom for her, and she nicked the lacy tablecloth from the dining table and tucked it under her arm before hurrying down the hill to the low stone cottages that huddled together against the sea.

The kindling girl was down on the shingle near the water, with her dress hiked up so she could paddle. Her bundle of salvaged driftwood had been carefully placed above the tide line. Sometimes she sold winkles and crabs as well as kindling, or pretty shells, or from time to time a fossil; once Jonah had bought an albatross feather from her and brought it back to draw and then to tuck into the frame of the mirror in the parlour, as a little gift. Viola saw her walking the steep streets, sometimes, her kindling on her back. Mrs Diggory had said that her father was a fisherman, but he had injured his back and could rarely go to sea, and the kindling girl, apparently the oldest of her siblings, had to make a penny or two wherever she could.

The rocks squeaked and echoed as Viola's boots stepped on them. The beach was made up of smooth rocks that looked like a solid surface until you stood on it. Then they sounded against each other, one rock upon another, spreading out as if the whole shore spoke in a hard, salty whisper.

The kindling girl scampered over on bare feet. Close up, her hair was whipped into elf-locks by the wind and bleached nearly white by the sun; her face was smudged with dirt and there was a rime of salt on her forehead. Her clothes were grey with many washings. It was difficult to tell how old she was; she was small, but that could be from poverty and deprivation. At a guess, she could be anything from six to ten.

'Winkles, miss? I got a cup of 'em, tasty and sweet today.' She held out a battered tin cup a quarter full of the shelled creatures.

'Yes, thank you,' said Viola, 'but I also wondered if you had some time to help me. I want to take a photograph of a girl.'

'A photograph? I ent never been photographed.'

'I'll give you a penny for the photograph, and buy your winkles and your kindling, too.'

The kindling girl's eyes grew wide with visions of riches and bread, and Viola resolved to feed her first.

'Yes, miss! Yes please, miss! Will you do the photograph here?'

'No; I need you to come to my house.' The girl turned and ran, and Viola thought she'd somehow frightened her, until she saw her pick up her bundle of driftwood. She came running back, not hindered by her burden or the smooth, fist-sized rocks that turned and protested.

'All ready, miss.'

'Don't you – what about your shoes?' She looked at the small dirty feet.

'Ent got any.'

'What's your name?'

'They call me Nan at home.'

Viola turned and started up Brandy Row towards her house. She was aware of what a strange sight they must make, Viola with her black silk gown and neatly-plaited hair, and this urchin in her shapeless dress which may have been, at one time, white.

'Well, Nan, I'd like you to pretend to be a fairy princess. Can you do that?'

'A fairy princess?'

'You'll have to wear a white gown and we'll make you a crown of flowers. Do you mind?'

Nan stopped, mid step, and gazed at Viola. For the first time, Viola saw her smile. It made apples of her wan cheeks and a twinkle of her eyes, and it filled Viola with a sharp longing.

'Do I *mind*, miss?' Nan said. 'This is the best day of my *life*.'

Viola sat with Nan in the kitchen as she ate. After she'd shoved a third slice of bread and butter down the bodice of her dress to hide it, Viola asked Mrs Diggory to make up a package for her to take home to her four brothers and sisters. It was an extremely cheerful and talkative little girl who accompanied Viola up the stairs to the studio. As Viola draped the child in the tablecloth and arranged the flowers around her, she was regaled with information about Nan's father, who drank to ease his pain, and her mother who had taken in washing until she ruined a lady's petticoat and now no one sent her anything any more, and the cottage where they lived that was half wrecked by the sea that came up over the beach during storms, and Nan's little brothers and sisters, one of whom was still an infant in arms, and none of whom went to school. 'I can get Michael to help me with finding wood, and Sissy will help me too once she's over her cold, and we'll make twice as much money, because little Sal needs milk every day,' Nan confided as Viola placed a crown of white flowers on her head.

'Now, I have to prepare the plate,' Viola told her, 'which will only take a few moments, but you must remain here, otherwise I'll have to rearrange everything and the plate will be spoilt.'

Nan nodded vehemently, and Viola went to her darkroom. The actions were as familiar as breathing to her; although she had lit the dark-lantern with its red shield, she hardly needed the light to pour the viscous collodion on the plate and tilt it to coat it evenly, and then to bathe it in the silver nitrate whilst she counted down the minutes in her head. When Viola returned with the prepared plate in its wooden case, Nan hastily straightened up. Her flower crown had slipped off her head and broken in two. 'Don't worry, miss, I'll mend it right away.' She bent over her task.

'Never mind – leave it on your lap, and sit still. That's right. Completely still, now.' Viola uncovered the lens, and at that moment, Nan put the crown back on her head. It fell off, scattering blooms, and with a cry of dismay, Nan began gathering flowers.

Well. Plate one spoiled. But that was to be expected. Leaving Nan to reassemble the crown, she went to prepare another plate.

Nearly an hour later, she had spoiled five more plates, and she knew much more than she had ever hoped to know about the lives of the children of fishermen in Chiswell. Nan was so lively and so good-natured, and so desirous to please whilst at the same time incapable of staying still, that Viola couldn't begrudge the waste of plates and chemicals; her throat was hoarse from laughing and talking.

'And Bess said to me, that's crippled Bess not Bess my sister;

she fell in front of a cart horse and she has to walk with a stick now, Bess said that when she's old enough she's going to marry a gentleman and live in one of the big houses like yours, miss, with servants, and I say "La, who will marry you with only one leg?" and she says, "They'll marry me for my cooking" and I say "You can only cook porridge, and a nasty thin porridge it is, with a fly floating on the top of it like a currant. Who will marry you for porridge with flies?"'

'That's a consideration,' said Viola quite seriously. 'You shall have to tell her to aim high, and marry a man with a cook.' She adjusted the focus, and slipped another plate into the camera. 'Now, Nan, this is the last shot we can take today, because the light is fading. When I take the cover from the lens, you must stay absolutely still until I say so.'

'I'll pretend I'm asleep,' said Nan. 'I'm good at doing that. Sometimes it's the only way I can get the little 'uns to stop pestering.' She arranged herself in the chair so her arm was draped across the back, laid her head on her arm and closed her eyes.

Viola took the cover from the lens, and counted twelve seconds' exposure. Nan, for the first time, did not move a muscle, until Viola covered the lens again and said, 'Finished. Well done.' Then the child sprang up, delight in her eyes.

'Is this one going to work? Can I see it being made into a picture?'

Viola calculated the effect of a whirling dervish in a small darkened room full of chemicals. 'I'll show you the fixing, because that can be done in the light, but you must wait until I come out.'

Nan was waiting directly outside the darkroom door when Viola emerged, so close that Viola nearly collided with her and spilled the tray of cyanide fixer down the front of her dress. 'Have a care, this is poison,' she said, though she couldn't help but laugh at the eager expression on Nan's thin face. She set the tray down on the wooden floor and the two of them knelt down beside it.

'Oh, that's me, but I look so strange!' cried Nan, spotting the plate, with its grey filmy image of her on it: negative, her white-clad figure dark against a light background.

'Watch,' Viola told her, and slipped the plate into the fixer.

It worked quickly, quick as breath. The grey image became blue, striated, like mist; it seemed to float over surface of the glass. And then as if by magic, the negative image coalesced into a positive, black and grey and white, crisp and clear.

Nan squealed with delight and Viola recalled a lifetime of kneeling by her father, witnessing this miracle when a moment became fixed in time forever. It was chemistry, pure science; but watching this, it was quite easy to believe that it was magic instead. Childhood captured, innocence inscribed on glass, a fairy made out of a living, breathing child.

A tear rolled to her lips. She licked it off, tasting salt and memory, and smiled.

Chapter Fifteen

Jonah was kept waiting at the door of Mrs Blackthorne's lodgings for over ten minutes, acutely conscious of the holidaymakers passing by him. He was about to leave when the silent blonde maid came down to admit him.

Mrs Blackthorne rose when he entered, holding out her hand. 'Mr Worth. Forgive me; I thought it was unlikely that you would come.'

'I'm not in the habit of dishonouring engagements,' he said, coldly. But he shook her hand anyway.

The truth was that he had thought of little but this appointment for the past three days. He had hardly heard a word that anyone had said to him: not Viola, not Mr Field, not his barber when he had a haircut and shave. He had wavered between the conviction that this was all nonsense, fury at the medium for toying with a stranger's emotions, and an unshakeable, burning need to know whether any part of the message had been true. The latter caused him no little measure of self-disgust.

The room looked much as it had the last time he had visited, with the addition of a screen in one corner, embroidered with Chinese dragons and lotuses.

'Would you like some refreshment?' she asked.

'No thank you. That is not what I came here for.'

'You're ready to meet Flora? I hope she'll come for you. I can't always guarantee it.'

'Do you have to be tied up again?'

She laughed, that low musical laugh. 'No. That's a piece of theatricality rather than a requirement. However, I do need to draw all of the blinds. Flora prefers it when it's dark. Will you help me?'

Jonah drew down the blinds on one window while Mrs Blackthorne did the other. It occurred to him as he did that there was some impropriety in a man being alone in the dark with a woman who wasn't his wife. The thought brought back memories, and he crossed his arms over his chest.

'What next?' he asked, rather too loudly.

'Be seated and make yourself comfortable, please.' Her voice came from the other side of the room, the corner with the screen. 'Meanwhile, I'll attempt to enter a trance state. Whether Flora will appear, we shall see.'

Absolute rubbish, Jonah thought, but he felt for the nearest chair and sat in it. As he waited, his eyes adjusted to the darkness: he could see the faint outline of daylight around the windows, and the shadows of the furniture around the room. He heard the rustle of Mrs Blackthorne's skirts as she presumably settled herself behind the screen, and then that ceased and he heard only the gulls crying outside, a distant accordion, and the soft sound of his own breath.

Minutes crawled by, and with every one he realised more and more the idiocy of his situation. He was in the lodgings of a stranger, a spirit medium, hoping to learn something about a person who was gone forever from a place that existed no longer. Delhi was a battleground, a wasteland. He'd left it behind him, and that was where it should stay. He should make himself believe that it had been another man who had lived those weeks; he shouldn't be waiting for an insubstantial spirit to remind him of everything and everyone he had lost.

Jonah closed his eyes and saw the stars in the blue velvet Indian sky.

His eyes flew open as he realised that he was breathing the scent of sandalwood. A subtle thread of incense, only a hint of it in the still air of the room.

When had that started? Had it been here all along? No – there had been the fragrance of the medium's perfume; he would have noticed anything else. Wouldn't he? Jonah breathed in deeply, trying to work out whether the scent was growing stronger, or if the whole thing was his imagination brought about from his memory. It was the scent of a temple; it made him think of flowers, offerings, entreaties at the feet of a god.

There was a white figure in the middle of the room.

Jonah started.

It stood perfectly still. He had heard nothing. He glanced at the corner where the screen stood, but he could see only shadows.

'Hello?' he said.

The figure didn't move. He remembered the hand on his shoulder in the Newhams' sitting room; that had substance, but he could not tell if this figure did. It appeared to be female, wrapped in a gown with a veil over her head, or perhaps the diaphanous outline was her actual form and not clothing.

'M – Mrs Blackthorne?' he stammered.

'I know you,' said the figure. Its voice was subtly accented, breathy and high, nearly a whisper, but it pierced the stillness of the room and he had no difficulty in hearing it even though he was several feet away. 'I have spoken with you before.'

'Yes.'

'You are a seeker. There is something that will not let you rest.'

Jonah half-rose from his chair, but the figure took a gliding step back and he subsided. 'I want ... you said before ...'

'Someone who wanted to speak with you. A "p", and white and red. Yes, I recall now. Whom do you seek?'

'Someone I once knew.'

'A secret.'

Jonah rubbed his eyes. The figure was still there. 'I don't believe in you,' he said. 'I thought you weren't supposed to appear to someone who doesn't believe in you.'

'I appear to those who need me.'

'Are you – do you call yourself Flora Bell?'

'I am many. Will you pray with me?'

'I don't believe in praying, either.' He stared hard at the figure, but could not make it out clearly. It appeared to have a slight glow. 'Prove to me that you are what you claim to be.'

'The confirmation of faith is not proof. It is faith.'

'I have no faith.'

'Not even in love?'

The incense was stronger.

'I have no faith,' he repeated.

'That must be very sad and lonely.'

The spirit's voice was gentle and full of compassion. Something about it made tears rise in Jonah's eyes.

'I am . . .' he said, but he wasn't able to finish.

'There is someone who wishes to speak with you,' said Flora. 'Would you like to speak with them?'

'Who is it?'

'I see red and white buildings,' said the spirit. 'The sun is hot. There are spices in the air. I see domes and minarets. This person is trying to reach you from a great distance.'

'Who is it?' he asked again.

'I see a man . . . and a woman.'

He drew in a sharp breath. 'Does – does this person have a message for me?'

Flora paused. Under her veil she tilted her head, as if she were listening.

'It is not your fault,' she said. 'None of it is your fault at all.'

Jonah choked. He stood up abruptly, toppling the chair over. It made a muffled sound on the carpet. The room was suddenly too hot, too close, too dark. He heard his own blood in his ears and he felt the slippery heat of blood under his right hand.

It was not real. Not any more. That was in the past.

'I – I must go,' he stammered, and rushed out of the room, down the stairs and out of the house into the weak sunlight of an English afternoon, the sound of an accordion. He walked rapidly down the length of the Esplanade, his heart pounding, and just as suddenly stopped. He looked at his right hand: it was pale and unmarked.

He turned around and went back the way he'd come.

When the maid admitted him and he climbed the stairs back up to Mrs Blackthorne's sitting room, the screen had been drawn back and Mrs Blackthorne was standing at the opened window. There was no sign of Flora Bell, though a trace of sandalwood remained in the room.

'Mr Worth,' she said with surprise. 'I woke and you were gone. I presumed your business was over.'

'I left abruptly,' he said. 'I – had hoped she would not be gone when I came back.'

'She told you something of use, then?'

'I – perhaps.'

'Sometimes the messages from the other side aren't fully clear. They have to travel a great distance, you understand.'

'I wanted to ask more.'

But was that true? Did he want to know more? He ached, and burned; felt wounds opening that had not yet healed.

'Come Friday at the same time,' she said, and smiled at him: a small, closed-lip, irritating smile of triumph.

An albumen print on paper from a wet collodion glass plate negative. Loose, with edges creased and torn, kept between the pages of a family Bible since 1858.

These are children. Their heads are strewn with flowers and wild samphire; they wear shawls and scraps of lace. Two of them have shoes. Their hands are blurred, and their faces, so the features aren't clear – shadows for eyes, streaks for lips – but their heads are tipped back in laughter. In the centre one child faces the camera. He is the only one who is still. He holds a drooping rose in one hand and in the other he holds a shell. He gazes ahead at the lens, at the person who holds this print. The print was found safe in a Bible at the bottom of a cupboard where it has lain since it was put away there and discovered years later, after a fire in 1923, when this boy, if he lived, would be seventy-three. He gazes as if he is saying to the future: I am here. No one knows his name.

Chapter Sixteen

It wasn't that he intended to sneak around, or to avoid his wife, exactly; but sleep was elusive and Jonah thought he may as well use the early morning light to do some sketches. A walk in fresh air would blow away a night spent tossing and turning, catching the faint whiff of imagined incense. Never mind that he had been taking rather a lot of solitary walks lately, with very few sketches to show for them. He skipped breakfast, left a note for Viola on the dining-room table, and opened the front door only to find a collection of urchins of various sizes standing on the pavement in front of their house.

'Please, sir,' said one, a young girl in a tattered dress with unruly curls, approaching him, with the rest of the children close behind, 'is Mrs Worth going to make any more pictures today?'

'I – excuse me, I don't know,' managed Jonah, and stepped backwards into the house in some confusion, shutting the door.

There was a footstep behind him on the stairs. 'Jonah?'

He turned around. Viola was coming down. 'There are several children waiting outside for you?' he said.

Her face did something quite extraordinary: it blushed and smiled.

'I meant to tell you last night,' she said, 'but you didn't return until late. I unpacked the studio and the darkroom yesterday and took some photographs.'

'How do these children know about it?'

Viola passed him and peeped out the window by the front door. Her smile was so unaccustomed and yet so ordinary that it made him feel both grateful that she was happier, and guilty that he hadn't caused it himself.

'Nan must have told them. You know Nan, the girl who sells kindling down on the beach? She was my model.'

Viola opened the door and was immediately surrounded by children. 'Am I to have pennies for all of you?' she asked, laughing as he hadn't seen her do since he left for India, years before. Not since she was a girl herself. Her hand lightly settled on a young girl's mousy curls.

'I don't care about no penny,' said a boy in stained trousers. 'I want to be a fairy like Nan.'

'Well. Go around to the back, all of you, and Nan, please tell Mrs Diggory to give you enough money to buy two dozen eggs. If you carry them back here, very carefully without breaking a single one, I will take your photographs and give you each a print on paper to keep.'

As if by magic, the children disappeared around the side of the house, leaving Viola flushed and happy in their wake.

'It isn't horribly extravagant, is it?' she asked him. 'I have all this equipment and they may never have seen a photograph before. It's like magic to them, I imagine, and they have so little in their lives.'

We have so little magic in our lives, too. 'Of course,' he said. 'I think it's a wonderful idea. I … I like seeing you happy, Viola.'

'You encouraged me to take photographs before. I should have listened to you.'

'You weren't ready.' He dared to touch the tips of her fingers; he saw now that they were stained with silver nitrate. 'Your father's hands were always like this.'

She raised her hands and looked at them; sadness passed over her face. 'Always. Yes. I-I think it's a better way of remembering him, if I do what we always did together. And the children are so full of life, and this is the only way I'm likely to—'

She stopped herself, but Jonah heard the rest of the sentence, unspoken. *The only way I'm likely to spend time with children, since you can't give me any.* He stepped sideways onto the path, and he wanted to answer her unspoken sentence with 'I'm sorry.' He wanted to take her hand again and offer to share her pain and her joy, all these memories that were written in silver nitrate on her skin.

Instead he said, 'If you're photographing fairies you'll need some flower crowns. I'll see what I can do.'

Chapter Seventeen

Fifteen years earlier ...

September, 1843
Upcross Hall, near Wareham, Dorset

After she had brought the fresh water up two flights of stairs and laid the fires for the night and brought the dirty water back downstairs and scrubbed out the cans, Hetty brought her single woollen blanket into the cramped room off the kitchen where the kitchen maid and scullery maids slept and spread it out on the floor. She didn't dare go back to her bedroom without Jane there. None of the women asked her why she did it, though she heard them whispering.

There was a party in honour of the new wife of the eldest son, Mr Gilbert Upcross, and the servants were all kept so busy cleaning and scrubbing that Hetty didn't have time to listen in on the children's French lessons, nor read her book. But she practised in her mind and under her breath as she dusted the bedrooms and polished the silver. 'Je m'appelle Harriet Smith. J'habite à Paris. Il fait beau, n'est-ce pas?' She pictured herself tall and upright, chin up, eyes sharp and glittering as jet.

The new wife was small and blonde and very rich. She simpered by her husband's side. She wasn't a patch on Madame, but then she wasn't the descendant of a headless nobleman: her family owned mills up in Lancashire. They were going to live in London.

Mrs Watson called her to the housekeeper's room. 'Jane's mother has died,' she told Hetty, 'and so she's staying at home to look after her younger sisters and brothers. I can't be a pair of hands down for this party so I've got a girl from the village, but she's even less experienced than you.' The housekeeper, wrinkled and solid, like a prune too hard to eat, glared at Hetty. 'I'm not promoting you to Jane's place, mind. I think you're a troublemaker, girl. Mr Diamond tells me there's been fistfights in the yard over your pretty, witchy face. I ought to let you go. But I need all the girls I can get, and at least you stay quiet about it. If there's a peep…'

'There won't be, Mrs Watson,' she said, grateful that she was having a bedfellow again and wouldn't have to sleep on the floor. Her black eye had faded to yellow.

But there was a hollow inside, knowing Jane wouldn't be back. It was worse than Charlie's betrayal. She'd miss the other girl's warmth. They used to sleep with arms around each other, breast to breast, feet laid on top of each other, whispering in the dark. They woke up in the morning still cuddled together. They spent those few moments before they had to get up awake with eyes closed, feeling safe.

The new girl was greasy and pious. The first night Hetty was ready with reassuring words and all the wisdom she'd learned working for seven months in this house (Keep quiet. Work hard. Don't eat the pilchard pie unless you like stomach ache. No one notices if you borrow books from the library, as long as you don't leave a space on the shelf) but the new girl was already on her knees, eyes screwed shut, praying. Hetty shrugged and opened her book. God could guide the new girl, if she didn't want Hetty's help.

When the girl crawled into bed, finally, she pushed herself up against the wall as far away from Hetty as she could get.

'Mrs Watson likes the fires laid a particular way,' said Hetty. 'I'll show you tomorrow, and then we can split the rooms between us. It'll be quicker for both of us.'

'I don't want you to show me nothing,' said the new girl to the wall. 'You're a whore. I don't want nothing to do with you.'

*

Parties meant work. The kitchen was a frenzy of cooking. Mr Moore, the butler, led his troupe of shiny-buttoned footmen in admitting guests and waiting at table. Upstairs, the ladies' maids and valets primped their mistresses and masters, squeezed them into corsets and curled their hair with tongs; in the yard, the grooms tended the guests' horses in between nips of beer. Hetty was safe from both Francis's leer and Charlie's contempt as she ran up and down stairs tending to a million last-minute requests. Several of the guests hadn't brought their own maids and Hetty was assigned to them. When she met another servant, she kept her chin up, her spine straight, like Madame.

Je suis une femme noble. Je suis intouchable.

The noise swelled and ebbed in the dining room and saloon – conversation, someone singing at the piano. The new wife was performing. Apparently her money wasn't enough, she must be accomplished as well and swallow her short Northern vowels. Hetty didn't envy her.

She'd avoided the servants' dining room and consequently hadn't eaten all day. In a five-minute break before she had to get the bedrooms ready, she sneaked down the main staircase, usually forbidden to her, so as not to meet any of the other servants. She was thinking only of bread and butter and did not hear the footsteps coming up to meet her until she was nearly face to face with Madame.

Madame was not dressed for the party; she wouldn't be attending. She wore her plain, well-cut dark green dress, her gold earrings and bangle. She held a book in her hand and she smelled of perfume, like bitter oranges.

It was the closest Hetty had ever been to her. She stopped short, confused and in joy.

'Bon soir, Madame,' she said without thinking, and Madame's arched brows contracted.

'Tu parles français?'

'Oui, I mean, no. Non. J'apprends à parler français.' She glanced down at the book in Madame's long-fingered hand. 'J'espère habiter à Paris.'

She had never spoken French out loud before, usually had to take a moment to compose sentences, figure out tenses, but Madame's presence inspired her. The foreign words flowed from her lips, every inflection copied from Madame.

Madame looked from Hetty to the book and back again. She looked Hetty up and down, from her worn shoes to the crown of her hair. Her expression was inscrutable, aristocratic.

In that moment Hetty imagined Madame offering to teach her, lending her more books. In the evenings after their duties were finished they would converse quietly in French in Madame's room. One night, recounting their childhoods, Madame would open her locket for Hetty and tell her who had owned that lock of dark hair. Her mother, her sister. Her lover, left long ago. Her great-grandfather, the duke, possessor of lost acres of precious land.

'Paris a l'odeur de merde,' said Madame. 'Va plutôt en Provence.'

And with a sweep of her emerald skirt, she proceeded up the stairs. Hetty, blinking after her, had never heard the French word for 'shit' before, and it was only after Madame was gone that Hetty understood what she had meant.

The bell rang while it was still dark outside. The new girl snored; Hetty felt as if she had only just fallen asleep. She prodded the noisy lump beside her but it only snorted and settled back into sleep.

She sighed and got out of bed. Pulled off her nightgown and dressed herself in the dark. She risked Mrs Watson's wrath and left off her corset.

The summons was from one of the guest bedrooms. Her discreet knock was answered by a half-dressed gentleman who looked half-drunk as well. 'Yes,' he said, 'we need some hot water, please, and could you get a message to the groom to ready our carriage. Mrs Beaumont isn't well and we must leave for home as soon as possible.'

Down to the dark kitchen to stir up the fire and warm the water. She yawned as she hauled it back up the stairs. No one else seemed to be stirring, either above stairs or below; the party had gone on until the early hours of the morning and the household was late rousing. When she brought in the hot water, she saw Mrs Beaumont sitting up in bed looking distinctly green around the gills, and didn't envy her the jolting carriage ride back to wherever they lived.

Francis, she thought as she went back down the stairs with the chamber pot (up and down these stairs, a thousand times a day, it seemed; her legs could climb them in her sleep). Or she didn't even think it; the idea of him occurred to her body rather than her mind, surrounded with a burning edge of fear. But surely he would be asleep as well. She couldn't imagine him up and eager to do a day's work before the sun rose. She'd wake one of the stable boys and pass on the message.

In the yard the sky was lightening, rose-tinted with sunrise. She raised her face and took a deep cleansing breath of fresh air. When was the last time she had even been outside? Hetty stretched her tired limbs.

Provence. She tried out the word silently on her tongue. She had little idea of where that was, but she had seen an atlas in the library and she would look it up later. A sunrise in Provence. Wouldn't it be glorious? Provence, providence, provisions, promise.

She was thinking about golden spires, fields of waving flowers, the sweet scent of clear water, and was almost to the stables before she heard the sound of men.

They were talking; she heard the slurred careful cadence of drunkenness and realised that they must have had their own party out here all night. Clatter of dice on stone floor, laughter, the thump of someone falling off a chair. Light glowed from the stable windows.

She hesitated. There were several of them; surely it was safer? The dice clattered again and she heard Francis swearing, and then the lower tones of another footman, John. A few other men talking. The male house staff must be out here too.

Well, she had no intention of walking into their party. She would see if she could rouse one of the boys, her original plan. But when she slipped into the far end of the stables near the horses' stalls where a boy usually slept on the straw, there was no one there. Only the horses standing side by side. There were more of them than usual, because of the party. Large incurious eyes turned in her direction; tails flicked. She had never been able to read horses. Their faces were frustratingly blank of expression. She touched the flank of one horse: a wall of living flesh.

'Now look who's shown up, just when Charlie's lost all his coppers.' Francis's voice was a low sneer. 'Lucky for him you're here to pay his debts.'

Hetty started and turned to flee, but someone else grabbed her arms. She twisted in the grip but he pulled her back against him so she couldn't see who he was. She kicked and struggled as the man dragged her along the stalls to where the other men waited. There was a group of them, some she recognised, some she did not. Smoking lanterns, tobacco, bottles of beer and spirits on a bale of hay. She saw Charlie and hope flared.

'Please, Charlie!' she called to him. 'I'm your girl. Only your girl. Tell them to let me go.'

He turned away from her and picked up the dice from the floor.

The man who held her flung her onto the straw-strewn floor and immediately straddled her, pinning her arms with his knees. She still couldn't see his face, just his stained trousers. She squeezed her eyes shut and swore to bite whatever came near her mouth, even if it got her hurt, even if it got her killed.

She would not bite. She did not want to die.

'Me first,' she heard Francis say, and the clink of a bottle.

Hands at her bodice, ripping the top of her dress. Hands on her legs, forcing them apart. Hands pushing up her skirt, hands pulling at her drawers. A tearing. The men had gone silent. How many were there? The only sound was harsh breathing, her own, the men, softer breath of the horses.

'What's going on here?' said a voice.

She was instantly released. The man scrambled off her and Hetty rolled and scuttled across the floor to piled bales of hay in a shadow. She tugged down her dress and held the top of it together with her hands. Mr Upcross was there in his riding clothes, young Mr Gilbert Upcross, the one who'd just been married.

'Just a bit of fun sir,' Francis was saying. 'This one came to find us.'

'There will be none of that on my father's property.'

'Yes sir, but she came here sir, she was looking for it.'

'Have you been gambling?'

'Not to speak of, sir, not for money.'

'And you are out here too? Charles, and John, and Ned? I am surprised at you.'

Mumbles.

'I shall certainly speak to my father about this. You have duties to do; do them.'

The men melted away. Hetty, in the corner, tried to slow down her heart.

'You? Girl?' called young Mr Upcross. 'Come here.'

She tried to stand as straight as she could, while holding her dress together. She knew the next step: she'd be sent back to the kitchen of the Red Lion, or worse. She'd end up standing among the women in the yard, pinching their cheeks for colour, waiting for travellers with a few extra coins to spend on pleasure. She walked out of the shadows already talking.

'Please sir, thank you sir, thank you for saving me.'

He squinted at her. 'Who are you? One of the housemaids?'

'Yes sir, please. He's been at me, Francis, he won't leave me alone. I only came to leave a message about Mr Beaumont's carriage, and they grabbed me. I didn't want to do that sir, they tore my dress.'

He averted his eyes. 'Yes. Well. I'll let Mrs Watson deal with that.'

'No, please sir, no. Mrs Watson will dismiss me, and she won't give me a reference, she'll say I was whoring though I was never. I'm a good girl. Please, sir.' An idea struck her and she nearly reached out to him, but then thought better of it. She needed both her hands to hold her dress together. 'You could take me to work for you. I'm a good worker. You must need maids in your new house.'

'Oh, well, you see that is not my concern, I …'

'Please, sir! If you leave me here, they'll get me again, or Mrs Watson will turn me out. Please, sir. You have to help me, I'll do anything.'

His gaze lingered on her loose hair, her torn bodice. She didn't have on her corset and her bosoms were half spilling out. 'Anything?'

And he's just been married to that poor girl, she thought, and sighed inwardly, and let her hand drop away from herself. He stepped towards her.

'Gilbert.'

Mr Upcross flinched, pulled his hands back as if he'd been hit. Madame stood in the doorway.

'Madame, I—'

'Your mother requires you. Qu'est-ce qui se passe?'

'I was … I was merely … this girl asked me …' His face flamed red.

'Tu vas employer cette fille à Londres. Tu ne la toucheras pas. Tu comprends?'

'Oui, Madame.'

'Vas-y.'

When he was gone, Madame stepped into the empty stables. She slid the door shut behind her. Hetty was clutching her dress again, eyes wide.

'How…' Hetty began.

Madame smoothed back Hetty's hair and tucked it into a neat bun behind her head, as if Hetty were one of her charges. She draped her own shawl around Hetty's shoulders to hide her torn dress.

'You mustn't do that,' she said in English, plain, everyday English, with the accent of hills and sheep. 'You're pretty, but you mustn't use your prettiness that way. Once you start it's very hard to stop.' She tilted up Hetty's chin. 'Listen to me. Are you listening?'

Hetty nodded.

'You must learn all you can and find the person with power; and you must make that power yours. That's the only way, for people like you and me.'

Madame stepped back, her hands at her side again. 'Pack your things. You will go with him tomorrow, when they leave for London. Gilbert is a coward, really. Make yourself instantly indispensable to the wife, so he won't have the courage to dismiss you. Don't find yourself alone with him.'

And then she was gone, into the dazzle of new sunlight.

Hetty was sixteen years old. She only saw Madame once more, and by then, she was dead.

Chapter Eighteen

June, 1858
Fortuneswell

Convicts were building the citadel on Verne Common. From where Viola stood on Old Hill, she could see them in their loose, colourless clothes, climbing scaffolding and hauling blocks of Portland stone. She told Jonah that she climbed up this hill to look at the view and breathe the air, but secretly she came to watch them. At this distance they looked like drab shadows. Identical, mere faceless bodies. It was impossible to read the crimes they might have committed to bring them here to hard labour on this hill overlooking the sea.

She had committed no crime. She should be free, but she felt confined. On an island, in a house, in a marriage where they never spoke. These convicts, at least, had useful work. After they died, the walls they built would stand. Her own meagre legacy was written in silver nitrate and glass and albumen-coated paper.

She'd just started her descent when she saw a small figure hurrying towards her. It wasn't difficult to tell who it was; Nan had started wearing flowers and feathers in her hair every day, and it made a halo around her small face.

'Ma'am!' Nan yelled, as soon as she was within hearing distance. 'Ma'am, you're wanted at the Mackeys'!'

Viola hurried down the slope to the girl. 'Who are the Mackeys?'

'He's got the fishing tackle shop in the High Street. Come quickly!'

'What's wrong?'

'It's his daughter. He's waiting at your house, I told him to stay there. Come on, quickly!'

Nan set off on her fleet bare feet and Viola followed as quickly as she could. Exertion still tired her, though less than it used to. When they reached her house there was a man standing at the gate in front. He was dishevelled and florid, with ginger hair and eyelashes and brows so pale they appeared not to exist. He seemed close to collapse: eyes wide, brow soaked in perspiration.

'Are you well, sir?' asked Viola, pressing her hand to her side where she had a stitch.

'It's my Mary.' He removed his hat to reveal sweat-soaked hair. 'That's my daughter. Last night she had a fever, and today she won't wake. The doctor says – the doctor says that she hasn't long, and I…' He twisted the brim of his hat in his hands.

'I will come,' she said, thinking of the times when, as the clergyman's daughter, she visited the sick. What foolish thing had she been thinking on the hill, wondering about her legacy? This was where she was needed. This important moment now. 'I can sit with her, and pray with you.'

'I want something to remember her. Something that will last forever. She's my only child. Her mother—' His voice choked off.

'He wants a photograph,' explained Nan. 'Like the ones you made of us. Before she dies.'

'Oh. I-I see. Is the house close to here?'

'On the High Street, Chiswell.'

She calculated distance and time. The fishing village of Chiswell blended into the more gentrified Fortuneswell; the High Street was only moments from her home. 'Yes. I can do that. Give me a moment to prepare the plate and gather my equipment. Nan, can you help me to carry it, please?'

She hurried into the house and straight up to the darkroom. She tapped her fingers as the plate soaked in silver nitrate solution, knowing that every moment was of the essence. Plate prepared, she put in the camera, threw the cloth over her arm, and gave the tripod to Nan.

Mr Mackey spoke little as he led her down the street; he was too distracted to offer to help her carry the camera. His hat was still in his hands and he turned it round and round as he strode forward. She had the distinct impression that he was finding it difficult to keep from breaking into a run.

He led her to a fishing tackle shop, which was closed and dark; the name over the door was Timothy Mackey. A door on the side led up a flight of narrow stairs to a clean if spartan sitting room. Tools and several long wooden rods and metal reels on the table revealed that Mr Mackey used his home as a workshop. A thin woman in a bonnet, possibly a neighbour, met them and she did not have to say a word for both Viola and Mr Mackey to understand what had occurred while he was gone.

The man stopped as if struck and dropped his hat on the floor. He buried his head in his hands.

'It's been minutes,' whispered the woman. 'You only just missed her.'

Viola remembered the moment of her father's death. The last shallow breath in the still air of the night when she sat with him alone. How when she had embraced him, even with the warmth remaining in his body, he had seemed so much less than what he had been.

She turned quietly for the door, to give him privacy.

Mr Mackey seized her elbow. 'Please don't go,' he said, in a strangled voice. 'Please, take her photograph anyway. Please. I need it even more, now.'

She inclined her head. 'If you wish it. But I have to work quickly, before the plate dries.'

He nodded and the kind neighbour led them both down a short corridor and into the bedroom at the rear of the building. Viola saw a narrow bed with a snow-white counterpane, a basin and a bottle, a roaring fire in the grate, the window closed so that the room was suffocatingly warm. The girl did not look sick, let alone dead. Her face still retained two spots of colour on her cheeks, the signs of her recent fever. Her hair was neatly plaited on either side of her head and her eyes were closed.

At the sight of the child her father let out a cry, quickly muffled by his arm over his mouth.

'I'll make her more natural,' said the neighbour. She went to plump up the pillows under the girl's head, drawing her more upright, laying her hands one on top of the other on her lap. Viola set up the camera on its tripod. It was all done in silence, in the heat and sour smell of fever and mustard.

What a sad difference between this child and the ever-moving Nan. Viola exposed the photograph, replaced the shield on the plate, and immediately packed her things to leave the man in peace with his daughter.

'I have to take this back to my darkroom quickly to develop it,' she explained.

'I'll help you with that, Mrs Worth.' He made to lift the camera.

'There's no need. I can carry it and Nan will help me. Stay with your daughter.'

'I need to do something,' he said.

Viola remembered the day following her father's death, when she had washed linen with her own hands, scrubbed and polished, thrown the windows of the house open, just so she would not cry. She nodded and bade goodbye to the neighbour.

At the door to her house she instructed Nan to help Alice carry water upstairs as quickly as possible, and turned to Mr Mackey, taking the camera and plate from him. 'When it's finished, I will bring the photograph to your house, if I may. I'd like to see how you are doing.'

'Oh,' said Mr Mackey. 'I thought... that is, I thought it would be finished today.'

'The development doesn't take long, but I will have to dry it and varnish it, and I would like to make some prints for you.' His brow furrowed, so she added hurriedly, 'It would be my privilege, as your neighbour, to make them a gift to you.'

'I was thinking – that is kind of you, ma'am, very kind, but I wasn't thinking of money, I was only thinking that perhaps – perhaps you would allow me to watch you.'

'But I am sure that you have many things to do at home?'

'They can wait. There's no hurry. She's gone.' He cleared his throat against the sob that she knew was there. 'I feel, somehow, that my Mary has gone inside the camera. The real part of her, not the body on that bed. And I want to see her.'

Viola nodded. She'd felt that herself, looking at the photographs that her father had taken of her: that he'd captured the truth of her. 'There's only room in the darkroom for one, but I'll fix it in the light for you so you can see it.'

She didn't bother to light the red-shaded dark lantern; she worked as rapidly as she could by feel in the darkness to remove the plate, pour over the developer, and rinse it. Then she opened the door and immediately dropped the plate into the tray of potassium cyanide fixer.

Beside her, Mr Mackey inhaled sharply. 'What is that?' he asked. He pointed to the plate.

In the centre, Mary was lying in bed, eyes closed, hands folded over each other. It was a good likeness, sharp and clear; she looked as if she were sleeping. But Mr Mackey was not pointing at his daughter's image.

He was pointing at the shrouded figure of a child who appeared behind Mary's left shoulder. In the negative, it appeared as a black shadow against the light-coloured walls. As they watched, it dissolved into misty blue, and coalesced into white.

'That wan't in the room when you took the picture,' he said, his voice breathless, his accent broad. 'That shadow. I didn't see it. Did you see it?'

Viola gazed at the plate in dismay. It wasn't a fault in the collodion, or developer burn: it was an actual figure. The features of the figure were blurred, as if moving. She tried to think back to the sequence of events that led up to taking the photograph. Had she used a partly exposed plate in the camera, an old one she hadn't cleaned properly? She'd been in such a hurry to prepare a plate, and she'd done it in darkness.

'I'm so sorry, Mr Mackey,' she said, her stomach sinking. 'I can't think how this happened. I'll take another photograph of your daughter.' But time had passed. Perhaps Mary would look less lifelike. Perhaps the neighbour had already started washing her and preparing the body for burial. There seemed little chance of gaining another picture half as good as this spoilt one.

'But this is … this is …' Mr Mackey reached for the plate, but did not touch it. His hands were shaking.

Viola removed the plate, putting it in a rack to dry, and turned to Mr Mackey to apologise once again, and to assure him that they could produce an acceptable image if they were given time. But she paused as soon as she saw his face. He was not angry or upset. His eyes were wide in wonder, his mouth turned up in a smile.

He looked like someone who had seen a vision of heaven.

'Mr Mackey?' she said gently.

'It's her,' he said. 'It's my little Mary. It's her soul there in the room with us, all that time.'

Chapter Nineteen

That evening, Viola looked up from her sewing and said hesitantly, 'Something happened today.'

Jonah put down his Gibbons. He wasn't making much headway on it, Viola noticed.

'I'd like your advice,' she added.

'Of course,' he said.

'Nan's been telling the village about the photographs I've been taking. Today a man – Mr Mackey, who owns the fishing tackle shop – wanted a photograph taken of his daughter.'

Jonah frowned. 'He sought to hire you? That's not appropriate.'

'No – no, his daughter was sick, and he was desperate. By the time we got to his house, the girl had died. I took this.'

She'd made several prints this afternoon. Most of them still hung in the studio, but she had one beside her sewing box. She passed it to Jonah, who looked at it.

'What a sad story,' he said. 'She's so young. It's a pity about the blurred figure, but I suppose her father won't mind. Who was that – one of her siblings?'

'That's what I want to talk with you about, Jonah. There was no one else in front of the camera except for the girl who had died.'

He lowered the print. 'What?'

'There was me, and Nan, and Mr Mackey, and a neighbour. We all stayed behind the camera. And yet, when I developed the plate, there was another figure.'

Jonah studied it more carefully. 'Did Nan wander in? It's about her size.'

'No. It was very solemn. Nan was quiet and still. And I watched the bed during the entire exposure. She looked so peaceful.'

'Then who is it?'

He was staring at the photograph. He held it closer to his eyes, then further away. He tilted the paper.

'It must be some sort of mistake,' she said. 'I may have used a plate with an image on it already. Perhaps I didn't clean a plate sufficiently. I was in a hurry, preparing it. I may not have seen what was there.'

'Have you ever made that error before?'

'No. But that's what must have happened, isn't it? There's no other explanation. Either someone walked in front of the camera, which didn't happen, or the plate had an image on it already. I've been thinking of how the plate could have been uncovered somehow as we carried the camera back here, to make a double exposure. But I'm sure that didn't happen. It was in the camera with the shield replaced.'

'It's very curious.'

'When Mr Mackey saw the image, he thought it was the soul of his child captured in a photograph at the moment of her passing.'

'The soul of his child.' His cheek had gone pale. 'We seem to be hearing a lot about spirits, lately.'

'It's nonsense, of course.'

'Of course,' he said quickly. 'Do you think it could be a trick of the light? A mirror in the room?'

'There wasn't a mirror, and this sort of image isn't formed by beams of light. It's very visibly a child.'

'Does it look like any of the children you photographed before, who might be on a used plate?'

'I can't tell. It's blurred. Mr Mackey thought it looked like Mary.' She rose and looked at the photograph over his shoulder.

'It's on the plate and on every print I've made, just the same. And Jonah – I'm certain I cleaned all of my plates that I decided to reuse. I cleaned them thoroughly before I put them back. I suppose I could have missed one, but why would I put it with the unused plates?'

'You're usually very methodical.'

'But the circumstances – a death bed. I may have made mistakes.'

He looked up at her, and she turned away from the pity in his face.

'Poor man,' he said gently. 'What did the girl's father say?'

'He said it was her. He was vehement.'

'A father would recognise his child. Wouldn't he?'

'But it's impossible.'

'Is that what you told him?'

'I should have told him that it wasn't her. That is, I *tried* to tell him that it wasn't her. I tried to tell him that it was from an earlier photograph, but he was ... I remember that pain, Jonah. I think that in the moments directly after my father died, I would have done anything to see him again. So I didn't insist.'

'Have you given him the prints?'

'Not yet. I didn't feel that I could, without knowing how this had happened. But I wonder – should I? Would it be a comfort to him, whatever is in this photograph? But it would be a lie – wouldn't it?'

'It could be ... It could be the girl's spirit. As her father believes.'

She turned and stared at him. 'But you don't believe in spirits.'

'I believe in a father's love for his child. Perhaps ... perhaps that could do extraordinary things.'

'Extraordinary enough to make a ghost appear?'

He chewed his lip, thinking, the same way he used to when he was a boy trying to do sums. 'Do you think it's kind to the father to let him have hope, even if that hope might be false?'

'I think that ... if I were to have a child – if *we* were to have a child, I mean.' She felt herself blushing. 'And we were to lose it. I would want to think about it in heaven, not lingering on earth.'

'But would lingering on earth be better than to be gone forever? There's some comfort in that, isn't there?'

He was fervent, and this was the most they'd spoken for days. Perhaps years.

'You think I should give the photograph to Mr Mackey, as proof that his daughter has an immortal soul.'

'Which is something you believe anyway,' he said. 'How is it a lie? The comfort is real, however the image was produced.'

'Faith doesn't require proof.'

'For people who have faith in the first place. For those who don't...' He looked away.

Do you? she wanted to ask. *Do you have any faith left after what you saw in India? Is that what's changed the boy I knew – did he see man's inhumanity and lose his God?*

She couldn't ask that, any more than she could speak about the way they had failed to make love.

'Perhaps,' she said kindly, 'those who don't have faith need hope even more than those who do.'

Chapter Twenty

For the space of a breath, leaning over Viola's shoulder as they watched the image appear on the exposed plate, Jonah both hoped and feared. Because it could not be true that Viola had captured a spirit in a photograph. But Jonah carried a spirit with him all the time. Every morning's waking, every word spoken, every step taken and meal tasted, someone stood and sat and lay beside him: someone invisible and precious. Sometimes he would forget, and in those times he would be light and free, and then the grief came back, and the emptiness, and the paradoxical sense that someone was there.

It was memory, but it was more than memory. It was not Flora Bell, but Flora Bell somehow spoke this person's words.

He bit his lip and his heart thudded loud in his ears and he saw himself appear on the plate, and no one else.

No one else.

Jonah swallowed back a sob and turned his back for a moment, ostensibly tightening the cap on the bottle of fixing solution. What did he feel? Relief or loss? Which was worse?

He cleared his throat. 'What next?' he asked Viola, who had lifted the plate to the window and was scrutinising it.

'I'll try to clean the plate of everything but your image, and expose it again. If that doesn't work, I can try walking into the frame with you for a second or two. But that didn't happen with Mary, so ... I could try a light in the darkroom before developing, but…' She frowned and turned away with the plate, still talking to herself.

What would he have said if a figure appeared beside him on the plate? How would he have explained it to Viola? How could he explain his feelings to her now, as she stood in the tiny darkroom with him, close enough for her dress to brush his legs and still not as close as the person he had lost?

There was nothing but him in the photograph.

The spirit of the one he loved – who he looked for in Mrs Blackthorne's rooms, who he dreamed of, who he felt beside him even now, just out of his reach – either existed but could not be photographed, or it did not exist.

Which was worse?

A clipping from the **Birmingham Mail,** *Wednesday, 13 February, 1858.*

WOMEN AND SPIRITUALISM
By Mr T Selby

It is perhaps not surprising that women, as the weaker sex, should be susceptible to these charlatans offering messages from 'spirits' for a shilling apiece. What is more disheartening is the prevalence of female mediums, often of the lower classes, who shamelessly present themselves as mouthpieces of Heaven, and who immodestly use their feminine charms to gull a desperate public. These women sell their talents to the highest bidder, and although the craze for Spiritualism has the perhaps laudable result of keeping these disreputable women off the streets, the messages of love and eternal life they pass on are no more genuine than the affections peddled by their more unfortunate sisters in back alleys and rented rooms. Even a medium of a better caste employs the wiles of a painted-face courtesan, simpering in order to flatter and tease, while her object is to fill her purse with mourners' coins.

Chapter Twenty-one

Henriette rested in her armchair, window open, a glass of wine and a plate of ginger biscuits on the table beside her. She fanned her face with a silk fan. One of her stays had come undone in her surreptitious transformation from Flora back to Henriette Blackthorne and it poked into her sweaty back every time she moved her arm. Even with the sea breeze this room was dreadfully hot. Not for the first time she wished she'd specialised in rapping walls and turning tables instead of materialising spirits. Although turning tables did require quite a bit of lower body strength and it wore out one's shoes.

'Were there any messages from little Priss today?' she asked Louisa Newham, even though she knew exactly what they had been, since she'd spoken them with her own lips not twenty minutes before.

'My sweet angel in heaven,' said Louisa. Her face was also sheened with sweat. It gave her a bit of a glow. 'Constance, too, and my dear Augustus. They were all here in the room with us. They spoke through Flora's voice, clear as day. I can't tell you how much good it does me to speak with my poor lost babies.'

Henriette smiled and nodded, and took a sip of wine, trying not to wince when the whalebone poked her. It did her good, too, when Louisa Newham spoke with her poor lost babies, though admittedly in her case the good was in a more material sense. She wondered when would be the right time to delicately mention that, as grateful as she was for her patroness's providing her with lodgings and recommendations to the cream of Weymouth society, she had certain financial obligations which she was neglecting in order to help the cream of Weymouth speak with their lost loved ones, and if Mrs Louisa Newham were good enough to spare her a small gift, it would doubtlessly enhance the reputation of Spiritualism.

It was only a matter of time before her creditors discovered where she had gone.

She surreptitiously wiggled her shoulders to try to shift the whalebone. 'Will you have a biscuit, ma'am?'

'Oh no, I couldn't possibly eat. I feel as if my babies' voices could sustain me forever. I wish that odious Erasmus Field could have been in the room, and his even more odious wife.'

'Why are they so particularly odious?' Henriette asked languidly, sipping wine. She found it wise to pretend not to pay attention when people passed on gossip, particularly if that gossip could be useful in the future.

'Sceptics,' said Louisa with a sour purse of her lips. 'They think they're cleverer than everyone else. Particularly Laetitia Field, with her six living children. From the way she talks, you'd think that no one but her had ever been a mother! As if *I* were not a mother, with three babies gone to heaven! I ask you, does that make me less of a mother than she?'

'Certainly not,' said Henriette. 'You love your children, even though they have passed over.'

'Of course I do! And Henriette!' Louisa blinked rapidly several times and leaned forward to tap Henriette on the knee. 'This all reminds me! I was too excited to speak with my babies to tell you before this, but this is extraordinary! You will never guess!'

'What's that?'

'Mrs Worth has taken a photograph of a spirit!'

'Is that so? Remind me, who is Mrs Worth?'

She knew perfectly who Mrs Worth was. A small slender

woman in full mourning, with lush chestnut hair that made her head appear almost too large for her neck. Grey eyes. There was an elastic strength in her, a surprising openness. Henriette had slipped her arm through hers and the young woman had smiled at her. She smelled of lavender water.

And her husband who was no less pretty, though righteous and weak. Unless Henriette was very wrong, Mrs Worth hadn't the slightest idea that her husband was making appointments to see a spirit medium.

Over the years she'd met many people like Mr Worth: sceptics who were nonetheless desperate to believe. They were almost as numerous as staunch believers, like Louisa Newham, or her own late husband, Ethelred. She'd met fewer like Mrs Worth, who took no convincing and yet had no hope.

And now Mrs Worth claimed to have taken a photograph of a spirit?

'She's the daughter of a vicar from Kimmerton in Wiltshire,' said Louisa, settling in for a good gossip. 'They've only been here on the coast for a short time. I believe the money comes from her husband's side. She's a very sweet girl, but he's the one who interests most people.'

'Because of the money?' she asked mildly.

'No, because he's a hero. You met him at your séance – he was the one who tied you up along with my husband. I told you about his story, didn't I?'

'I don't recall. Remind me?'

'He snatched a girl from the very jaws of death in India, during the Revolt. The natives were killing every white man, woman and child they could get their filthy hands on and Jonah Worth smuggled a girl out of Delhi under their very noses. He was dressed in white, and put a turban on his head and smeared his face with dirt, and got her out hidden in a laundry cart. They wandered on the plains without any food or water for days and days, close to death, until they were rescued by English troops. It was in all the newspapers.'

'Oh yes,' Henriette said vaguely. 'That sounds familiar.' She had heard almost every detail in almost these same words from Louisa when she first arrived in Weymouth. Why else would she have chosen Jonah Worth to tie her up? 'I was in Geneva of course, so the English news was very slow in arriving, and there were so many incredible stories at that time. I recall Cawnpore, that horrible tragedy in Cawnpore. On the day of that tragedy – that very day, Louisa – I was conducting a séance and Flora, when she appeared, was able to do nothing but weep. We discovered later what had happened. All the women and children slaughtered. And Mrs Dawlish, who was in the room that day, had lost a cousin. Such a waste of life. Did Mr Worth escape from that massacre in Cawnpore?'

'No, this was in Delhi.'

'Oh yes, you said. My knowledge of geography is shocking. And was it the vicar's daughter that he rescued, and she married him in return? It's a romantic story, if so.'

'No, he rescued the daughter of the family he was staying with, the Hamiltons. Every one of them was killed except for the daughter. Butchered.' Louisa shuddered, but not without pleasure. 'The natives are animals.'

'And what happened to the girl? Does anyone know?'

Sometimes people's lives were like tangled lengths of string and all it took was patient picking at, until it was all clear in front of her, ready to be taken up and used to her benefit. Sometimes it was more complex, like a pictogram puzzle – one of those amusements that bored ladies passed to each other in the parlour. Her dear Ethelred had been fond of them. He used to draw them for her, because he enjoyed watching her solve them. The information was all there, some of it plain, some of it obscure. Often she could reach the solution through instinct alone, and then trace, after-wards, the steps that her logic had taken without her knowing it.

But sometimes she needed to sift through the pieces. She would try on several different interpretations, each as possible as the last, until she found the right way of seeing. Very often, she needed to allow herself to be comfortable with the idea that part of the puzzle might remain a mystery to her, and that the person who had come to her for answers could fill in the blanks by themselves. That was half the skill of her chosen profession: to say just enough to give the illusion of knowledge, but not enough to risk being wrong. Vagueness had a practical merit.

In this case, she'd thought she knew what had happened to the girl, so when Louisa answered, Henriette sat up in surprise, the whalebone jabbing her. 'She's alive?' she said.

'Yes, living with her aunt and uncle in Exeter. She's a distant relation of Mrs Stanhope – you remember I spoke of her, the one who is a martyr to rheumatism?'

If the girl he saved was alive, Worth wasn't paying visits to Henriette to speak to her. It was someone else he loved. Had it been the mother that Worth had loved in India, then? Under the husband's nose, their affair cut short by the war and her death, while the beautiful Viola pined away in her holy father's house? And now, despite his double betrayal, Worth was so righteous?

Few things made her disgusted – she had seen too much of the world – but hypocrisy was one.

'Of course the Worths must be in constant contact with this girl and her relatives,' Henriette said. 'She must be almost part of their family.'

'Oh no,' said Louisa, 'Mrs Stanhope says that they have not even met him to thank him. The girl went back to England almost immediately after the Rebellion, and Mr Worth stayed in India for some little time – I believe he was ill after his ordeal.'

'What a pleasure it would be to reunite them,' said Henriette lightly, wondering what such a reunion would look like. Whether it would turn the puzzle pieces to the correct angle … especially if the girl looked like her mother.

'But this isn't what we were talking about,' said Louisa, sitting forward again. 'We were talking about *Mrs* Worth. I called on her yesterday, because the poor thing has so little society, and we were sitting in her drawing room drinking tea, when the maid announced this... this *woman*, who barged in without so much as a by-your-leave, and started demanding that Mrs Worth come and take a photograph of her boy.'

She recalled talking about photography with Mrs Worth during their short walk together. Mrs Worth had said she no longer took photographs.

'Did you know the woman?' Henriette asked.

'Indeed I did not! I don't associate with that class and I advised Mrs Worth not to do so either, but she spoke with the woman and went so far as to give her a cup of tea. It transpired that this woman's son had passed away, and the woman wished Mrs Worth to take a photograph of the child because she had taken a photograph of another child soon after its death and captured its spirit on the plate.'

'Captured its spirit? How?'

'Well, I couldn't understand it either, and Mrs Worth said the woman was mistaken, but this woman insisted. "You did it for Mr Mackey and his Mary, why won't you do it for me?" This person was in tears, nearly in hysterics, right there in the parlour, and poor Mrs Worth was white as a sheet. So, as you can imagine, I got rid of this person. Mrs Worth was so upset that it took a very long time for her to come back to herself.'

'And then she showed you the photograph of Mr Mackey's daughter?'

'No, poor dear, she was far too shaken. I left her to rest and I went straight to Mr Mackey's house. He owns a fishing tackle shop in Chiswell, it's quite well known. And he was only too happy to show me the photograph.'

'What was it like?'

'It was the girl, surely enough, and there was a spirit standing behind her plain as day. Mr Mackey said it looked exactly like his daughter in life. I offered to buy the photograph from him, but he would not give it up. I was saying to Thaddeus last night, it's incontrovertible scientific proof! Erasmus Field can put that in his pipe and smoke it.'

Incontrovertible scientific proof. Created by a woman who didn't believe in spiritualism, married to a man who was secretly seeking the ghost of a mystery lover. This was a puzzle indeed . . . but a puzzle that could, with careful handling, become lucrative for a canny dealer in the uncanny. She imagined that people would pay a great deal for a photograph of their loved ones who had passed.

'Where did you say Mr Mackey's shop was?' Henriette asked. 'I have a great curiosity to see this photograph.'

Chapter Twenty-two

The front doorbell rang several times quickly in succession, and Viola was just rising to find out what the urgency was and why Alice hadn't answered it when the parlour door opened and a woman rushed into the room. Without ceremony she crossed the room and took Viola's two hands in hers. It was Mrs Blackthorne, the medium.

'Bless you, my child,' she said, fervently. There was a spot of pink on each of her cheeks, and her eyes were sparkling. 'You are a wonder, an absolute wonder.'

Viola blinked at her. 'Mrs Blackthorne, I—'

'Mrs Worth?' said a timid voice from the door. Viola glanced at Alice and nodded a dismissal. Mrs Blackthorne seemed not to notice; she stood holding Viola's hands.

'I'm too forward and familiar. I know it. But I couldn't stop myself, as soon as I heard what you'd done. It's glorious, glorious in every way, it will usher in a new era of happiness and faith. Who can doubt the immortality of the soul when it's documented in a photograph, clear as the eye can see, created by chemicals and light?'

'Oh. You have heard of Mr Mackey's photograph.'

She squeezed Viola's hands. 'Heard of? I have seen it! I went to Mr Mackey myself and saw it. It's kept in a box which he made with his own hands. Exquisite work; he's done nothing else since his daughter died. You can't imagine the comfort it gives him, Mrs Worth. May I call you Viola?'

'I—'

'I must see all your work. Immediately! And please call me Henriette. I think we're going to be such great friends. It was fate that brought me to Weymouth, so that I could meet you.' Henriette's eyes were shining. 'You have a great and unique talent.'

'It was a mistake,' said Viola. 'We're not sure how it happened, but two images were put onto that one plate somehow. I've tried to replicate it. I haven't managed yet, but I will.'

'No,' said Henriette. 'It was no mistake. I conducted a séance in Mr Mackey's home and Mary's spirit told us without any doubt that it was she in that photo.'

'She told you? How did you know it was her?'

'She was able to tell us several things about her late mother which satisfied Mr Mackey as to her identity. But Viola, we mustn't talk about my talent for contacting spirits – we must talk about yours for capturing them! It is really most extraordinary and hugely exciting! Please, show me your other work. Please.'

'But I . . . none of my other photographs contain spirits.'

'Let me be the judge of that, please.'

She still held Viola's hands; her own hands were warm and strong. One of the very few memories Viola had of her mother was of her hands holding hers, or stroking her hair.

'I have an album,' Viola found herself saying. 'It's in the library. I'll fetch it for you.'

'Oh no, I'll come with you,' said Henriette, releasing Viola's hands and drawing her arm through her own, almost leading her out of the room. 'Do you know, I have quite a fancy to see your house, if I may. I hear that your husband is quite a famous man; everyone here calls him the Hero of Delhi.'

'He doesn't like to talk of it,' said Viola, feeling quite swept up by this person who was so at ease with physical contact and making requests.

'No true hero does. Oh, is this one of yours?' She paused to look at a framed print of Lacock Abbey, which had hung over the dining room fireplace in the vicarage in Kimmerton.

'It's one of my father's.'

'Talent clearly runs in the family. It's very evocative – those high windows and the shadows. I remember you spoke of your father the night I met you.'

'What you said prompted me to start taking photographs again. It helps me remember him. I really didn't look for any of this excitement about supposed spirits.'

Viola led her into the library. The album of her own photographs lay on a low shelf next to a similar album of her father's. She lifted it out and Henriette immediately took it from her and threw herself down in a leather armchair to pore over the photographs. She opened it in the middle.

'Oh!' she exclaimed. 'Oh, these are delightful. You have a gift for the theatrical, I see.'

'I like costumes. That was my favourite part of posing for my father's photographs.'

'Costumes and emotion. This one is so beautiful.' She gazed at a photograph of Mrs Chapman sitting in a chair in the garden, peeling apples. 'There's a simplicity to it, something we can see every day, and yet I glimpse this woman's entire life in her posture.'

Without quite knowing why, Viola was hovering by the arm of the chair, watching the other woman leaf through the album. 'Oh, it's … it's just our old housekeeper. She went to live with her sister.'

'And you miss her.'

'Well, my mother died when I was a child, so …'

Henriette looked up. 'I see. You truly do miss her. You must be very lonely.'

Sudden tears. Viola blinked them back, and turned away. For a moment she thought that her unexpected guest was going to stand and try to comfort her, even embrace her with that strange familiarity and warmth. For a moment, she half hoped that she would.

But she didn't. Viola took a handkerchief from her sleeve, wiped her eyes, and heard Henriette turning pages behind her.

'This,' said Henriette, after a silence. 'This one, here. This is what I was looking for.'

Viola tucked away her handkerchief. The photograph that Henriette was gazing at was a portrait she had done of Jonah a few days before he set off for India, just after his twenty-first birthday. A summer's day, bright sunlight dappling through leaves. He sat on the grass in front of a bed of peonies which in reality had been scarlet red, wearing Viola's cashmere shawl wrapped round his head like a turban. He leaned his elbow on a toy elephant which Viola had borrowed from a family in the village and smiled a frank, bright smile, straight at the camera.

She had not looked at that photograph since before her father died. She had almost forgotten that Jonah could smile like that.

'It's my husband,' she said, though of course that was obvious – Mrs Blackthorne had met him at the séance. 'Just before he sailed to Calcutta. We thought the elephant was quite funny, since he was going to be seeing real ones soon.'

'Yes, I love the humour in it. But I was referring to this.' Without touching the print, Henriette hovered her finger over the top left corner of it, behind Jonah's head. Through the dappled effect of the leaves, there was a filmy white streak.

'Yes, an impurity in the collodion,' said Viola. 'It happens sometimes, but I liked the image well enough to keep it even though it was flawed.'

'It's not a fault. It's a face. It's distorted, but can't you see the eyes, and the mouth?' She held the album up for Viola to examine. There was something there: three smudges, dark shapes, two circular and one elongated.

'I don't – I assumed those were leaves.'

'It's unmistakably human. Has your husband lost someone close to him?'

'Well,' said Viola, 'his parents both died in India, but that was a very long time ago.'

'What were their names?'

'Edward and Julia.'

'Edward and Julia,' she repeated thoughtfully, as if tasting the names. 'Isn't it the most likely thing in the world that they should be looking out for him before he embarked on such a hazardous journey to the place where they passed away? Indeed, a journey that would nearly kill him?'

'I-I don't know. But Edward and Julia Worth aren't the cause of that fault. It's the chemistry of the collodion. It's quite a delicate mixture.'

'Has he lost anyone since? Anyone whom he loved?'

'Well ... my father, of course.'

'What about the family he lived with in India? The girl whom he saved?'

'I have no photographs of them. He didn't know them before he went to India, and we haven't seen Emilia since. That was a terrible loss, of course. So many people died in the war, both English and native.'

'But you say your husband never speaks of it.'

'No, never.'

'What were their names? The family? If I may ask?'

'The Hamiltons, Robert and Patience, and the children who died were Toby and Christian, the baby. So sad.'

'Patience is a beautiful name. I suppose she was a beautiful woman?'

'I wouldn't know. They were certainly kind to Jonah.'

'So often, it's the kindest who pass too soon.' Henriette turned her attention back to the album. She examined each photograph in turn, particularly the ones of Jonah, and paused at one of Viola's father near the front of the book. 'Here it is again,' she said, pointing to a light area in the background. Viola had always assumed it was the sunlight reflected off the garden wall. 'Can you see the figure?'

Viola squinted. That could just be a head and shoulders, with shadowy features. 'I …'

'Does it look familiar to you? This is your father in the foreground, is it not? I can see the resemblance between you. Does this form in the background look like your mother at all?'

'I don't know.' She tried to recall her mother's face: not as it was in her father's photographs, but as it was in her memory. 'It could resemble her. But I really think it is a reflection.'

Henriette put down the album and gazed up at Viola, her eyes soft with wonder.

'You have a gift,' she said. 'I believe you have a true talent, given by God. I never knew it was possible to capture spirits with a camera.'

'I couldn't say that these were spirits. I never even saw these figures until you pointed them out.'

'You weren't looking for them. But you saw the spirit in Mary's photograph.'

'I didn't – I don't believe it was a spirit.'

'Oh, Viola!' Henriette started to her feet and took one of Viola's hands again. 'How can you possibly doubt the power of your gift?'

'Well, because it could have happened another way. It could be a double exposure, or a faulty plate.'

'Is this something that happens often?'

'No.'

'Have you tried to replicate it using purely mechanical means?'

'Yes. But none of them have worked, so far.'

'And if it did happen, would it be likely to produce the image of a person strongly resembling someone who has passed over into death?'

'I-I have no idea.'

'It seems much more plausible, does it not, to take the simplest and most direct explanation for this phenomenon: these images are of the spirits who walk among us every day, but who can only be seen and heard by those with special talents. Such a one are you, Viola.'

It was easy to see that Henriette was utterly convinced of the truth of what she said.

'I really don't know,' said Viola.

'Why do you deny it? Do you doubt that human beings have immortal souls?'

'No, I believe it with all my heart. My father was a clergyman.'

'So you told me, when we first met. You said that you doubted that immortal souls would care to play tambourines. But surely they *would* care to watch over the people they love?'

'I—'

'Love is not destroyed by death. It lives forever. You believe that?'

'Yes, of course.'

'So it follows that the spirits of our loved ones are with us, always, until we join them in heaven.'

Which would mean that after all of his fondest and highest hopes, Viola's father knew about the reality of her marriage to Jonah. How lonely she was, how far apart from each other they were, even further than they had been when Jonah was in India and she was in Kimmerton.

'Heaven must be very crowded,' said Viola. 'Sometimes it seems to me that everyone I meet is grieving.'

'Then why do you have so much trouble believing that you can capture the image of spirits?'

'Because I've taken so many photographs of people *without* ghosts in them. Photography is a chemical process, not a spiritual one. It's about silver salts reacting to light. It's about outward appearance, not immortal souls. It seems like magic, but it's a prosaic process. I have faith, Mrs Blackthorne, but photography doesn't require faith. Only the correct technique.' She sighed. 'Look, I'll show you. Come up to the studio now and I'll take your likeness. Then you'll see: I have no special talent. It's light and silver and glass and paper. That's it. No more.'

Chapter Twenty-three

Henriette had been thinking cartes de visite, framed originals, photographic prints at three shillings each. No – five shillings. She had been thinking bound albums, newspaper articles, the irreplaceable gloss of scientific validation. She had assumed that Mrs Worth's photograph of the Mackey girl was a subtle form of revenge upon her husband, Mr Worth, who had fallen in love with another woman in India, and who snuck furtive hours with yet another woman in a stuffy room on the Weymouth seafront.

She had not thought about how the photograph had actually been produced. She assumed an accomplice dressed in a shroud, or a trick in the chemical process; a streak on the plate or a length of swabbed muslin. Experience had taught her that the process of deception was less interesting and glamorous than the outcome: that a battered tambourine could lead to sovereigns and a cheese-cloth veil could lead to guineas.

She had not expected Viola Worth to be stammering and guileless, and to deny that the spirit in the photograph was real.

And Viola didn't know her husband had a lover who had passed away. Henriette had asked a direct question about who he had lost, and there was no self-consciousness when Viola spoke of Jonah's parents or the Hamilton family. She doubted that Viola knew of her husband's visits with Flora.

Why, then, did she take the photo of the ghost in the dead

girl's room? Was it indeed a mistake? And if it was a mistake, not a deliberate fraud, how could Henriette turn it to her advantage?

Henriette sat on a stool in the studio attic of the house, in the pool of light streaming through the overhead windows. She gazed around the room: the periphery was cluttered with trunks and boxes, but the place where she sat was tidy. A screen sat behind the stool; it had been draped in a linen sheet. The camera stood on a tripod in front of her. It was a wooden box with an extendable glass eye. Henriette had had her photograph taken in Paris with Ethelred years ago; this camera was smaller than the one the male photographer had used, but to her untrained eye in other respects it looked the same.

People used science and ritual and religion to dazzle, but Viola was not seeking to dazzle her. 'I'll use a new plate,' she had said, unwrapping it from paper, and holding it up to the light in front of Henriette. 'It's completely clear, isn't it? You can watch me pour the collodion, here.'

She tipped viscous liquid over the plate, tilting it with her fingers, dextrous and focused. Henriette, used to misdirection, watched her, but there was nothing to be seen except for her expertise. This woman had been uncertain when talking about spirits but she was sure-handed when it came to this delicate chemical process. 'The next part needs to be done in the darkness,' Viola told her. 'You can do it yourself, and then you'll know there's no trickery.'

They went together into a sort of closet – not dissimilar to the cabinets she sometimes used for her séances – and Viola lit a red-shaded lamp. She showed Henriette how to test the collodion for tackiness with the tip of a finger, how to grip the plate by the edges, place it in a holder to dip in a bath of liquid.

'Your father taught you all of this?' Henriette asked as Viola turned over an egg timer and turned to pour a chemical into a glass beaker and another into a tray. They stood close enough that their skirts pressed together. In the red light, the other woman's black-clad body was almost invisible, but her face was smooth and young. Henriette wondered about the effect of introducing a red-shaded lantern to her séances.

'It's unusual for a girl,' Viola said. 'A few parishioners objected to his teaching me. My education was slightly unusual, I think, because I had no mother to guide it. A girl should paint or draw, but I'm no good at either of those. Jonah's an accomplished artist, and he gave me many lessons and I always failed. I'm much better at this. Mr Fox Talbot called it The Pencil of Nature, indeed, published a book by that title, which I always took to mean that we allow light and chemistry do all of the hard work. You may raise the plate from the bath, now. Here's a cloth to clean the back of it.'

Under Viola's direction, Henriette placed the plate in a wooden holder with a sliding cover, which fitted into the wooden camera. And now she sat on the stool in silence as Viola silently counted the seconds of exposure.

'That should turn out well,' Viola said, covering the lens and sliding the cover back onto the plate. She seemed to have waited for the photograph to be done until she spoke again, as if the camera could detect noise as well as light. 'You're a good sitter. Some people are stiff or self-conscious, or find it difficult not to move.'

'I've always found it easy to control my body. Other people's bodies can be a problem, however. I'm more at home with spirits.'

Viola laughed. 'Did you feel the presence of any spirits? I only see you.'

'I feel them always.'

'Who would appear next to you, if I could photograph one?'

'Flora, most likely, I would suppose. Or perhaps my late husband, Ethelred.'

'Oh, you're a widow. I'm sorry.' Viola removed the plate holder from the camera. 'I'll develop this now, though I'm sorry you won't see your husband on it. Come and watch.'

Back into the darkroom, where Viola lifted the plate out of the holder. 'Your husband doesn't assist you?' Henriette asked, watching those slender fingers holding the glass. It was very satisfying, she found, to watch a woman being competent at something other than sewing, cooking, cleaning, gossip.

'Not usually. He knows the process, but he prefers to draw.'

'He isn't at home today?'

'No, he is … he is often away.' Viola turned away and with a swift capable movement, poured the beaker of rusty-looking liquid over the plate. After a few seconds Henriette saw shadows developing in the red light. Her own figure, seated. And another.

'Oh!' gasped Viola, beside her, and turned quickly to pour water over the plate. Henriette peered over her shoulder. That was her seated on the stool with colours reversed, her dark hair white, her gown white, and beside her a tall, dark shadow.

Henriette knew who it was merely from the posture: upright, straight, chin up, shoulders set. It could be herself. It was not.

Viola didn't speak. She rinsed the plate and put it into the tray she had prepared earlier. Henriette watched as the negative image became positive, white became black, shadows and depths appeared. It felt as though her heart had stopped beating.

It was only when the photograph was removed from that tray and placed into a tray of water that Viola drew the curtain to allow natural light into the room. She extinguished the lantern.

'There was no one behind you when I made the exposure,' Viola said. 'I saw no one. No one entered the room.'

Henriette did not answer. Her eyes were fixed on the plate under the water. On that person whom she had not seen for so very long.

'That isn't me,' said Viola. Her voice was high. It sounded upset. 'It was a new plate. This shouldn't happen. This is impossible.'

It was impossible. This was not a trick. Henriette stared at the image. In this moment she was not Henriette Blackthorne but someone else, someone smaller and more afraid, someone whom she had not known for a very long time.

'Do you know who this is?' Viola pointed at the surface of the water, which rippled and shone and did not conceal anything.

'Yes,' said Henriette. The words came from a long distance. Miles and years away and under another name. 'Yes, I know who it is.'

In the photograph Henriette Blackthorne gazed calmly at the camera, hands folded on her lap, her eyes steady, her chin high. To her right and behind her – eyes steady, chin high – stood Madame.

Chapter Twenty-four

Eight years earlier...

April, 1850
London

A theatre off the Strand. Most nights, the stage was occupied by tight-dressed singers, loose-dressed dancers, male sopranos dressed as women, female actors dressed as men, occasionally a conjuror, a clown. Last night's performance had featured a dancing bear and the room still carried the meaty animal smell of its fur.

The audience tonight was not all that different from on most nights, although the show was different. The posters called it A SCIENTIFIC WONDER and A MEDICAL MIRACLE and THE EXTRAORDINARY EFFECTS OF ANIMAL MAGNETISM.

A gentleman sat in the front row. He was neatly dressed, with white whiskers and a luxuriant crop of silver hair, a watch chain on his waistcoat catching the light from the stage. A silver-topped cane rested against his thigh. He was a physician, a member of the Royal College, sixty-three years old and still in prime health, his own body a wonderful advertisement for his professional services. He believed in the merits of cold baths, bracing walks, rare meat, sea air. He was also the leader of a very enthusiastic group of amateur spiritualists who spoke with the ghosts of the dead on a weekly, if not daily basis. He had travelled to Massachusetts to meet the Fox sisters; he had met Madame Blavatsky. His name was Dr Ethelred Blackthorne.

The man on stage also claimed to be a doctor. Dr Blackthorne listened as he listed his accomplishments – his time studying with Armand Bacon, who had trained under the Marquis de Puségur who was a student of the great Mesmer himself.

Dr Blackthorne pulled out his watch and consulted it. In his experience, the amount of time that a person had to use to explain to you what an expert he was, was in inverse proportion to that person's expertise. He began to regret the curiosity that had brought him to the theatre. Animal magnetism, as yet, had no proven benefit to health, and Mesmer had never made claims that the procedure had anything to do with spirits. It was an interesting topic, on the scientific frontier between the known and unknown, but this Ferguson came across as a charlatan. Blackthorne thought that perhaps he would slip out and dine at his club instead.

'And now for the practical demonstration,' said Ferguson. (Blackthorne doubted that he was indeed a doctor.) 'Albert, if you will?'

A man carried a wooden chair to the middle of the stage. He went backstage again and this time returned with a young woman. She was tall, healthily built with a slender waist and a full bosom, and pretty. Her lustrous brown hair twisted around her head. Her neat but plain clothes marked her as a respectable working-class woman or servant. Her eyes were downcast, her demeanour modest. Mr Ferguson invited her to sit, which she did, folding her hands in her lap.

'Tell us your name, please,' he said to her gently, and she replied, 'Harriet Smith. People call me Hetty.'

'May I call you Hetty?'

'Yes, sir, if you like.'

Her voice was soft, and barely carried across the hushed theatre. Dr Blackthorne put his watch away and decided to stay for a little longer.

'And what is your age and your position, Hetty?'

'I'm a lady's maid, sir, and I'm twenty-two years old.'

'Are you married?'

'No, sir.'

'In good health?'

'Except for the fainting, sir.'

Ferguson turned to the audience. 'Hetty has been suffering fainting spells. How often will these happen, Hetty?'

'Two or three times a week, sir, at first. But then they started happening more and more, and my mistress, that's Mrs Upcross, she had heard of your work, and she brought me to see you. She's ever so good to me, Mrs Upcross.'

'Indeed she is.' Ferguson addressed the audience again. 'I have had considerable success treating hysteria with animal magnetism. I found that Hetty is particularly susceptible to the effects of the procedure. With your permission, Hetty, I will demonstrate now.'

'Of course, sir.'

'Please stand up.'

Obediently, she stood. Hands still folded, her eyes now on the so-called doctor, the picture of demure acquiescence.

'I pass my hands over her, like so. Not touching. But passes over the patient produce a magnetic alignment. Complete silence, please, as we conduct this demonstration.'

There was already complete silence. The doctor floated his hands over her face, her shoulders, her breasts. He traced her shape in the air. The young woman's bosom heaved once. Twice. And then she sagged, as if she would fall. Despite himself, Dr Blackthorne drew in a sharp breath.

She caught herself before collapsing. She stood, but her hands were no longer folded; they dangled by her sides, limp. Her head lolled slightly to one side. Although she was upright, it appeared as if her limbs were sagging.

'Can you hear me?' asked Ferguson.

'Yes sir,' she said. Her voice was dull, whispery, as if she were talking in her sleep.

She has been coached to act this way, thought Dr Blackthorne. He had met and treated many hysterics in his years in practice, all of them, of course, female. They were above all eager for attention – sometimes inappropriately so. He had learned not to shut his consulting room door and always to have a female nurse nearby.

Despite the appeal of this patient and the strangeness of the demonstration he decided to give it five minutes longer, no more. She would probably manifest a fit, or fainting spell: the sort of symptoms he had witnessed hundreds of times, only in this instance brought on by some pseudo-scientific mumbo jumbo.

'Tell us where you are,' said Ferguson.

The girl raised her head. It was, suddenly, as if she were transformed. Her limbs grew firm, her eyes opened. She stood straight, her chin up, gazing at a point above the audience. 'Je suis en France,' she said in a loud, clear voice. 'Nous sommes dans un théâtre, n'est-ce pas?'

The audience, as one, gasped. The girl's accent was faultless, her posture almost regal. It was as if between one moment and the next she had shaken off the demure lady's maid, the young modest girl, and become a Frenchwoman.

Dr Blackthorne leaned forward, entranced.

'If we are in a theatre,' said Ferguson, 'would you please sing for us?'

The girl stepped forward, her hands clasped in front of her, and began to sing in a high, clear voice.

> J'ai descendu dans mon jardin
> J'ai descendu dans mon jardin
> Pour y cueillir du romarin.'

And Dr Blackthorne was a young man again, nineteen, listening to a sweet voice singing from a window above the street. The scent of bougainvillea, the taste of deep red wine. A young and beautiful woman named Fleur, whom he had loved, who could sing until the consumption stole her voice, and then filled up her lungs, and took her life. She had sung this song, 'Gentil coquelicot'.

The audience sat in utter silence. There wasn't a cough or a single rustle. Only the young girl's voice. When Ferguson clapped his hands to break the trance, Dr Blackthorne started as if he, too, were being awakened.

And there she was again, Hetty the lady's maid, hands folded, shoulders rounded, head bowed.

'When will you start the demonstration, doctor?' she asked.

Applause, loud and genuine, from the audience. Ferguson buoyant.

Dr Ethelred Blackthorne lingered behind to speak to Ferguson. Permission was sought, money changed hands. The next afternoon there was a private demonstration of mesmerism in Dr Blackthorne's home for a select audience of one.

Dr Blackthorne, sixty-three, a lifelong bachelor, presented the young lady's maid with flowers.

'For you,' he said to Hetty. She looked nothing like Fleur, who had been blonde and small, with the hectic cheeks of her illness. But the night before, the resemblance had been uncanny. Not in appearance, but in essence.

'I've never had hothouse flowers before,' she said, and breathed deep of their exotic scent. 'Not for myself.'

'They suit you,' Dr Blackthorne said, looking at her work-roughened hands.

He explained spirits to her, how sometimes they came to people who were in trances and spoke through them. He explained that a person who did this was called a *medium*, and that they were gifted individuals who had the power to help all of mankind.

Ferguson put the lady's maid into a trance again, and he discreetly left the room. Dr Blackthorne drew a chair close to the young woman's.

'Will you sing for me?' he asked her gently.

She sang 'Au clair de la Lune'. And then they spoke in French for half an hour.

Although she had left Madame behind, Hetty had improved her French in her new position in London. To make up for her deficient Northern education, young Mrs Upcross had lessons in elocution and French, and she liked having her favourite clever maid in the room so that they could practise together. Hetty had discovered her talent for acting almost by mistake, when she began affecting fainting spells to escape the renewed attentions of young Mr Upcross.

Ferguson, the mesmerist, had been ridiculously simple to gull, although at first he had tried to fob her off with two shillings per 'demonstration'. Now he gave her a percentage of the takings, which she was saving for travel. She thought she'd like to be her own mistress for a little while.

She found this Dr Blackthorne to be polite and almost unbearably easy to read in his grief for a woman he had lost long ago.

'Are you my Fleur?' he asked her in such tones of hope and reverence that she had never heard from a man before, that seemed as exotic and precious as the hothouse flowers.

It was no effort at all to answer, 'Oui, je suis ta Fleur.' And to take his warm hand in hers.

Hetty was unsurprised to receive a letter from Dr Blackthorne the next day. *You have a very great talent as a medium*, he wrote to her. *I would be honoured if you would visit me again.*

Mr Ferguson – he wasn't a doctor, but a barber surgeon who found mesmerism much more lucrative than cutting hair and lancing boils – objected to Hetty visiting someone else without him, most especially for free. But Dr Blackthorne, although he offered no payment, had something much more intriguing for her than anything Mr Ferguson could offer: open adoration and gentlemanly respect. She went to his home many times, and he always had flowers waiting for her. He never touched her when she was Hetty, but when she pretended to be Fleur, he always held her hand and kissed it.

'I have so much I can teach someone of your natural gifts,' he said to Hetty. 'Have you ever attended a séance?'

And Hetty, who was beginning to understand how she could painlessly and pleasantly escape her life as a servant, smiled and said, 'No, but I would very much love to.'

She was a widow at twenty-seven, and for two of her married years she had lived in Paris. She found the smell of shit more than bearable. They had lived in Copenhagen, too, and Vienna, places where she was known as Mrs Blackthorne, where no one knew she had once been Harriet Smith.

When they visited London, no one recognised her. Ethelred had seen nothing wrong in concealing her humble past, especially as she carried his beloved Fleur within her. At his age, he had no relatives to object to his marrying beneath him. And he never treated her as anything less than his social and moral equal.

She performed often as a spirit medium, though never for payment and never in public. Ethelred would not hear of it. Her séances were in salons and drawing rooms for Ethelred's wide circle of spiritualist friends. Fleur was private, for her husband; when she appeared in front of others, she became Flora Bell.

Dr and Mrs Blackthorne spent the last year of their marriage in Aachen, because of Ethelred's failing health. She was glad to play nursemaid, to be able in some way to repay his kindness. The day that he died she wept, remembering this good and gentle man who had only ever been full of hope, who had loved her sincerely and who had invested her with all the virtues of a woman whom he had loved a lifetime before.

And then she dried her tears and sat down and wrote a letter, in French, to Madame, addressing it via the Upcross family. She told Madame that she had followed her advice. That she had observed and imitated, and given what was needed without giving too much of herself in return. It had been no cost at all to give Dr Blackthorne her faithfulness.

She wrote that she was free now, without a single relative or dependent, a gentlewoman and a widow of independent means, and that if Madame wished to leave the service of that wealthy family, Mrs Blackthorne would welcome her as a companion and friend.

'I have not yet been to Provence,' she wrote, in English, at the bottom. 'Perhaps you and I could visit it together.'

She sealed the letter and posted it, giving the return address of her husband's house in Sussex. She thought of sunshine and fields of lavender, and Madame's quick, nearly hidden smile.

Hetty Smith, now Henriette Blackthorne, had been a thousand different people in the séance rooms. She had learned how to escape ropes and play a tambourine without seeming to touch it. She could tell any story that she could invent, be anyone she wanted to be, but perhaps, in Provence with Madame, she could be purely herself.

She travelled with her husband's body by train and boat and carriage and buried it in his family plot in Sussex. Young Mr Abernathy, her husband's family solicitor (he was fifty years old if he were a day, but the son of Old Mr Abernathy, who had also been her husband's solicitor) came back with her to the house afterwards and told her frankly of her husband's estate.

Like the accent and diction she had learned from listening to Mrs Upcross's elocution lessons, the straight-backed pose she had learned as a girl was so natural to her now that she held it without thought or effort. But as Young Mr Abernathy read to her, her head bowed.

'Nothing left?' she said, when he had finished. 'Ethelred told me that I would be secure when he was gone.'

'Dr Blackthorne perhaps had an inflated view of the value of his investments. His treatment in Germany was very expensive, he made several large donations to the advancement of causes which he espoused, and he travelled in style for many years. He had no heirs, and so his wealth was his own. If he had consulted me when he married, I would have advised him to plan in greater detail for the future. Especially with such a young wife. But he did not consult me.'

'I see,' she said.

'This house remains, but it has several loans taken out against it. If you were to sell it, you would be able to repay the debts and have a small amount to live on.'

'A small amount?'

He gave her an estimated figure.

'It is … perhaps just as well that you did not have any children,' said Young Mr Abernathy, who had five.

'Perhaps,' she said on a sigh. 'Yes, it is just as well.'

She stayed in Sussex long enough to sell the house. She never received a reply from Madame.

Chapter Twenty-five

June, 1858
Weymouth

Jonah Worth sent up his card at the appointed time, and Henriette was ready for him according to her custom. She had set up the screen and drawn the curtains, prepared everything she needed.

The only thing that was different was the print of the photograph Viola had taken the day before. It was propped up on the mantelpiece between a pair of candlesticks and an arrangement of dried flowers under glass. Henriette had spent all morning picking it up and gazing at it before setting it back down.

What did it mean? How could it exist? Viola Worth could know nothing of Henriette's past, or of Madame. Up until the moment the figure of Madame appeared on the plate, Viola was insisting that she couldn't take photographs of spirits at all. Of course this could be a ploy – what better way of seeming genuine than to express scepticism? – but Henriette had years of experience in reading people, and she was certain that Viola Worth was guileless. Viola had been as honestly shocked as Henriette had been.

Madame had not been in that room. And yet the image of Madame appeared on the plate. If this image was of a spirit, then it meant that spirits were real. It meant that Henriette had spent the best part of a decade ignorantly aping something that truly existed.

And if spirits were real, the photograph meant that Madame was dead.

She told Greta to admit her visitor, and Jonah Worth entered her room. He shuffled his hat from hand to hand, guilty and full of desire. Men – and sometimes women too – came to her like this, as if she were their clandestine lover.

'Mr Worth,' she said, holding out her hand. 'I was at your house yesterday.'

His cheeks grew pale. He shook her hand but his was cold. 'You were? I was not aware of that – were you looking for me?'

'No, I was having a very enjoyable conversation with your wife.'

'About me?'

'About photography. I saw Mr Mackey's photograph of his daughter's spirit and I wished to talk with Mrs Worth about it.'

'Oh,' said Worth, twisting the brim of his hat. 'Did you …'

She took pity on him. 'I didn't mention that you have been to see me.'

'Oh.' He seemed to sag a little with relief. 'Do – do you believe that it is indeed a spirit in that photograph?'

'Yes,' she said, and she knew, as she said it, that she did believe. She had gone to the Worths' house looking for a trick and found the truth. 'Did you see the photograph that Viola took of me?'

'I … have not seen my wife today.'

Henriette took the photo down from the mantelpiece again and gave it to Worth, who scrutinised it. 'Is this someone you know, who has passed over?' he asked.

'It is someone I know.' She took it from him; it felt too intimate, somehow, for a man to hold this memory of hers. 'Despite this evidence, your wife doesn't believe that she can take photographs of spirits.'

'She is … perhaps she doesn't need to believe.'

Did Henriette need to believe?

She never would have said she did, until this photograph.

Henriette replaced the photograph and took a deep breath.

'But you did not come here to discuss Mrs Worth's photograph with me. You want to see Flora, and hear any messages she may have for you.'

'Yes. Yes, please.'

'If you will draw the curtains, please, and take a seat?'

She stepped behind the embroidered screen. She waited until the curtains were drawn and she could hear Worth settling into his seat, and then she waited silently for a little while more before she slipped off her shoes and unfastened her gown.

Long ago, when she first started doing this, she would undress hurriedly, risking being detected by the rustle of her clothing. These days, her dress was specially made with concealed fastenings at the front that she could undo at a touch, but she took it off more slowly. Anticipation worked in her favour. Underneath her outer silk gown she wore a lighter, diaphanous garment: not a petticoat, but a draping dress in a Grecian style. She had sewn it herself out of gauze soaked in diluted phosphorescent paint. It was almost transparent; in full light it would be positively indecent, but in darkness it glowed. She pulled a bundle of the same stuff from under her chemise and draped it around her head as a veil. A few drops from the phial of sandalwood oil concealed in her bosom shaken over the hot dark-lantern behind the screen, a few more on the hem of her veil, and Flora Bell was ready once again.

Henriette paused, her hand on the edge of the screen. All of this – all of this falseness – was habit to her now. What did it mean, if spirits truly existed?

'You must learn all you can, and find the person with power, and you must make that power yours. That's the only way, for people like you and me.'

If spirits truly existed, Madame was dead, and Henriette had never been able to tell her how much she meant to her. How Madame had changed her life forever. She did not even know Madame's true name.

Her eyes stung suddenly with tears. She stepped out from behind the screen and went silently to the side of the room. Worth was a shadow in his chair, his back to her.

'Jonah?' she said, making her voice lighter. A thrilling whisper. Sometimes when she was Flora, it was not an act. In her stocking feet, in the darkness, she spread her arms wide like a blessing and forgot everything about the past. She felt loss and hope and love, all the emotions of the spirits that she claimed passed through her. She felt herself light, bodiless, as if she could float away, out of the closed window, into the sky.

'Jonah, is that you?'

He started and turned his head. 'Flora?'

'I am not Flora,' she said. 'I am the other. The person whom you seek.'

'I . . . cannot see you. It's too dark.'

'We met in darkness, did we not?'

She thought of the shadow of that staircase, the stables once all the men had gone.

'Yes,' he whispered.

'Did you receive my message before? That I do not blame you for what happened?'

'Yes. But why – why are you here now? After all this time, after everything that's happened?'

She approached him.

'Why did you not wait for me?' Henriette said. She was Flora, and she was Jonah's lover. No. She was Hetty, with her dream of Provence, and Henriette, who wrote to Madame and never had a reply.

She knelt at his feet. Underneath her veil, she felt a tear fall.

'Why did you go away?' she said, to him and to the spirit who floated behind her, which had been captured in Viola's photograph, and whom she could not see. 'Why did you go, and leave me all alone?'

Chapter Twenty-six

Fifteen months earlier ...

March, 1857
Delhi

Forms and figures. Money in, money out. Duties, levies, weights and measures, names he did not recognise from places he couldn't even pronounce.

Jonah pushed the heavy ledger back on the desk. His solicitors in London and in Delhi had tried to explain all of this to him, over and over, and yet it was making no impression at all. Whenever Jonah tried to make sense of it the figures danced in front of him. They seemed to be different every time he looked at the page. And yet this was his family's property and investments which had led to the money that had paid for his education, the very clothes he wore, and that was meant to sustain and support him and Viola for the rest of their lives.

'It's no use,' he moaned, dropping his head in his hands.

'Excuse me. May I help?'

The voice made him straighten quickly. Pavan Sharma stood in the study doorway holding several rolls of foolscap and a bottle of ink.

'Oh, Pavan. Hello. Please, come in; you have more business here than I do.' He stood up from the desk to cede it to the young man. 'Are you here to do some work for Hamilton?'

'Yes,' Pavan said. 'May I?' When Jonah nodded, he placed the ink and the paper on the gleaming mahogany desk, but did not sit. 'This was your father's desk, was it not?'

'My father's desk, my father's chair.' He tugged a corner of the ledger over and turned back the pages, going back years. 'This is my father's handwriting. I can't understand any of it. I suppose it's all clear to you.'

Pavan hesitated, as if awaiting permission, and then tilted his head to read the words and numbers. 'Clear enough, yes. Your father was a very good bookkeeper. A very shrewd investor in the concerns of the East India Company.'

'You're too young to have known him, surely?'

'I can see him through these figures.' Pavan ran slender fingers over the ledger page.

'I can't at all. I never knew that part of him, and I think I never will.' He gazed at the bold, precise handwriting. 'Even in school, I was never any good at numbers.'

'What is your interest?'

'I draw. Botanical illustrations, mostly. I've had some small commissions and hope to have more. But this ... my father wrote to me before he died. He created all of this for me, he said. He left it for me in his will – appointed trustees to administer the estate until I reached my majority. But now that I'm here ...' He closed the heavy book. 'I don't understand this ledger, and I don't understand India. I was born here but it doesn't belong to me at all.'

'Mathematics, poetry – they are for everyone who can study and understand them. A country, however ... that is beyond understanding.'

'But you've lived your life here. Surely it's as clear to you as this ledger?'

Pavan smiled, and shook his head. He gestured to the desk. 'May I?'

'Of course.'

The young Indian sat at the desk and unrolled his foolscap. Jonah knew he should leave him in peace to work, but he lingered. He wasn't sure that he believed what Pavan said, about a country being beyond understanding.

'Can you show me?' he asked suddenly.

Pavan looked up, putting his finger on the paper to keep his place. 'Show you the ledgers? Of course, though they are yours to see.'

'No – I mean India. Can you show it to me?'

'You are in India. Again, it is yours to see.'

'I'm in India. But I live in an Englishman's home, and go to an Englishman's church. The people I meet are English, speak English.'

'India belongs to England and to Englishmen. You have the proof in this ledger, here.'

'That's not what I mean. There's so much more to India than I can see.'

'There is more than you can see in England, too, I am sure. But you know your place there, and so you feel that you understand everyone else's. It seems to me that the trick is not to know a country, but to know one's self.'

'But…' He felt that he was being rude to this young man, to refute something that he clearly knew better than Jonah himself did, but the frustration had been bubbling for weeks. 'Ever since I've come here, I've felt as if I've been battering up against a glass windowpane. I can't get through. I see everything through my own expectations, and all of my own expectations are wrong. I feel as if I could see something that is real, something that is authentic, perhaps I could begin to understand.'

'But what is authentic, sahib?'

'I don't know.'

'You told me you were born here, and then went to England as a boy. Yet you say you understand England, and not India. What made you understand England?'

Viola.

He hardly remembered his childhood journey from Delhi to Bombay, from Bombay to Dover, from Dover to London. But he recalled in vivid colour stepping out of the carriage in Kimmerton into the lush green of a vicarage garden, and how the small, rosy-cheeked girl, draped in pink and orange with a feather sticking up from her frizzy hair, ran up to him and took his bigger hand in his, as if she were his guide.

'A friend,' he said. 'I had a friend, and she helped me have a home.'

'Then that is what you need.'

'Will you?' Jonah asked, impulsive. 'Will you be my friend? I mean – is it allowed?'

'It is not normal.'

'But it surely must be possible. Will you?'

Pavan smiled.

'Yes,' he said. 'I will try to be your friend, sahib.'

'Please don't call me "sahib".'

'Mister Worth, then,' Pavan said, laughing a little, exaggerating the accent.

'No, no. Call me Jonah.'

A letter dated 13 April 1857, folded around a sketch of a man squatting in a doorway, surrounded by baskets of spices which have been tinted with watercolours: vivid red, orange, yellow. The man wears a richly patterned shalwar kameez, tinted in indigo; he holds a pair of scales.

Dear Viola,

My new friend is Pavan Sharma, and he was born in the same year as you. He took me to the market in Chandni Chowk today and he tells me that I was quite shockingly cheated by the merchants there, because I would not bargain but paid the first price they asked me. 'They see you are an Englishman,' Pavan told me, and I laughed and said, 'Perhaps you can dress me as a Hindu.' He assured me that there was more to being a Hindu than clothes, and I would still be cheated. It seems I must learn to haggle as an Englishman, or else I will be very quickly poor.

Chapter Twenty-seven

April, 1857
Delhi

Every dawn she awoke loose and unbound and, in the moment before she opened her eyes, she felt as if she had no borders or limits, as if her hair spread around her, and her four languid limbs, could be as powerful and bodiless as light.

Then she sat up and her world began; and with it, the ritual of winding herself in.

First, her hair. Cross-legged on her bed, she smoothed her hair with a comb made of bone, and then she began to plait and to twist. As she did this, she thought about fractional exponents and recursive self-similarity. *The straight line is a curve, any part of which is similar to the whole.* The infinite inscription of circles. She liked poetry, but not when it was related to hair. Hair had enough meaning of its own.

Pulled up off her neck and piled up on the top of her head, tucked under itself in glossy coils, her hair was heavier than when it was loose. When she was in a hurry she thought it would be easier to cut it off – imagine the lightness, the lack of this burden, the cool air on her scalp! But of course she would not, any more than she would cut off her own arm.

After her hair, then the two lengths of white cloth. First, the turban, which she wound precisely and, like her hair, by touch. She had a mirror but these days she was practised enough not to need it, and she did not use it until this process was complete. She did not like to see herself in a half state. Then the second cloth around her chest, binding her breasts tight and flat. Sometimes she tied it too tightly and later she found herself panting for breath, far from any private place where she could loosen her bonds. The sensation reminded her of how she had felt as a girl, hearing the well-meaning statements that suffocated her, bound her, trapped her. *Of course you will give up all these studies when you are married and have children.*

Only men could study at the college. So a man was what she became, every morning. These bonds made her free. They defined her outlines, created a fiction, and made it easier for her to be unnoticed. It was also a trap, but one of her own choosing.

Finished, Pavan put on her clothes and gathered her books and went to join her family for breakfast before setting off to the college, as she did every day, a sole woman hidden in plain sight.

'One day, may I see where you live?' Jonah asked her. (It had taken some time and many mistakes, but she had got used to calling him Jonah.) They were in the Hamiltons' library. It was cool in here, and Pavan had found a copy of *Villette*. She looked up from the scene where quiet Lucy Snowe watches as her employer Madame Beck methodically and clandestinely goes through Lucy's every belonging. The novel's theme and Jonah's request were so similar that Pavan's reply was a little testy.

'Seeing where I live will not teach you how every Indian lives,' she said. 'I cannot always be your model.'

'No,' he said. 'It will teach me how *you* live, and that's all I want to know.'

'Perhaps I don't wish for you to see how I live.'

'Then that's fine,' he said without offence, and went back to his *Lyrical Ballads*, she to *Villette* as Lucy Snowe thought: *Loverless and inexpectant of love, I was as safe from spies in my heart-poverty, as the beggar from thieves in his destitution of purse.*

She put down the book with a sigh.

'Come tomorrow,' Pavan said to him.

What would he see, after all? All that she had to hide, was not concealed in her home. It was concealed here, in her own self.

He had chosen her as his friend, not knowing how unusual she truly was. Being chosen, she had chosen him as a friend in return. He was unusual too, an Englishman who seemed to want to use his wealth and power by pretending not to have it. At first she'd thought it was a game, but as she knew him better, she realised that the pretence was in earnest. They were both trying hard to be something they were not.

She told him a time when Rajesh would be working and his wife Lakshmi would be at market with little Roopitha. In the morning, though, she regretted the invitation. This house was the only place where she could be herself, a safe space that was created not by the walls and doors and curtains, but by the love of her family. And yet she hurried that family out the door, so that they would not cross paths with her visitor.

When Jonah arrived, he handed her a box of jalebi from Abu-Mohammed's sweet stall. Pavan had confessed to him that she sometimes bought a pocketful after lectures and ate half of them by herself before she could get them home to her niece. For her sister-in-law he had a bouquet of hibiscus from the garden of his house, wrapped in a length of red silk.

'I'm sorry they're such modest gifts,' he said, giving them to her. She took the apology for what it was: an acknowledgement that he would not shame her family by bringing her something expensive that they wouldn't be able to afford for themselves. A poorer man, or a man who wasn't conscious of his own wealth, would have given something that cost him more. These were the ways that pretence broke down.

'I'd hoped to meet your family,' he said.

'Unfortunately, they had to be away. I will have to suffice.'

'I also have something for you.' He gave her a page from his sketchbook, with a drawing of the temple of Radharani. He was so skilled with his pencil that the leaves of the peepul tree seemed to be moving. Just inside the door, half in sunlight, half in shadow, were a pair of sandalled feet. The body was an indistinct shadow reclining on the floor. Pavan could just make out the outline of a book splayed on the sleeping person's chest.

'It's me,' Pavan said, tracing the figure on the paper. It was a very convincing young man.

'I'm better at drawing flowers than people,' Jonah said.

'I have never been drawn before.' But it was a familiar feeling, Pavan thought, to see yourself as someone else saw you, to borrow their eyes – to have that distance, while at the same time knowing that a figure on paper could never show the entire truth.

Pavan had thought that the house would feel smaller with Jonah in it, but it didn't. The Englishman wasn't as tall as Rajesh and, unlike some small men, he didn't try to make his presence larger. He asked her permission before entering any room, and he exclaimed over their collection of books, which was much smaller than the one at the haveli but more eclectic: volumes of poetry and philosophy and mathematics in English, Hindi, Urdu and Sanskrit … and Pavan's carefully hoarded Dickens novels.

He walked around Lakshmi's garden and admired her plants and her skill; he paused to take a sketch of a gourd in the sunlight. They drank cool water in the shady part of the garden.

'This is beautiful,' said Jonah. 'My family's house is a little too grand for me. This is cosier, like the vicarage where I grew up. Perhaps one day you can visit Wiltshire. I think you and Viola would like each other.'

Then he yelped and his cup went flying, spilling water across his lap. He brushed his arm and a gecko plopped off and scurried into a flower bed. Jonah's blue eyes were so large and his face so comically shocked that she began to laugh.

'Are you laughing at me?' he said, laughing.

'I am laughing because you are the only person I've had to visit me here, and the first thing you do is fling my sister's cup across her garden.'

He scrambled to retrieve it. 'The only person? Really?'

'I have not had many friends,' she said, realising as she said it that it was true. 'None at all since we left Agra. I never thought I needed them.' And it was too risky, of course.

'Have you been lonely?'

'I never thought so.'

He examined the earthenware cup for chips or breaks, and then set it back on the little table.

'I was lonely too,' he said.

They changed the subject then to Dickens, and argued the relative merits of *Oliver Twist* against *David Copperfield*.

When he left, she hid all the gifts he had brought.

Chapter Twenty-eight

April, 1857
Delhi

They climbed to the top of the ruined temple with the help of a vine hanging from the peepul tree and sat there, legs dangling over the side, slapping at the mosquitoes that buzzed in their ears. From here, Jonah could see the shadows and fires of the city spread out beneath him. Above, the stars glittered like diamonds on velvet.

'I can't get used to the idea that these are the same stars that I see back home,' said Jonah. 'Almost everything seems different here in India, and yet there is the Plough, and the Little Bear, and Orion the warrior.'

'They are the same stars, but we have different names for them,' said Pavan, pointing to the stars of the Plough, one by one. 'These are the seven sages, Rishis. They make the sun rise and set, and they were married to seven sisters.'

'*Were* married?'

'According to legend, only one was faithful. Arundhati. There she is – the smallest star.' Pavan pointed. 'The other six are there, the Krittika.'

'The Pleiades, in English. So many stories, about balls of gas and fire.'

'This is the definition of what it is to be human: to invent stories to explain what we see around us. A monkey will accept. A human will mythologise.'

Jonah leaned back on his hands, tilting his head back, kicking his heels in the air like a child. 'Which do you believe? The Plough, the sages, the balls of gas and fire?'

'In a sense, I believe them all. I was taught one meaning as a child, and as I grow I learn more and more.' Pavan's voice gained a familiar note of humour. 'I am a Hindu in a city ruled by Christians and Mohammedans. It is advantageous to me to be flexible in my beliefs whenever possible.'

'Some would say that choosing one's beliefs according to advantage means that none of the beliefs are true at all.'

Pavan paused for a long time before answering at last, speaking slowly as if formulating his own beliefs as he expressed them.

'I believe them all, and none,' he said. 'I am more than one thing, you see. I am a Hindu; I make offerings at this temple for Radharani. I am also a scholar at the college, discovering another story about the Universe that does not include Shiva and Rama. Which is true? I cannot choose one – how can I, when there are so many? All stories are true, or none. I find more beauty if they are all true.'

'Listening to you, I feel as if I wasted my education. I went to Oxford but I was never very good at anything except for drawing.'

Pavan smiled. 'My brother says that once I start on a topic I am like a horse who has been stung by a fly. I must learn to rein myself in.'

'Viola says that one of the reasons she likes taking photographs is because to those who don't understand the chemistry, the process is indistinguishable from magic.'

'Will…' Pavan paused. They rarely discussed personal questions. Jonah thought Pavan was more comfortable with mathematics and philosophy. 'Will Viola come here, or will you return to England?'

'I don't know. It would be hard for her to be away from her father.'

'If you are in love with her, I wonder that you could leave her for so long.'

'We've been engaged for a very long time,' said Jonah. 'We've known each other from childhood, you see.'

'Your parents wished you to marry?'

'My father and her father were close friends.' He thought about what Pavan had said about being separated from Viola. 'I miss her, of course, but it's not – if we were in the full flush of first love, it would be painful to be apart, but we've spent nearly all our lives together. I know Viola so well that I feel that she's with me always.'

'She *is* with you always,' repeated Pavan. 'And of course, you are under the same stars. That must be a comfort.'

Jonah nodded, though the Kimmerton of gentle spring, of crocuses and daffodils and the first buds on trees, seemed very far away. He'd had a letter from Viola that morning; she had mentioned that her father was unwell. *Only a slight cold from being out in the rain*, she had written. *He believes it is nothing that cannot be cured with a basin of gruel and a sermon by Kingsley.* He knew her well enough to understand that she was worried. But the letter had taken so long to get here, her father was probably better by now.

'What about you, Pavan?' he asked. 'You speak as if you understand love.'

'Oh. Oh, I did not mean to – this was very impertinent of me. I am sorry.' Pavan scrambled to his feet on the wall.

'No. Please, Pavan, I am the impertinent one. I was merely teasing. I should have asked, more politely: are you yet thinking of marrying, or do your studies take up all your time?'

Pavan sat again. 'I am engaged,' he said slowly. 'Or I am meant to be. I have been engaged since I was six years old. Our parents arranged it.'

'Why do you say you're "meant to be" engaged? Have you broken it off?'

'I came to Delhi instead of being married. My brother was good enough to move here with me so I could attend the college.'

'But you intend to go back? Or will she come here to join you?'

'I ... there is a great discrepancy between our ages. If I'm honest, I do not wish to marry. I would prefer to study.'

'Surely one can do both?'

'Our temperaments are very different. We have little in common, aside from our parents' wishes. And yet I'm honour bound to marry.' Pavan folded his hands on his lap. 'Like yours, my parents are dead. It's more difficult to ignore the wishes of the dead than the living.'

'Why should you feel this way, if you are a scientist?'

'You are also trying to follow your father's business, even though you are an artist.'

Jonah gazed at his friend. In the darkness, he was a glow of white clothing and turban and a liquid light of eyes.

'You're right,' he said. 'Our lives have a lot of similarities. I'm glad you're my friend. If I go back to England again, perhaps one night you'll look up at your seven sages and think about me, looking up at the Plough.' He took Pavan's hand in his and squeezed it, as he sometimes did with his school friends, as he sometimes did with Viola.

Pavan disengaged himself and stood. 'I should go. I have work to do tomorrow.' He swung himself down into the limbs of the tree.

'I've a book for you,' called Jonah. '*Aurora Leigh*, by Mrs Browning. I'll finish it tonight.'

But Pavan had climbed down, and had already disappeared into the shadows.

She ran towards home. Pavan wasn't afraid of Delhi at night; her male garb made her safer, she was faster than most men, and she knew every back alley and shortcut. She wasn't running away from the thieves and bored soldiers that lingered in the city's shadows. She was running away from that moment when Jonah and she were looking up at the same stars and he took her hand, his arm brushing against the cloth that bound her chest.

She should have left as soon as the conversation turned to love. She should not have talked about her engagement. It was too close to the truth. She should never have mentioned Jonah's fiancée. But she was curious to know what kind of a woman Jonah could care about.

She was running away from this curiosity, too.

Pavan rounded the corner, breathing hard, sweat soaking through her bindings. She was unsurprised to see Rajesh waiting in the lit-up doorway of their house.

'You don't have to stay up waiting for me,' she grumbled, panting and pushing past him.

He put out an arm to stop her. 'I'm your elder brother. Where were you?'

'Jantar Mantar,' she lied. 'Making celestial calculations.'

'Sahib Worth is also an amateur astronomer?'

'Stop being an old woman, Rajesh.'

'An old woman would have put an end to this long ago.'

'Let me pass. I have to study.' She pushed at his arm.

He withdrew his arm, but only enough to show her what he held in his hand. It was the sketch Jonah had done of her sleeping in the temple, signed with his name.

'How did you get that?' she asked, feigning outrage despite the anger in her brother's eyes. Rajesh was so rarely angry.

'It fell out of one of your books. This needs to stop. Why are you spending time with this man?'

She lifted her chin. 'He's my friend.'

'Friend?' A low bark of a furious laugh.

'He treats me as an equal.'

'You are not his equal. All of that is an illusion.'

'It's not an illusion. A woman can be the equal of a man. You say all the time, brother, that I'm cleverer than you are.'

'That's not what I'm talking about.'

'But he understands – he feels—'

She understood all at once why she wanted the illusion to be true, and she averted her eyes from her brother's.

'You can't,' Rajesh said, more gently now. 'We gave up so much to come here. You would lose all that you have worked for, my sister. You can't live as a man and still love as a woman. And of all men, you can't love one like him.'

'I don't,' she said. 'You think I'm foolish, but I'm not.'

She was lying. Every hour of every day, she was lying to everyone, and most of all to herself.

She snatched the drawing from him and ran off to her room before Rajesh could see her cry. Of all the humiliations of this night, that would be the worst.

But when she had stopped crying, and was lying on her bed face down, breathing the scent of damp cotton, she heard soft footsteps entering her room. Her sister-in-law Lakshmi sat beside her on the bed. Pavan heard her quiet breath. No one ever came into her room.

'He only wants to protect me,' Pavan said into her pillow. 'You all do. I understand. But I wish you'd leave me alone.'

Lakshmi, the quiet, the gardener, who never asked questions but who nourished her family and her plants and honoured secrets, said nothing.

'I don't know who I am. I've learned so much and I still don't know, and no one else does either. So what is the use of all this pretending?'

'You're you,' Lakshmi said quietly.

'I wanted to think, just think, and never have to worry about my body or what it was or who it wanted. I never wanted to love.'

'Why do you love him?' she asked.

'Because … because I thought I didn't want to be noticed, and he noticed me. I showed him a lie, and he saw myself.'

'We see you too.'

'Is that enough?'

Her sister-in-law didn't answer. There wasn't an answer. She laid her hand on Pavan's shoulder, and left it there until Pavan fell asleep.

Jonah had the copy of *Aurora Leigh* under his arm when he knocked lightly on the study door and entered without waiting for Pavan's light and courteous invitation. Someone else looked up from the desk, someone taller and broader, with a black beard and without the snow-white turban.

'Oh,' said Jonah, halting midway through the door and blushing at his own rudeness. 'Hello, Rajesh. I was expecting your brother.'

'Pavan could not come today.'

'I hope he is well?'

'Quite well, only unable to attend.'

'Oh,' said Jonah again, disappointed. 'I'm glad to see you, of course. I have this book that I thought Pavan would enjoy.'

'Sahib, my brother has very much work to do with his studies. He cannot accept any other books.'

'Oh. I see. Well... thank you.' He tucked the slim volume under his arm again and retreated.

Usually he walked home from church on a Sunday, enjoying the chance to look about him and explore, but today he joined Mrs Hamilton in her carriage with the children, while Hamilton rode behind. It was an open carriage with a shade to protect from the sun, but it was still hot; the horses barely kept a pace great enough to cause a breeze, especially when the driver paused so that Mrs Hamilton could exchange some words with her passing acquaintances, which she did often. Jonah waited until she had finished chatting with the Coopers about the news of the day. Miss Jennings had become engaged to Captain Roberts, and a rebellious native soldier had been hanged at Barrackpore the day before.

'Is Pavan Sharma ill, do you know?' he asked when the Coopers had passed on.

'I haven't heard that he is,' replied Mrs Hamilton. 'We'll ask Rajesh when we see him.'

'I saw Rajesh last week, and he said that his brother was well.'

'Then what makes you think that Pavan is ill?'

'Because I can't think of any other reason why he would stay away.'

Mrs Hamilton had been gazing idly at the passing scenery. Now she turned to Jonah. 'You had an engagement with Pavan?' she asked.

'We didn't have any specific engagement, but we're friends.'

'You and Pavan are friends?' said Mrs Hamilton. Her hands were clasped in her lap, and she rubbed her thumbs together. Jonah had the impression that she was choosing her words carefully.

'It is quite easy to forget,' she said at last, 'how enormous is the gap between the natives and us. We have so many points in common, and we live so close together, it is easy to assume that we think the same way. As you know, I was born in India and have spent almost all my life here. But every now and then one comes up against this fundamental difference. Our gods are different; our language is different. It must form us, in a way that cannot be altered.'

Their carriage stopped; Jonah rose to see why. There was a cow in the road. He sat again beside her.

'My foster father taught me that every human being is equal in God's sight,' he said, irritated. 'I assume this means Indians as well.'

'I will never forget something I witnessed when I was a child of only six,' she continued, as if he hadn't spoken. 'My family and I were travelling to Calcutta by boat. We came across a group of natives who were starving. They had collected by the shores of the Ganges so that their bones would be washed away by the holy river. Men, women, children. Infants. Their skin hung off them like rags, and their eyes ... I saw an infant crawl up to its dead mother ...' She closed her eyes for a moment. 'My father, naturally, offered them food. But their religion forbade them to taste food that was given to them by an Englishman. They would rather die, and see their children die, than violate the rules of their faith.'

He winced at the idea of dying children. 'But many Christians have died for their religion, and seen their children die. That's not so different.'

'The principle may be the same. But the religion is different. I remember that one of the men, at last, was so driven by hunger that he approached our boat. He said he would eat and live; he cast off the cord he wore about his neck and threw it into the water, renouncing his religion. My father immediately gave him food. But after starving for so long, it was too much for the poor man. He died from the very thing he needed. Our Christian charity, however well meant, killed him.' The carriage started again with a jolt, but Mrs Hamilton seemed not to notice. She was looking at Jonah now, seriously. 'There is a gap, always, over which we can never quite meet, no matter how much we would like to.'

'You're telling me that Pavan Sharma and I are not friends.'

'I am telling you that perhaps it's best not to think of him that way, and perhaps he has good reason for putting distance between you.'

'But what reason can that be? Have I offended him in some way? If so, why won't he tell me?'

'You may never understand the reason. And forcing it without understanding may cause much more harm than good. We each have our place in this country. It has been this way for hundreds of years, and it always will be. We are not the same.'

Chapter Twenty-nine

June, 1858
Weymouth

He did not move from his chair as Mrs Blackthorne walked through the room, turning up the gas and opening the curtains. His face was buried in his hands, his palms slick with tears. He didn't dare move.

'Mr Worth? Are you unwell?' Her voice was not unkind, but brusque. The opposite to the sweet voice of the spirit who had spoken to him. She paused beside him, and he felt the brush of cloth against the back of his fingers. 'Here is a handkerchief.'

He had his own, but he did not want to take his hands away from his face to reach for it, so he took hers and wiped his face with it. Although it was an obligation he would owe her. Although it was a clear sign of weakness and unmanliness.

The spirit had cried. A single tear had touched his hand. He could still feel the burning of it.

'Did you hear what was said?' he asked, through the cloth, not looking up at her.

'I've told you several times, Mr Worth – what occurs when I'm in a trance is beyond my comprehension.'

He nodded. He put her handkerchief into his pocket. Thankfully, when he looked up she was at the window adjusting the curtain. The room still smelled faintly of sandalwood.

'Thank you,' he said. 'I'll return this.'

'No need. I've seen plenty of grieving people. There is no shame in it.'

The shame was like bile in his throat.

'Please,' he said. 'I need to ask you not to tell my wife that I am visiting you.' He stood and fumbled in his pocket. 'Perhaps it's customary for your – ' Clients? Supplicants? ' – visitors to offer you a fee, or a gift, in gratitude for your—'

'You do not need to pay me to keep your secret,' said Mrs Blackthorne, coldly. 'It is your secret, not mine. I advised you when you first came to see me that you should not conceal your thoughts, feelings and actions from your wife. I've known far too many faithless men.' She seemed to collect herself. 'However, if you wish to leave a donation to further the cause of Spiritualism, I will be happy to make certain it reaches the place where it will do most good.'

He nodded and took out a guinea, which he placed as quietly as he could on the table. On second thoughts he added another.

'Why are you helping me?' he asked. 'You clearly don't like me.'

'I'm helping you because you believe you need help, and I promised myself, when I discovered these gifts, that I would use them to comfort others.'

'I … am not comforted.'

'But you find something that helps you, or else you wouldn't return.'

'I don't know.' It was more a compulsion than a desire. He had not wanted to hear the spirit, whoever it was, ask that question: *Why did you go, and leave me all alone?* He did not want to breathe the scents of incense or see a slender figure dressed in white whom he could not touch but whose tears were real.

He swallowed hard.

'Also,' said Mrs Blackthorne, 'I like your wife. She has a talent which is … extraordinary. I hope that whatever you learn here, even if you cannot tell her about it directly, helps you to help her to become less sad.'

'I don't know how to make my wife less sad,' he said.

'In my experience, a husband almost always knows how to

make his wife happier, if he will allow himself to understand her.'
Mrs Blackthorne finished with the curtains and turned to him.
'I'm a little tired.'

'Of course,' he said, picking up his hat and making for the door.
But before he left, he paused.

'May I see you again soon?' he said, hating himself for needing
the pain and the guilt, and most of all for needing to speak with
the spirit of Pavan, who may not have blamed him, but whose
death, nonetheless, was on his hands.

Chapter Thirty

When Viola developed the photograph of herself it was a poor one – blurred where she had moved, with her bottom half out of focus and the light striking her all wrong – but it was also only of her. She pored over the plate while she was rinsing it, held it dripping up to the light looking for a streak or a spot, something, *anything* that could be her father, but there was nothing there.

Of course there was not. Of course.

She wanted to laugh at her foolishness, but the image of herself on the plate stopped her. She rarely looked in a glass, but this photograph was a captured reflection of ten seconds of her life this morning. Even with the image being such bad quality she could see that her hair was untidy, her dress unflattering, her eyes too large, her mouth too small. Her face was a pale smear, and yet it was so hopeful.

Did she want so badly to believe? Was her future so hazy that this was all she had left, the hope of an image from the past?

A knock on the studio door. She discarded the plate and went to the door, wiping her hands on her apron. 'Mrs Blackthorne is here for you, ma'am,' said Alice, who had been trained well never to open the door to the studio.

'Again?' she said, but her heart thumped. She took off her apron and followed Alice down the stairs, smoothing her hair back as she did, though she thought that it was probably a lost cause.

Henriette, despite her familiarity with spirits, had been as astonished as Viola when one turned up in her portrait. It was that almost as much as anything else that had made Viola wonder whether these things she had produced were real. There was something about Henriette – a strength, an enthusiasm – that made one feel as if anything could happen.

Perhaps if she sat with me, I would see Papa, Viola thought, and shook her head, and went into the parlour to greet her waiting guest.

'Viola,' Henriette said warmly, as soon as she came inside, and took her by both hands as if this were Henriette's own house and she was welcoming Viola as a guest. 'I had to see you. I think I was in shock the last time we spoke, because I was so astonished by your photograph. It's one thing to see such a wonder, and another to experience it.'

'But you see spirits all the time, don't you?'

'They appear, and then they dissolve. But you've fixed them in time, forever. Your skill is far greater than mine.'

'I really don't think it is,' said Viola. 'Shall I ring for some tea?'

'Let's walk,' said Henriette. 'I've been doing nothing but talking with spirits for two days. I feel as if I'm still in a cabinet. I need to breathe sea air.'

'All right,' said Viola, and went to fetch her hat and coat. As soon as they were outside, Henriette linked her arm with hers and started striding down the hill towards the sea.

There was something exhilarating about walking so quickly and confidently, arm in arm with this woman. It was a fine day and the water was a deep turquoise blue, several shades darker than the sky. Viola's usual walk was up the hill to gaze at the view towards the mainland and the convicts building defensive walls, but Henriette took another direction, along the top of the beach to the end and then along the stony path between the coast and the cliff. It was too narrow for them to walk side by side, so Viola relinquished Henriette's arm and followed, gazing upwards at the striated cliff and downwards at where the water crashed against the rocks that appeared to have been scattered there by the careless hand of God.

'This is near where Jonah has been sketching,' she said. 'His friend Mr Field has excavated a fossil of a dinosaur.'

'Oh? He hasn't taken you with him on his expeditions?'

'I … no.' *We don't do much together.*

Henriette didn't press her. Instead she said, after a moment, 'You came to the coast for your health?'

'Yes – I was weak after my father died. I'm much better now.'

'Have you bathed in the sea yet?'

'Here? I don't think—'

'Not here, this isn't suitable for bathing. Weymouth, however – I can see the machines from my window, and I've been longing to bathe. There's nothing better. We shall go together.'

'I … yes, let's.' She felt breathless, both from the brisk walk and the force of Henriette's personality.

Henriette glanced over her shoulder. 'Are you, perhaps, in an interesting condition? Sometimes it can enhance a woman's communications with spirits, if she's with child.'

'No. No, I'm not expecting a baby.'

'Not yet. Or perhaps you don't want children?'

'I do want children. Of course I want children.'

'So did I.' Henriette paused and turned to press Viola's arm again. They stood together on the path looking out to sea. The sky was just as bright, the air just as fresh, the sea as sparkling, but the talk of children had dulled it all a bit for Viola.

'You and your husband never had children, then?' Viola asked, after several moments.

'No. We didn't have enough time.' Henriette smiled sadly. 'I would have liked to have Ethelred's child. He was a kind man. But he was older than I, and his health started to fail. We lived in Germany and Switzerland because of the air. I had to nurse him. I don't begrudge him that. Even when he was sick, we were happy together.' She stopped and gestured with her free arm to the sea. 'He showed me my first glimpse of the ocean. Every time I see it, I think of him.'

'That's lovely.'

'He gave me many gifts, but perhaps that was one of the most precious.'

'I nursed my father,' Viola told her. 'His doctor advised sea air, but he wanted to stay at home with his parishioners, where he could be of use. His life became smaller and smaller, limited to a single room. He used to walk all over his parish when he was well. By the end he could barely sit up in bed.'

'Illness is terrible, Viola, but it has an end. Grief can be more terrible if you cannot believe that you will be reunited with the person you have lost.'

'But that photograph. And the others. They're proof, aren't they? That the soul lives beyond the body. That nothing ends.'

'From that rock,' Henriette said, pointing, 'it will feel as if we are flying.'

'Mrs Newham says that *you* can fly.'

Henriette laughed. 'Come on.'

She hitched up her skirts and instantly began to climb the large boulder of white Portland stone perched over the foaming sea. Viola looked around; she saw no one except for a solitary fisherman far down the distant beach and a pair of gulls swooping in the empty sky. She had not climbed anything since she was a little girl and she and Jonah had climbed every suitable tree in a mile's radius of the vicarage, and some that were not suitable, too.

She pulled up her skirts with one hand and pulled herself up with the other, finding toeholds in the rock. It left white streaks on her black dress, but when Henriette reached down and helped her up to the top of the rock and the two of them stood there together, the sea roiling beneath them, nothing but sky before them, Viola did feel as if she were flying.

The world, so colourless and cold, had changed around her in a single instant to something fresh and vibrant and infinite.

'It's beautiful,' she gasped.

'There are moments when we touch the sublime,' said Henriette. 'And those moments confirm everything that we have always hoped to be true. Your photograph changed something in me.'

'My faith has wavered,' confessed Viola. 'I thought it was strong, but it wasn't. My father's death crippled it.'

'Have your photographs restored your faith?'

'I don't know,' she said. 'But my father taught me this, and I do know it: love never dies.'

'Never. And if we truly live, our lives echo out to touch the whole world.' Henriette turned to her. 'You must continue to take the photographs, Viola. Think of all the people you could help.'

'Help?'

'Those whose faith has been tested by grief. As yours was. If you can give them material proof of life after death, what a comfort they will find it! It will make it easier for them to believe again.'

'But I ... I don't know how it's happened, the times I've done it. I haven't meant to photograph spirits. They've just been there. I've taken plenty of photographs without any spirits at all.'

'You have a gift. If the spirits are there, they will show themselves.'

'What if they don't, and these people are depending upon me?'

'I can help you, if you like. I have many years' experience in manifesting spirits. I believe that they will come for you alone, but it may give you more confidence to have me in the room.'

'My photographs have always been private things, for my own pleasure. I'm not certain I could put myself forward, show myself off. I'm not ...' *Like you*, she was about to say. Not a show-woman who allowed herself to be bound in front of an audience.

But then again, she had used to be that girl who climbed every tree.

'Sometimes,' said Henriette, 'we think our lives are going to go in one direction, and quite suddenly something happens, and we have to adjust and to change. There's been a change in both of our lives because of your photographs. Your father had a ministry, and this is yours. I can feel it inside my bones. Can't you?'

Henriette was taller than she, and stronger. Her eyes were a deeper blue than the sky and brighter than the ocean. A lock of her dark hair had come loose and it blew between them, touching Viola's face lightly; there were strands of silver in it that caught the light.

Perhaps I can do anything, Viola thought. *Perhaps I am not meant to have children. Perhaps Papa didn't appear in my photograph because the photographs themselves are a message that I am meant to do this instead.*

'Yes,' she said. 'I can feel it, too.'

Viola Worth

From Wikipedia, the free encyclopaedia

Viola Worth, née Goodwin, b 1837, was a British amateur photographer, widely credited with creating the world's first spirit photographs in Fortuneswell, Dorset in 1858.[1] Between the months of June and August 1858, at times working in collaboration with later-discredited spirit medium Henriette Blackthorne[2], Worth took a series of six photographs of living and dead subjects which included so-called spirit images of recognisable individuals who were deceased. Although contemporary accounts, including Worth herself [citation needed], suggest that Worth took the photographs for private consumption, the photographs quickly caught the attention of the Spiritualist community in England and thereafter in wider Europe and the United States, with some claiming that the photographs represented scientific proof of life beyond death, and others (notably Theodore Selby[3] of the English Society for Supernatural Research) alleging deliberate fraud.

[1] ^Smith, Nathaniel (2006). *Victorian Photographic Pioneers.* Oxford: Oxford University Press, p 92.

[2] ^Nwabara, Elisabeth (2012). *The Spirit Moves Me: Spiritualism and Feminist Spectacle.* University Park, PA: Pennsylvania State University Press, pp 114-156.

[3] ^Selby, Timothy (1975). *Theodore Selby, Seeker of Truth.* New York: Sell-Bee Press, pp 450-502.

Chapter Thirty-one

July, 1858
Weymouth

Jonah fumbled down the stairs of Mrs Blackthorne's house, jamming his hat back on his head. He emerged onto the wide, bustling Esplanade and blinked at the bright sunshine, rubbing his eyes free of the trace of tears. He hurried across the road, dodging carriages and holidaymakers, and stood leaning against the railings overlooking the beach.

Today he and the spirit – it wasn't Flora, and it wasn't quite Pavan either, but rather a strange, tantalising version of both at the same time – had stood together, side by side, and in the darkness the spirit was a glow of white and a gleam of eyes, as Pavan had been when they sat on the roof of the temple together and gazed at the stars. And Jonah had followed the impulse he had not quite understood on that night in Delhi, the night that preceded all that followed, and he took the spirit's hand in his. It was warm; far warmer than he would have expected of a ghost.

In that moment, he felt complete. Not without grief, but as if his grief had been transmuted into something else, something pure, stripped of all the many layers of betrayal. The touch of two hands in the darkness.

Jonah gripped the railing and closed his eyes. He ignored the shouts of children and the cockle-sellers, the scent of horses and seaweed. He willed himself back fourteen months in the past and halfway across the world, when the stars had looked exactly as they did here but had different names.

All stories are true, or none. I find more beauty if they are all true.

'Worth!' boomed a familiar voice. His stomach sank. Jonah swallowed, opened his eyes and slowly turned to Admiral Newham, who was making his way towards him like a ship in full sail.

'Good luck running into you here, I've been trying to get a word in with you. It seems like our womenfolk are tight as thieves, eh? That photograph Mrs Worth took of Louisa with little Augustus in her lap – I'm telling you, Louisa has not let it out of her sight. She has framed the prints and had them placed in every room. I have never seen her so happy, sir. Your wife is doing God's work.'

'Viola is happier, too,' he replied, giving into the inevitability of this conversation with Newham, and feeling the precious sensation of purity wisping away from him like fine mist.

'Good to keep women busy,' said Newham. 'They get into all sorts of trouble otherwise.'

If Viola was busy, there was certainly less pressure on him; she had company, work to do, and plenty of conversation. He felt less as if her entire happiness rested on his unworthy shoulders. But it was strange, at the very least, to have Mrs Blackthorne in their house so often. She never spoke a word of their clandestine meetings, and he'd grown less nervous about her keeping the secret; in fact she seemed an entirely different person with Viola than she did with him, and she treated him with a cheerful courtesy that showed that she was very skilled at social dissembling. He could only be grateful for it. In contrast, their dealings together in her shadowed room felt furtive, somehow tainted, something he would never have believed he would stoop to. No eye contact, coins left on a table ...

Black Maria, he thought, and shook his head.

'In any case, Worth, I wanted to talk to you about India. I lost friends in Delhi myself, you know. Altrincham, cousin of mine, killed at the Kashmir Gate. Probably by one of his own native men with a British gun.'

'I'm sorry to hear that.' Jonah stepped back, averting his face, drawing on his gloves. 'I regret that I have an appoint—'

'Bloody treacherous savages, what? Our own guns! You saw it first-hand, didn't you – the slaughter of all those innocents? Should have burned that city down, wiped it off the earth and started again, in my opinion.'

A long breath. And another. He had endured a dozen conversations like this, a hundred, in the hospital in Calcutta and on the steamer crossing the ocean, in polite sitting rooms and private members' clubs and church halls. He reached for well-worn phrases, bland in their calm reason.

'It's much more complex than in the newspapers. You have to take into account a people who have had their self-rule taken—'

'Women and children, man. What sort of monster does such things in a war?'

'We killed theirs!' Jonah burst out. 'We killed them all, afterwards. Women, children, old men, everyone. The British killed them all, and more. The Indians were fighting for independence, and we were fighting for money and for pride. If they're monsters, then we're worse.'

'Now you're sounding like "Clemency" Canning,' said Newham, comfortable in his beliefs and this conversation, like thousands of conversations like this, a million, in Jonah's hearing and out of it, conversations that only made Englishmen even more convinced they were eternally correct. Newham leaned on his stick, a man who would not be moved. 'No point in reconciliation, my good man. It's common sense. We have to draw a line in the sand. The British simply can't be bullied.'

Jonah passed a shaking hand over his mouth and said, 'Please excuse me, as I said, an engagement . . .' He looked desperately around him and with relief, spotted a familiar figure at the other end of the street, mounting into a carriage. 'Ah, there he is, Mr

Field. I'd better run to catch him. Good day, Admiral Newham.' He bowed to the other man and hurried down the pavement, holding on to his hat against the wind.

'Mr Field!' he called, and the naturalist paused at the door of the carriage and slowly descended. He left the door open, however, and as Jonah drew up he could see Mrs Field and at least five little Fields crowded inside together. 'Forgive me,' Jonah panted. 'I don't mean to interrupt your time with your family. It's been weeks since we've gone fossil-hunting together and I was wondering if—'

'Mr Worth. I regret to say that I cannot, with good conscience, continue to associate with you.'

'I – what?'

'I believed you were a man of good sense and science, but I learn that I was mistaken. I may possibly blame myself, as the cause of your introduction to the Newhams and their circle, but these photographs of so-called spirits are beyond the pale.'

'Are you – Mr Field, are you saying that my wife is a fraud?'

'It is pointless to argue with someone against their irrational beliefs, but when it comes to opening one's house to such people, to writing letters to the papers! My cousin is my family, but I can choose with whom I spend my leisure time. Good day, Mr Worth.' Mr Field bowed coldly and climbed into his carriage. He shut the door, knocked on the roof, and the coachman drove away, leaving Jonah staring after the carriage. In the back window, a child's tiny hand waved at him.

Chapter Thirty-two

July, 1858
Fortuneswell

'Mrs Worth! They're coming!'

Nan tumbled through the doorway, out of breath. Alice followed closely behind her in dismay. 'I'm sorry, madam, she came to the front door and she wouldn't go round to the back nor wait. Come here, you little hussy.' The maid reached for the girl's ear and Nan darted out of the way. She had a bright new ribbon in her bedraggled hair.

'Don't worry, Alice,' said Viola, rising to her feet and putting aside her book. 'What is it, Nan?'

'Mr Smy finally died.'

'Ah. I see.'

Alice wrinkled her nose. 'Madam, this one smells of fish. If you'd let me take her round to the back, I could—'

Nan scowled. 'I don't want no bath.'

'And do they want me, Nan? Did they send you?'

'I was outside when they hung the crêpe on the door and I ran straight here. I'm the fastest girl in Portland, and that's a fact. Beat some boys, too.'

Viola winced. 'Nan, I think it's best if we wait to see if they contact me again. I appreciate your enthusiasm, but not every recently bereaved person wants a photograph taken.'

'It's not recent, he's been hanging on for weeks, Cora says.' She dodged Alice again by ducking behind the sofa. 'I don't want no bath!'

The doorbell rang and Alice gave a huff of exasperation before going to answer it. Nan stuck out her tongue at the housemaid's back.

'Come out from behind the sofa,' Viola coaxed, anticipating Alice's reaction to the dirty handprints on the upholstery. 'Come and have a sugar lump.'

Nan instantly emerged and stood by the tea table. 'Do I use them?' she asked, pointing to the silver tongs in the sugar bowl.

'Yes, so your fingers don't touch the sugar.'

Squinting with concentration, Nan picked up a lump of sugar from the bowl and ate it straight off the end of the tongs. Her face melted into bliss and she reached for another.

'Where'd you get the ribbon, Nan? It's very pretty.'

'Bought it,' said Nan, which Viola took to mean she'd found it, as Nan used the stream of pennies that now came her way from Viola to feed and clothe her siblings.

Alice came back in, bearing a note on a silver tray, and exclaimed aloud at Nan. Viola shook her head at her and took the note.

'It's from Mrs Smy,' she said, reading it. 'Nan, I need you to carry a message to Stephen to take to Mrs Blackthorne, please.'

'Told you,' said Nan through a mouthful of sugar.

'After you've given the message, come back here – to the back entrance this time, please – and Mrs Diggory will give you some cake.'

'But—' protested Alice, before remembering her place.

'Cake and *no baths*,' said Nan.

'Baths are really quite pleasant, you know,' said Viola, going to her writing desk.

Nan stuffed two more lumps of sugar into her mouth.

'But,' Viola said, staring at the paper in dismay, 'I didn't intend any of this to be in the *Dorset Echo*. How did they find out?'

'Mrs Newham wrote to the Spiritualist Society and enclosed one of the photographs of her and Augustus,' said Henriette, adjusting the draperies on the studio screen. 'Mr Wattle of the Society then wrote to the *Echo*.'

'But – did you know she was going to do this?'

'I encouraged her. And Mr Wattle, to be truthful.'

'But we discussed this, and I said I didn't want anything in the papers.'

'A talent such as yours should be known by the world.'

'That's – I don't *want* to be known by the world, Henriette.'

'You may not be able to avoid it, Viola. There will be an article in *Spiritualist News*, as well.'

'Oh dear. I wish you hadn't.' Viola sat on the hard-backed chair that her photographic subjects used. 'What can we do?'

The door to the studio opened and Jonah stepped in, though seeing Henriette he stopped, seemingly in some confusion, his cheeks flushing. 'Ah, Viola, I – my apologies, I did not know you were not alone.'

'It's only Henriette,' said Viola, standing and holding out the newspaper. 'Though Mrs Smy is coming in a quarter of an hour. Jonah, look at this.'

He took it and glanced over the letter. 'Ah, yes, Field told me something of the sort yesterday. I hadn't had a chance to see it. Viola, did you say a *Mrs* Smy was coming?'

'Yes, to have her photograph taken. She lost her husband yesterday, poor woman.'

'Well, she's here. And so are all her friends and relations – including, if I'm not mistaken, Mr Smy himself.'

'*Mr* Smy?'

'I told Alice to show them all to the parlour. You'd better come down and see.'

The parlour was loud with conversation and full of people Viola had never seen before, at least twenty, every one of them in bright colours, hats with feathers, winking tiepins. Children, clutching currant buns, circulated around the adults' knees. Viola caught the distinct whiff of alcohol.

'Mrs Smy?' she said doubtfully, and a rounded grey-haired woman in a pink gown pushed through the others, her cheeks rosy with smiles. Although the others were strangers, Viola had seen her once or twice in church.

'Thank you so much for having us!' she said, taking Viola's hand. 'You must think we're a crowd, but Christopher's entire family came from Buckinghamshire, and then there are the rest. They are all so eager to see your work. You're welcome to come to our house afterwards, to join us for some cake and a glass of cider to celebrate his life.'

'Oh. That is very kind of you.'

'Christopher laid on the drink especially. He had all of this planned, you know. The wake, the funeral, all of the food. My Christopher always liked to take care of things.'

'I'm very sorry for your loss,' said Henriette, who had come up behind Viola.

'He was in a lot of pain,' said Mrs Smy in a matter-of-fact tone. 'He was ready to go. We had the best doctors, but they said there was nothing to be done, and Christopher always liked to have things settled. "Lalage my love," he said, "see if you can get my picture taken by that ghost woman." That's why I wrote to you.'

'I like to help people if I can,' said Viola. 'This is Mrs Blackthorne, the spirit medium.'

'Of course I've heard of you,' said Mrs Smy, shaking her hand. 'Thank you for coming. Mrs Worth, you remember my husband, don't you? Owned three quarries up this way, two more on the mainland. John, move out of the way so that Mrs Worth can see your grandfather.'

A young man in a bright red waistcoat obligingly shuffled out of the way to reveal a bald gentleman sitting quietly in a wooden chair, hands folded in his lap. He appeared to be asleep.

'That's Christopher,' said Mrs Smy.

He was in an impeccable suit, with a candy-striped waistcoat and a flowing tie in electric blue. A diamond tiepin winked at his neck. A certain pallor to his skin, his closed eyes, and his immobility were the only indications that Mr Smy was no longer living.

Viola had to resist an impulse to greet him. 'He looks very… peaceful.'

'Oh, he is. We decided to use a chair to take him here, thought that would be easiest in the cart. We could just pop him in, carry him in, pop him back home afterwards.'

Viola exchanged glances with Henriette.

'He looks wonderful,' said Henriette. 'Almost still alive.'

'Thank you. I dressed him and combed his hair, and Bernard, that's my son, arranged him in the chair. He's not stiff yet so we had to use half a broom handle. The Smys have always been ingenious and Bernard gets it from his father. Christopher owned his first quarry before he was twenty-five.'

'Very admirable,' said Henriette.

Now that she was closer, Viola could see the thin silk cords that crisscrossed over Mr Smy's chest, holding him upright in the chair. She wondered how the enterprising family had contrived to ensure that the man's mouth and eyes stayed shut, and suppressed a shudder.

'Bernard was wondering about painting circles on his eyelids,' Mrs Smy continued, 'so it would look as if he were awake. What do you think, Mrs Worth? Would that show up in the photograph? Or is it better if he looks as if he's sleeping, so when the spirit comes, it's easy to see who it is?'

'I think… he looks so peaceful now.'

'It's very lovely as it is,' added Henriette. 'The photograph will be a wonderful memory of the husband and father you all loved.'

'And grandfather,' added Mrs Smy. 'Twelve grandchildren, and two great-grandchildren. They're here, most of them. My Enid came all the way from Doncaster. Mrs Blackthorne, do you go into a trance?'

'It isn't necessary. My presence is merely to facilitate the appearance of spirits, if they need me.'

'Oh, that's too bad. I've never seen anyone in a trance before.'

'Perhaps ... perhaps we should take the photograph here rather than carrying Mr Smy all the way up the stairs to the studio,' said Viola.

'Your studio is upstairs? Bernard and his son Miles can carry Christopher, it's no problem. Strapping lads, both of them.'

'No no no, I'll prepare the plate and we can bring the equipment down here. You do understand that we can't guarantee that a spirit will be captured on the plate?'

'Oh, it will happen,' said Mrs Smy comfortably. 'Christopher said to me, "Lalage my love," he said, "I'm looking forward to Heaven, but I'll linger behind to see you again." And he's hardly cold yet, are you, dear?' She leaned over and pressed a quick kiss to the dead man's cheek. 'Hardly cold at all. Well, I'll round them all up for you.'

'You all want to be in the photograph?'

'Of course!'

'We'll need some more chairs,' said Viola, turning to Jonah. But Jonah wasn't there.

'I'll get the strapping lads to find the chairs,' said Henriette. 'And one to help you carry your camera and tripod.'

By the time Viola returned with her equipment, the conversation in the room had grown, if anything, louder. Several young men and brightly dressed young ladies arranged themselves around the wooden chair. Sofas had been pulled up to accommodate the older ladies and gentlemen. A bevy of children settled at the corpse's feet and one of the young ladies draped herself over the back of the chair as if she were about to kiss the gentleman on his shiny head.

Someone plopped a fat baby onto the dead man's lap. The baby stuck its thumb into its mouth.

'Are you ready, Mrs Worth?' called Mrs Smy, from her seat next to her husband. She also held an infant in her lap.

Viola adjusted the focus of the camera. 'I think the ropes may be visible,' she murmured to Henriette, who was standing beside her. 'Do you suppose they'll mind?'

'If I may…?' said Henriette, and approached the gentleman in the armchair. With light touches, she made adjustments to his clothing and the angle of the armchair, and the costume of the baby on the corpse's lap. She pinched its fat cheek and it gurgled at her.

'Please try to stay still,' Viola said, aware of the terrible irony in saying this in the direction of Mr Smy. From experience, she knew it was nearly impossible to get a photograph of a party this large, especially with children, without someone's face or hand moving. 'Silence, please. Watch my hand.'

She raised her hand and silence fell, aside from the gurgling of the babies. With so many people and the light only from the parlour windows she had to guess at the exposure time.

'All finished,' she said, lowering her hand, and there was a cheer before the conversation swelled again. There was the pop of a bottle opening and the children erupted into some sort of noisy game of tag. One of them knocked against Mr Smy's chair and the body listed to one side.

Mrs Smy jumped up, more flushed than before. 'Thank you so much,' she said, over and over again. 'This is for you.' She pressed something into Viola's hand.

Viola shook her head. 'No. I don't accept payment for this.'

'But the plates, and the prints, it must cost money. You shouldn't be out of pocket. Don't worry, my husband has left me plenty.'

'I couldn't possibly.' She tried to give the folded notes back to Mrs Smy, but the other woman backed away with a grin, holding up her hands out of Viola's reach. 'Mrs Smy, I…'

Henriette touched Mrs Smy's arm. 'Do you know, your

husband's spirit is very close. He says he has a message for Lalage in private.'

Her face lit up even more. 'Is that so? That's just like him, you know, to have something to tell me. Forty-six years we were married, and we always had something to talk about with each other. What does he have to say, then?'

Henriette took the money discreetly from Viola's hand. Winking at Viola, she drew Mrs Smy aside.

Viola, flustered, removed the plate from the camera and turned to go upstairs to develop the image. Behind her, she heard a childlike squeal. Someone cried, 'Hortense! Don't untie your grandfather, the party isn't over!'

Mr Smy stood in the back of the photograph, faint but clear between a young relative in white lace and a middle-aged one wearing a peacock feathered hat. Bernard Smy promised to call to collect prints in two days' time before he and his son hoisted his father, chair and all, out of the parlour and into the waiting cart, followed by a stream of chattering Smys. Mrs Smy pressed Viola and Henriette to join them for the party, but Viola gave the excuse of needing to tend to the drying plate. When they were gone, she rang for Alice and sank onto the sofa that had so recently been occupied by Smys.

'Tea?' she said to Henriette, who shook her head and said, 'Something stronger, I think.'

'Wine, please,' Viola told Alice when she arrived. 'Is Mr Worth in?'

'No, ma'am,' said Alice, gazing with dismay at the rearranged furniture. 'He said not to hold dinner for him.' Alice left, and Viola closed her eyes, leaning her head on the back of the sofa, feeling again the stab of disappointment.

Mrs Smy's husband is dead, she thought, *and she's still more happily married than I am.*

She felt Henriette sit on the sofa beside her, and she opened her eyes. 'Thank you for your help,' she said. 'I found that all a little bit overwhelming.'

'I have to admit it was the first time I've ever been in a room with a corpse tied to a chair.'

'What was the message you told Mrs Smy? Or was it private?'

'It was private,' said Henriette, 'and also quite crude. But Mrs Smy seemed to know just what her husband meant. I think they had a very healthy enjoyment of each other.'

'Oh.' Viola bit her lip. 'Are you – I mean were you – did your husband ever send you any messages? After he died?'

'Only one,' said Henriette. 'It was unexpected. And nothing like Mr Smy's.'

'Did he believe in spirits?'

'Oh, yes. He was an ardent believer. He knew Flora in life, you see.'

'Is that what brought you together? Flora?'

'Partly. She was his first love, when he was a young man. We met at a séance, and he recognised her. At first, he only wanted to speak with her. Eventually he noticed me.' Henriette laughed, her light musical laugh.

'He … loved you, and your spirit guide? Both of you?'

'He knew her before he knew me. And love isn't depleted by being given to more than one person in a lifetime. He learned to love from loving Flora so long ago, and I reaped the benefits in the tenderness of his heart.'

Alice came back with wine and glasses and Viola poured a glass for each of them. The first sip warmed her throat and made her lips tingle.

'Jonah and I were childhood sweethearts,' she said.

'Then you have the first flush of each other's love.'

'Was your husband your first love?' Viola asked.

'No,' said Henriette. 'I loved someone else, first. But they never knew how I felt. At least, not until it was too late.'

'It's not too late now. You're a widow. If this person isn't married, then…'

'Perhaps. You're a romantic.'

'You should find him,' Viola said. She was surprised to hear that her voice was both strong and urgent. 'Life is short, and maybe he's lonely too. No one should ever be lonely.'

'I've never said that I was lonely.'

'But you are, aren't you? That's why you and I like each other.'

Henriette didn't say anything for a moment. Then she turned her eyes on Viola.

'Are you lonely, Viola?' she said at last.

'Every day. I mean – perhaps less, now. Yes. Less, now that…' *Now that you are my friend.* She hurried over that. 'I never had a mother, and my father is dead, and I've left everyone I know behind. And people are so kind here, but I didn't grow up here and I'm not part of their lives, not the way I was up in Kimmerton.'

'You have Jonah.'

'But Jonah is…'

Henriette didn't say anything, didn't press her. She merely waited quietly for Viola to finish her sentence. And Viola didn't know why she wanted to tell her – maybe it was how quiet the room seemed, or the fact that she finally at last had a friend. Maybe it was just because speaking the words out loud would be such a relief.

'He loves me,' said Viola. 'We've known each other all our lives, and he's careful of me. He cares what happens to me. But since we've been married, we've grown apart. It's as if there's an invisible wall between us. Jonah's a good man, I would trust him with my life, but somehow he doesn't seem to trust himself. He's often far away, and yet he won't tell me what he's thinking. And he hasn't…' She took a deep breath. 'He hasn't touched me. Hardly at all, since we've been married.'

'I thought you wanted children.' Henriette's voice was gentle.

'We do. Or I do, and he says he does, but we sleep apart. We have separate rooms. And he's only come to my room once, and when he did it was ...' She put her glass down. 'I'm afraid that I'll never have children, and Jonah and I will grow further and further apart. I'm afraid I'll be lonely for the rest of my life.'

'Oh, my sweet girl,' sighed Henriette, in compassion. She gently stroked Viola's hair back from her face. 'I understand what it's like to have to be strong and to have no one to rely on. Always walking a tightrope between who you seem to be and who you are. It's exhausting to keep your feelings to yourself, all the time. It's lonely, even in a room full of people.'

Her friend's warm hand was so kind ... Viola felt tears coming into her eyes and shook her head violently to clear them.

'I'm sure it will be fine,' she said hurriedly. 'It can take some time for a husband and wife to know each other. Can't it? Did you and your husband – you said he loved someone else before. Did he ever hesitate?'

'Never,' said Henriette. 'Ethelred had a healthy appetite. And Flora had passed over so many years before.'

'Did ... you like it?'

'Oh, Viola. When you love someone, their love is the most wonderful feeling in the world.'

Viola nodded. She didn't trust herself to say any more. She feared she'd start crying again, and demand more of Henriette's comfort, and embarrass herself with her own neediness. She simply wanted to be touched, so badly.

After a moment, Henriette asked a question about printing the photograph, and they spoke of that instead, but the question still hung on Viola's tongue, in her mind, though she knew she would never ask it. She suspected even if she did ask it, it could never be answered adequately enough for her to understand.

How does it feel?

Chapter Thirty-three

July, 1858
Upcross Hall, near Wareham, Dorset

Henriette's first impression was that the house was smaller than she remembered. In her head, it covered acres and acres; the narrow passages of her memory stretched on for miles.

But she had seen many houses since she had been a young housemaid fresh from the scullery of the Red Lion.

The carriage stopped, and she adjusted her hat and veil and pinched colour into her cheeks. She doubted that anyone would recognise her; it had been too long and she had changed too much. Not that the Upcross family would recognise her anyway – people never looked at servants, not properly. But that didn't stop her from being nervous in a way she hadn't felt for a very long time. Not the same nerves as before a séance, where she knew she could rely on her wits, or the nerves she felt when she looked at the bundle of bills she owed and compared them with the money in her purse. She was used to both of those.

No; this was the fluttering stomach and sickness of simultaneous hope and despair.

Despite the evidence of Viola's photograph, she kept thinking that there was a chance that Madame might be alive. Perhaps the plates, in Viola's hands, captured yearning rather than grief.

And she did yearn. She was lonely; after all this time she craved someone who understood her, with whom she wouldn't have to hide and to lie. Viola's sad admission of her own loneliness had made the feeling in Henriette's chest keener.

The driver she had hired with Mrs Smy's money helped her out of the carriage and Henriette walked to the front door, head high, back straight, in the posture she had learned all those years ago. Her heart pounded but her hands were steady.

Mr Moore, the butler, answered the door. His hair was greyer than the last time she had seen him. 'I'm not expected,' she said, and gave him her card. 'I've come to call on Madame.'

She wore her veil, and she detected no recognition in his face. 'I will see if she is at home,' said Mr Moore.

He led her to a saloon to wait while he took the card up. She didn't sit in one of the uncomfortable chairs, but instead stood in front of the marble fireplace, remembering without touching it how it had used to feel: cool and eternal. As a housemaid here she'd used to wonder why people would decorate their rooms with the same materials that were used on graves. The vase on the mantelpiece was new and ugly; there were two porcelain figurines of dogs which had no purpose other than to collect dust.

She rehearsed once again what she would say. Her letter had gone unanswered, but letters were easy to misplace or ignore. Her circumstances had changed since she had written, in any case. She had no real proposal to make; she wanted merely to talk to Madame. To honestly tell her all that had happened since they had last met; how Madame's words had led her to places that she could never have imagined.

Perhaps to say, as Viola had said to her: *Life is short. No one should ever be lonely.*

'You may come up,' said Mr Moore, reappearing, and she followed him. They went up not the dim back stairs but the grand front stairs. She paused momentarily on the step where she had first spoken to Madame. Then he showed her to the morning room on the first floor, in the east of the house where it caught the most sunshine. It was the place where Mrs Upcross received visitors; perhaps she was allowing Madame to use it? Perhaps

Mrs Upcross thought it was etiquette to see all visitors to the household first?

'This is Mrs Blackthorne, madam,' the butler announced to the occupant of the room. Or did he say 'Madame'? He stood aside to allow Henriette in. She took a deep breath and stepped into the light and airy room.

The lady who sat in the window, embroidery in hand, was not Madame. It was not Mrs Upcross either, not the old one or the young one. It was a stranger.

'Mrs Blackthorne?' The lady rose. 'I'm very sorry; have we met?'

'N-no,' said Henriette, recalling herself and crossing the room to her hostess. 'I am very sorry, I must apologise. I expected someone else.'

This woman was heavily pregnant. She bore no resemblance at all to the people whom Henriette had known before.

'Whom were you expecting?' the woman asked.

'When I was last at this house I knew the Upcross family.'

'Ah. That was some time ago. I am Mrs Phillips. We bought this house four years ago.'

'I am so very sorry. I . . . all the furniture is the same, and with Mr – with Moore answering the door, I assumed—'

'We bought the furniture at the same time, and many of the servants stayed on. We were relocating from Ceylon, you see, and it made everything much easier.'

'Oh. I understand. Are you related to the Upcross family?'

'Not at all.'

'You must understand my surprise. I was under the impression that this house had been in the Upcross family for many generations.'

'Did you know them well?' Mrs Phillips asked, settling back in her chair with a sigh of relief and motioning for Henriette to do the same. 'The Upcrosses?'

'Not particularly well, no,' she said, perching on the edge of a chair. She had never sat down in this room before. 'We were acquaintances.'

Mrs Phillips leaned forward and lowered her voice, though there was no one else in the room to hear them, except perhaps her unborn baby. 'Mr Upcross lost everything. Bad investments. Mrs Upcross died soon after, I heard. I never met either of them. He had to sell the house. It was quite the scandal, apparently. And then his younger son died in a riding accident. Mr Upcross was a broken man. He went somewhere up north, and died of influenza. There's a married son in London, I heard, but I never met him either. Our agent met with him to arrange the purchase. His wife had money, apparently, so they escaped the family ruin.'

'Oh. That … that is very sad news.' She thought about Eloise Upcross and her casual kindness, her self-conscious timidity. She was like a child. In London Eloise had taken lesson after lesson in elocution and etiquette, to try to leave behind all the traces of her life as the daughter of a mill owner, but even after years, she never lost her curt, northern vowels.

Henriette would never dare to visit Eloise, of course – she was the only member of the family who would recognise her instantly, despite all the changes that time and effort had wrought.

Mrs Phillips picked up her embroidery again. 'When I saw on your card that you were a spirit medium, I thought perhaps you'd come offering to get in touch with their ghosts! Do you think this place is haunted? That would be fun. Just like in a novel.'

Henriette wondered what kind of a person could buy up a whole house because of someone's misfortune, and live quite contentedly among their furniture, without changing a single thing, and then be delighted with the prospect of the place being haunted.

'I do feel a certain presence in particular,' said Henriette. 'I've felt her quite strongly since stepping into the house.'

Mrs Phillips perked up. 'Who is it? Is it the tragic mistress? They think perhaps she killed herself, you know.'

'No, it's someone else, who speaks in French. She wears black. She tells me she knew the children, but she didn't belong to the family. A governess, perhaps?'

'Our governess is from Surrey. Did the Upcrosses have a governess? I'll ask Moore.' She rang the bell pull next to her chair, and Moore appeared almost immediately. 'Did the Upcrosses have a French governess, Moore?'

'They did for a time, madam.'

'What happened to her? Is she dead?'

'I couldn't say, madam. She left before their misfortunes, when the children were grown.'

'Do you remember her name?'

'No, madam. It was some time ago.'

Mrs Phillips turned to Henriette. 'Too bad. If we knew her name, we could track her down and if she were alive, we'd know she wasn't a ghost.'

'Places – and people – can be haunted by the memories of people both alive and dead,' said Henriette. She stood and inclined her head politely to Mrs Phillips. 'Thank you for your time. I won't bother you again.'

On her way back down, she brushed her fingers against the spot on the banister that Madame had touched. She wondered if Madame had ever read her letters, or if she had left long before they ever arrived. She wondered if she were in Provence, or dead under the ground. She wondered if she knew how important she had been to Henriette.

Moore held the door open for her. 'You've changed a bit,' he said in a low tone.

She held her chin up. 'These days, I look to the future. Thank you, Moore.'

She dropped one of Mrs Smy's coins into the butler's hand and swept to her hired carriage with the bearing of a queen.

Chapter Thirty-four

July, 1858
Weymouth

Henriette took charge of everything: the day, the hour, everything. She strode across the sandy beach as if the seaside belonged to her personally; led Viola to a wooden hut, and said to the woman sitting inside on a wooden chair, 'My friend and I would like to bathe, please, Mrs Bissle.'

'One or two?' said the woman, who wore scarves around her neck and a hat pulled down over her eyes, despite the heat.

'One,' said Henriette. 'And we don't need a dipper.'

The woman grunted in disapproval. 'Any valuables?'

Viola had left her locket with curls of her father's hair at home, terrified of losing it to the sea, but she still wore her wedding ring. She had not thought to remove it until now. It had not been off her hand since she was married. But it was loose on her finger.

'Perhaps, to be safe, I should take this off,' Viola said. She slipped the ring off her finger and gave it to Henriette, who gave it to the attendant.

'Thank you, Mrs Bissle,' said Henriette with special emphasis on the name. The woman put the ring into a small box and then onto a shelf.

'Number four,' said the woman, and Henriette passed her some money and then she was leading Viola off again, through the people scattered on the beach, the children playing ball on the sand.

'She won't take my ring, will she?' Viola said, struck by guilt both about having taken it off and for not having left it at home, safely, with her locket.

'She knows that I know who she is,' said Henriette.

Number four was a white-painted bathing machine on high, wide wheels. Henriette went up the steps and opened the door, and Viola followed her in. Inside there was nothing more than a wooden bench on either side, a shelf high up on one wall, and a single salt-crusted window on the opposite wall, also set high up. Two folded white towels sat on the benches. Henriette put her bag on one bench and closed the door behind them, and it was instantly murky dark inside. The shouts of playing children and the rumble of the surf sounded very far away.

'Much easier with two of us,' said Henriette, taking off her hat and placing it on the high shelf. She took out two flannel swim dresses from the bag and shook them out, draping them on the bench. 'We can help each other, and have more time for bathing. You first. Here, turn around; I'll do your buttons and you can do mine.'

Viola took off her bonnet, turned her back to Henriette, and tilted her head forward so that Henriette could unfasten the buttons on the back of her dress. It was a simple day dress without a crinoline, that she'd chosen for ease of putting on and taking off, and Viola was perfectly capable of taking it off herself, but in this strange situation she was inclined to follow Henriette's suggestion.

'You always know what to do,' Viola said as she felt her friend deftly unfastening the jet buttons on the back of her frock.

'Oh dear. I hope this isn't your way of saying that I'm overbearing.'

Viola laughed. 'No. You're not overbearing. Mrs Newham is. She always makes me feel like an errant, foolish child.'

'Doesn't she? She's a kind woman, but she rather likes to be the loudest in the room.' Henriette finished unbuttoning the dress and helped Viola pull it over her head. She carefully folded it and placed it on the high shelf. 'Of course we can forgive her that, for her generosity.'

'Of course. But when I'm with her I feel bullied and prodded. When I'm with you, I feel as if I'm on an adventure.'

Viola had her back turned to Henriette still, but she could almost hear her smiling. 'It *is* an adventure,' said Henriette. 'Life is an adventure, and so is death.'

Viola felt a small tug as Henriette untied her corset laces. She was close enough behind Viola in this small enclosed space that Viola could feel her soft breath on the back of her neck.

Cool fingers, loosening what held her in tight. She could feel them through the thin fabric of her chemise. The corset fell away and Viola took a deep breath full of sea air and Henriette's perfume. She expanded: lungs and ribs and breasts and air.

'You've such a slender waist, Viola.' Her hand rested briefly on Viola's waist and Viola had an almost irresistible impulse to lean back into the touch. Then it was gone, and Viola thought about how Henriette was the only person who had touched Viola freely, affectionately, since Viola's father had died. She touched Viola all the time. She took Viola's hands, touched her shoulders, tucked her arm under hers as they walked. And now these small touches, the unlacing of a corset, a hand on a waist.

This was what female friends did, she knew. But she had never had a female friend, and the simple sensation of a gentle hand on her body was enough to make her burn for more. Her cheeks flamed; it was embarrassing to be so naïve. To make something so universal into a craving for just one person.

Not wanting to turn around and show herself to the other woman, she pulled her chemise over her head and groped blindly for the flannel swim dress that Henriette had lent to her. It was loose on her shoulders and waist, and too long. She rolled up the sleeves and did up the simple hook-and-eye fastening herself. By the time she'd sat on the bench and removed her shoes and stockings, she felt a little less flustered, especially when she glanced up at Henriette and saw that the other woman wasn't watching her but was instead taking the pins from her hair so that it fell in dark curls down her back.

'Do you need me to help you?' Viola asked.

'Please,' said Henriette, and turned her own back, catching her hair up in one hand to hold it away from her neck.

Henriette's buttons were mother-of-pearl, and each of them gleamed like little moons in the shadows. Viola had never before unbuttoned another woman's dress, and this everyday act felt strange. Henriette's perfume was stronger as her dress shifted and fell from her shoulders, along with a slight scent of sweat. She wore a corset with no chemise underneath, fastened with hooks and eyes and she must have her maid fasten it for her each day, unlike Viola's with the long laces she could tighten and tie herself. The material was stiff; even in the semi-darkness Viola could see the pink marks it made against the pale skin of Henriette's back.

'Ah! It always feels so wonderful to shake this off,' Henriette said, raising her arms and twisting her body so that the corset flopped down over her skirt and she was bare to the waist. She reached back, unfastening her skirt herself and stepping out of her clothes, leaving them as a pool on the floor, unselfconsciously reaching for her own flannel swimming dress. Viola saw the curve of a naked hip and full breast, a shadow of hair between her friend's legs, and she turned to busy herself folding up her clothes and placing them on the high shelf.

What must it be like to inhabit your body so fully? To not be ashamed of someone else seeing it, to feel wonderful to take your clothes off and be naked? Perhaps because Henriette had been happily married, she could see her body as something to enjoy. Was this what love could do, this transformation into someone adventurous and unashamed and whole?

'Henriette,' Viola began, not sure how she could ask this question but needing more than anything to know, when at that very moment the world shook around them. The floor juddered, the walls tilted, and Viola stumbled and fell into Henriette, who caught her and laughed.

'They're pulling the machine into the sea,' Henriette told her, and together they sat on the bench. Viola held tight to the wooden seat as the machine tipped and slid in the sand. Then she heard water sloshing around the wheels and directly below them and she jumped up to stand on the bench and peer out the window. 'Oh! We're in the water.'

'The first time I bathed in the sea,' Henriette said, 'it was an isolated cove, and there were no bathing machines, no swimming costumes. It was myself, alone. I took off my dress and I left it on the rocks and I walked out into the sea, step by step, until my feet could no longer touch the sand, and then I swam. I had no concept I could do it before.'

'Weren't you afraid?'

'I think that might have been the first time in my life that I wasn't afraid at all.'

The machine stopped. The only sound was the water sloshing below them. Henriette got up and opened the door in the front of the machine, allowing sunshine to flood into the interior. Viola joined Henriette in the doorway and after her eyes had become used to the dazzling light on water and in sky, she saw the silhouette of a man, fully dressed and in water up to his waist. As they watched, he unharnessed a horse from the machine and led it away through the surf, without so much as glancing in their direction.

'Now,' said Henriette, a broad smile on her face. She stepped out of the machine and instead of climbing down the stairs into the water, she launched herself into the air. Dress flying, hair loose and blowing around her head, for a moment Viola expected her to fly. Then she landed in the sea with a splash and a scream of laughter. Her head disappeared for a moment beneath the waves and then resurfaced, her hair now sleek.

'It's freezing!' she called to Viola. 'You must come in immediately!'

'Those two statements don't seem to go together,' said Viola, clinging to the doorpost. From this perspective, she couldn't see the shore, just the sea, spread out in front of them in all directions, vast and endless. It was like when they'd stood on that rock together and Viola had decided to take more photographs. How much had changed since that day… and how much hadn't changed at all.

'Now, Viola! Hurry! I'll catch you.'

Henriette stood and held out her arms and Viola didn't allow herself to think. She closed her eyes against the dazzle and she jumped.

Viola exploded into the water, or the water exploded into her. A blast of cold, a sudden cessation of noise that was a noise itself, a low boom, an immersion unlike anything she'd had in bath or stream. For a second she was free and floating, airless and weightless, and then she felt arms around her pulling her to the surface and she emerged, laughing up into Henriette's face.

'Isn't it wonderful?' Henriette said, and Viola gasped 'Yes,' clinging to Henriette's shoulders. Her feet didn't quite touch the bottom but Henriette anchored her in place against the waves that pushed against them both.

'Lie back,' said Henriette. 'Don't worry, I'll hold you.'

This time she didn't hesitate. She lay back in the water as if it were a bed, spreading her arms wide, letting her legs stop seeking the ground and float to the surface. Henriette held her by the waist with one arm and with the other she reached up and tugged at Viola's hair. 'No pins,' she told Viola. 'Let it float free.'

She felt the plaits and twists undoing; felt her hair fan out in the water around her like seaweed; gazed upwards at the blue sky. The water touched all of her: back, breasts, belly. It lapped under her skirt and between her toes, warmed the small space between Henriette's arm and her waist. It no longer felt cold. It felt like a part of herself.

'See?' said Henriette, smiling down at her.

'Yes,' said Viola. She closed her eyes and let herself be unafraid.

*

Back in the bathing machine, waiting for the bather to harness the horse and drag them back to the shore, they shivered and stripped off wet clothing and rubbed themselves with the towels until their skin was pink and tingling. Viola, hair dripping and turned mahogany with water, forgot about modesty in her rush to get dry and warm. She pulled her chemise over her head and reached for her corset, glancing at her friend.

Henriette was naked save the towel around her, hair shielding her breasts. She was built on a bigger scale than Viola, but perfect, like a statue of a Greek goddess in a book. Viola put on her dress and watched out of the corner of her eye as Henriette pulled on her dress with nothing underneath at all. Without being asked she stepped behind Henriette to do up the row of mother-of-pearl buttons. Henriette's skin was still damp and the material clung to her.

'I spent the first part of my life doing as other people told me,' Henriette said, facing away from Viola, speaking to the closed door between them and the sea. 'I followed orders and I was only free in my mind. When I floated in the ocean I told myself: never again.'

The bathing machine suddenly jerked and started moving, sending them laughing into each other. They helped each other onto the bench and then sat there as the machine was towed back to shore, pinning up each other's wet hair, straightening each other's clothes. Viola was warm, her skin tingling and alive, and when the machine stopped she wanted to open the door and tell the man with the horse to pull them out into the water again, so they could bathe some more.

They put on their shoes, collected their wet clothes and the wet towels, and walked together back across the beach to the hut. Viola, free, took Henriette's hand as they walked.

'It's a rebirth,' said Henriette. 'The ocean washes us of our past, and we can start afresh.'

'I feel wonderful,' said Viola. 'I see why people bathe for their health.'

'We shall do it again. Every fine day, if you like. We can't be taking photographs and seeking spirits all the time. Sometimes our eyes need to fix on life, not death. I wish we could do away with the dreaded machine and have a cove all to ourselves.'

'I rather like the machine,' Viola said, though she didn't mean that she liked the machine. She liked the intimacy, the laughter, the small space between sea and land where she was not quite herself. 'I wish I could—'

They'd reached the hut. Mrs Bissel, grunting, took the wet towels and gave them the small box with Viola's ring.

Viola had almost forgotten about it. She took it from the box, cool metal, and slipped it back on her finger. It was a slender ring, not heavy... but she felt weighted down, suddenly, in a way she had not for the past hour.

'What do you wish?' Henriette asked her, as they walked towards the Esplanade.

She'd been about to say *I wish I could float there forever with you*. But her ring reminded her.

'I wish I could bathe like that with Jonah,' she said instead.

'You could. There's no impropriety in a husband and wife bathing together.'

'But we don't – we haven't – our marriage isn't like that.' Not loose, and free, and intimate, and unafraid.

Henriette frowned. Small tendrils of her hair had come loose, or not been tucked away properly in the first place, and they danced around her head in the sea breeze. 'Doesn't he touch you at all, Viola?'

'Not unless necessary. No. He doesn't even seem to like speaking to me very much. You saw what happened the other day, when the Smys were there – he disappeared.'

'Was he always like that? You said you were sweethearts, once.'

'I think... perhaps it's me. I've changed since my father died.'

'Or perhaps it's he who has changed?'

'I don't know. It's – he does seem different to me. But perhaps that's because I'm different.'

'What happened to him in India could change any man. All that death and violence – and saving the life of a young girl.'

'Yes, Emilia. Poor girl.'

'And you have never met her?'

'No. He doesn't speak of India, ever.'

Henriette tapped her chin with her finger thoughtfully as they walked. 'Sometimes fear and horror can be trapped within us. If we never speak of them, or share them with another human being, they fester and turn everything to rot. He should enjoy being a hero. He should enjoy his new life. But he can't, as long as all of that is poisoning him.'

'But he won't speak of it. I have tried.'

'Perhaps … No.'

'What, Henriette?'

Henriette glanced over at her, almost sly. 'I was going to suggest that perhaps seeing Emilia again could work as an inducement for him to talk about what happened. Very often when my clients see their loved ones who have passed, it allows them to talk about their cares and their grief in a way they could not before. How much better could it be, for your husband to see the young girl he saved, alive and well, a reminder of the good he has done?'

'I could invite her to visit. But what if he would rather not be reminded? He doesn't write to her, or mention her at all. If I invited her, it might make him angry.'

'The family who have adopted her are friends of the Newhams. If they gave the invitation … ?'

'I don't know,' said Viola. The freedom of just half an hour before had dissipated, leaving fear to gnaw her once again. 'Maybe it's a bad idea.'

'I'll arrange everything. Don't worry. We all need a fresh start, Viola.'

Viola nodded miserably as they climbed the steps to the Esplanade. But Henriette was right: seeing the child, Emilia, could be the thing that explained Jonah's behaviour to her. Perhaps greater understanding was the key to their marriage. She didn't know what else to try.

'If tomorrow is fair, shall we walk or bathe?'

'Either,' she said, though she corrected herself immediately. 'No, bathe, if it isn't too cold. Henriette?'

'Yes?'

'You said that for the first half of your life you followed orders, and in the second you've been free. What did you mean by that?'

Henriette smiled. Her hair, caught by the sun, made a halo around her head.

'Oh, that's a story for another time,' she said.

Flying had been a party trick that she learned from a drunken magician, backstage during the days of Ferguson the mesmerist. He'd taught her how to escape ropes, too – but flying was more impressive. Appearing to be weightless was an enormous effort; after two carefully managed and even more carefully publicised attempts, Henriette retired it from her repertoire and enjoyed the reputation she'd earned.

Today, in the ocean with Viola, she'd been on the other side of that illusion. As she helped Viola float, she watched her face. Though Viola's eyes were closed, Henriette saw the exact moment when the young woman let go of her cares and let herself go weightless.

Viola's camera truly saw ghosts, and Viola herself, free of unhappiness and loneliness, flew more truly than Henriette had ever done. What made her able to do it? A purity of soul?

Back in her rented rooms, Henriette didn't undress or wash the salt from her face and hair. She went straight to her desk and took out a sheet of writing paper, pen and ink.

She had already started this note, requesting that Mrs Newham invite her young friend Emilia Hamilton. Last time Jonah Worth had visited her rooms, he had taken hold of Flora's hand. She didn't usually allow this: it was better for Flora to remain as incorporeal as possible. But, as suspected, he gave Henriette twice as much money afterwards. Soon, she was going to run out of generalisations about exotic India and universal truths about forgiveness and departed love. If she wanted to keep this particular source of income, she needed to learn more about what had happened to the Hero of Delhi. Viola didn't know the true story and Jonah wouldn't tell her. Emilia Hamilton was the next logical step. And now Viola had given her permission to send for the girl.

Learning more about her husband would help Viola. It was the same reason why Henriette had written to as many newspapers as she could about Viola's photographs, even though Viola had asked her not to. Viola needed to have more confidence in her talents. The net benefit to her friend outweighed any personal scruples.

The fact that Henriette was able to exploit both of these situations for her own financial gain, was a fortunate side effect.

What do you think of a surprise party, perhaps, to honour the Hero of Delhi? she wrote. *I will leave the particulars up to your superior organisation. Shall we discuss it, the next time you visit to speak with Augustus, Constance and Priss?*

She sealed the letter, thinking again of Viola Worth. Poor Viola, whose husband did not touch or trust her, who confided in Henriette out of friendship and not any hope of gain, who took such delight in the sea and her own, naïve body. In the wide view of Viola's eyes, souls existed and Henriette Blackthorne was a good woman.

Until she had met Viola, Henriette did not much care whether souls even existed. Now, she wondered … if she, Henriette, could see her own soul, what would its texture be?

Chapter Thirty-five

You should tell your wife, the spirit had said. *Allow her to comfort you.*

Jonah accepted another cup of tea. If he was drinking tea, at least he didn't have to speak.

The parlour was crammed to the gills with Spiritualists. They all looked eminently respectable, though some had possibly seen better days. There was a man in a rusty suit with rusty whiskers to match, a woman in a frayed bonnet, a man with a jacquard waistcoat and gleaming gold watch chain; a grey-haired woman whose jet buttons winked, and her daughter in identical jet; a man who held a Pekingese dog on his lap and fed it bits of cake as he spoke; a young man, as young as Jonah, with the earnest ink-spotted hands of a clerk. They all, perhaps unsurprisingly, wore mourning.

They passed Viola's photographs from hand to hand, marvelling. The rusty man occasionally read phrases from the latest *Spiritualist Telegraph*, which he held in one rusty-haired hand.

'"Spiritualism will rally all those who dare to think for themselves on all points of Theology – for in it, philosophical test and research is open to all – to investigate the phenomena of Spirit manifestations and to understand and make known the modes and realities of our existence – present and future. For the mind's existence after physical death is here treated as *a Question of fact – not as a form of belief.*"'

A low murmur of approval.

Viola sat on the other side of the room. Mrs Blackthorne sat beside her. Yesterday the spirit had held his hand again and said that he should tell his wife about what had happened. But this was impossible; a betrayal of everything. And who was his wife? Was Viola truly his wife? They had spoken vows, but they lived as brother and sister. They weren't even as close as siblings were. There was a wall between them and it grew taller and thicker every day. She sat here now, in the same room, cradling her camera in her lap in the same way that the spiritualist beside him cradled his little dog, and she was someone other than the person he'd known as a child. She was even other than the person he'd married. Independent, unknowable.

He filled his mouth with tea and did not speak. Field shunned him; Newham was a bigot; Mrs Blackthorne, though she kept his secret and took his money, disliked him. He knew every inch of this island – had walked it, sketched its flora and its dead fossils, breathed its air and worn its mud – and not a single inch of it was his. It was connected to the mainland by a slender thread but he was connected to no one. He could only ask the spirit for advice, and the advice, when it came, was impossible.

Newspaper, wadded into a pad and stuffed into the crack of a wall. **The Bristol Mercury,** *29 August 1857.*

The intelligence from India reaches this country in a rather puzzling complication. We have, first, electric telegraphs; then copious narratives in Indian journals and in the private correspondence of the London press; and, thirdly, masses of letters from residents in India to friends in England. Thus the reader of all that appears travels, often unconsciously, the same ground three or four times over; and everything seems to be surrounded by a continuous dense, murky atmosphere, universally tinged with blood.

Chapter Thirty-six

1 May, 1857
Delhi

Jonah stood outside Delhi College, sweating in the sunlight. Under his hat, his hair was wet and his collar was nearly soaked through. He watched the stream of students emerge from between the columns of the building and walk down the steps, all of them talking to each other on topics he did not know, in a language he did not understand.

He missed Pavan. And despite what Mrs Hamilton had said, he couldn't help wondering why he had chosen to cut off their friendship. Because it *was* friendship. Several times a day he had to check himself when he thought of something he would like to say to Pavan, or to ask him. And each time, he went back over their time together, everything he had said to Pavan, trying to work out what he had done to offend him. Was it, as Mrs Hamilton had said, an irreconcilable cultural difference? Surely Europeans and Indians could become true friends?

In his time here, he had met an Englishman who had taken a Muslim wife. They seemed to live quite happily, raising children who were half Indian and half European, refraining from eating pork, and offering prayers to Allah and to the Christian God. There must be many others. And these people were still admitted to Christian society; they were regarded as eccentric, perhaps, but not outcasts. If a marriage worked, surely a friendship was permissible?

He must have done something wrong, said something. He

could not leave it as it was, not knowing whether he had offended Pavan in some way.

Jonah removed his hat and wiped his brow. A group of bearded students emerged from the building and Jonah's heart thumped as he recognised the slender figure of Pavan walking slightly behind them. Among these Muslims, Pavan wore a red dot on his forehead marking him as a Hindu.

This was not his only difference. In the daylight amongst the other men, Jonah could see how Pavan was different: his face was beardless and soft in contour, his stature shorter than most of the other students. For the first time, Jonah wondered if perhaps he had lied about his age in order to be admitted to the college. As a stranger coming from Agra and mixing with men of another faith, it would be easy for him to do so.

Pavan exchanged a word or two with his fellow students. At the bottom of the steps he turned to walk in Jonah's direction. He held a book in his hand, which he had opened and was reading as he walked, so he was nearly upon him before Jonah said, 'Pavan Sharma!'

He stopped as if struck, and looked up. Jonah saw his eyes widen.

'Sahib, I did not expect—'

'Jonah. I'm still Jonah. Can we talk, please? Just for a moment?'

Pavan wavered, but then nodded. He pointed to a low wall in the shade of a tree and they sat there together. Jonah was glad to get out of the sun.

'What are you reading?' he asked.

Pavan showed him the book. 'Mathematics. A universal language. They say that if there were people on the moon, we could communicate with them through numbers only.'

'Have I upset you in some way?'

Pavan didn't answer. He put the book in his lap and bit the inside of his lip. There was a flush on his cheeks. His eyelashes were long and dark.

How old was he? He'd said he was twenty, but was he more like sixteen? Younger? And yet he was clever, wise beyond his years. No wonder Rajesh was protective of him.

'I believed we were friends,' said Jonah.

'We are,' said Pavan quietly.

'Then why did you stop coming to meet me?'

Pavan said nothing.

'Is it because I'm English, and you're Indian?'

He shook his head, though the movement was so small that Jonah would have missed it if he weren't watching him carefully.

'If I have done something,' said Jonah, 'or said something that has offended you, I apologise. It was unintentional, and I would like to learn what it was so I won't do it again. I've enjoyed our talks very much. I thought that I'd finally found someone who I could—'

'You have not offended me. It is not your fault, sahib.'

'Jonah. If we are friends, call me Jonah again.'

'I cannot. And we cannot meet any more. Believe me, it is best that we do not.'

'Is this your brother's idea?'

'It is... it is mine.'

'But why?'

He shook his head, more vehemently this time.

'Surely there's no harm in us meeting to have discussions about astronomy and religion and literature?'

'If we are friends, that is not all we are discussing.'

'What are we discussing?'

Pavan didn't reply.

'This silence,' Jonah said. 'It's not like you. It's as though there's a wall there I can't get through. Why?'

'Perhaps I have been this way all along.'

'But you haven't. You *haven't*. You said you believed in everything, and nothing. You believed you could do anything you wanted to, or at least you could try. Something has changed you. Why won't you tell me what it is?'

'I may have seemed certain about what I believed. But I was wrong.'

Jonah removed his hat and ran his hand through his damp hair. He wiped it on his thigh. 'Pavan, are you afraid I am going to expose your secret? Because I am the last person—'

Pavan dropped his book onto the dusty ground. His cheeks, flushed before, had gone pale.

'You know?' he whispered.

'I suspected, and this has confirmed it.'

'You said nothing.'

'Do you think I care? That it matters to me? Two people, such as ourselves, who have a meeting of minds—'

'It is never only minds,' Pavan said. 'Never. I – I must go.'

He jumped up from the wall, turning to go, and Jonah gasped. There was a large patch of bright red blood on the seat of Pavan's white pyjamas.

'Where are you hurt?' he asked, rising and grabbing Pavan by the arm. 'Are you in pain? What happened?'

'I'm not hurt.' Pavan tugged on his arm. 'Let me go. I'm leaving.'

'Not when you're bleeding.'

Terror crossed Pavan's face. He looked down at himself, first his front and then twisted to peer at his back. As soon as he saw the red stain on the white fabric he turned around, quickly, and pressed himself up against the wall, sitting so the stain was covered.

'Why are you afraid?' asked Jonah. 'Why won't you let me help you?'

'I can't…' he whispered.

'Why are you bleeding?'

'You know why.'

'I don't, because you won't tell me!'

'My secret…'

'Why would your age cause you to—'

And, all at once, Jonah knew Pavan's true secret and why their meetings had stopped. Not age, or illness, or the gap between their culture and religion. Not anything that Jonah had done to offend.

He stripped off his jacket. 'Here,' he said, holding it out. 'Tie this around your waist. It will cover the stain.'

Pavan took it and tied the sleeves with hands that were shaking. Small, neat hands, with delicate fingers.

Pavan and Rajesh Sharma were strangers, in a strange city where no one knew them. And Pavan had a thirst for knowledge, a desire to study at the college where only men could go.

'Please don't tell anyone,' Pavan whispered.

Jonah could do nothing but shake his head.

'Promise me.'

'I will tell no one,' said Jonah. 'I promise.'

Pavan tightened the jacket and turned to flee.

'Your book,' Jonah called, stooping to pick it up from the dust where it had fallen.

But she was gone.

Jonah sat on the wall of the temple, tracking Venus moving across the sky, east to west in an arc, separated by velvet night from her red lover Mars.

It had been a week since he had discovered Pavan Sharma's secret. In that week, he had eaten and slept, admired art and scenery, read books and written letters; conversations had gone on around him and he had participated in them. But he had retained nothing. He was thinking about Pavan Sharma.

He thought about how she must have tied up her hair, or shorn it, and wound it in a turban. The cloth she must have used to bind her breasts. Her careful efforts to modulate her voice, the pains she must go to every month, so she could learn and be free.

She was man and woman, scientist and deceiver, body and mind, everything and nothing.

He wanted very much to see her again. It burned somewhere inside his chest. Watching Venus, he tried to understand what this burning meant. It was more than curiosity. She'd been deceiving him, but she'd been truthful with him, too. He'd talked with her in a way he'd never spoken with anyone before. This yearning was a little like homesickness: a craving for the one person in this strange country who didn't seem strange to him.

A bat flitted close to his head, gone as soon as he heard it.

'Jonah,' said a voice below him.

He peered into the darkness. 'Pavan?'

A white sleeve, a white turban. Pavan climbed up onto the wall with Jonah and stood on it facing him.

'I didn't think I would see you again,' said Jonah.

'You came here to be alone?'

'I came here hoping you would come here too.'

'Yes. So did I.'

She was a slender figure, clad in white. Jonah reached out his hand for her and then thought better of it.

'What's your real name?' he asked her.

'My real name is Pavan Sharma. I had another name, when I was born. But Pavan is my name, now. It is the name I have chosen.'

'Are you angry with me?' he said. 'For discovering your secret?'

'Are you angry with me for deceiving you?'

'No. Not at all.'

'We could not have met here, like this. If you had known.'

'No, we couldn't,' he agreed. He added, perhaps against his judgement, 'Yet we are meeting now.'

'I wanted to explain to you, for the final time.' She sat on the wall, her feet dangling over the edge. 'Almost everything I have told you is true. I do come from Agra. My father was a man of learning. He educated me at home. After our parents died, Rajesh and I came here together.'

'Who knows, besides your brother?'

'His wife Lakshmi also knows. Outside the family, only one person. My father worked for the Lieutenant Governor. After my father's death he wrote me a letter of recommendation for the college here in Delhi. He told me that Amrit Sharma's child deserved to learn everything about the world and he did not mind whether it was the son or daughter. He is an unusual Englishman.'

'And the person you were meant to marry?'

Pavan bowed her head. 'We were promised to each other since we were children. He's a kind man, but he has no curiosity. He needs a partner in his faith. I like him, and I care about him a great deal, but I could never be his wife.'

'You plan never to go back to marry him.'

'I have broken my promise to him. It is my one regret. One *of* my regrets,' she corrected.

'What did you tell him when you left? Is he waiting for you?' Jonah thought of Viola waiting for him in England. Her faithful letters, two or three each week, all the news from home put into the same envelope to save postage and arriving months and months after they had been written so that when he read them all the news was old and the world had moved on. They could have each become completely different people.

'I wrote to him when I reached Delhi,' Pavan said. 'I told him that although I could not marry him, I would never marry anyone else. I made him that promise, and it is one that I can keep.'

'But what if you meet someone you would like to marry?'

'How could I?' Pavan spread her hands wide. 'Here in Delhi, I am a man. I cannot marry a woman. A wife would help me keep up appearances, it is true, but I couldn't trap a woman in that way. Even if she agreed to it, I could never be a true husband or give her children. But I don't want to marry a woman.'

'What if you fell in love with a man?'

It was not a question he would ever ask of a woman other than Pavan. But the two of them had been so friendly, so equal. They had already spoken of love, in the darkness – a conversation that had new meaning to it, now that he knew her secret.

'I cannot allow myself to do that, either,' Pavan said. 'And in any case, who would want a wife like me? I don't want to keep a home, or cook, or bear one child after another and raise them all. I want to learn and teach. I want to see and understand.'

'That's the sort of wife I would want.'

Pavan shook her head. 'The sort of wife you want is waiting faithfully for you at home with her father.'

'I wasn't comparing you to Viola.'

'No,' said Pavan. 'Viola is not selfish. She does not neglect her duties. She follows her faith, not her own wishes.'

'I meant that I would want to marry someone with passion. Someone who looks at the stars and doesn't see mere points of light. Someone who looks at numbers and sees a language that they could understand on the moon.'

'And what does Viola see?'

'I don't know. I ... perhaps I don't know her that well.'

Pavan tilted her head back to look at the heavens, and Jonah did the same.

'Will this be the last time we meet?' he asked her.

'Yes.'

'But why? I won't tell your secret. Nothing has changed from when we met before.'

'Everything has changed, Jonah.'

'Why should it?' As soon as he said it, though, he knew the answer.

'I should not have come here tonight,' she said, 'but I wanted to explain to you.'

'I feel as if I'm only starting to understand you.'

'And yet I feel that I have known you for a very long time.' She sighed. 'Hindus believe that we live many lives. It is our punishment for being too attached to the world. Perhaps you and I knew each other a very long time ago.'

'Do you believe that?'

'No. And yes. Do you believe what Christians do – that if my soul were Christian, though we might be parted from this day onward, that we would be reunited in heaven?'

'Yes.' He gazed at her. 'And no.'

'Then we have our answers.' She stood. 'Goodbye.'

She immediately climbed down the vines hanging from the peepul tree.

'Wait!' He scrambled to his feet and swung down too, scraping his hands on the wall. He landed beside her inside the temple, near the dais, out of breath. 'Before you go, I would like to see you once as yourself.'

'You see me as I am. I have nothing else to show.'

'I mean ... without this. Please?' He could not resist touching her white cotton turban.

It was darker inside the temple, but the ruined roof let in the starlight. Her eyes were a liquid gleam. He remembered how they had looked in the day: how her irises which now appeared black were in fact a rich, warm brown.

'Do you know what you are asking me?' she said, her voice as matter-of-fact as it had always been.

'Yes.'

She did not take her gaze from his as she unwound the cloth from her head. Slowly she let the uncoiling cloth pile upon itself in a jumbled heap on the packed dirt floor. And then she removed pins, or a clasp, and she shook her head and her hair fell around her face, over her shoulders, down to her waist. Darker than the sky, thick and heavy. The scent of incense was released into the air, along with a warm rich smell: perhaps an oil she used on her hair, perhaps her hair itself.

'It's beautiful,' he said, and he touched it as he had her turban. Warm and soft and deep. It lay around her face like a veil.

'It would have been easier to cut it,' she said.

'Why didn't you?' He held a lock of it between his fingers.

'For many reasons. Perhaps this was one.'

Her hair fell over her face and, with his other hand, he stroked it back so he could see her eyes.

'This?' he murmured.

'This,' she said. She stood on her toes and clasped the collar of his jacket and kissed him on the mouth. Full on the mouth, here in this place built to worship a marriage.

'I've got something for you.' Emilia danced over to him, hiding something behind her back. 'Can you guess what it is?'

'A monkey,' said Jonah, setting down the book which he had not been reading. He caught the sparkle in the young girl's eye and smiled. He had been smiling nearly constantly this morning. He had crept back to the house before dawn, to the sound of the muezzin calling the faithful to prayer, his lungs full of the scent of Pavan's hair, his hands warm with the texture of her skin. He hadn't bothered going to bed, merely had a wash and changed his clothes and gazed at himself in the light of the rising sun, in the mirror above his washstand, trying to trace in his face the momentous discoveries he and Pavan had made together.

Despite the lack of sleep he was not tired; he felt reborn.

'No,' said Emilia, 'better than a monkey.'

'An elephant?'

'Better.'

'What could be better than an elephant?'

'I think you already know,' said Emilia.

Pavan Sharma, eyes dark as forever, whispering in his ear her stories of the universe.

As they lay under cover of the stars he had asked Pavan, 'Do you feel like a woman? Or a man?'

'I have the body of a woman,' Pavan had said, 'and the mind of a human being. I don't relish deception, but I have no other choice if I wish to be myself.'

'And your heart?' Jonah had asked, tracing a slow finger along the swell of Pavan's breasts, released from their bindings.

'That,' Pavan had said, 'is only mine.'

His heart already belonged to her.

'A mango?' he guessed now, to Emilia's teasing.

'Even better than a mango. Stop being silly, you know what it is already. You would not look so happy at the prospect of anything else.'

'Do I look happy?'

'Radiant. Doesn't he, Mama?'

Mrs Hamilton glanced over from the portrait she was sketching of little Toby as he played with a skein of wool. 'He does indeed.'

'I hope one day a man will look that way because of me.'

Jonah's smile melted. He glanced from Emilia to her mother, but both of their faces were as normal.

'You have plenty of time to find a husband,' said Mrs Hamilton to her daughter. 'There's at least a year before you're an old maid.'

'Mama, I'm only *eleven*.'

'Perhaps six months, then.'

Emilia sniffed and turned her attention back to Jonah. 'Promise you'll read it aloud to us. All of it, even the parts where she praises your manly virtues and your sky-blue eyes.'

'Emilia!' reproved her mother. The girl giggled and dropped an envelope in Jonah's lap. He saw the familiar handwriting and his stomach sank.

Viola.

'Well?' prompted Emilia.

'I'll read it later,' he said, slipping it into his pocket.

'But you promised.'

'Emilia, he did no such thing. Stop teasing our poor guest.'

Emilia pouted and turned away. Jonah picked up his book again. The letter lay in his pocket like a stone.

Chapter Thirty-seven

August, 1858
Weymouth

Warm weather meant that Mrs Newham's tea party was held in the walled garden instead of in their drawing room. Gulls wheeled and screamed overhead. Jonah sweated under his starched collar.

'Used to this heat in India, what?' opined Admiral Newham, who was red-faced and fanning himself with a napkin. Jonah murmured something vague and polite and, as usual when it came to Admiral Newham, walked away as soon as he could. He didn't want to be here, in the company of the Newhams and the cream of Weymouth society, whoever they were. He couldn't help but remember that the last time they'd been here had been the séance, where they'd met Mrs Blackthorne.

She was with his wife now, talking in the shade of a rhododendron bush. The medium's dark head was bent to Viola's chestnut one. As he watched, the two of them whispered something to each other.

What did they talk about? Had Mrs Blackthorne kept her word to him?

Last week, the spirit had said nothing. A brush of light fingers against the back of his hand, and that was all. Half a whisper, words that could have been 'I shall see you soon.'

Then it was gone, and Mrs Blackthorne was stirring behind her screen, and it was time for him to leave his furtive tribute and go, so that when they saw each other again, they could pretend it had never happened.

All of the spirit's words haunted him, but these more than usual. They were almost a blessed promise. But the only way he could see Pavan again would be to die.

In some ways death would be a relief. The end to this necessary deception, a reunion with the person whom he yearned for above all others. But dying would betray Viola even further. She would be left with no one. She hadn't wanted to come to this tea party without him – how could he leave her a widow?

When he looked again, Viola was standing alone. He made his way across the lawn to her.

'You aren't too hot?' he asked, with that furrow of concern between his eyebrows.

'No, it's fine in the shade.'

'I can take you home.'

She shook her head. 'No, I'm fine. Mrs Newham has yet to announce her guest of honour.'

Guest of honour. Jonah sighed under his breath and wished himself back on the island, in the abandoned quarry by Easton, sketching a wort.

'What were you and Mrs Blackthorne talking about?' He couldn't help but ask, though Viola and Mrs Blackthorne were always talking about something. In some ways, it took a burden from him – he no longer felt as if he were solely responsible for her. Craven as that was. He was her husband; he should be her all in all. They should be all in all to each other. Wasn't that what they had vowed to be?

'The guest of honour, as it happens,' she answered, with an odd smile.

'Speculating on who it might be?'

'I know who it is. Henriette is the one who asked Mrs Newham to invite her.'

'Ah. Between the two of them, Mrs Blackthorne and Mrs Newham seem to have their fingers in every pie.'

Viola seemed to straighten her shoulders. 'Why do you dislike Henriette, Jonah?'

'I don't dislike her,' he said. 'She is a very civil person.'

'But you make excuses not to be in the same room with her.'

'Do I?' Of course he did; always. 'I'm sure I don't. Has Mrs Blackthorne said anything?'

'Well, no. But she must have noticed, and is too delicate to say anything. It's bordering on rude, Jonah. I like her so much. You must admit it's done me good, being friends with her.'

'I can't disagree with that.'

'I've never had an intimate friend before.'

'You've had me.'

'I mean, a female friend. There's a certain ...' She hesitated, and he saw a faint flush on her cheeks. 'Sympathy.'

'Evidently.'

She shot a quick glance at him which was quite out of character. Almost a direct imitation of the medium's keen gaze, quite disconcerting from her mild grey eyes.

'Are you jealous?' she asked.

'How could I be anything but glad that you have a friend here?'

'Is it the photographs, then? Do you think it's not a suitable occupation for a woman?'

'I know they give you pleasure. You're so much happier than you were.'

'The subject. Do you find it morbid?'

'I think you're helping people,' he said, with total honesty.

'But you blame Henriette for that article in the papers.'

'I know that Mrs Blackthorne is no stranger to publicity.'

Viola pressed her lips together, but she looked herself again, with a sadness that prickled at his skin. 'I wish you'd like her. Or at least tell me why you don't. Do you remember when we used to agree on our opinions of everyone?'

Walking home after church, her hand in his, the two of them whispering and laughing about Mr Adams' gloomy face, Mrs

Welling's naughty children. Viola hiding her smile behind her hand as if that would stop God from seeing her gossiping. It had used to be so simple.

Now, it felt as if they were always on the edge of a quarrel and he feared that if they started they would never stop. He knew that the fault was in him, but he was afraid that he would be weak enough to find his faults in her.

How could he disclose some of his secrets to Viola without disclosing the whole? He could confess his visits to the medium – that would ease this precariousness of trusting Henriette Blackthorne to keep those visits secret – but Viola would be sure to ask her friend about it, and what if, despite what she claimed, the medium did know what the spirit had said to him? What if she said, 'He talks to a person whom he loves'? His thoughts had been going around and around this subject for weeks.

'I only want to know you,' she said to him. 'Both of us have changed, Jonah. My father's death changed me, and what happened in India changed you. But we never talk about it. We never talk about what happened, or what... what you and I haven't done. I want to be your helpmate, Jonah. I want to be your wife. But how can I do either if I don't know you any more?'

Her voice was quiet – in this shady corner of the garden, no one but him would be able to hear her – and tears swam in her eyes. He fumbled for a handkerchief and with his own feelings of guilt.

'You haven't changed at all,' he told her, pressing the clean handkerchief into her hand. Aware that he was not answering her question. 'You are always the same. You've always been the same, good and kind.'

'But I have changed, Jonah. I have questions that I never thought I would ask of myself, and feelings that I never suspected could—'

A tear fell. 'You are unwell,' he said hurriedly. 'I will fetch you a glass of water.'

He crossed the sunny lawn, giving the other guests a wide berth and avoiding the refreshments table where several people had congregated. He slipped through the French doors into the hot, still house.

A servant was nowhere to be found. He decided to head for the kitchen, but he had only reached the parlour door when he heard a voice that made him stop still.

'Thank you for inviting me, Mrs Newham. It is very kind of you.'

It couldn't be. Not possibly. It must be some other young girl.

'You'll want to freshen up,' said Mrs Newham in her fussy way. 'Please, come with me, and then we can take you outside to meet the guests, who are all eager to see you. Particularly Mr and Mrs Jonah Worth.'

He peered carefully through the parlour doorway to the entrance hall. Mrs Newham was talking to an elderly woman, standing next to a slender girl of twelve or thirteen in a pink dress. As he watched, the girl removed her straw hat to reveal blonde curls tumbling in familiar waves over her shoulders.

He did not hear her reply. After the first terrified glimpse he did not see the child, or at least he didn't see her as she was now. Cold struck him, cold and a pain that he had tried to bury but which lived inside him and stabbed him at every breath. The sound of a gun, death in a dark place in a field of slaughter.

Jonah saw Emilia Hamilton in her torn nightgown, the blood on the white fabric, the gun in her hands, the dreams that haunted every sleeping hour and the figures that would not leave his mind. He gasped a strangled sound of fear, stopped his mouth with his hand, and stepped backwards into the parlour as Mrs Newham and this girl, the girl whom he had driven safely out of Delhi in the bottom of a laundry cart, walked past on their way to the stairs.

In a moment they were out of sight, and he fled the house, out through the front door and running blind through the street.

Chapter Thirty-eight

When Jonah did not return with a glass of water, Viola went to the refreshments table and took a glass of punch. She wasn't particularly thirsty anyway; she knew full well that her husband had used the glass of water as an excuse to get away from her expressing her feelings and the unpleasant truth. Viola was not often cross, but she was feeling distinctly so now.

What hope did they have of any sort of successful marriage if Jonah couldn't bear to hear how she felt?

Such a contrast to Henriette, who had prompted Mrs Newham to arrange this entire affair just so that Viola might have some small answers to the mystery that surrounded her husband. She looked around for her friend, and spotted Mrs Newham instead, emerging through the French doors with a young girl in pink. She beckoned Viola over to them.

'This,' she said with great pride and satisfaction, almost as if the invitation had been her own idea, 'is Miss Emilia Hamilton. Miss Hamilton, this is Mrs Worth.'

The girl was pretty, pink-cheeked, very young, and clearly embarrassed. Viola held out her hand in true friendliness, and half a lie. 'It is very good to meet you, Miss Hamilton. My husband has spoken with fondness of your family and the kindnesses they did for him.'

'It's nothing compared with the kindness he did for me,' said the girl. 'They were all killed by those filthy sepoys and he saved me. I would have been rotting in the stinking Indian earth with my family if not for Jonah.'

Viola blinked at this vehemence of language. 'Well … he will be very glad to see you again, I'm sure.'

'Yes!' said Mrs Newham. 'Where is he? Where is the Hero of Delhi?'

'He went inside the house for a glass of water, I believe. I'll go see if I can find him.'

The house was silent. All of the guests were outside. Viola checked the parlour, the saloon, and then the kitchen, which was hotter than the sun-drenched garden, with servants sweating over plates of cake dripping icing. She stopped a maid whom she recognised from her previous visits, who was carrying a tray. 'Lottie, have you seen my husband? He came inside to fetch me a glass of water.'

'No, ma'am.'

'If you do, would you say I'm looking for him?' She nodded thanks and went back outside. By this time Mrs Newham and Emilia had moved to another part of the garden, and Viola had to negotiate several intercepting groups and their requisite small talk before she reached Henriette, who was coming back towards her.

'Have you met Miss Hamilton?' she asked Viola, looping her arm through hers so they could talk more intimately.

'She's quite … outspoken for someone her age.'

'That's a kind way of putting it. She managed to damn all dirty Indians to hell within five minutes of our meeting.'

Viola bit her lip. 'Well, her family were all killed by Indians, I suppose, which must make one …'

'Mr Worth witnessed the same events she did, and I've never heard him speak so.'

'No. But Jonah is a grown man, and didn't lose anyone he loved.'

Henriette leaned closer. 'Has he seen her already?'

'Maybe. I can't find him. Have you seen him?'

'No. I'll confess I've been keeping an eye out. I hoped to witness their reunion. I'm a terrible busybody.'

'I looked inside for him, but—'

A clatter of glasses, and Lottie was beside them with her tray. 'Mrs Worth? Beg pardon, but you said you were looking for Mr Worth and Barnaby just told me that he saw him leaving through the front door a little while ago.'

Viola's stomach sank. 'Oh, I must have forgotten the time. Thank you, Lottie.' She waited until the maid had left them before turning to Henriette and speaking the truth. 'He's run away.'

'Perhaps he's ill.'

But she remembered when he had fled after receiving some sort of message at Henriette's séance. That time she had found him and he had shifted the focus to her instead, but she was beginning to recognise that for the evasion it was.

'Something is horribly wrong.'

Henriette's arm tightened on hers. 'Shall we go find him? That is – he's your husband, I have no business.'

'Yes,' she said. 'No. I want you to come with me. Please.'

He had not taken the carriage. He was not along the south side of the harbour or on the Town Bridge, where they had found him before. They weaved through holidaymakers and boatmen, Viola's gaze darting back and forth hoping to catch the familiar slender figure, with the hair that still curled like a girl's. On a hot August day there was hardly any room on the pavements to move; Viola stopped, suddenly, near the Custom House.

'What if he – what if he jumped in the water?'

'Why would he do that?' asked Henriette, but their eyes met and Viola could see that she understood. The fact of Jonah's sadness came upon her all at once. She had only been able to think of herself. But that was why there was a gulf: he was sad, and he couldn't tell her why.

'It's too busy here,' Henriette told her. 'Someone would see him. Where else would he go? Has he a club? Would he go to a pub or a church?'

She shook her head. 'Perhaps he walked home. Or the Nothe– there's a cliff…'

That thought was too much. They retraced their steps, looking into the pubs on either side of the bridge fugged with smoke and fumes of ale, where the men went silent as soon as they stepped inside. The two churches, cool and dark and empty. She thought about climbing the steep steps to the Nothe and she balked. Instead they returned to the Newhams' and Viola waited outside, neck craned and eyes sharp for a glimpse of Jonah, while Henriette asked for the carriage and left a note for Mrs Newham, pleading Viola's sudden illness.

They didn't speak during the journey to Fortuneswell; Viola stared out one window, Henriette the other, watching for a figure on the road or, once they reached it, on the beach. He was sad; why hadn't he told her? Why hadn't he taken her hand, and told her the truth?

Her hot hand was taken by Henriette's cooler one. Viola held tight to it, while she searched for Jonah.

When they reached the house, Viola knew without any doubt that Jonah was not there. He couldn't have got there faster than they on foot, so it was logically impossible, but more than that: she had become so used to a house without Jonah in it that she could tell from the mere feeling of the air inside.

'We can wait for him,' she said, discarding her hat with hardly any thought of where she put it. 'He will be here soon.'

She went to the parlour and sat on the sofa that looked out towards the water, Henriette beside her. Alice brought a tray of drinks; Viola hardly noticed.

What if he never returned?

A rap at the door and Viola was up, rushing to the door before the maid could answer. A boy was there, holding a slip of paper. 'Message for Mrs Worth, ma'am?'

She held out her hand. The paper was heavy, a page torn from Jonah's sketchbook and folded in half. 'Where did you take this message?'

'From the station, ma'am, my pa's a porter there. Gentleman taking a train.' He smiled, clearly angling for a tip, and she put a coin in his hand and closed the door so she could read what her husband had written, in pencil, to her.

I am so sorry.

A sob ripped through her and she covered her mouth with her hand. Someone came up behind her – Henriette. She took the paper from her and then whispered, 'Viola.'

'What did I do?' she asked, hand still over her mouth, staring at the blank shut door. 'What's wrong with me?'

'There is nothing wrong with you.'

'He won't talk with me. He won't touch me. He will barely even look at me. And now he's gone. Why am I so flawed? What should I have done?'

'Nothing. You are not flawed. You are perfect. Oh, darling girl.' Henriette touched her shoulder and Viola turned to her, tears falling.

'All I ever wanted,' she said, knowing she was crying, that she should hide her face, but Henriette looked at her so kindly, her own dark eyes swimming with tears, 'was to be his wife. It's what my father wanted more than anything. It was the last thing he spoke of before he died. And I've failed.'

'*He's* failed you. He's the one who's left.'

She shook her head. And whispered, 'If I were only beautiful…'

'Oh Viola. My precious Viola. If you could see yourself as I see you.'

'How do you see me?' Blinking up at Henriette, her guide, her protector, her only friend. The only friend, besides Jonah, she had ever had.

Henriette put her fingers under Viola's chin. Tilted it up, dipped her own head. And kissed her on her tear-wet lips, soft and warm.

Viola had not been expecting this and yet in that moment it was the thing she most wanted in the world. She found herself pushing up on her tiptoes, pressing closer to Henriette's mouth, lip against lip, tears still rolling down her cheeks but arms raising to wrap around Henriette's neck. This, she thought. This is what it is meant to feel like, this tender shock of flesh against flesh, the warmth of Henriette's breath on her cheek, the silk of their gowns rustling. A sound, half a sob, half a moan, gathered in her throat and escaped against Henriette's lips.

The sound startled her more than the kiss had done and she stumbled backwards. Lips burning, staring at the other woman. Her friend.

'What's wrong with me?' Viola whispered.

'Nothing is wrong.' Henriette's voice was lower than Viola had ever heard it. When she pushed back a curl of hair that had come loose, her hands were trembling. Calm, collected Henriette was as shaken as Viola herself, and this realisation sent a bolt of longing through Viola.

Despite this, because of it, she said, 'You're a woman. It's unnatural.'

'Do you feel unnatural, now?'

A breath, barely caught. 'I – you're the only thing I can hold on to. The only person.'

'Please choose to let me help you. I want, so much, to help you.'

Tears in her eyelashes, heart beating hard enough to hurt, Viola stared at her friend.

So much of her life, it seemed, had been determined for her. Whom to love, whom to marry, where to live, what to wish for. Her only choices what to have for dinner, what dress to wear, in which small ways to spend her time. Even the photographs and the way they had changed her life, had been done at the request of others.

Now, she had a decision to make by herself. Two paths: to walk away or to step forward. Loneliness, or something more frightening by far.

Viola was used to loneliness. She was not used to those stolen glances in the dark of the bathing machine, a gentle hand on her skin, the pressure of an arm around her waist. Or the taste of another person's mouth, another woman's mouth.

Henriette's mouth. This woman who smiled and laughed and spoke kind words, words for Viola alone. Maybe this is what Viola had always wanted, exactly what she lacked.

Viola hurled herself into Henriette's arms. Clasped her head in her hands, thick coils of hair in her fingers, and kissed her hard enough for their teeth to clash. Henriette drew her closer, hands on her waist, so their bodies pressed together. Through layers of cloth and whalebone Viola felt every one of Henriette's breaths, felt the rapid beating of her heart. Kissing, unable to stop now, she blindly searched with fingertips for the pins and combs holding up Henriette's hair and pulled them out so it fell heavy and warm into her hands. Henriette sighed and tilted her head back, shaking her hair free as Viola kissed her chin, her smooth cheeks.

'Let me,' whispered Henriette, and she loosened Viola's hair too, combing it out with her fingers. Viola remembered the sea that first time, floating in Henriette's arms, safe in the grip of something much larger than herself. That was exactly how she felt now. Viola, wet-mouthed and hungry for something she didn't quite yet fully understand, tilted her head as Henriette had done and closed her eyes for a moment with the pleasure of Henriette's hands in her hair.

'No,' she said, not denying this touch but where they were touching: in the hallway next to the umbrella stand.

Henriette nodded. Viola took her hand. The short note

fluttered to the tiled floor and they went up the stairs to Viola's bedroom and shut the door.

They had undressed each other before, in the damp murk of the bathing machine. Now they unbuttoned, unfastened, revealed in daylight. Neither one of them drew the curtains. Viola wanted too much to see, wanted this to be different from the failed guilty fumbling in the dark with Jonah. Without spoken agreement, Viola undressed Henriette first. Her eyes open, she gazed at Henriette's pale flesh, the curve of her spine, the dimples at the base. When the dress had parted and slipped to the floor and the underclothes after it, Henriette turned around and Viola looked at her, not touching. Henriette stood, was looked at. Her hands by her sides, half a smile on her lips. The way she stood naked was a wonder even greater than her beauty to Viola. She could be in a salon, fully dressed and veiled, stared at by supplicants. No blush, no shame, no Venus-modest hand to cover herself.

'How does it feel?' Viola asked her. Still not touching.

'How does what feel?' Henriette asked gently.

'To know you are beautiful.'

'Let me show you.'

Henriette put her arms around Viola, close enough so Viola could breathe the scent of her skin, and unhooked her dress. She unlaced her corset and Viola felt herself loosening. Piece by piece Henriette unwrapped her from her layers and with every part freed from fabric, she touched and kissed. Lips on bare shoulders, a kiss between uncovered breasts. She knelt to kiss Viola's belly and Viola's hitch of breath was loud in the bright room. Henriette drew down all her clothes, chemise to stockings, and Viola stepped out of them, leaving this husk of herself on the floor. And Henriette still knelt, looking up at her.

Her father's house had no full-length looking glass, only a small square on the wall of her bedroom. Her glass here was on her dressing table, and showed her only from the waist up. She had never seen herself from head to foot except in photographs, and then she was dressed. Viola's view of her own body was what she had gazed down on in her bath, or glimpsed while changing. The expanses and textures learned by her own hands at night under her nightgown when she dared. She was a person of parts.

Now, she saw herself in Henriette's face and Henriette's fingers. How Henriette lay her palm on each of her ankles and stroked up her pale legs, making the fine hairs stand up as if touched by electricity. Viola swallowed, looked down and saw herself formed by how she fitted into Henriette's hands. A spirit willed into existence by this dear person.

She pulled Henriette onto the bed where she slept alone every night and there in the afternoon sunlight they loved each other. She closed her eyes at the pleasure of it, muffled her cries against Henriette's skin so the servants wouldn't hear. Nonsense words of lovers, quick laughter, Henriette her teacher, hand and mouth and skin and breath. And again. In this new knowledge, finally alive.

Chapter Thirty-nine

At breakfast Henriette was careful not to take the seat at the head of the table. It sat empty between them as Viola poured them each coffee and Henriette watched her. A great transformation had happened to both of them.

This morning they had woken early in each other's arms and exchanged kisses and pleasure before the sun was fully risen. Now, though, Viola was pale and timid where last night she had been rosy and bold. Henriette remembered far too clearly how easy it was for a maid to learn an employer's secrets. So she waited until Alice had left the dining room and her footsteps had retreated to say, quietly, 'What worries you, Viola?'

Viola screwed up her eyes and whispered. 'What do the servants think? We spent last evening in my bed together.'

'It's perfectly reasonable,' Henriette said, reaching for the toast rack. 'Mr Worth has been called away suddenly, and you didn't wish to be alone, so I, your friend, stayed the night. After all, that is what happened.'

'But... do you think they can tell? What we did?'

Henriette could tell. Viola's lips were pink and swollen from kisses; there was a pliability about her body that had not been there before. She was nervous now, but even in her discomfort there was a knowledge, a sureness, a certain languid satisfaction that couldn't quite be dispelled by manners or formality or fear. It was quite extraordinarily beautiful. Henriette couldn't take her eyes off her. She wanted to take her hand and lead her upstairs again, forget appearances and deception, relax back into that world that contained only the two of them.

'Are you sorry for what we did?' Henriette asked.

'I didn't even know that it was possible,' Viola said. 'I looked at you while we were swimming, and I thought about your body, but … it never crossed my mind.'

'Selfishly, I'm glad that it has now.'

'We should have taken off the bedsheets,' said Viola, biting that swollen lip. 'You only have to look at them to …'

Henriette buttered a slice of toast and put it on Viola's plate. 'They will suspect nothing,' she said. 'They may see, but they don't observe. Most people are far too conventional to see two women together as anything more than friends. It's illegal for men to lie with men, and immoral for a married woman to be with a man who's not her husband. There's no law about women. Women loving each other … don't even exist.'

'Men do that to each other?'

Henriette couldn't help but laugh at Viola's astonished expression. 'Oh, you are a perfect vicar's daughter.'

'Other people do that? Other women? What we did?'

'They must. I've heard of it.'

'Have *you* done it before?' Viola's face turned from pale to bright red.

'No.'

'Have you wanted to?'

'There was a woman once, who I think I loved. I never touched her. But I loved her.'

'Was it the woman in the photograph?'

Henriette nodded.

'How did you know her?'

Henriette lifted her cup of tea and noticed, almost dispassionately, that her hand was shaking. She put down the cup.

'I worked in the same house as her. She was the governess, and I was a housemaid.'

Viola stared. 'How long ago was this?'

'Years. Madame hardly noticed me. I can't think that she cared about me. But she saved me once, and I never stopped thinking about her. Or – or about another girl,' she added, though she surprised herself by saying it. 'A girl called Jane. We shared a bed, and she always made me feel safe.'

'Do you know what happened to her?'

'No. Perhaps she's still alive. Married, with a houseful of children. I've … never told anyone about this.'

'About the love, or about being a servant?'

'Ethelred knew I'd been a servant. He didn't care. He helped me hide the fact.'

Viola leaned her elbows on the tablecloth. 'You've loved so many times before. Madame, Jane, your husband. You're so lucky.'

But none of these were anything like Viola, with her elbows on the table. Viola, breathless and eager, curious and tender, modest and frank. Viola, who kept her eyes open at the peak of her pleasure, seized Henriette's head to kiss her, had no fear of daylight, who tasted of sweet clover and seawater, who fell asleep curled into Henriette, hand tucked inside hers.

'I'm lucky to have met you,' said Henriette. 'I've been alone for so long.'

'I've been so lonely. Even though …' She glanced at Jonah's empty chair and her eyes filled with tears. 'I haven't thought of him at all, not all night. Oh, Henriette, how awful. I'm a terrible wife.'

Henriette abandoned her toast. She got up and went around the table to Viola's side, kneeling by her chair and taking her hand.

'You are not a terrible wife,' she said. 'You care deeply about him.'

'But you and I—'

'What you and I did has no bearing on your love for him.'

'Because I love him as a brother. Not a husband. I understand that now. And he must feel the same. That's why he's never touched me, except for that one time when he couldn't. But poor Jonah. I forgot to think of him. I've betrayed him that way. Where do you think he's gone? Why do you think he's gone?'

'I think,' said Henriette, honestly, 'that he is running away from his past. I think that Emilia Hamilton reminded him of a very unhappy time. So unhappy that he finds it easier to leave than to tell you.'

'Henriette – that awful note. Do you – what if he's harmed himself? What if he threw himself in front of a train?'

Viola's eyes, huge and frightened and wet. Henriette squeezed her hand, hard.

'We would have heard by now. He's gone to London, or somewhere without associations, where no one knows him.'

'I don't know him. I thought I did, but I didn't even know myself – how can I know what he would do?' A tear fell from Viola's eye onto their joined hands, and Henriette had the impulse to kiss it from her skin. 'Can you tell, Henriette? If he'd passed into the world of spirit, you'd know, wouldn't you?'

'I…'

'Flora would know. You could ask her?'

Henriette gazed at this other woman, so vital and so desperately innocent. Despite yesterday's sunlight, despite the caresses shared and thoughts spoken and air breathed together, mouth to mouth, skin to skin – every single part of this life between them was built on deception.

For a moment she considered telling the entire truth. Being as frank with Viola as Viola had been with her, as frank as Viola was being now. What they had done together should reset their relationship, shatter it and rebuild it on a new foundation. How long had it been since she had been honest with anyone, Henriette Blackthorne who was born Harriet Smith? Including herself?

But in Viola's eyes she saw what she'd seen in so many other people: pain, loss, an uncontrollable craving for reassurance.

She squeezed Viola's hand and lied once again.

'Jonah's alive,' she said. 'I know he is. I would know if he had passed into the world of spirit.'

Chapter Forty

Viola sat on a glossy pew in the empty church, her hands folded in her lap.

When she was a child she'd thought that God lived in the rafters of her father's church. She pictured Him perched on an oak beam, watching her with benevolence as she prayed. She'd been confused to discover that there were other churches in towns all over the country, cathedrals built in the shape of vast crosses, churches nestled in streets of the teeming cities, in places all over the world. Gilded temples, echoing monasteries, shabby shrines by the side of the road. 'God is everywhere,' her father had told her, taking her on his knee and opening a book to show her pictures of Michelangelo's paintings, God soaring over the whole world and yet also over a small particular room in Rome.

Yet sitting here, in this particular room, she gazed up at the rafters. She was not looking for God but for her father, though her father had always been the way in which she had understood God. Since she had started to photograph spirits she also understood that empty air is not empty, and that the eternal is able to manifest in any room, great or small, sad or joyous.

Still, a church felt like the right place to ask this question. Eyes lifted, Viola whispered, 'Father, I know it's a sin to love Henriette the way I do. But this is a sin that hurts no one – at least, I hope it hurts no one – and it makes me so very happy. If you think it is wrong... will you give me a sign?'

She waited, gazing up at the rafters, the high ceiling and shadows where she once believed God watched.

All was still. No one spoke at all.

Chapter Forty-one

Jonah fled to London as if he were running from the Devil instead of a twelve-year old girl and the woman he had married. He scribbled a note to Viola, hardly aware of what he was writing; shoved it into the hand of a porter, along with money and an address; caught the train and sweated in a second-class compartment, hat pulled down over his eyes, to Dorchester and thence to Waterloo Bridge station.

The streets were grey and close, the clear skies of the seaside replaced by a humidity that tasted of mud, the dank odour of the Thames, the filth of horses and gutters. He wandered the narrow damp streets as foetid water leaked into his shoes. He had come to London only to avoid throwing himself over the cliff and into the sea but now that he was here, he had no idea what to do except to keep moving and to stay away from water. He kept south of the river, avoiding the bridges and the docks. He walked, rehearsing over and over again that sight of Emilia Hamilton through the doorway of the Newhams' house, remembering the sight of her in the ruined temple with blood spattering her white nightgown. The baby on the floor. And Pavan...

He walked faster, seeing nothing except black and white and red. No one spoke to him here in the teeming morass of London; he was just another person, a transient or a native, with no one to look closely enough to see the story written on his skin. He thought of the crowds of people when he had landed in Calcutta, how shocked he had been to see so many human beings at the same time. Here was the same, except colourless, bleak and wet. A damp shadow of the life he'd glimpsed in India.

But that was all dead and gone. This was his life now, this drear and these secrets. This ring on his finger that seemed to weigh down his soul. He had shared so little of his heart with his wife that she had thought he would want to see Emilia Hamilton. What must she be thinking now, poor Viola, who had never done anything wrong?

With the thought of his wife, he stumbled on the kerb and finally stopped to look around him. It had grown dark and he recognised nothing; soot-streaked walls, peeling posters for pills and ointments. He was in a narrow street. At the end, light shone weakly through hazy windows onto a sign: a pub. Something about the sign and the frontage looked familiar. Realising he had neither eaten nor drunk anything since that morning, he made his way to the pub – The Bunch of Grapes – and pushed through the door into the lounge bar.

Tobacco and beer fumes almost choked him. At the bar, a small man with slicked-back hair and a port-wine birthmark looked him over and poured him a pint in silence. He took it to a small battered table in a corner, gulped half of it, and then looked about him by the light of the guttering gas lamps and the smoking fire. It was a workingman's pub. The sparse clientele sat in shirtsleeves and tarnished jackets, each one intent on his own pipe and pint. None of them so much as glanced at him or at each other. One played cards by himself. Occasionally someone grunted a greeting.

He could be invisible: he with his fine waistcoat, his garden-party tie, his new hat. When he went to the bar for a second pint he asked the landlord: 'Do you have any rooms?'

The room was neither clean nor spacious. It had an iron bedstead with a narrow mattress covered only by a yellowing sheet. The single window looked out upon the alley where Jonah had stumbled. But within five minutes of his being shown the room, a girl knocked on his door with a fresh jug of water, another jug of hot gin-and-water, and a plate covered with a grey napkin, all of which she placed with extreme nervousness on the small rickety table under the window. She retreated before he could offer her a coin, and he sat on the bed, fully dressed, and poured himself a measure of gin. And then another. And another. He stared at the cracked blank walls, trying to wash away the remembered taste of Delhi dust and blood and guilt.

He did not remember his own father well enough to know if he ever drank; Viola's father hadn't been teetotal but he drank very little, keeping a bottle of port only to offer visitors. Jonah had never taken to the habit. His friends in Oxford drank, but he usually fell asleep.

This gin didn't make him sleepy. It made him feel more awake, gave him more uncomfortable edges. He stood up and paced the room: it was only big enough for four steps in one direction, three in the other. He thought it had probably been used by working men and whores for their transactions. In this moment, he envied them their straightforward needs: lust and money.

His fault had been to marry Viola. No; his fault had been to allow himself to love Pavan. If he had not loved Pavan, she would be alive and Jonah would be free of the double weight of grief and guilt. Viola might have had a child by now. He could have accepted this watery version of love, seen the good in his daily life.

Or would he have always known something was missing? Was the fault not about any choice he had made, but in himself, running through him like the cracks through this wall?

He made a wordless sound, a choke of despair, and left the room, half-empty tumbler on the table. Outside the night was darker but the streets seemed even busier. Gin had cleared his vision and he knew where he was now: Vauxhall. He had been here once before, to meet his friend Blandford. He saw a group of gentlemen in evening dress and glossy hats, fresh from the Pleasure Gardens; he heard a cackle from two women dressed in ruffles and feathers. A young girl stood alone, hardly older than Emilia, with rouged cheeks and a dirty pink dress. Jonah crossed the road and hurried away, but he stopped abruptly when he saw a green-painted door.

He knew this house. He'd been here years ago before he went to India, back when he had been able to predict everything about his life: his marriage to Viola, his children, his seamless accession to his father's wealth. An innocent young man who, despite the deaths of his parents, nevertheless believed that everything always went as intended.

Before he could stop himself, he rang the bell and heard it ring deep inside the house. A clatter of footsteps, and the door was opened by a young boy in a too-big hat.

'Black Maria?' Jonah said, and the boy said, 'Number six,' and then disappeared back into the shadows of the house. Jonah stepped inside, closing the door behind him.

The flight of stairs was just how he remembered it, threadbare carpet and smeared banister. The first door on the first floor had a brass number six on it. Jonah, who was feeling a strange dislocation from himself, almost as if he had stepped into his own body three years before, knocked on it.

'Come in,' said a deep, low voice, and he opened the door.

It was Maria, just as he remembered, except she was wearing a red dress, low-cut in the front. She had gained some weight, perhaps, but her long dark hair was the same, and her rosebud lips. She was even nearly in the same pose in which Blandford had drawn her, lying on her bed on her side so that the curve of her hips showed to advantage.

'Do I know you, love?' she asked in her low drawl from her bed. 'I thought you was my friend, from your tread, but I don't recall seeing you before.'

'No,' he said. 'That is, I was here once. But we never – I never …'

'That's all right, sweetpea,' she said with the manner of a patient mother. 'I'm not busy tonight. But I don't know you, so you'll have to put the money on the chest there first. Sorry to have to ask, but some of 'em try to run off without paying. It's a sovereign for a hand, two for the full.'

He fumbled two coins out of his pocket and put them in the chipped porcelain dish on the wooden sailor's chest. Maria crooked a finger at him and like an obedient schoolboy, he came to her and sat carefully on the bed.

'Now,' she said, her hand solid on his thigh, 'what was that? One sovereign or two?'

'Two,' he said, feeling as if the voice came from someone else. 'But I don't … I can't …'

'You can do what you paid for, sweetpea. I don't mind.'

'I'm married.'

She laughed, though it wasn't cruel. 'Oh, honey, my best customers are married.'

'No,' he said. 'I mean I can't. I can't do it.'

'You tried with your wife, and you couldn't?' She didn't wait for an answer; she sat up on the bed and pulled him into her arms for a hug. 'Oh, love. I'm sorry. Let Maria take care of you. Would you like a drink? Help you relax?'

He nodded and she got up from the bed and went to a cupboard, where she pulled out a bottle and poured two measures of some clear spirit. 'Ain't the finest,' she said to him as she handed him one glass, 'but it works.'

He took a fiery drink, and then another. Maria took a small sip and placed hers on the bedside table before she lay down beside him again. In a brisk way that he could no more have resisted than the sun rising and setting, she unfastened his trousers, pushed aside his underthings and took him in her soft hand. He didn't look; he gazed at the flowered curtains covering the window, a curving intricate design of roses and thorns, so sinuous that it could go on forever. He took a drink and felt himself growing in her hand.

'There you are, my love,' she cooed in his ear. 'Nothing wrong with you.' She was practised, firm and efficient. Jonah finished his drink, lowered his glass, careful to keep his gaze at the curtains. Roses, thorns, a wall of roses like the one in the fairy tale protecting a sleeping maiden … His breath grew short.

'Nearly there,' Maria said, movements quickening. 'Let me take care of you.'

Roots digging deep into soil, thorns digging deep into flesh. He closed his eyes for a moment, saw blood-red blooms, opened them again. Maria whispered in his ear and he gasped, half a sob.

'There you are,' she said, taking her hand from him and reaching for a cloth on her bedside table next to her glass. 'Nothing wrong with you at all.' She wiped her hand and Jonah dared to look at her, which was a mistake, because his eyes filled with tears.

'Oh, love,' she said, drawing him down to her. Weak, spent, he laid his head on her soft, half-naked bosom, unable to control the tears. She patted him on the back with the hand that held the cloth. 'Don't cry now. There's nothing to worry about. Next time you're with your missus you'll be fine, and if you're not, you just come back here to Maria.'

He breathed in powder and sweat and the tang of other men – and for a single moment, crying in her arms, he felt more comforted than he had in many years. He used to lie like this after a bad dream. He would leave his sleeping ayah and creep through the silent house to his parents' room and put his head on his mother's breast, listening to her breath. In her sleep, her hands would comb through his hair.

When his mother had a fever, that final fever that took her life and then his father's, he had been in England. For months afterwards, at school and at the rectory, he dreamed about lying in that narrow coffin with her, his head on her cold breast, and he would wake crying in his empty bedroom. Sometimes Viola heard him and she would creep down the hallway to his room, crawl into bed with him, hold his hand in her small cold one.

Jonah sat up suddenly, wiping his wet eyes with his hands. 'I – I'm so sorry.'

'No need to be sorry. Lots of 'em cry afterwards. I don't know why, it's a release, like. I don't mind.'

Sitting so close to her, he could see where the make-up was caked in the lines of her face, see the sweat stains under the arms of her gown. Nothing like his mother, nothing like Viola, nothing like Pavan – nothing like the naked, alluring woman he had seen sprawled out waiting for Blandford to draw her – a stranger who traded sex for money, and yet she had just been kinder to him than he deserved. She was more decent than he, who had used her.

'You can take your extra money back, now,' she added. 'I won't charge you for the full. Some would, but not Maria.'

'I – no – I must go.' He stood and dashed for the door, fastening up his clothes with clumsy hands as he ran downstairs and into the night.

On the street, nothing had changed. He hurried through the crowds, looking at no one, nothing, pulled towards the Thames, wiping his face over and over to rid himself of the traces of tears. The buildings became larger, more solemn and he passed between them like a shadow until he was halfway across Westminster Bridge.

Then he stopped. Jonah gazed down at the dark water and he thought that if Earth had nothing to show more fair, he might as well jump here into the crawling Thames.

He remembered reading Wordsworth with Pavan. Pavan had spoken the words in a musical lilt that made this most English of poets sound like an Indian.

He remembered the story that Patience Hamilton had told him, about the starving Brahmins on the river bank, how they would not eat to save themselves because they could not accept food from an Englishman. When Mrs Hamilton told him that story, he had been appalled that fellow humans could waste their lives on something that seemed to him so small. But now he understood it more. How it was better to die than to be degraded, to betray everything that one believed.

If he jumped, he could erase those last moments in the temple. His mind could stop from replaying them again and again, twenty or thirty seconds stretched out into hours and sleepless nights. There would be the silty water closing over his head, and then it would be over. Viola would have his name and his income. And she would be alone.

Dear God! the very houses seem asleep;
And all that mighty heart is lying still!

He seemed to hear Pavan saying it, invoking the name of a God she did not believe in, the image of a city she had never seen. Pavan had saved his life. Pavan's spirit had said he was forgiven.

If he threw away his life, however small and wretched it had become, however riddled with grief and inadequacy, these gifts would be for nothing.

Jonah breathed deep the damp murky air. As he turned and walked back to the Bunch of Grapes, the sun rose slowly, peeping through buildings in the watery sky.

A faded yellow clipping from **American Medicine**, *April 1907.*
Pasted into a scrapbook. In handwritten ink above, the title:

**Hypothesis Concerning Soul Substance Together
with Experimental Evidence of The Existence of Such
Substance, by Duncan MacDougall, M.D. of Haverhill,
Mass.**

My first subject was a man dying of tuberculosis. It seemed to me best to select a patient dying with a disease that produces great exhaustion, the death occurring with little or no muscular movement, because in such a case the beam could be kept more perfectly at balance and any loss occurring readily noted.

The patient was under observation for three hours and forty minutes before death, lying on a bed arranged on a light framework built upon very delicately balanced platform beam scales. At the end of three hours and forty minutes he expired, and suddenly, coincident with death, the beam end dropped with an audible stroke, hitting against the lower limiting bar and remaining there with no rebound. The loss was ascertained to be three-fourths of an ounce.

In this case we certainly have an inexplicable loss of weight of three-fourths of an ounce. Is it the soul substance? How other shall we explain it?

Chapter Forty-two

Viola had never known this: to lie abed as the sun rose and shone through the open window, as a bee stumbled and buzzed on the wisteria outside; to hear the sea distant on the breeze and skim her hand, slowly, along valleys and swells of flesh. All her life she had lived according to the ticks and chimes of the clock that had stood on the landing of her father's house, and which now stood in the parlour of hers. Time to rise and dress, time to worship, time to visit, time for kindnesses, for letters, for hours of idleness without purpose but which must be endured until time for supper, time for bed.

In this bed now, she couldn't hear the clock downstairs. They were alone out of time, with the door closed and the window opened, their clothes draped on a chair like discarded duties. Had this always been possible and she'd never seen it?

Henriette, eyes closed, caught Viola's hand and brought it to her lips to kiss the fingertips, one by one. Viola opened her mouth to say something soft, inconsequential, when there was a tentative tap at the door.

She sat up, bedclothes falling away from her. 'Yes?'

'Mrs Worth, there's a gentleman at the door says he wants a photograph taken of a spirit.'

A visiting card slipped under the door. Viola sighed and left the warmth of the bed to pick it up. *MR T. SELBY*, it said on the front, and on the back, in pencil: *I would like a photograph of my father.*

'Tell him to wait in the studio,' she called through the door to Alice. 'Take him up the back stairs, if you don't mind. I'll be up directly.'

'Come back to bed,' said Henriette. 'It's early and no one is up.'

'It's late and everyone is up,' corrected Viola with a smile. She put the card on the chest of drawers and went to the heap of clothes, untangling hers from Henriette's. 'The poor man has lost his father. I should help him.'

Henriette sat up. 'You're too good.'

'No, you stay here. You've had enough early mornings to last a lifetime, I think. Besides, I'd like something to come back to.' She dressed herself, letting Henriette fasten her buttons, and gave her a swift kiss on her lips before slipping the card into her pocket and leaving the sunny room.

Mr Selby was a small man, barely taller than Viola, with a claret waistcoat, a black moustache and fine black hair greased back from his forehead. When she entered the studio he pursed his lips at her as if disapproving and Viola wondered if, somehow, he could read the marks of Henriette's lips on her cheeks and mouth.

'Mr Selby,' she said, holding out her hand and only remembering after he had shaken his small dry one that she had not washed since being in bed with her lover. She felt herself blush, and said, 'I am sorry about your father, though you are not recently bereaved, I do not think?'

'I am not,' said Mr Selby, drawing his brows down and taking his hand back very quickly.

'Well, I must tell you right away that I don't always capture spirits in my photographs so I apologise in advance if I disappoint you. Have you come far?'

'London.'

London. She had spoken with Henriette yesterday about

writing to Jonah's friends in London to ask if they had heard from him. They had decided to wait another day or two, to save Jonah any rumours if he came back earlier. Unspoken was the fact that the two of them didn't want their idyll spoiled too early.

'If you will please take a seat on that stool in front of the screen, I will prepare the plate and be with you in a moment or two.' She gestured to the stool, but Mr Selby didn't move.

'I want to watch you prepare the plate,' he said.

'Oh. I-I can certainly show you the plate before I prepare it, but it is light-sensitive you see, and I have to prepare it in a darkroom, which is quite small for a gentleman and a lady together.'

'Then I will see the plate, please.'

'Yes, of course.' She fetched an unused plate, unwrapped it and held it by the edges so that he could inspect it. 'It's just clear glass. Are you interested in photography, sir?'

'I am interested in your photography.' And he fixed her with his pale, slightly protuberant eyes. She was glad she had refused to allow him in the darkroom with her.

She kept up a running explanation of what she was doing through the darkroom door. Once she emerged she continued explaining the process while she placed the plate in the camera, settled Mr Selby on a stool. She fell silent when she took the image out of courtesy to her subject as she counted the seconds of exposure. But she doubted she would have tempted him to speak, anyway; he sat like a toad, almost unblinking. When she went back to her darkroom he followed her and stood outside the door.

'Next, I pour developer over the plate,' she said, doing so, 'and the image appears.'

She stammered and stopped her commentary.

Mr Selby sat in the middle of the image, staring, his mouth a small line. A figure stood behind him.

The figure was not a stranger. Even before she looked closely she recognised him not with her eyes but with her whole being.

'Mrs Worth?' came Mr Selby's voice.

'I . . . yes, it's all fine, just a moment.'

She lowered the plate into a water bath and stared at it, her vision rippling and red and in negative, white appearing as black.

The figure standing behind Mr Selby was her own father.

He looked alive. Kind and well. His face was healthy, his eyes bright, his whiskers threaded with grey. He was not the man in her last photograph of him taken when he was dying, the one she still looked at sometimes when she could bear it. It was the man she remembered, the man who taught her how to read and write, how to mix chemicals and coat a plate, how to keep a moment alive forever.

'Father,' she whispered. He was with her. The red light was his touch, the ferric scent of developer his breath. In a trance, she transferred the plate to the bath of fixer and gazed as his image misted and became positive.

'Mrs Worth, what are you doing?'

Mr Selby's voice was almost a shout. She started, physically shook herself, and opened the door. 'I'm sorry, I have to rinse the plate several more times and dry it before—'

'Let me see the photograph, please.'

She showed it to him. Her hands were trembling.

'Is this a spirit in the photograph?' he asked.

'Yes.'

'It is not a double exposure or a fault in the plate?'

'No, no, sir, it isn't.'

'Do you claim this is a photograph of my father?'

He was staring at her, not at the plate, and she understood him. How terrible would it be to hope for a message from your loved one, and someone else's loved one appeared instead? It was exactly what she had been feeling herself, until this moment.

Gently, she said, 'Your father is with you, always. I know it.'

His face relaxed and she knew that she had given the correct answer, the one that gave him some comfort.

'I would like to take this plate please.'

'No,' she said, quickly. 'No, I will make you a print. Several, if you like.'

He nodded. 'When will they be ready?'

'Can you come back tomorrow? I will have them ready then.'

She hardly knew what she said as she accompanied Mr Selby downstairs to the front door. She went immediately back upstairs, to the message that had been left for her. Henriette found her, some time later, in the darkroom staring at the plate as it dried.

'That is not his father,' Viola said, hearing Henriette approach but not looking up. 'It is mine.'

Henriette's hand settled on her shoulder as she gazed at the photograph, too. Papa was smiling directly at where Viola had been standing as she uncovered the lens.

'What does it mean?' Viola whispered, but Henriette did not answer.

Chapter Forty-three

The next afternoon, when the knock came on the front door, Henriette and Viola were outside in the garden. They had spent the time after lunch carrying wide-mouthed jars of silver nitrate solution down the stairs and outside to be sunned while the warm weather lasted. The night before, Viola had woken Henriette with her crying. 'I thought it would be a relief to see him,' she sobbed as Henriette held her.

Henriette knew from experience that revisiting the past could be painful, even when you wanted to. Even when you craved it enough to seek out spirits and miracles. She could, if she chose to, tell Viola how Jonah had felt the same way: how he had returned to her over and over to try to find the thing he missed, but when he saw it again, he had to run.

But she didn't. Secrets, even the ones not her own, were too sticky and dangerous to unwind. And this one had become her own, too.

Today, Viola was muted, but she seemed at peace. She tended the glass containers of chemicals as if they were flowers, or children, and Henriette tended her – holding a parasol to shield Viola from the sun, brushing a cloud of pollen from her black skirt.

Alice came out through the French doors. 'The gentleman from yesterday is at the door, ma'am.'

'Oh,' said Viola, straightening and touching her hair. 'I …'

She glanced at Henriette. They had discussed this last night;

Viola had wavered about whether to fulfil her promise to the man, seeing as the spirit wasn't his father after all.

Henriette had no such scruples. 'It will help him,' she told Viola, and when Viola bit her lip, she said, 'Stay out here in the sunshine. I'll give him the prints.'

They had been left on the table near the front door, wrapped carefully in paper. Henriette barely glanced at the short man with the frog eyes as she handed them over and he tucked them greedily under his arm.

'How much do you charge for this?' he asked.

Henriette, thinking of how Viola had handled every image with reverence and love, said, not without some spite, 'We take a donation at your discretion to further Spiritualist causes – say, five pounds?'

It was a ridiculous amount, and she expected him to sputter and object, and be embarrassed to haggle, but he merely took out a purse and handed her the notes.

She took the money and tucked it into her bodice. 'Good day,' she said, shutting the door on him.

When she returned to the garden Viola was sitting on the grass, her face turned to the sun. Henriette sat beside her, mindless of her skirt or the gaze of stray servants, and kissed the faint freckles on her cheek.

'How did Mr Selby like the prints?' Viola said, smiling, and Henriette paused in her caress.

'Mr Selby?' she said carefully. 'That is his name?'

'I think so. I still have his card.' She took it from her pocket, and showed it to Henriette: the name in plain capitals, *MR T. SELBY*.

'He was so matter-of-fact, I thought perhaps he had been sent by someone we knew. But he was not very conversational. Do you know him?'

She had never seen Mr Selby in person, but she knew him. The address was the same as on all those letters she had never opened.

'No,' lied Henriette, aware of the paper money folded into her bodice. Her own flight from Geneva. The careers of women ruined, the words of vitriol written in the national press. 'No, I do not know him.'

Chapter Forty-four

Jonah stayed in the small bare room above the pub for several days; he couldn't tell how many. The window was nailed shut and for the first few days the room was unbearably hot, and then the weather turned and it was miserably damp. The young girl brought him food and water and gin. He barely touched the food. He slept and paced and slept again, tamping down his dreams with the gin. He knew this could not last but he was trying to resist the lure of the bridge, of the Thames below.

Finally, he woke one day and felt that the walls were too close. He got out of bed, dizzy and weak, and splashed his face with water. Then he stumbled down the stairs. The wan light dazzled him. He craved fruit, something cold and sweet, the mangoes he used to eat sliced on a dish in India, like they gave him in hospital in Calcutta when he woke from his fever. But he did not know where to get such a thing in London. He gravitated towards the station, looking for a fruit seller.

'Worth? Good God, is that you?'

A hand on his arm. Jonah pulled back, but when he focused on the man in front of him it was his friend, Blandford.

'Saw you from across the street, couldn't believe my eyes,' Blandford said. His voice was loud, his neck thick, his face ruddy with good health. 'I thought you were in Dorset. I say, are you quite all right?'

'I…' His voice, unused to speaking, was harsh, and as he spoke he swayed, faint. 'Yes.'

'You're a liar. You look as though you're about to drop dead.'

'What are you doing down here?'

'Still got a soft spot for Black Maria. Remember her? Her rooms are near here. But you're more urgent, good chap.' Blandford whistled for a taxi, and when it came, he practically pushed Jonah into it. He considered before he gave the driver an address. 'Can't take you to the house in Mayfair, Mama's full of questions. I'll vouch for you at my club even though you look like the Ancient Mariner. No razors in Dorset, are there? No washerwomen? Never mind, don't explain, you can tell me later.'

In the rattling cab he was protected from the lure of the river. Then there were trees, white buildings, and he was being chivvied through a glossy door and up mahogany stairs to a leather arm-chair, a glass of whisky and soda. Jonah's hand trembled, barely able to hold the crystal to his mouth, but the liquid warmed him, seemed to make him breathe better. As if by magic, food appeared: a bowl of soup, a soft white roll with butter, a chop. It was the magic of money, of position. All the ways idle Englishmen like Jonah poisoned the world. He turned his head away, sick.

'Give this to someone who deserves it.'

'You deserve it. You're my friend.'

Blandford sat close beside him and coaxed the food into his mouth as if Jonah were a child. Then, without allowing Jonah to say another single word in protest, he brought him upstairs to a bedroom with a fire and a bath and towels and a razor and a decanter of port and another of sherry on the sideboard.

'I'll be back tomorrow,' Blandford told him. 'I expect to find a human being when I return.'

He felt more like an echo than a human being, but the next morning he was washed and shaved and wearing fresh clothes that had been brought to him. He thought they were probably

Blandford's, as they were distinctly too large. Jonah looked in the gilded mirror and saw an approximation of that terrible creature: an English gentleman.

And yet something had shifted. It was not the clothes or the room, the readmission into a world of privilege; it was the kindness of his friend.

He could think beyond the next hour. He would have to explain, somehow, to Blandford. He would have to write to Viola.

He did not know what to say.

But when Blandford arrived, in a magenta tie and a cloud of cologne, he didn't ask Jonah for any explanation, at least not right away. He merely settled in the armchair opposite, poured them each a glass of sherry ('Medicinal, get it down you,' he said) and offered Jonah a cigar. When Jonah refused, he lit one himself, and sat there smoking in silence while Jonah sipped his sherry.

'Thank you,' Jonah said at last. Blandford waved it off in a cloud of smoke.

'Have you been staying somewhere in London?' he asked. 'I can't imagine anyone let you on a train looking like you did.'

'The Bunch of Grapes, in Vauxhall. I need to settle the bill.'

'I'll do it. Have you got a bag there? I'll have it fetched and the contents burned. Along with the clothes you came in. Bound to be infested.'

'No, no bag. I came ... unexpectedly.'

He had decided last night not to mention his visit to Maria. Blandford might not judge him, but he judged himself.

Blandford settled back into his chair, cigar tip glowing. 'Listen,' he said. 'Don't blame you for doing a flit. It'd be a lot of pressure on anyone. But don't you think you should go back to Dorset?'

Jonah felt sick. 'I ... no. Viola is better off without me.'

'Without you?'

'I'm a coward. I know it. But she's a strong woman, and she has friends now. I'll write to her with an explanation of course, but for now, she'll be fine on her own.'

His friend's thick brows contracted. 'Hardly thought you were the type to abandon his wife when she's in a tight spot, Worth.'

'I can't explain to her. I can't explain to anyone. I've done things, seen things, that ...' Jonah stopped, suddenly realising what his friend had said. 'Viola is in trouble?'

Blandford put down his cigar. 'Don't you know, man? See here, when did you leave Dorset?'

'A few days ago – a week, maybe more – I can't tell. What's happened to Viola?'

'It's in the papers. You haven't read them?'

'I haven't read anything. I've been ill. What has happened? Tell me!'

Blandford rose. He rang the bell pull. 'I'll let you read it for yourself.'

Chapter Forty-five

In the end it was weather that made all the difference.

After days of sunshine, clouds moved in, and a chill rain. They cancelled their morning walk on the cliffs and Viola sat down to write letters to Jonah's acquaintances and his solicitor in London. Henriette, while encouraging this, privately had her doubts. She knew very well how easy it was to disappear without a trace when one wanted to, and although Jonah Worth had less experience than she did in this regard, there had been no word from him for nearly a week. If he were with friends, he would have written.

Henriette, in the meantime, went back to her lodgings in Weymouth. She wanted clothes and to check her post, and Mrs Newham had her long-standing appointment to speak with her babies. She had cancelled every other engagement to stay with Viola, but she felt that she owed Mrs Newham and besides, she wanted to check the state of Weymouth gossip as it pertained to her and to Viola and Jonah Worth.

Viola was confident that Jonah was alive, because Henriette continued to say that he was. Henriette certainly hoped he was. Although Jonah and she had never been fond of each other, his only sin was in not adequately loving his wife. If he died, his blood would be to some extent on her hands, and Viola's hands too, for forcing the crisis. She worried more about Viola's sense of guilt than her own.

There were no letters from Mr Selby at her lodging, nor had he left his card. It seemed that the two of them, natural enemies, had come face to face and failed to recognise each other.

There were, however, fresh bills. She wandered her lodgings, feeling how empty and mercenary they were compared with the rooms she had been sharing with Viola. In the Worths' home, Henriette felt almost like a newlywed, far more than she had with Ethelred when she'd been learning the new business of being a wife. In contrast, domestic bliss with Viola was almost effortless. She felt more as if she had a wife than if she were one. There was no sense of obligation or duty; she did not have to earn Viola's tenderness.

If Henriette's life had taught her anything besides how to dissemble, it was to know that happiness couldn't last, any more than the sunny weather could. She did not have to earn Viola's tenderness, but she had already betrayed it.

She summoned Flora for Mrs Newham, though the spirit was spiritless, and her patroness's talk afterwards was mostly about when she and the Admiral would return to London for the winter. Mrs Newham did not mention whether she hoped to take her pet medium with her, and posing the question took more charm and energy than Henriette had to spare.

She had been telling lies for so long, living from hand to mouth. She had reinvented herself so many times. A few days with Viola had made her see how very tired she was. How much more peaceful it was to be purely herself. All she wanted to do was to go back to Viola and forget everything else.

'When will you be back here, Mrs Blackthorne?' Greta the maid asked as Henriette packed some clothes, and Henriette thought, *That is the question.*

'Certainly not until Mr Worth returns,' she said, sounding (as usual) much more assured than she felt.

'When will that be, madam?'

'We shall see.'

But on the journey back to the isle of Portland, under lowering skies and beside restless waters, Henriette felt less certain. If

Jonah returned, would he and Viola settle back into their imitation of a marriage, and would Henriette be expected to quietly withdraw? Although she had met many men who found it easy to ignore their wedding vows, in her observation these men didn't extend that moral elasticity to their wives.

And if he didn't return, what then? Could this last any longer than the summer, two women living together, with no discernible source of income? They could charge more for the photographs – but would Viola agree to that?

All of her instincts told her to leave an uncertain situation, where she could not see her advantage. But Viola…

She thought of grey eyes and warm lips. The touch she had not felt for so long, like the ghosts of all her desires come to life again. Together they lived on an island, a new country, somewhere meant only for them. Madame had appeared and chosen Viola for her. The photograph was real. So how could this emotion possibly be an illusion?

She alighted from the carriage and hurried up the path to avoid getting spattered by raindrops. She let herself in the front door of Viola's house, smiling despite herself, ready to find Viola and cover her with kisses, to dispel all her doubts, if only for an hour.

Alice stood in the hallway, leaning with her ear to the door to the parlour. The maid straightened up as soon as she saw Henriette and whispered, 'Oh, Mrs Blackthorne – something has happened.'

'Is Mrs Worth all right?'

The maid wrung her hands. 'A man came to the door, a police constable. Do you think it's news about Mr Worth? It can't be good news can it?'

'How long has he been there?'

'Only a minute – I can't hear what they're saying.'

Henriette put her finger to her lips and pressed her ear to the door. She heard three words, a part of a sentence, a name. Then, without hesitation, without making a sound or speaking a word to Alice, she turned and walked out of the house and into the rain.

A letter never finished and hastily folded. The ink has run from rain or tears or sea water, and the edges are tattered and stained. Dated 28 August 1858.

My dearest H,

I am meant to be writing to Jonah's friends, & I will. But you have gone for an hour and I cannot stop thinking about you, & something that I want to tell you but which I am not certain that I dare to say.

Papa feels very close to me now since I have seen him in my photograph. In the garden yesterday, while I was sunning the solutions, I thought I heard his voice. He used to quote Mr Fox Talbot to me, & I remember it word for word: 'The most transitory of things, a shadow, the proverbial emblem of all that is fleeting and momentary, may be fettered by the spells of our "natural magic", & may be fixed for ever.'

I have been thinking of these words ever since. I did not understand why Papa was appearing now, when he has not appeared before, but now I do. I know what natural shadows I have fettered. It is not ghosts that I photograph. It is love.

I love you. My love for you is what has brought my father's love back to me.

Chapter Forty-six

When they arrived the magistrate was at lunch, and Viola stood waiting in a back hallway with the police constable beside her in silence, small puddles forming around them on the floor. All she could smell was the wet wool of the constable's jacket and the distant scent of stew.

'I'm worried that my friend will return and I will be gone,' she said to the constable. 'Do you think I might write a message to—'

'No paper,' said the constable, and glared at the wall opposite.

She gnawed at her lip. She had paper; she had a letter hidden in her bosom, shoved hastily between her skin and chemise when the knock had come on the door. It crackled when she breathed. But she could not take that letter out in front of a policeman.

Of course she wouldn't be here for long, she'd be back home in an hour or two, but she hated to think of Henriette arriving and hearing a garbled account of a police constable from Alice. She was about to suggest that possibly there was a boy who could be sent, when a servant swept past them, knocked on the mahogany door, entered, and emerged a few moments later with a tray bearing used crockery. 'You can go in now,' she told the constable.

Viola did not know the magistrate, who sat behind a glossy desk and did not rise when they entered, but she recognised the man in the armchair next to the desk. 'Mr Selby,' she said, approaching him with her hands clasped, 'I did not sell you any photographs, sir. This is some sort of error.'

'Do not speak to the complainant,' barked the magistrate through his drooping moustache, and Viola fell silent. She tried to think back to the servant's tray and how many dishes had been on it, and whether Mr Selby, who was apparently her accuser, had been having lunch with the magistrate, while a police constable was sent to her home.

'Sir,' she began, to the magistrate this time, but he glared at her and she subsided again. He picked up a paper from his desk.

'This gentleman, Mr Selby, alleges that you did sell him photographs which you claimed depicted the ghost of his father. Is this true?'

'I did not sell the photographs, sir.'

'Mr Selby's statement says that he paid five pounds for these photographs. Are you denying this?'

'I never ask for money for my photographs. I make them to help people who are grieving.'

'Are you calling Mr Selby a liar?'

She was very conscious of the eyes of three men upon her, and she wished the servant had stayed behind in the room, so at least there was another female present. 'No, sir. He must be mistaken about money changing hands.'

The magistrate grunted. 'You take photographs, then, do you? You don't deny that?'

'Yes, I do take photographs.'

'Not a suitable occupation for a woman, I would have thought. Chemicals and darkrooms. Who gave you permission to engage in this hobby? Your husband?'

'My father taught me, and my husband encouraged it. He knew it made me happy.'

'It's the business of a woman to make the home happy, not to go inviting strangers in, establishing a commercial enterprise in her parlour, and taking advantage of grieving people. Why are you not looking after the welfare of your children?'

'I have no children.'

'Hmph.' He held up Viola's print of Mr Selby and her father. 'Did you take this photograph?'

'Yes sir, I took the image and I made the prints from the plate. That is one of them.'

'Do you claim this is the photograph of a ghost?'

'Yes, sir. It is Mr Selby in the foreground of the photograph, and in the background it is a spirit.'

'You told Mr Selby that this was the spirit of his father, did you not?'

'I …' She couldn't remember exactly what she had said, and it suddenly seemed very important to know the exact words. 'I told him it was a spirit, I think, and he was seeking to see the spirit of his father, and believed that this was him.'

'His father is alive!' thundered the magistrate. 'He lives in Surbiton! You are lying!'

Regardless of Surbiton, he was right: she was lying to a magistrate. It occurred to her, with a horrible sinking, that perhaps Henriette had taken money from Mr Selby when she handed over the packet of prints. But why would she do such a thing? And how could Viola implicate her for what they were calling a crime?

'You have no answer to this?' The magistrate's face was deep purple.

'N-no, sir,' stammered Viola.

'Can you explain, please, your version of events?'

'I – this gentleman, Mr Selby, arrived wanting a photograph of his father, whom he gave me to understand was dead.'

'I said no such thing.' Mr Selby spoke for the first time. The magistrate glanced at him, and he said no more.

'Well – perhaps I assumed he was dead, as I am known in some places for taking photographs of spirits.'

'You have taken others?'

'Yes, a few. Mr Selby sat for me, and this spirit appeared on the plate. I showed it to him, and … and he seemed to accept it was an image of his father, and requested prints of the photograph, which I prepared for him that afternoon so he could collect them in the morning. I took no money for them,' she added, hoping that this would not harm Henriette. 'Perhaps – perhaps he left some money, but I did not find it.'

'Where is your husband?'

'I-I do not know, sir.'

'Well, when was the last you saw him?'

'Five – no, seven days ago.'

'Are you in the habit of losing your husband?'

'He went to London I believe, sir. But I do not know where he is, or when he will be back.'

'You can see spirits, but not your living husband? How odd. And your father?'

'He is dead.'

'Have you a brother, or an uncle, or another responsible male relative to look after you?'

'No, sir. But my friend – if I may send her a message …' In some confusion, she realised that if Mr Selby saw Henriette, he might recognise her as the person who took the money, and she might be arrested too. She did not finish her sentence.

'I am charging you with fraud,' said the magistrate, dipping his pen and beginning to write. 'If I were your husband, I would be inclined to have you admitted to the Dorsetshire County Asylum because of hysteria and delusions. But this gentleman wishes to press criminal charges. As you have no responsible male relative into whose custody I can release you, I am sending you to Dorchester, which is our closest prison where women can be accommodated. You will be tried at the next Assizes, which is in October, and if you are found guilty you will face hard labour. Do you understand?'

She did not understand. She stared at him until the constable took her by the arm and led her away.

*

The cell was coffin-narrow, made of shadow, with a vaulted ceiling, stone cold walls. The door, open, looked half a foot thick. Viola balked, wrinkling her nose at the scent of sweat and soured milk and the sound of weeping. 'I can't go in there,' she said.

'La-di-da,' said the officer holding fast to her arm. 'Ain't what you're used to?'

She had arrived at night, hardly able to make out the shape or size of the prison from the vast, unlit walls, but as soon as she was inside the echoing corridors she knew in her bones that this place was foreign. All metal and stone, carbolic and urine, no comfort anywhere. 'I need to write a message,' she had said to the hollow-faced warden in grey who admitted her, and the warden laughed. They took her locket and her wedding ring. When they searched her, they found the letter she had written to Henriette.

'That's private,' she said, her face burning, and the warden shrugged, glanced over the letter, and put it into the cardboard box with her jewellery.

'Will I get them back?' she asked.

'If you're found innocent.'

Passing door after door, she was taken up a flight of steps and along a narrow walkway on one side of a tiered gallery lined with cells, one on top of another. Someone was crying, a wordless cry of pain over and over with no stopping. It got louder with every step she took. An infinite loop. So many cages, and this one, it seemed, was hers.

She made out two pallets. A dark figure was curled on one. This was the source of the weeping.

'She does it all day and all night,' said the guard. 'Driving us all round the twist.' She raised her voice. 'Leave off, Sukey. Cryin' ain't going to bring your smothered baby back.'

The weeping continued without pause.

Viola edged into the room. There was a covered pot in the corner, and the two pallets, one with the weeping woman. A high window which let in the darkness. Nothing else.

'Will I be able to send a message to my friend tomorrow?' she asked the guard, who shrugged and said, 'If you've got money for paper and ink.'

Then the door closed and Viola was alone with a stranger in tears.

She went to the empty pallet and sat down. There was a blanket on it, which Viola wrapped around her shoulders. She was hungry and her limbs ached from the cart ride to Dorchester and the only thing she could think to do was to sleep or to pray, but she could not bear to close her eyes, though they burned, and praying seemed almost blasphemous in a place like this.

Where was Henriette? Viola tried to imagine Henriette here in this prison somewhere. She couldn't imagine it, didn't want it to be true. And yet she knew it would be easier if Henriette were beside her. She might be innocent of what she was charged, but she was guilty of this sin: to want a companion in Hell.

She could hear nothing aside from the crying. She peered across at the other woman, Sukey, whose baby had died. Had been smothered. Now that she was closer and her eyes were more accustomed to the darkness, she could see that her cellmate was no more than a girl. Her hair was blonde and lank; she sat with her knees curled up and her thin arms around them, rocking back and forwards with her sobs, almost as if she were still holding her baby. If Viola had her camera with her, the baby might appear on the plate in its mother's arms.

Earlier in the day – it felt like a million years ago now, but it was this same day – when she'd sat in her warm parlour and Henriette had left her, with a kiss, to fetch some more clothing, Viola had written the letter that now sat in that cold cardboard box. It was the first love letter she had ever written, and it had been interrupted by a knock on the door.

Henriette had brought her father back to her. That was what love could do. A prison did not change that.

Viola stood. She took the three steps to the girl's pallet and sat beside her hip to hip. She held out a side of the blanket. The girl, hardly more than a child, who had lost her baby, who may have killed her baby, stopped her sobbing and turned a moon-pale face to Viola. She hesitated for a moment, and then scuttled against Viola's side underneath the blanket. The girl said nothing but Viola very quietly began to whisper the words of the twenty-third psalm. The girl's head drooped against Viola's shoulder and she began to cry again, but more softly. Viola prayed and held this lost girl, and hoped that wherever Henriette was, Henriette her love, someone was offering her comfort too.

Chapter Forty-seven

They brought Jonah's wife to him in a bare, whitewashed prison room. When she saw him she cried out and ran towards him, arms outstretched, then checked herself before they touched.

'You're alive!' she said, and of all the greetings she could have given him, those simple words were the ones that made him feel the worst.

'I'm sorry,' he said to her. 'I'm so sorry for running away. I am a coward. I betrayed you. I came as soon as I heard.'

'Henriette told you?' She craned her neck as if she were looking for someone else in this empty room.

'No, I read in the paper and came straight from London. I should have gone to the house first, to get you some things.' He looked her over, head to foot. Her hair and dress were neat, as always, but the hem of her dress was dirty and her hair was dull; her face was pale, eyes large and with dark shadows. It looked as though she'd lost most of the weight she'd put on since coming to Dorset. 'At least a shawl and a hat. I'm sorry.'

'I don't need things,' she said. 'I am so glad to see you, Jonah.' And then she did take his hands in both of hers and squeezed them before she released them. 'Henriette said you were alive, but I doubted. I shouldn't have.'

'They let me post bail for you. I've come to take you home.' He gave her the packet with her jewellery in it, and she turned it over as if she didn't know what it was. Then she opened it, took a folded sheet of paper from the packet and held it tight in her hand.

'Has Henriette been arrested, too?'

'I don't know. It wasn't in the papers, if she was. Viola, are you about to faint?' He put an arm round her shoulders to keep her steady.

'No. I am well enough. Please take me home.'

She slept against his shoulder, like a child, for almost their entire journey. When they got back to their house she wandered from room to room, touching objects as if she had forgotten them and was learning them again.

He wanted to ask what she'd seen in gaol, what she had been through before that, while he was gone, but his own confession was so large that it seemed to block his throat. 'What can I do for you?' he asked her, following her as she picked up books and papers and ornaments, and set them back down again.

She turned her eyes on him as if she'd forgotten he was there. 'Will you pray for me, as I prayed for you?'

He swallowed and felt his face grow hot.

'I don't think I believe in God, Viola,' he said. 'I don't think that I can any more. Not after everything that's happened.'

She nodded. 'That's what's changed in you.'

'Only one of the things.'

'Will you tell me the other things that have changed, later? The other things you've lost?'

'Yes. I haven't been able to tell you before. But I will tell you.'

'Then you haven't lost faith in everything.' She passed him the photographic plate she'd been holding. It was a photograph of a man he didn't know, and behind him, Viola's father.

'Oh,' Jonah breathed. 'It's …'

'Yes.'

'How did—'

'I'll tell you everything, too. But first, I'd like to take a bath.'

While he waited for her, he washed and changed into his own clothes and gave orders for tea and toast and cakes to be put on a tray. Mrs Diggory said, 'We're glad to have you back, sir,' but she and Alice looked anywhere but at his eyes. He supposed this was normal enough, when the master of the house disappeared without so much as packing a bag, and the mistress was arrested in his absence. He could only imagine the gossip that was floating around.

'If, after all that's happened, you'd prefer to look for a new position,' he said, 'I will be happy to write you a reference. We wouldn't blame you. But Mrs Worth and I are grateful for your loyalty, and for keeping the house so well whilst we were gone.'

'Thank you, I'd just as soon stay, sir,' said Mrs Diggory, but she said it to his left shoulder.

'I found this outside the door, for Mrs Worth,' said Alice, and gave him a packet wrapped in a smudged sheet from the *Dorset Echo*. 'The children have been asking for her every day. They threw horse droppings at Constable Peebles after he arrested Mrs Worth, but I put a stop to that when I saw them.'

He put the packet on the tray and brought it upstairs to her room. When Viola came to answer his knock on the door she had a comb in her hand, her hair was wet, and she was wearing a white nightdress.

'Not here,' she said, when she saw him. 'I'll come down to the parlour in a minute, and we can talk there.'

He gave her the packet, though, and when she came downstairs a little while later she had put on a dressing gown and slippers, but her hair was loose and drying all around her shoulders, and she wore around her neck a sort of necklace made from twisted wire, wrapped around smooth pebbles and shells, with bits of feather woven through.

'From Nan,' she said, and she curled into an armchair, looking for all the world like a mermaid who had grown legs.

'Do you feel better?' he asked her, pouring her tea and buttering her toast, as she had used to do for him.

'Yes. I've made up a bundle of things to be taken to the prison – a comb, and underthings, and handkerchiefs, and I'd like to put in some sweets if Mrs Diggory has them. My cellmate, Sukey, killed her baby because she could not feed it, and I would like her to have some small comfort.'

He winced. And thought of himself in London in that upstairs room, a self-inflicted prison, while his wife was in a real one.

'You should not have been taken to gaol,' he said, taking his chair across from hers. 'I should have been home to protect you. It's my fault.'

She shook her head. 'I lied to Mr Selby. I said that it was his father in the photograph – or I implied that it was – when it was mine. But I didn't put that in my statement. So if I'm punished, it's what I deserve.'

'You don't deserve to be punished. I do, for what I've done.'

'I'm not angry with you for running away. I only wish I understood why, that's all.'

'No. I betrayed you before that. When I was in India. And since, by not telling you.' He took a fortifying breath. 'I've been visiting Mrs Blackthorne to speak with a spirit.'

'Henriette? She didn't tell me.'

'I asked her not to. But I shouldn't have kept it from you.'

'Whom did you speak with?'

'Someone ... someone I loved.' He nudged her plate closer to her. 'Please, eat something. You must be famished.'

He'd been hoping for a moment of distraction by offering her the food, but she neither ate nor drank. 'You loved someone who died?' she asked gently. He had dreaded seeing pain on her face, or even anger ... but all he saw there was pity, and kindness. He swallowed hard.

'Yes. I loved ... I loved a person called Pavan. I tried not to. I didn't even know I was falling in love until I had done it. And then it was too late. And Pavan was gone.'

'Oh, Jonah.' She rose from her chair and knelt at his feet, taking his hand. 'Tell me everything.'

And so, with his wife kneeling before him as if she were saying the prayers he could no longer bear to utter, he told the story he had told no one before. From the moment he met Pavan, until the day that death came to Delhi.

A letter from Charles Dickens to Baroness Angela Georgina Burdett-Coutts, on blue paper, written in blue ink with a goose-quill pen. Held in the collection of the Morgan Library, New York.

... I wish I were the Commander in Chief in India. The first thing I would do to strike that Oriental race with amazement (not in the least regarding them as if they lived in the Strand, London, or at Camden Town), should be to proclaim to them in their language, that I considered my Holding that appointment by the leave of God, to mean that I should do my utmost to exterminate the Race upon whom the stain of the late cruelties rested; and that I begged them to do me the favour to observe that I was there for that purpose and no other, and was now proceeding, with all convenient dispatch and merciful swiftness of execution, to blot it out of mankind and raze it off the face of the earth.

Chapter Forty-eight

Eighteen months earlier...

10 May, 1857
Delhi

Mr Toyne's sermon was about family and duty and faithfulness to one's country. Jonah sat beside Hamilton in St James's church in Delhi and his thoughts were not about God but about two women in two different countries.

He owed a duty to them both. He loved them both, although in different ways.

If he asked Mr Toyne, the vicar's advice would be clear: go back to England and marry the Christian woman he had promised to wed. Jonah had made a promise which he was honour-bound to keep. A Hindu and a Christian could never be married, unless the Hindu converted to Christianity.

The vicar would be wrong. The religions they had been born into were not what separated them. It was the oaths that they had made to others. Pavan had vowed never to marry. But Jonah knew that, along with his promise to Viola, he had also made a promise, though an unspoken one, to Pavan. A kiss – or at least such kisses as he and Pavan had shared – was a promise; an oath as unbreakable as an engagement.

The pew was hot. The air in the church barely stirred, despite the fans the ladies fluttered in front of their sweating faces.

Which of his oaths was the most sacred? Which of Pavan's?

'We must strive to do what is right, even when it is difficult,' said Mr Toyne from his pulpit. 'Here in this country we see examples of loyalty among the natives. Who among us has not known a loyal family retainer? A servant who will forsake his own family for our sake? And yet we see faithlessness as well. Even today, in Meerut, judgement is being passed upon the members of the Third Bengal Light Cavalry who refused to bear arms for their officers. We Christians must show ourselves to the natives as shining beacons of true faith. Through the example of our lord Jesus Christ we know what it is to be steadfast and true. Through His passion we may suffer any torment, knowing that His death has provided us with life everlasting.'

Why was a soldier's death pointless, Jonah thought, *but a Christian's a shining light of faithfulness? Wasn't any death a tragedy?*

How could duty be a higher calling than life itself?

The cross behind Mr Toyne stood for suffering and redemption. It stood for duty and faith. It did not stand for joy.

Pavan had taken him by the hand and they had lain down together on the cool floor of the temple. He had kissed her skin and felt her heart beating, hard and fast, under his palm. She had held him and whispered into his ear. He had watched her silhouette, moving above him, against the stars.

Steadfast and true. He knew what they had done was wrong, but he could not feel it was wrong. His heart had been full to bursting with happiness. It still was, when he thought of it.

She might be carrying his child. They may have started a new life together. That was another oath they had both taken.

'Worth?'

With a start, he realised that the service was over and everyone had stood up to leave.

'Good service,' said Hamilton at the door of the church, gazing down the steps at where the grooms hurried to get the carriages ready for the sahibs and their mems. 'The sooner we convert these natives to Christianity the better for all of us. They'll be assured of their place in heaven and we'll be assured that they won't murder us all in our sleep.' He tapped his hat more firmly onto his sweaty head and laughed.

The papers piled up around Jonah's feet. He knew he could not write this letter to Viola. He knew this was not a suitable subject for a letter. He had to tell her in person, face to face. He would have to travel back to England. And yet writing it made it more real.

I am so very sorry, Viola. I care for you a great deal, and you will always be my sister, but I cannot marry you. I promised before I understood what love is.

But what was love? If he married Viola he understood what his life would be. What kind of life would he have with Pavan? Even if she were willing to forswear herself, how could they marry? As a wife, she could not study at the college. As a man, she could not marry Jonah. Living with her, unmarried, would be disrespectful to her. She would be labelled a concubine, or if she remained dressed as a man, it would be assumed that she was his servant. They could never be social equals in either of their cultures; they would be violating the rules of both of their religions.

Jonah wasn't sure of what he believed, but he couldn't subject her to scorn. He couldn't live with her unless she were his partner in all things.

But if this was impossible, how could he live without her?

She had said that last night would be the last time they would meet. But that was before they had touched. She had left him with no words, only a final soft kiss.

The thought that she might not want to meet again, that last night might have been the only time they could see each other for what they truly were, filled Jonah with panic.

He crumpled up his letter to Viola and dropped it on the floor with the others, took a fresh piece of paper and wrote quickly on it.

P – I have not been able to stop thinking about the conversation we shared last night and cannot bear to think this might have been the last time we will talk together. I know there are barriers and difficulties but between us we must be able to solve them. For myself, I care nothing about the rest of the world; the topic we have discussed is the most precious of my life and I would be willing to sacrifice a great deal to learn more, here in India, or in England, or in another country. I cannot imagine abandoning it. Please meet me tomorrow night, or the night after. I will wait. – JW

He read it over to ensure that it would not betray her secret if it were intercepted or read by another person. Then he folded and sealed it and went through the sleeping house to find someone to carry it.

Several of the servants sat on the ground in the courtyard, sharing a simple meal of chapattis and lentils. It was Ramadan, and they were not allowed to eat during daylight hours. They sat in a tight circle, talking in low voices to each other; when Jonah drew closer, he realised there were several men he didn't recognise as part of the household. Samir, one of the house servants, stood as Jonah approached. 'You need something, sahib?'

'Yes please, Samir. I wondered if you knew where Rajesh and Pavan Sharma lived?'

'I do,' said a boy, one of the grooms. He scrambled to his feet and held out his hand for the letter, and for the coin which Jonah added to it.

'Thank you. It is for Pavan Sharma. Please give it into his hands. If there is an answer, please bring it to me immediately.'

The boy scurried off.

'I'm sorry to interrupt your meal,' said Jonah. The men remained silent as he returned inside.

*

First, the gongs from the Jama Masjid to rouse the faithful before sunrise. The darkness fading, slowly, into pink pre-dawn light. Jonah stood by the window watching for a reply to his letter. He heard the household stirring, always early to be up in the coolest part of the day. The distant bells from the shrines along the river as the Hindus made their morning prayers. Then the cannon from the fort to mark the hour of sunrise and fasting for the Muslims.

Pavan would write back to him, or if not, she would meet him. He kept telling himself this would happen. They would meet and together, they would decide what they would do, whether she would stay and wait for him or if she would come to England while he returned to settle his business there, to explain to Viola. He had to believe that she would not stay away. She would not tell him they could never meet again.

There was a scent of burning. He peered out of the window. A group of natives ran down the street beyond the garden wall. Some of them were holding sacks, some had sticks. Downstairs, he heard raised voices talking quickly, though he could not catch the words. The boy who had taken his letter rounded the corner at a sprint and came running full pelt through the gate to the house.

Jonah's heart leapt. He hurried downstairs and, as he did, he heard a series of pops, like a knot of wood exploding in a fire. Mr and Mrs Hamilton were near the front door with the steward, talking rapidly; Mrs Hamilton held the baby in her arms and the ayah stood beside her with her arms around Emilia and the boy. The scent of burning was stronger now, and he heard the pops again, closer. Outside, people were shouting.

'Worth,' said Hamilton as soon as he reached the bottom of the stairs. 'I was just coming to find you.'

'What's happening?' Jonah looked for the boy but he was nowhere to be seen.

'A rabble of sepoys have come into the city from Meerut and are killing every Christian they see and looting their houses.' Hamilton's tanned face was chalk white. 'It'll pass, the army will subdue them, but we'd best lay low until it all blows over. The servants will protect us. Go, Patience. I'll be five minutes. Worth, come with me.' Mrs Hamilton instantly hurried off, taking Emilia's hand. Toby clung to his ayah's skirts, crying, as they followed.

'I don't understand,' said Jonah.

'We haven't a moment to spare,' Hamilton said. He was walking rapidly to his library, with Jonah on his heels. 'Can you fire a gun?'

'What? No. That is to say – I went hunting once, but—'

'No matter.' He bent under his desk to open a case and took out two rifles and a pistol. 'You take the pistol. It's loaded.'

Jonah held it gingerly, as if it were about to explode merely from being touched. 'Surely things aren't that bad?'

'Adil says that he saw Dr Jacobs shot in the street by a gang of soldiers and everything stolen from his body, even his clothes.' Hamilton was stuffing ammunition into his pockets. 'Quickly, now. Let's go. I don't want Patience to be frightened any more than she already is.'

They went out of the house to the front gate. The steward, Adil, was standing beside it, feet planted as if he were daring an entire army to shift him. Hamilton handed him one of the rifles. The street outside was empty – eerily empty, as it never was – but smoke billowed from somewhere close by and Jonah heard yelling and what he knew now to be shots. He looked around and saw the boy who'd taken his letter, standing barefoot in the shade of a tree just inside the gate. Jonah went to him.

'Did you see Pavan Sharma?' he asked him urgently. 'Was he well? Was he in danger?'

'I saw him.'

'Worth, come with me! They're killing Christians, not Hindus!'

'They are killing everyone,' said the boy quietly, his head down, looking at his bare feet in the dust. 'They are looting the bazaars and breaking down the doors of the Jain moneylenders. They are killing whomever they like.'

'Worth!' called Hamilton. He was already hastening around the house. 'The devils are coming! Come with me!'

'I will join you,' he called back, 'but I need to do something first.'

'Quickly!'

The sound of hoofbeats and thundering footsteps, a cry from a crowd. Not far away, a woman's scream. Jonah hesitated, glancing at Adil and the tall metal gates.

'Let me through,' he told Adil.

'But sahib, it is too dangerous.'

'Let me through!' He tugged at the latch, rattling the metal. Adil, muttering under his breath, unlocked it with the keys at his waist and Jonah ran through, holding the pistol pressed to his side.

He didn't dare take the main road; he ducked into the maze of alleys and pathways between buildings, heading in the general direction of the Sharmas' house. Every door was closed. The sun had risen and the heat beat down on him; Jonah's hand was slick on the gun. Smoke rolled heavy in the air. He ran down a narrow passage slippery with filth, crumbling walls looming windowless on either side. He heard a shout ahead, close, and at the end of the alley glimpsed white clothes and the gleam of metal.

His foot caught on a stone and he tripped, landing hard on his hands and knees. The pistol skittered out of his hand. He groped for it, found it again, his breath loud in his ears.

He crept to the end of the passageway to the wider street. It was deserted, now; no one moved. A hand-drawn cart lay overturned in the road, its contents spilled out over the dirt.

Jonah caught a glimpse of white out of the corner of his eye and swung the gun around to point at his enemy.

'Jonah!'

There in front of him, intact and safe, dressed neatly as always: Pavan. He staggered towards her.

'You're alive,' he gasped.

'Why are you here? Why haven't you fled?'

'I was looking for you.' He clasped her arm with his free hand and she gripped his wrist.

'I came to find you,' she said. 'You should be gone. Far away, out of Delhi. You are in terrible danger. Where are the Hamiltons?'

'They're hiding in the house. The gate is guarded.'

'Your house is closer than mine. We must go there immediately. They are coming this—' She stilled and listened, eyes wide. Without a single word she pushed Jonah backwards into the alley he had just come from. She came after him, pulling at his jacket with frantic hands.

'You must take this off,' she said to him, 'all this black, you will be spotted in an instant.' She pushed his jacket off his shoulders and Jonah fumbled with his trousers, still holding the pistol in one hand. His trouser legs caught on his boots so he kicked them off, tore off his socks, and wore only his white shirt and white knee-length drawers. Pavan pulled off his collar and discarded it on the ground, grabbed handfuls of red dust and rubbed them on his face, his neck. 'You can't pass, you can't pass,' she muttered. 'We must be quick. Quickly. It is quiet. Quickly, go now.'

She tugged on his hand and they threaded through the alley, footsteps quick, back the way Jonah had come.

'If I lose you,' she said, her voice low and urgent, 'if we are separated, go north. Find where the English have gone, get out of the city.'

'I won't leave you.'

'I will find you.'

The smoke was billowing around them now. It provided some cover but it made Jonah's eyes water and Pavan cough. She pulled a fold of her kameez up over her mouth and nose and Jonah did the same with his shirt. More shots rang out around them and shouts that Jonah could understand only by their tones of hatred and fear. She pulled him down behind an abandoned ox cart as a crowd thundered past them in the opposite direction. Crouched near the ground, Jonah could see the feet and calves of the people passing. Some were soldiers, in boots; others wore sandals or slippers or were barefoot.

'It isn't only the army,' he whispered to Pavan.

'Some want freedom. Some want money.' She tugged at his sleeve. 'We must go now, before another gang comes.'

The street was deserted. They ran towards the Hamiltons' gate. 'Adil has a gun,' Jonah panted, 'we must make sure he recognises us so he won't shoot.'

But when they reached the gate, Adil wasn't there. No one was there. The gate hung open.

Silently, they entered. Everything appeared as usual – the yard was well-brushed and neat, reed blinds covered the windows to keep out the heat of the day – except that the property was deserted and there was no sound, not even a bird.

Lying in the centre of the path to the front door was Emilia's doll.

Jonah stooped and picked it up. Its dress was hardly soiled but its porcelain head had been cracked in two.

Cold flooded him and Pavan touched his elbow.

The front door was open; they went through into the courtyard. One of the dining-room chairs lay shattered on the ground as if it had been tossed from a balcony. Crockery crunched under Pavan's feet. In the centre lay a jumble of possessions, hardly recognisable out of context. Cooking pots, blankets, clothes, candles, broken bits of furniture. A small fire smouldered in the corner of the courtyard. Jonah could detect the scent of burning meat. Poking out of the ashes was something that looked like Mrs Hamilton's rose-patterned shawl. Heedless of his bare feet and broken crockery, Jonah strode around the courtyard towards the staircase and up to the bedrooms. All the doors were unlocked, most of them open, and all of the rooms were empty. In the library, books carpeted the floor.

'They must have escaped,' he said to Pavan, who was close beside him. 'They must have run, and then the house was ransacked.'

'We should check the back,' she said. 'The temple. They might have hidden there.'

He didn't want to. But he nodded, and they went together around the haveli.

The raiders had been here, too. He could hardly believe they had caused so much destruction in such a short time: clothes and blankets were strewn over the grass, thrown from windows. Shattered plant pots. His father's old ledger lay broken-backed on the ground like a felled bird. He skirted around it, heading for the temple, and stopped short.

What he had taken for a bundle of clothes lying on the ground, was not.

Hamilton had been shot at close range. There was a charred hole in his chest and another in his forehead. Blood soaked into the earth below him. His eyes were open and several flies had settled there.

Jonah staggered backwards. Pavan was close behind him.

'His gun is gone,' said Jonah. 'He – who shot him? Those men we saw – or was it Adil? He was supposed to guard ...'

'One cannot stand for long against many,' said Pavan. 'Mrs Hamilton and the children. We must make sure they are safe.'

Hamilton's fourth and fifth fingers were gone. His wedding ring had been cut off.

'Jonah,' said Pavan. 'We haven't much time. We must find the rest of the family and get away.'

'Yes,' said Jonah, but he didn't look away from Hamilton's hand. 'Jonah!'

He tore his gaze away and looked at Pavan instead. Her

beautiful face, hair tucked away under her white turban, her eyes keen and quick and beloved.

'Yes,' he said. He thought of the shawl smouldering in the corner of the courtyard and tried to remember if Patience Hamilton had been wearing it this morning. He did not want to go to that fire, with its smell of burning meat, and investigate.

Instead he strode to the tree-roofed temple. The inside was shadow. Were the family huddled in the dark, afraid to move, listening for Hamilton to come back to them?

Or was that where the person or people who killed Hamilton had gone? Had they killed everyone and were now waiting in the darkness for more?

He paused in the doorway and listened. There was no sound.

He handed the pistol to Pavan. 'Stay outside,' he whispered. 'Take this.'

'No. I will come with you.' She tried to give the pistol back to him.

'It's too dangerous. They could have heard us. They could be waiting inside.'

'I will not make the choice to leave you.'

'I'll go first, then.'

She nodded. 'Patience?' he called through the doorway into the silence. His words fell dead.

Pavan's eyes flicked from him to the house. He knew what she was thinking: would another gang come while they were in the temple? She seemed to make a decision and raised the gun, held it in both small hands, pointing it past him into the temple.

He felt a rush of fierce tenderness for her, this woman braver than any man he had known, and he stepped inside.

It was very quiet. Cool and dark. As always, it took a moment for his eyes to adjust. 'Patience?' he said again and then he saw it.

The baby lay face down in the middle of the floor in front of the altar. Lay unmoving in his white gown, bonnet half off his head and trailing strings.

Jonah cried out and fell to his knees to touch the child, to shake it and try to wake it, but the little arm was limp in his hand. Still warm, as he had been in his mother's arms. His head lolled unnaturally to the side.

A hurried noise behind him and he heard Pavan's sharp intake of breath. He turned his head to see her standing in the doorway, pistol in her hand, face stricken with shock and horror and grief. A white-clad figure, slim and stark with the daylight behind her.

Then it all ended.

A flash of light, blinding; an explosion bigger than the world, a physical blow to his ears that toppled Jonah onto his back and away from the tiny corpse on the floor. He felt no pain, but for a moment he thought he had been killed.

Then his vision cleared and he saw Emilia Hamilton holding a rifle nearly as tall as herself.

'They're dead,' the girl said. Her nightgown was torn and covered in blood. 'Mama, Toby, the baby. Papa left us his gun and went up to stop them and we hid but they came and killed us all.'

'Emilia,' Jonah said. He got to his feet. His ears rang.

'They had swords. They stabbed Toby first and then they took the baby and threw him. They were laughing. Mama was ... and then she ... and I ...'

The girl's face was dead white but she was not crying. She was standing as tall as she could, holding the rifle.

'They were laughing and one hit me so I fell on the floor and then Mama fell on top of me and I lay there. Mama was dead. And they left, and I lay there and then I heard you and saw that one and killed him. I've killed him. Haven't I?'

She raised the gun and pointed it behind Jonah.

His heart stopped. His lungs ceased. His eyes burned and did not want to see.

Jonah turned around and Pavan was lying on the floor, next to the baby. A slender figure, dressed in white. Her eyes were closed.

Red blood blossomed on the white clothing she wore. More and more of it, everywhere.

He could not scream. He could not say her name. He fell to his hands and knees and crawled to her. She did not move.

'He was going to kill you,' said Emilia, quite calmly, 'and then he was going to kill me. So I shot him like Daddy... like Daddy...'

He could not breathe. He touched Pavan's shoulders, her cheek, the lock of hair that had escaped her turban when she fell. He put his hand on her chest, on the blood, red on white. He felt nothing. No life in her or in him. This was the end, their grave, their parting, this place where they had met.

Standing next to an altar to lovers, where her mother and brother lay dead behind her, Emilia began to cry.

The sound made him move. A crying child, alive. Jonah took his hand from Pavan's body. He picked up the pistol that she had dropped, and he stood.

'We need to leave,' he told her. 'I need to take you out of the city.'

He held out his hand, covered in Pavan's blood. The little girl, still clutching the rifle, took it.

Chapter Forty-nine

September, 1858
Fortuneswell

By the time Jonah had finished his story, Viola was holding both his hands in hers. She raised one, then the other, to her lips and kissed them, tears in her eyes.

'Oh,' she said. 'Oh Jonah, I am so very sorry.'

He had been staring straight ahead as he told his story, but at this he looked at her.

'You don't hate me?' he asked.

'You found love,' she said. 'How can I hate you for that?'

'But I'm your husband.'

'You married me, but you belonged to Pavan first. You are Pavan's husband. You are my brother. You've always been my brother.' She kissed Jonah's hand again. 'I only wish I'd known what had happened.'

'I thought – I didn't want to hurt you.'

Viola shook her head. She felt no pain, not in the way Jonah clearly expected. She didn't feel betrayed – how could she be betrayed if Jonah was never hers in the first place? The only pain she felt was for Jonah and for Pavan, and for Emilia, too, losing her whole family.

For herself, she felt only relief. Jonah's pain wasn't her fault. The failure of her marriage wasn't her fault. And her love for Henriette wasn't a betrayal of Jonah.

'Did Flora contact Pavan for you?'

'Yes. She – I spoke with Pavan's spirit.'

'Was it a comfort to you?'

'Not a comfort, no. It was more a – a necessity.'

'Is that why you asked me to take your photo?'

'Yes. But she didn't appear.'

She leaned her cheek on the back of Jonah's hand. 'I don't know where Henriette is. I asked Alice and she said that she was here, when the policeman came, but that she left right away. I don't know if she's been arrested too. I didn't take any money from Mr Selby – she must have taken money from him, for the photographs. I don't understand it.'

'She . . .'

'Did you pay her? When you saw her in secret?'

'I gave her money.'

'Oh, poor Henriette.' She thought of what Henriette had told her, about having been a servant and educating herself secretly, modelling herself after this woman whom she loved. How keenly she must have felt the sting of being a gentlewoman now, and walking among gentlemen and gentlewomen, and yet still furtively asking for coins in exchange for her talent. Just as she must have been tempted to tell Viola about what she knew about Jonah, and yet her honour kept her from betraying another's secret. 'She is so proud. I would have given her money, if I'd known.'

'She told me, again and again, to confide in my wife. I was too afraid, but she was right.'

'I love her,' Viola burst out. 'I love Henriette.'

She had never said this aloud, never to Henriette herself. She watched Jonah's face as she spoke and she saw nothing – no comprehension, no betrayal. Just as Henriette had said: love between two women was so invisible that in normal everyday words, it did not exist.

It only existed in her heart. And now she did not know where Henriette was.

'I know,' said Jonah. 'She's your friend, and she has been here with you while I abandoned you. I won't do it again, Viola.'

'You don't understand. I love her as a woman loves a man. As a wife loves a husband. In the way you and I have never been able to love each other. Do you understand?'

'You love ...'

Watching his face so closely, this face that she had known for so long but which had been in some way guarded from her since their wedding day, she could see the exact moment when he fully understood.

'You're in love with her? You've—' His eyes narrowed in bafflement and anger. 'Since when?'

'The day you left.'

'And did you – this whole time were the two of you planning to—'

'No. It just happened. I didn't even know it was possible for women to love each other. But she ... showed me.'

Jonah stood and walked to the window. She stayed on her knees, watching him.

'You're my wife,' he said, not looking at her.

'Jonah,' she said gently, 'we both know that I was never truly your wife.'

'I don't know what any of this means.'

'It means that we haven't failed each other.'

He bowed his head. She waited as he struggled.

When he turned around, she went to him. He held out his hand and she clasped it. Almost the same way they'd stood at the altar to marry.

'I'm glad that you found someone to love,' he said.

'Will you find her?' she asked him. 'She must know I was arrested, and yet there's no message from her. Will you take a message to her lodgings for me? I'm so afraid that she's in prison somewhere, alone.'

'Yes,' he said. 'I'll find her.'

Chapter Fifty

But Henriette was not at her lodgings. Her belongings had all been packed up and taken away. The servant did not know why she had left. Jonah was frostily informed, when he asked an incandescent Mrs Newham, that Mrs Blackthorne had absconded without saying goodbye, without a single thank you, without leaving a forwarding address. When he enquired with the police, they said she had not been arrested, and was not being sought.

She had gone, disappeared as suddenly and completely as if she had been a ghost.

In the days that followed, Jonah looked after Viola. They both knew that she had to regain her strength for her trial and whatever might come afterwards. She was weak, not only physically but with worry about where Henriette had gone. He coaxed her to eat, made nests for her in the sitting room in front of the fire, read her Mrs Gaskell. Sometimes he merely sat with her as she cried, and he felt tears in his own eyes, remembering how she had never cried as a girl. Whenever there was a knock on the door, she would start up out of her chair, hoping that it was Henriette; but it was most often Nan, who came cheekily to the front door and sat with them, nicking the cakes that Mrs Diggory made and chattering endlessly about her brothers and sisters. She went away every time with a large parcel of food, a very small price to pay for the faint smile she brought to Viola's face.

The police had been through their house, and most especially the studio. While Viola took her frequent naps, he quietly set everything right, or as right as he could make it, despite the missing photographs, the spoiled equipment, the broken plates.

Both of them stayed, as far as possible, in the house. Maybe a braver man than he would walk the streets with his head held high, proclaim his wife's innocence to the world. But Jonah felt that he had spent far too much of his marriage to Viola running away. His place, in this strange interim period between her arrest and her trial, was by Viola's side.

For the first time since they'd been married, and for ironic reasons, he and Viola were entirely in harmony, though they were not happy. Both of them loved someone else, who was gone.

Love was love, and it was not in your control. He had fallen in love with someone whom he first understood as a man, and his wife had fallen in love with a woman. They each loved a person, a soul, and the body that was attached to that soul. There was nothing wrong with him. There was nothing wrong with Viola.

Both of them had loved and they had lost.

They did not talk about the future.

The future came to find them with a knock on the door two days after they came home. Viola started up, and Jonah said hurriedly, wanting to protect her from disappointment or the idly curious, 'I'll answer it. It's probably Nan.'

It was not Henriette or Nan. It was Mr Field, holding his battered hat in his hands, twisting the brim.

'Ah, Worth,' he said, more to his shoes than to Jonah. 'I wondered if I could have a word.'

'Yes?' He didn't step back to let Field into the house, remembering how he had humiliated Jonah in the street.

'I heard about what happened with your wife, of course. Everyone's talking about it. She's to be tried at the next Assizes, yes?'

'Yes?' he said again, with a growing dismay that this man had not only cut off all association with him, but that now he came to gloat about how he had been right all along.

'Well, I don't know if you – if you have a family barrister, as you are not from these parts. But I was thinking, that although I am mostly in retirement from the bar now, as you know, to follow my scientific and paleontological pursuits, and spend more time with my family, that as your neighbour, and friend of course, though that has somewhat fallen by the wayside of late, you might consider allowing me to represent your wife.'

'You ... want to represent Viola in court?'

'Just so, yes.'

'But you don't believe in spirits, and my wife is accused of committing fraud by taking spirit photographs. You must believe she is guilty. Why would you want to represent her?'

'Well. That is.' He twisted his hat harder. 'According to the law, every person is entitled to justice. These are large questions to debate in court, about religion and science and life after death, and I would not want them to be decided by prejudice and bias, rather than by rationality. Besides,' he added, nearly ripping his hat in half, 'it may be advantageous to Mrs Worth to have counsel who is a sceptic, as I can anticipate the arguments against her better than someone who unquestioningly believes.'

'I will have to speak with my wife about it,' said Jonah. 'But I thank you.'

He held out his hand and Field took it without hesitation.

'You are my neighbour, and my wife feels in her heart that Mrs Worth is a fine person,' said Field. 'The feelings of women are often the best indication of what is correct to do.'

'The feelings of women,' Jonah said, gently, 'are most often based on as much logic and reason as the arguments of men.'

'Perhaps. Perhaps. All I know is what I have felt strongly myself. If there is no God, then we all have a responsibility to look out for each other.'

Chapter Fifty-one

October, 1858
Dorchester

In the small hours of the morning Viola woke in her prison cell. Dampness under her cheek, the blanket unbearably hot and itchy. She threw it back but instead of cold, dank prison air, she was hot. So hot.

She sat up, opening her eyes and seeing nothing but darkness and a rosy glow through a crack in the wall. The prison was on fire.

She reached for Sukey, who slept beside her, and shook her shoulder. 'Wake up,' she croaked, unable to scream as she wanted. 'Wake up, we have to escape.'

'Viola?' Sukey sat up. Her form, poorly lit by the rosy light, was odd: too thick, with hair standing up in wild curls. 'What's the matter?' Her voice was wrong too.

'Jonah?' Viola said. 'Why are you here? The prison is on fire, we have to leave.' She pushed her legs out of the bed, arms out to feel her way across the dark cell, and stumbled.

Arms caught her. 'Oh, goodness, Viola, you're burning up.'

'It's on fire! Can't you see the flames? We need to escape, we need to call the warden, we'll burn alive.' She tried to push away from Jonah but he held her fast.

'It isn't fire,' he said to her. 'It's the sunrise through the curtains. You're hot because you're ill.' He gently made her sit on the bed and pulled open a pair of curtains. The light outside was pink and yellow.

He was wearing his nightshirt, and this was what made her

realise that they were not in the prison, because a man in a nightshirt would not be allowed in a cell for women. She looked around the room and remembered: this was the King's Arms in Dorchester. They had come down the afternoon before so that they would not have to travel on the day of her trial.

He poured her a glass of water from the jug and sat beside her on the bed. 'You had a dream.'

'My trial is today,' she said, unable to take a sip. Her neck felt hot and swollen, and it was hard to swallow. 'Maybe it's not a dream. Maybe it's my future. In a few hours I might be in prison again.'

He touched her face lightly. 'You're burning up. We will have to ask for a delay till the next Assizes. I'll go find Field.'

'No,' she said, grasping his wrist. 'No, I can't take any more waiting. One way or the other, I need to know today.'

But she knew. The dream had told her. She was going to be convicted.

She was shivering when she was taken from Jonah and led to the dock. She wrapped her shawl around herself, tight as an embrace, and stood there, looking out over the courtroom.

Hers was not the only or the first case to be heard today. People packed the room: sitting on benches, leaning on walls, crowded up together. They passed snacks back and forth and whispered and pointed and when their eyes fell on her, every eye in the room, of people whom she knew and strangers, she felt a wave of heat but she didn't drop her shawl.

It's like being noticed by God, she thought, and she stood as straight as she could, though her legs were weak and her ears roared and her head throbbed and burned.

Jonah was there, near the front, and there was Mr Field in a wig and gown. But everyone else was hard to make out; there was a veil over her vision, possibly the fever, possibly the fact of being in the dock. She wished for a camera so she could take a photograph and understand who was here. A plate would not move so, and shift and change every moment.

But she knew who was not here: Henriette. She would be able to see Henriette through fever and crowds. She would be able to sense her through walls. Their spirits would call to each other, but she did not feel Henriette, and that was why she could stand here so still in the dock without moving, without thinking, only able to hear some of the words that were said as if from a great distance.

'Representations were made to me which were not fulfilled as promised. Mrs Worth promised to give me a photograph of a relative or of someone deceased near in sympathy to me. This she failed to do. And I therefore consider that this was a fraud practised on me.'

That was Mr Selby. He stood near the front. His eyes bulged in his head. Mr Field, in his fluffy regimented wig, said something and Mr Selby frowned and said, 'No. I may have implied that my father was deceased but I did not state it, sir. These fraudsters will go to any lengths to deceive their victims, who are people in mourning and among the most vulnerable. I am well versed in dealing with spirit mediums and I understand that they seize upon facts like vultures upon carrion, and make full use of them.'

Vultures upon carrion.

She hadn't been able to eat today, nor yesterday either, but that image made her bow her head and swallow hard, battling sickness. When she looked up again, a different person was speaking, a person in a dark frock-coat and a dove-grey waistcoat. He was speaking about double exposures, faults on the plate, extra plates in the camera, figures made with muslin and paper, accomplices who enter a room and pose secretly behind a subject.

'And in your opinion, could these photographs have been produced through these methods?'

'A double exposure, or an altered plate, or an extra subject, could all produce the effect in these photographs.'

That was what she had thought had happened, with that first

photograph of Mary Mackey. She wanted to explain to this room of people how she hadn't believed it at first either, not until Henriette came and showed her what was possible. But she wasn't allowed to speak. Mr Field would read out her statement when the time came, and those were the only words of hers that were permitted to be heard in this room. Meanwhile, the words of others went on and on.

'Is this the photograph that Mrs Worth took for you?'

Mrs Smy, round and befeathered, stood at the front of the courtroom. The prosecutor was showing her a photographic print. Viola could not see it, but she knew what it was, of course.

'Yes, that's a print of it.'

'And she claims that this photograph includes the spirit of your deceased husband?'

'She don't claim it, he *is* there. Right there, in the back. There's his corpse, sitting in the chair, and his spirit off to the side there, standing next to cousin Ethel.'

'There are quite a few people in this photograph. How are you certain that one figure is a spirit?'

'Because it looks just like him.'

'Did Mrs Worth put anything in the frame of the photograph before she took it?'

'No, sir, Mrs Worth was standing behind the camera.'

'Did she have an assistant, or an accomplice?'

'Mrs Blackthorne was there to help the spirits arrive.'

Viola had let her attention wander to the prosecutor's white wig, but at Henriette's name, she looked at the witness, Mrs Smy.

Mr Smy, her husband, was standing beside her. He looked just as he had in his photograph except that instead of monochrome, he was in colour. He was smiling and the wall of the courtroom was faintly visible through him.

'Did you see the plate being prepared or developed?' asked the prosecutor.

'No, she went to another room to do that,' said Mrs Smy,

apparently unaware of the ghost standing beside her. No one else seemed to see him except for Viola.

She touched her burning forehead, and screwed up her eyes. Mr Smy was still there.

'How much did you pay for the photograph?'

'Three pound. And worth every penny.'

That wasn't right. She had refused Mrs Smy's money. But she couldn't speak.

'How would you feel if you discovered the photo had been faked?'

'Well, I would be devastated. But it's not faked. Anyone can see that's my Christopher standing there.'

'We've had an expert photographer here to testify that this effect could have been achieved with a double exposure, or muslin.'

'I've been married for forty years and you think I can't tell the difference between my husband and a muslin?'

The spectators laughed. So did Mr Smy.

Viola had the sensation of floating. The judge said something, and the spectators fell silent, but Viola's attention was no longer on who was speaking or what was being said. Instead she gazed around the room and saw that the number of people had doubled, at least. In between the spectators, witnesses, judge and jury, stood and sat a host of others who had not been there before. Their clothes were old-fashioned or modern, knee breeches and crinolines; one or two were wrapped in shrouds. Silent babies nestled on mothers' laps and small, grave children crowded their parents' legs.

So much death and loss and love.

A voice intoned a familiar rhythm, well-known words, the first chapter of Samuel, spoken by her lawyer the unbeliever:

And the woman said unto him, Behold, though knowest what Saul hath done, how he hath cut off those that have familiar spirits, and the wizards, out of the land: wherefore then layest

> *thou a snare for my life, to cause me to die? And Saul sware*
> *to her by the Lord, saying As the Lord liveth, there shall be no*
> *punishment happen to thee for this thing.'*

She wiped her eyes and for the first time she looked beside her
in the dock, and her father stood there. He smiled at her. He had
always liked the books of Samuel.

'I will go to prison, Papa,' she whispered to him. 'I can bear it
if you're with me.'

And her father, silent and loving, shook his head. He raised a
hand and pointed to the back of the room, to where Henriette
Blackthorne stood surrounded by ghosts.

Chapter Fifty-two

Jonah sat between a plump woman in dusty black, a member of a Spiritualist society who twisted a worn pamphlet between her fingers, and a lean, sandy-haired gentleman with frayed cuffs and bushy sideburns who muttered 'Nonsense!' under his breath every time the word 'spirit' or 'ghost' was mentioned.

Slender and pale, Viola stood in the dock with her hands folded in front of her. There were hectic spots of colour on her cheeks and a sheen of perspiration on her lip and forehead. He wished he had insisted that this be delayed until she was well. Even if she endured the entire trial, her illness made her look nervous, as if she had something to hide. And what if she were found guilty and sent to prison while she had a fever?

Although he didn't allow it to show in his features, although he'd hardly been able to admit it to himself, he was almost entirely convinced that she would be found guilty. To believe in spirit photography was a leap of faith; to believe in it in a courtroom which was built on the premise of rationality was a leap too far. The witnesses meant to support Viola came across as credulous and foolish.

In the courtroom, Viola's photographs looked so flimsy. Prints on paper, documents of a fleeting moment. He had once believed that photographs were permanent records of an undeniable truth. But since then he had seen photographs of a Delhi that no longer existed. He trusted Viola implicitly, and knew she could not lie;

but he also knew that what was being argued in this courtroom was the wrong argument, the wrong truth.

All photographs were spirits. The record of something that had once lived and was now dead. A moment, a human being, an emotion, a city. All of them were paper ghosts.

Among the whispers and rustles of the audience, through all of the questions by the barristers and the shuffling of witnesses, Jonah only watched Viola. She was his childhood friend and his sister, the sole constant in his life since he was eight years old.

So it was in his wife's face that he saw when everything changed.

She was gazing quietly out over the courtroom, her hands folded in front of her as they had been the entire time. She turned to the side, and he saw her lips moving, as if she were saying a silent prayer.

Then she straightened, and a bolt of joy came into her features, as if a light had shone through the dusty windows on her and on no one else. Jonah turned in his seat, following her gaze to the back of the room, and he saw Henriette Blackthorne. She wore an electric blue dress and a hat that made her appear even taller. While Viola's face had been transformed by love, Henriette's was regal and impassive, almost stern.

Unnoticed by the rest of the people in the courtroom, and certainly by Field, who was quoting Scripture in an attempt to show that spirit photography was acceptable to Christian law, Henriette strode forward down the centre aisle, leaving whispers behind her like a wake. She stopped only when she stood in front of the judge.

'My name is Henriette Blackthorne and I am a spirit medium,' she said as boldly as she spoke at the beginning of her séances and loudly enough so that she could be heard by every person in the room. 'I was present when nearly all of Mrs Worth's photographs were taken. I would like to speak as a witness in this trial.'

In the dock, Viola was vibrating with happiness. Her hands

clenched the wooden rail in front of her, as she leaned forward as if to drink the other woman in. Henriette looked only at the judge. She was magnificent.

She had broken his wife's heart. She had convinced Viola to take these photographs in the first place. She had captured Viola's love and then run away and left her to the mercy of prison and the court and yet Viola, his wife, loved her more than she could ever love him.

In that moment, Jonah hated Henriette Blackthorne.

'My name is Henriette Blackthorne. I work as a spirit medium, which means in the simplest terms that I communicate with a guide, Flora Bell, who is the spirit of a young Frenchwoman who died forty years ago. In a séance, which is the performances I undertake, usually for pay, my guide facilitates contact with other spirits of deceased people who are known to my audience. In this way, the dead can pass on messages. I have performed these séances all over Britain and also on the Continent. The fees that people pay me to contact their dead loved ones are my main source of income, and allow me to live independently.

'At times I manifest spirits physically, by doing things like playing instruments or knocking on furniture. Flora Bell usually appears in a physical form, and sometimes so do other spirits, which appear to be semi-transparent. In short, I create in actual life the effects which you see in Mrs Worth's photographs.'

She paused, reading the room as if she were performing. Field opened his mouth to speak, to ask her a question, but before he could, she said, 'I am a liar.'

The room had been utterly silent, transfixed by this new development. At this, it exploded. Henriette merely stood still, waiting until the clamour subsided, until the red-faced bailiff and the steel-eyed judge had silenced everyone in the room. Then without waiting for a question or a prompt, she said, 'There is no such person or thing or spirit as Flora Bell. Or at least, there was, but she died long ago and has never been heard of since. I provide the messages from the spirit world through a mixture of educated guesswork and knowledge I have gathered from other sources. Flora Bell's physical form is me, in disguise. While my clients believe I am in a trance behind a screen, I play the instruments, I knock on the walls. And when a spirit appears, it is this.'

With a movement of her arm so quick as to be nearly un-detectable, she flicked a small length of some white stuff from her left wrist. With her other hand, she pulled on it, and it unravelled itself into the witness stand, draped over the railing, trailing down onto the floor below.

'Cheesecloth or muslin, at times silk. Anything that will fold up small and will unroll to be diaphanous will do. I soak it with a phosphorescent mixture so it will glow in the semi-dark of a séance space. I wear clothing made of this under my gown, so I can change quickly from myself to a spirit.'

'Mrs Blackthorne,' said Field, raising his voice, 'what is the purpose of these theatrics?'

'Viola Worth did not fake these spirit photographs, or take money for them. I did.'

Henriette Blackthorne at that moment was the centre of every-one's attention except for Jonah's. He was, once again, watching his wife. And at Henriette's announcement he saw her, for the first time, sag in the dock, as if her legs couldn't keep her upright, and he knew exactly why.

Viola hadn't known. This was a worse betrayal than Henriette's disappearance. She had believed in Henriette, believed everything about her, risked her own reputation on that belief. And it was all a length of silk.

The judge banged his gavel on his desk for order, but it was a long time before he got it. During this entire time, Henriette gazed steadily out at the courtroom. Not at Viola, not once.

'Why?' said the judge, when he'd restored order.

'Why did I fake the photographs that Mrs Worth was taking?

Partly for monetary gain, and to enhance my own reputation as a medium. Partly for the challenge of fooling the camera. Largely, in order to spend more time with Viola Worth, who is a pure-hearted woman of integrity and who had no idea whatsoever that I was the one committing fraud. Not her. Never her.'

'And why have you come forward now, to make your confession in such a way that your own reputation and livelihood will both be ruined? If what you say is true, you have been deceiving people for years. What could possibly be your motivation to confess now?'

'Because I love her,' said Henriette.

At this, for the first time, Henriette turned her head and looked at Viola, who flushed and held fast to the railing and gazed back at her, and Jonah saw that no matter what Henriette had done, his wife loved her. Viola forgave Henriette's betrayal without her asking it, just as Viola had forgiven his.

This good woman, Viola Goodwin Worth, was the woman he himself had not been able to love well enough. This miraculous woman.

And all at once, Jonah knew exactly what he had to do.

A clipping from the Dorset Echo, *22 October 1858. From the private collection of Mr Timothy Selby, Brooklyn, New York.*

Verdict in Spirit Fraud Case Amongst Courtroom Chaos

A case which, although the sums of money were low, has excited considerable interest in our readers, due to the questions of Spiritualism and the novelty of Spirit Photography, has come to a surprising and dramatic conclusion at the Dorchester Assizes yesterday, under the auspices of Judge Hart Davies.

Chief witness for the prosecution was Mr Theodore Selby, who is well-known in certain circles for various publications denouncing the authenticity of Spiritualists. It was his claim that the accused, Mrs Viola Worth, had defrauded him of the sum of five pounds in exchange for a photograph which she claimed represented an image of his dead father, who is nevertheless alive. Mr Wills Fletcher, a photographer, provided evidence outlining how the image of a so-called 'spirit' could be produced by means of trickery. The witnesses for the defence, various clients of Mrs Worth, were largely notable for their credulity but were nevertheless vehement that the photographs in their possession depicted deceased loved ones.

Mr Field, barrister of the accused, in his summary remarks, gave all assembled a lesson in the presence of spirits in Scripture, further emphasising that this case touches not only on everyday matters of law and truth but on the great questions of Religion and Truth.

The judge was preparing to deliver his instructions to the jury in a courtroom crowded with onlookers, when he was interrupted by the dramatic appearance of the person often mentioned in these proceedings, but never seen: Mrs Henriette Blackthorne, the celebrated spirit medium. Mrs Blackthorne insisted upon taking the stand where she made her sensational confession: 'I faked Mrs Worth's photographs without her knowledge.' Mrs Blackthorne demonstrated for the judge, jury and onlookers how she had fraudulently created the appearance of spirits using phosphorescent cheesecloth and silk, artfully concealed about her clothing until such time when they were needed.

Her astonishing revelation was brought to a close by another dramatic event: Mr Jonah Worth, the husband of the accused and popularly known as 'The Hero of Delhi' for his rescue of a young girl during the Sepoy Rebellion, collapsed, no doubt due to the strain of the proceedings. Bailiff and spectators alike rushed to his rescue, carrying him outside for air. Meanwhile several altercations erupted between members of Spiritualist societies and various representatives of the scientific community, with numerous blows being struck on either side.

By the time Judge Hart Davies had re-established order and the offenders had been taken away, Mrs Blackthorne, who had been left on the stand while this disturbance took place, had vanished as mysteriously as she had appeared, and as surely as any of the spirits which she claimed to manifest.

After such an unexpected denouement, the jury quickly returned its inevitable verdict: Not Guilty.

Mrs Worth, who has been a picture of modest silence throughout her ordeal, more suited to a parlour or a church than the dock, cried tears of joy as she was released.

No serious injuries were reported as a result of the altercations between spectators. The whereabouts of Mrs Blackthorne are still as yet unknown, though Dorchester police have issued a request for any information which the public may have about her. Meanwhile, it is difficult not to conclude that the cause of Spiritualism has been dealt a bitter blow by this court's proceedings.

Chapter Fifty-three

Fourteen months later...

December, 1859
Northern Wales

They lived quietly in a small house on the edge of a wood, with few neighbours except for the farmer and his family a mile down into the valley. Winter was harsh here and summer was damp, and they had no visitors, but their parlour was cosy and warm. No English language newspapers reached this valley; no one here had heard of the Hero of Delhi, or the spirit photographer, or the famous medium.

Viola studied Welsh. She took photographs only of Jonah, in their cramped parlour, training the camera closely on his face and developing the photographs in the cold shed in the back. In the evenings she pored over the prints. In them, his face was a landscape of its own: hills and valleys, plains and pools, all the territory of his love and his suffering. In her photographs, as in life, all was finally laid bare to her. Viola saw him, at last, her brother, and loved him as she had always done and as she had always meant to.

The photographs were only ever of him. They never saw the ghost of Pavan or anyone else. It was as if in her final fever dream, in the courtroom where her father smiled at her, she had seen all her ghosts at once.

'She didn't fake the photographs,' Viola had told Jonah, in wonder on their way home from Dorchester after the trial. 'She wasn't even there when I took the one of Mr Selby, or the first one of Mary. And none of those effects could have been produced with muslin. A double exposure, possibly, but I would have known if that happened. The photographs are real. She lied to save me.'

And yet, without Henriette, all of her photographs were without spirits at all.

The light here was slanting and low, but it was strong when it came between rain clouds, transforming the hills from shadows to shocking green. They were landlocked here. Viola no longer wore her wedding ring but kept it on the chain by her heart along with her locket. It wasn't a reminder of promises made, but of promises that had died long ago but which were nonetheless the most precious things she had.

They spoke to each other of Pavan and Henriette. When they had first come here a year ago to this remote place, setting up their house together in the dead of winter, finding a girl to come in the mornings, they had settled into silence but only for half a day. At their first meal Viola put down her fork and knife and said, 'We didn't talk to each other when we got married and it made me very unhappy. I want to know what you're thinking now.'

Jonah, surprised, said exactly what he was thinking. 'I was wondering how two women loved each other.'

And Viola, laughing for the first time since she had been taken to prison, told him.

He had nightmares, sometimes: talking about Pavan had stirred up memories that burst free in the darkness. When he did, Viola came from her bedroom into his and held his hand and stroked his forehead as he dimly remembered his mother doing back in India. He cried and she sat with him.

Jonah was working on a commission for a book about Welsh wild flowers. In between, he studied Welsh, too. Although they had no visitors, sometimes he walked the four miles to the nearest pub and sat listening to farmers speaking. After a few months he tried hesitant phrases of his own. He loved the lilt and the music of it, the hoarded vowels and liquid consonants. It was nothing like Hindi but it was like Hindi in that all languages were like each other, and with strange words on his tongue he felt more at home than he had in a very long time. The farmers, for their part, although they distrusted the English as an entity, didn't dislike Jonah. They asked after his cariad, his gwraig bert, and when he asked them to sing him their songs, they put down their glasses and sang loud enough to wake the valley.

So passed winter, and spring, and summer, into autumn and winter again.

Before Christmas a letter came addressed to Viola. From the crossings-out on the envelope Jonah could see that it had been sent to Fortuneswell and redirected via their solicitor in London. Sometimes, she had letters from strangers asking her to photograph their relatives; often she had letters from Spiritualists who wanted to express their support; once she had had an invitation to speak to a group called The Society of Sceptics. She ignored the invitation and the letters from Spiritualists, but she did write back to the mourning relatives, brief notes, declining their requests but offering her condolences. Her only regular correspondent was Nan, who was learning how to read and write and wrote sprawling letters across the paper Viola sent her in bundles, detailing the lives of the village children and their continuing attempts to sabotage the career of Constable Peebles.

This letter looked like none of those. It had an American stamp and a return address in Philadelphia. He brought it to Viola where she sat in their tiny parlour, sewing in the weak light. 'It looks as if you have an admirer in the United States,' he said, holding it out to her.

She finished her hem and put down her work, reaching for the letter. 'A devotee of the Fox sisters, maybe.'

But as soon as she saw the handwriting on the envelope, she knew.

She thought of Henriette daily – hourly. But she had trained herself not to think about Henriette's betrayal: the months of deception, the cheesecloth in the sleeve, the manifestation of Flora, the earnest words about spirits. She did not know how much of what Henriette had told her about her past was true. She tried not to think about how Henriette had insisted that the spirits had told her that Jonah wasn't dead, and how she disappeared when Viola was in prison.

She had thought, instead, of those words Henriette had spoken in the courtroom, and how Henriette had told one last great lie about the photographs, to sacrifice herself for Viola's freedom.

Because I love her.

Those words were true and plain, and yet no one in that courtroom had understood them except for Viola and Jonah.

Henriette's final words, and Jonah's steady, patient, brotherly love, were what helped her pass the days, the reasons for the small light in her heart in this dim place. Henriette did love her. Jonah had helped Henriette to escape and she had to leave, to protect herself. Somewhere, Henriette was in the world, and she loved Viola.

And now, although the name on the return address was not hers, this letter was from Henriette.

Hope and a great painful longing made her hands so weak she could barely hold the envelope. 'Jonah,' she said, and he took it and opened it, carefully, and handed the single sheet of thin paper back to her without reading it.

Viola, my love,

  I don't expect you to forgive me, though I know you're good enough to find forgiveness for me, in time. I am only so very sorry: for deceiving you, for taking money when it was offered, for making you think I saw spirits when I did not. I am not sorry for the other things we shared.

  This letter may never reach you, or you may rightfully tear it up without reading it, but in case you are reading these words, halfway across the world ... I left England very soon after

*your court case and have, after some travelling, found myself
in Philadelphia. I live here now under the name of Hélène
Gailliard.*

*This is not my true name. The name I was born with is
Harriet Smith. I was born poor of a mother who died from
drink and a father who beat us. I was a scullery maid and then
a housemaid, until I met the man who was good enough to
marry me and then I changed my first name and took his last.
He was the only person to know my true name. Now you are
the second.*

*I know we'll never meet again, but Viola, my Viola,
although I am a liar, I never spoke truer words than when we
were together, and when I said that I love you. The moments
we spent together were the sweetest of my life. With you, I felt a
goodness that I did not believe still lived in this world.*

Ever yours,

H.

Viola read through the letter once with hands shaking the paper.
She read it again. Then she gave the letter to Jonah to read, and
when he had put it down, she said, 'I must go to her.'

'Yes,' he said, without hesitation. 'You must.'

Viola had never travelled alone, and never by water, but she sailed
from Liverpool on the steam packet without a maid to assist her,
walking the decks for most of the daylight hours. She spoke to
few people, watched seabirds, stared at the churning sea with its
chunks of ice. 'You're brave,' said a fellow traveller to her one
evening at dinner, with a narrowing of the eyes that conveyed
that *brave* signified *foolish*, but Viola did not feel either foolish or
brave. She felt necessary and impatient.

Because the Delaware River froze it took almost as much time
for the ship to reach Philadelphia from the coast as it had taken
it to cross the Atlantic. The riverbanks were lined with trees and

melting snow. When they landed in Philadelphia she hardly saw the docks or the warehouses, the scurrying porters, the shuffling Irish and English families who had come in steerage – all the machinery of emigration and hope. She sent her trunk to the Girard Hotel and took a cab to the address that Henriette had written on the envelope of the single letter she had sent.

I know we'll never meet again, the letter had said. Halfway across the ocean Viola had thought, with a cold edge of despair, that perhaps this was a prediction rather than a lament. Henriette wrote about their moments together in the past tense. She had always been worldly-wise, much more than Viola. Perhaps she knew, more than Viola with her quick and naïve yearning, that it was impossible for women to live together. Perhaps she had already found someone else, had married for security or for love. She had loved before, after all.

Henriette had spoken her love in a crowded courtroom, in front of a judge, under oath. But it wasn't a vow. And Viola hadn't been able to answer.

The streets of Philadelphia were unnaturally straight. They were set out in a grid and lined by uniform red-brick houses with flat roofs and white steps and green shutters and slanting cellar doors. To Viola it looked more like a model city than a real one. A stage set. From the boat it had seemed like winter, but here in the city it was warm, and the air felt like spring.

Henriette might not even be here any longer. It had been months since she'd written the letter, and as far as Viola knew, she'd never written another.

Henriette had never read the love letter that Viola wrote to her on the day she was arrested, and which had been taken from her in prison. For the whole journey Viola kept it folded between her corset and her chemise, next to her mother's wedding ring and the locket with her father's hair. The ink had smudged and the creases grown soft with wear.

The cab set her down outside a brick house. It was perhaps

smaller than some of the other houses she had seen, in the middle of a joined row of similar houses, and it had a terracotta pot of daffodils on the steps. Viola rang the bell and she fiddled with her bonnet strings; found her bonnet too constraining so took it off and immediately felt exposed, messy – and very far from home.

The girl who opened the door was not much older than Nan, but she was almost painfully neat, with starched cap and stiff apron. 'I'm here to call on Mrs – Madame Gailliard,' stumbled Viola. She was suddenly aware that she was unannounced, she had never spoken the French name aloud, and that Henriette, running from the past, was perhaps wary of strangers at her door.

'Do you have a calling card?' asked the maid.

'No – tell her that my name is—' A thought struck her and she reached inside the bosom of her gown for the folded, worn letter. She held it out to the girl. Tattered and poor, the entire contents of her heart.

'Give her this,' she said.

The girl disappeared into the house, letting the door shut behind her. Standing on the white doorstep, Viola took a deep breath of the Philadelphia air, scented with mud and horse dung and burning coal and new grass. The sun broke out between clouds. It painted the red brick in light, set the daffodils ablaze. She could wait no longer.

She walked into the house without an invitation, stepped across the entranceway and through the open door into the parlour at the front of the narrow house. It was neatly furnished, feminine and airy, but she did not see that.

Henriette stood in sunshine with the letter open in her hands. Her head bare, her gown a muted green. She looked up.

'Viola,' she whispered. She held out her arms. 'You came.'

Viola went to her and pressed her face into Henriette's bare, warm neck. 'I did,' she said. 'I do.'

An extract from **Remembering Victorian Philadelphia,**
by Frederica T. Matthews, published by Cox & Co, 1962,
page 133.

*A photograph of two elderly Edwardian women in white
shirtwaists. The taller, with white hair in a long braid over her
shoulder, wears wide-legged trousers, while the shorter, a slender
woman with grey hair in a neat bun and a locket around her
neck, wears a dark skirt. They stand side by side in front of a
Philadelphia brownstone with two terriers, one black and one
white, on leads on the step below them.*

Madame Gailliard's School For Girls was a popular
and increasingly stylish place for the affluent families
of Philadelphia to educate their future debutantes in
a Continental fashion. The proprietress, pictured left,
a native of France, taught French, dancing and music
while Mrs Goodwin, an Englishwoman, handled moral
and religious education. A keen amateur photographer,
Mrs Goodwin kindled the love of this art in many of
her students and it was a common sight to see her
in Washington Square with a bevy of young ladies all
carrying portable cameras. Madame Gailliard's popu-
larity was such that parents of strictly religious families
ignored the rumours that the proprietress occasionally
hosted a séance, or a game of piquet, in her parlour.
Notable students include Isabella Palmer (née Mullins),
the violinist; Mercy George (née Prospect), the essayist
and suffragette; and of course Juliet Sutton, the photographer whose portraits of Philadelphia women and

children may be seen in the Woodmere Art Museum. The two women ran the school in a Chestnut Street brownstone, together with a succession of tutors and terriers, for forty years until Madame Gailliard's death in 1902.

Epilogue

1861
Delhi

He had studied Felice Beato's photographs of Delhi after the siege, but nothing quite prepared him for the way everything and nothing was different. The skeleton of the city was the same and yet he could turn a corner and not see a row of buildings he expected; a wall could be identical except for the spray of bullet holes. Although the Jama Masjid still stood, other mosques and temples had been razed. The Mughal's palace had been gutted and turned into a British barracks; the old king himself was in exile in Rangoon. The very air was wounded. And yet men in market stalls sold spices and clothing and food, children ran and scrambled over the ruins, and the English took tea in the cool of the evenings.

The Delhi soil was red, as it had always been, regardless of the blood spilled: the English hunted, the Indians slaughtered. Life went on, built and bought and sold and loved and died, and, perhaps what surprised him the most, when he came back to Delhi after Viola left for America, was that in the four years since he'd been gone the place had never been frozen in time. Everything he thought he knew about it was busily in the process of being proven wrong.

His haveli, the house where he had fallen in love and learned about death, was empty. No one had lived in it since the Hamiltons and Pavan Sharma died there. The gate was rusty and the courtyard had been used for a bonfire. Every book in the library was gone. Someone had been sleeping in it, but the blanket was musty and stiff, and Jonah thought that whoever it belonged to was long gone, driven out by ghosts and memory.

The temple was demolished. Only the peepul tree remained, spreading roots in the rubble, reaching for the sun.

He could have sold the haveli and disposed of his assets from the safety of London, or even Wales. But that would be cowardly. His parents had died here, and the person he loved. He owed Delhi, at least, a few months more of his life. And he owed Rajesh Sharma something more.

He knew no one – all of his acquaintance in Delhi were dead. For all he knew, Rajesh was, too, but on the third afternoon after arriving Jonah found his way through grass-grown streets to the house where, one morning long ago, he and Pavan had sat in the garden and talked about Dickens' orphans.

The garden, unlike so much he had seen, was tended and orderly. A woman sat among the fruit and flowers and squashes reading a book to three small children. Jonah approached and bowed to her, palms together; she stood and silently returned the greeting, face wary.

'Are you Lakshmi Sharma?' he asked. She nodded and the children clung to her clothes. 'I'm Jonah Worth. I wonder if I may speak with Rajesh.'

She nodded again, and went inside the house. A few moments later Rajesh emerged, wearing white as usual, wiping his hands on a cloth. His beard was longer and his eyes looked so like Pavan's that Jonah almost turned around and walked away.

'Sahib?' said Rajesh. He was also wary, but his voice was polite. 'You are back in India.'

'I'm disturbing you,' said Jonah. 'I am very sorry.'

'No, no, not disturbing at all.' He gestured to a pair of chairs in the shade of a guava tree. Jonah thought they were the same ones where he had sat, that morning, with Pavan.

'It's been so long since we met,' said Jonah, unsure of where to begin, even though he had rehearsed this conversation in his head. 'When you were working for Robert Hamilton. It was my house that … where …' He felt breathless.

'I remember you, sahib. They say you saved the young girl.'

Lakshmi came out carrying a tray of sherbet and sweetmeats which she put on a low table beside them. Then she returned to her book, and the children gathered around her once more.

Rajesh offered a cup of sherbet, and Jonah took it.

'Yes, I – I couldn't come back, not right away, after …' He took a gulp of the sweet, cool drink. Rajesh was clearly not happy to see him. And yet he was still offering hospitality. Jonah gestured to the jalebi on the plate. 'Pavan used to love these.'

Rajesh didn't answer. The craving to talk about Pavan was like clawing hunger; but how could Jonah do so? He wasn't even certain which pronouns to use. Even though Rajesh knew the truth, would it be a betrayal of Pavan for Jonah to admit he knew her secret?

He wished he had written to Rajesh first, explaining everything. He hadn't known the exact address, or if the house still existed, but here in this garden that seemed like a feeble excuse.

He averted his eyes to the garden, searching for a topic that was less painful. 'You have had more children. Congratulations.'

'I have been blessed with a growing family.'

Jonah gazed at the children: it looked like two girls with straight hair, and a boy with curls. The oldest girl was clearly in charge of the younger two, who were still toddlers; as he watched she said a sharp word to the boy, who was pulling leaves off a bush.

There had been so much death in this city, and yet children still played and leaves still grew. What would it be like to stay here and to help make this place new? To try to do what his wife had done with glass and silver and paper, and see the past as a gift to the present, a lesson that love can teach us?

But Viola had gone to a new country, and this country was so old. He could imagine a time, far in the future, where languages and beliefs, nationality and race, did not matter. When the stories told about the stars, the feeling behind the prayers, mattered less than the stars and the prayers themselves.

That time was not now, in the year 1861, in a land that was scarred with too much hatred that had been caused, he believed, by people who looked like him.

'I have a job for you, if you will take it, Mr Sharma,' he said. 'I need your help.'

Rajesh had been raising a cup to his lips. He lowered it.

'Pardon me, sahib?'

'If you will ... I would like you to help me decide how to give away my property and investments here in India.'

'You mean sell them?'

'No, I mean give away. Or perhaps sell, and then give the money away. I don't understand business, you see. I've never been good with numbers. Pavan used to say numbers were a universal language, but I've never been able to speak it. I would like you to decide how to use the money to help build Delhi again. Build schools, preferably.'

'You wish to give charity?'

Rajesh's voice was very cold. What had Jonah expected? Had he thought that Rajesh would welcome this unsolicited offer with open arms?

'Not charity. Reparation. I owe a great debt to Pavan. And the only way I can pay it is to – the only thing I have to give is property. I believe sh ...' Faced with Pavan's brother's stony face, he stumbled over the pronoun. 'I believe Pavan would want the money to go to education. It has been a terrible time in this city, a terrible time between your people and mine. Perhaps it will get better in the future but we don't know, do we? We only know the present. We can't escape it any more than we can escape ourselves. But Pavan would want people to be able to learn.'

'What debt do you believe you owe to Pavan?'

'She died because of me.' This time he was able to say it. 'She saved my life. And I loved her. I love her still.'

Across the garden, a childish voice protested. Jonah couldn't understand the words, but the meaning was clear – a plea of dismay. He glanced over again; Rajesh's wife had lowered her book and was staring at him.

Rajesh, too, was staring at him.

Jonah pulled the roll of papers that his solicitor had given him from his jacket and held them out. 'Look. I don't understand any of this, it's all legalese and numbers, but you will understand it much better than I can. I don't know whether—'

And then he stopped, papers still in his hand, because a young man came into the garden from the street. He was dressed in white, wore a turban, and held a stack of books under one arm. Despite his youth and beardless face, he walked with a limp.

The slender young man did not see Jonah and Rajesh sitting under the tree; he went straight to the children, put his books down, sat upon the low wall and opened his arms. The children exclaimed in joy and climbed onto his lap.

Jonah stood. He had seen ghosts. He did not know how it could be true, but this slender figure, dressed in white, was not one.

He let go of the papers and they fluttered to the ground.

'Pavan?' he said, slowly and with a new kind of faith.

Author's note

I've taken a lot of historical liberties, including with the facts about spirit photography. The first well-known spirit photographer was William Mumler who practised in Boston and New York in the 1860s and who was himself tried for fraud in New York in 1869, in a sensational trial where the lawyer quoted Scripture and P.T. Barnum was a witness. Mumler was found innocent (for different reasons from Viola) and, in a strange twist of fate, later invented the process that enabled newspapers to print photographs. Thus, perhaps prophetically, a fraudster was directly responsible for the way in which we still experience news today.

The first known English spirit photographs were taken in London by Frederick Hudson in 1872. Although early spirit photographs were – like most photographs – taken by men who were popularly supposed to be more naturally competent with the science involved, the everyday business of mediumship was largely conducted by women. There's an examination of this collision between gender, science and faith in *Nature Exposed: Photography as Eyewitness in Victorian Science* by Jennifer Tucker.

The facts in Patience Hamilton's story about the starving Brahmins were taken from Harriet Tytler's memoir *An Englishwoman in India*. This memoir is not only a fascinating read about a brave woman's life in India in the nineteenth century and what it was like for an Englishwoman to be caught up in the events of May 1857 and the subsequent Siege of Delhi, but also an illuminating portrayal of imperial entitlement at this time. The timeline of events on 10–11 May 1857 was taken from William Dalrymple's *The Last Mughal*. I also recommend *Inglorious Empire:*

What the British Did to India by Shashi Tharoor and *From Plassey to Partition and After* by Sekhar Bandyopadhyay.

I learned wet plate collodion photography from Daniel Barter who was an inspirational teacher and who helped me brainstorm elements of the plot. Sadly, he informs me that cyanide is no longer used in the process.

Thanks to my dear friend Bhavya Singh and the historian Sona Singh who helped me with the Delhi sections of this book. All errors are mine, not theirs.

I wrote sections of this book cherished and nourished at Chez Castillon, France, Retreats for You, Devon, and Ponden Hall, Yorkshire – where I was assisted by a Chopin-hating ghost.

Elizabeth Haynes, Steve Wade, Deborah Barker, Callie Langridge and the staff at the Berkshire Records Office were immensely helpful in pointing me towards archives and resources about Victorian criminology, newspapers and daily life.

Thanks to Fiona Wilson, who donated to CLIC Sargent's Get In Character charity campaign to have the name Lalage Smy appear in this novel, and to Mrs Smy who was good-humoured enough to lend her name and her husband Christopher's to a widow and a corpse.

I wrote the first draft of this book when I thought my writing career was over. Oddly, the novel turned out to be about faith. Thank you to my family, my friends and the publishing professionals who had faith in me, especially my agent Teresa Chris, my editor Harriet Bourton, and everyone in the credits on the following page.

Credits

Julie Cohen and Orion Fiction would like to thank everyone at Orion who worked on the publication of *Spirited* in the UK.

Editorial
Harriet Bourton
Olivia Barber
Clare Hey

Copy editor
Kati Nicholl

Proof reader
Linda Joyce

Audio
Paul Stark
Amber Bates

Contracts
Anne Goddard
Paul Bulos
Jake Alderson

Design
Rabab Adams
Joanna Ridley
Nick May

Editorial Management
Alice Davis
Jane Hughes
Charlie Panayiotou

Finance
Jasdip Nandra
Afeera Ahmed
Elizabeth Beaumont
Sue Baker

Production
Ruth Sharvell

Marketing
Cait Davies

Publicity
Leanne Oliver

Sales
Jen Wilson
Esther Waters
Victoria Laws
Rachael Hum
Ellie Kyrke-Smith
Frances Doyle
Georgina Cutler

Operations
Jo Jacobs
Sharon Willis
Lisa Pryde
Lucy Brem